A Valentine's Anthology

The Lending Library
C.L. Kraemer

Chasing Rainbows
Genie Gabriel

The Gift
Christine Young

Published by Rogue Phoenix Press
Copyright © 2009
ISBN: 978-1-62420-534-7

The Lending Library

C.L Kraemer

Dedication

To my husband Larry who is my forever prize.

Prologue

Follow the highway that hugs the shoreline of the river about fifteen miles into the dense forest. A covered bridge spanning the water appears on the right side. Turn your vehicle slowly onto the creaky, wooden single lane passage and after holding your breath and praying the bridge holds your vehicle, follow the narrow lane for three miles. The transport through a rainbow of greenery is unlike any other spot on this planet. Towering pines reach their evergreen arms to the sky creating a canopy that provides a cool shelter for the creatures of the forest. As the fading blue of the overhead sky begins to morph into inky darkness, the road wends itself past a slatted building tucked into a crook within the wooded landscape. The clapboard siding could do with a coat of paint and visitors must wonder if the shaky building will stand another year in this coveted haven. Much of the outside bears the weathered scars left by years of rain and a slight green sheen to the sides indicate the moss which cushions the foot on the forest floor has decided to overtake the structure thus returning the elements back to their beginning. The one inconsistent in this picture is the sturdy, new porch hosting miniscule tables and chairs.

A sign out front bears white, chipped letters of explanation:
The Lending Library--open 24 hours. Welcome.

Linda Brown moved to these woods so long ago she'd forgotten the actual date. She hated the isolation at first, but after spending ten years being miserable, she realized she had a choice to make--move or learn to adjust. She adjusted.

It was after she'd adjusted to her situation she discovered mail order catalogs and book clubs. When her husband Donald passed away, she gave away all the earthly things he had felt so important and built shelves in every room except the kitchen to store her books and create her library. She moved her small bed into the old pantry adding a small window so she might see the "little people" when they came to visit her before she fell asleep.

Friends from her socializing days stopped visiting. People in town began calling her the Witch of the Woods and quit passing by the house. Linda didn't care. She had her library and the wee ones.

Chapter One

Ailidh wobbled precariously on her high heels.

Kayne smirked. "Having problems, dear?"

"Shut up!" she snapped. "I need to practice this until I get it right. We don't really have many options left open to us, Kayne. You had better practice, too."

He stopped and steadied himself on the railing of the porch. He wriggled his feet out of the closed leather shoes that encased them.

"I don't know why you insist we wear these ridiculous articles of clothing. This long-sleeved shirt cuts off the circulation to my hands not to mention the lack of space for my wings and these long pants chap my legs.

"Worst of all, are these horrendous leather shoes. They pinch and make my feet swell. Why do we have to go through all of this? I don't understand." Kayne grumbled.

Ailidh sighed and slowly, *patiently* explained to him, once again, why they were practicing.

"Remember last Wednesday when Keegan and Connal lost their dwelling? The sound of their tree crashing to the ground was deafening. The Others are moving out more and more. We will lose our home if we don't act first. Now, put your shoes back on and walk for just five more minutes."

Kayne wrestled his shirt off and threw it to the porch's deck. He pulled the long pants off his body and left them in a heap next to the shirt. Bending forward, he touched his toes gingerly as he gradually unfurled his lacey wings. Slowly, he pulled himself to an upright

3

position. Shoulders back, wings completely expanded, he lifted his 18-inch form to its full height and looked at Ailidh defiantly.

"I don't need to fit into the Others' world. They need to adjust themselves to my world and leave us alone."

Ailidh, teetering, grabbed the lower railing of the porch and shook her head.

"Kayne, most of the Others don't even know we exist. How can they adjust to something they don't even believe?"

"They adjust to animals, don't they?"

"The animals chose to be seen. We did not. Remember? Our great, great grandfathers took a vote and decided we would endanger ourselves more if we continued to be visible to the Others. At that time, they didn't have all the machinery they have now. They moved into our lands at a slower pace. Now, put on the clothes and try to adjust."

"No." Kayne kicked at the clothing on the porch. "I'm going to get a magazine and a cup of coffee. You can stand here and practice day and night for all I care."

He turned on his heels and lifted himself off the ground with his delicate appendages. He lazily winged his way into the open window of the building marked *Lending Library*.

Hovering until he landed on the balls of his feet, he folded the wings tight to his torso and walked to the corner of the building signed Coffee Shop. He sat in a small chair snugged close to the matching table. Sliding the Newsweek someone had tossed on the table toward him, he flipped through the pages. Minimized for easier handling, the magazine was still large enough to require both of his hands to turn the pages. A diminutive nymph in a waitress uniform with a "Chrissy" nametag took his order for a latte. Ten minutes later, she returned with the steaming liquid in a cup.

"Thanks, Chrissy." Kayne picked up the cup carefully and took a sip.

"No problem, Kayne," she had a surprisingly deep voice for a nymph. "Where's Ailidh?"

Kayne jerked a thumb over his shoulder toward the front porch.

"Practicing," he grunted.

"Oh," Chrissy mopped the table next to Kayne's with a wet rag then flew daintily to the kitchen with the dirty cups and saucers she'd picked up. One of the resident dryads of the valley, Chrissy was living in the tree behind the Lending Library. Her home across the meadow had been one of the first destroyed.

Ailidh is right. Kayne frowned at the silent admission. The Others were invading his world with frightening, swift, uncaring swaths into the forestlands. Soon there wouldn't be an Ancient tree left. While, at a glance, their movements seemed random, even careless, Kayne had noted a pattern, albeit haphazard, to their actions. Months earlier he'd watched from a safe distance as the huge screeching yellow machines ripped up his ancient wood friends and squashed their bodies beneath armored tracks. He could never be sure whether the squealing had been the old trees or the vicious yellow machines. After the first occasion of watching as they destroyed a sea of Ancients, Kayne had left on shaky wings and flown home. Ailidh was furious at him, thinking he'd been with his friends drinking honeysuckle wine. He couldn't stop throwing up long enough to tell her what he'd seen.

When the thunder and growl of the angry yellow tree destroyers rumbled over their living room ceiling several months later, Kayne sat Ailidh down and explained what had happened that fateful night.

He took her soft, dainty hand in his and looked into her sparkling moss green eyes.

"We must be prepared to move from our home."

Ailidh's exquisite wings trembled. "Why?"

The earth near the entrance to their home groaned and bits of dirt drizzled from around the doorway.

Kayne pointed up. "That--that--monster will reach into our home and pluck us up with no regard whatsoever. I've seen it rip out the Ancient trees in the glen over by Drystan's home.

"The night you thought me so drunk I could not speak, I was ill from watching The Others kill the Ancient trees and destroy homes of our friends. I couldn't stop being sick long enough to explain to you. When I finally got the horror of that picture out of my mind and stopped throwing up, you'd gone to bed--angry. I didn't want to disturb you."

Ailidh's face blanched and she slumped to the cloth-covered chair Kayne had so carefully carved from a branch the Ancient tree had gifted them.

"Wh-wh-why? We've not harmed them. Why do they want to rip out our homes and make us move?"

"I don't know my love, but we've got to find a way to fight back or we'll be next."

Kayne had soothed Ailidh's fears that night, but she began a campaign to move to Faetown and get out of the meadow and woods they called home.

Kayne sighed. She'd get her way and they'd move, but he wasn't going without a fight.

He felt a soft rush of air caress his cheek and looked up to find Ailidh alighting gently on her bare feet, her toes inflamed and angry looking.

He nodded to her. "Better get the Librarian to wrap those before they swell too much. Wouldn't want to put your *shoes* in the rubbish bin." Licking several fingers, he turned the page, the crinkle of the slick paper echoing off the wall of books.

When his smarmy comment met with silence, Kayne looked up to see a large tear meandering down Ailidh's cheek. He dropped the magazine to the table and hung his head, pushing out air between his lips. He'd done it again. He'd hurt the one woman who put up with his attitude and still loved him. Most women of the Fae would have kicked out his boastful self long ago not tolerating his pride and pomposity. Not Ailidh. She'd just look at him with those enormous sparkling moss green eyes, pat his hand and kiss his cheek. Kayne, unlike most Fae men, preferred one mate and one mate only. He never had understood the need to wing from inviting mossy bed to inviting mossy bed.

He reached out and grabbed the wayward drop heading toward the fine line of Ailidh's jaw.

"I'm sorry, my love. Let's see if the Librarian has something to ease the pain." Kayne lifted himself from the chair and fluttered to the back of the building.

On the door was a sign. It read: "Rap loudly. Human hearing."

Kayne pounded on the door, settled himself on the floor, and waited.

Slowly the big door opened; before him stood a giant of a person. He sucked in a deep breath and felt his wings tremble.

Pulling up a stool, the giant Librarian sat. She was nearly at his eye level. A gentle smile touched her lips and crinkled her gray eyes. The essence of wild roses swirled lightly on the air.

"Kayne. How can I help you?"

Her soft voice purred quietly to his keen hearing.

Kayne opened his mouth but nothing came out. He coughed, stepped back then winged himself up a foot. At this level, he was looking in to the kind eyes.

"Ailidh… Ailidh has been practicing with those high heel shoes, and now her feet are swollen and hurting. Do you have something that would help?"

Linda thought for a moment. "I do believe I have something to ease her pain. I also have some Epson salts you can take with you so she can use them tonight. Wait here."

Rising from the step stool slowly, she walked to the back of the small room and opened a cupboard on the wall. Taking out a box and a bottle, the Librarian returned to the doorway.

"May I come out and administer to her?" Gray eyes questioned as she stood with the medicine in her hands.

Kayne hesitated. Ailidh liked the Librarian, but he still didn't trust her. After all, she was one of the Others. He turned his head and saw his mate trying to stifle the large tears meandering down her cheeks by swiping at them with the back of her hand.

"Yes. Please. She's in such pain."

Linda was surprised. Very few of the wee folk had become comfortable with her presence. Ailidh was the exception, so getting their permission to move about her own home was necessary if she was to keep them coming into her library.

"Lead the way, Kayne." She wasn't above playing to his male vanity.

As they got closer to the tiny faerie, Ailidh straightened in her chair and sipped from her coffee drink. She was a bit startled to see the Librarian out in the building. She didn't come out in the daytime for fear of scaring away the wee folk that gathered. Something must really be wrong for her to take such measures.

"Librarian." The sweet sound of Ailidh's voice carried to the odd pair approaching her.

"Ailidh. How are you today?"

"I'm well, thank you. What brings you out of your room?"

"Kayne asked me to see to your feet. He mentioned you were suffering and asked if I could help."

Ailidh shot Kayne a glare. "My toes are swollen and hurt a bit, but they will heal without help, thank you."

Linda could sense a fight brewing and opted to take the diplomatic way out.

"Well, let me give you some of my healing helpers. Use them if you like and if not, hang on to them. At some point in the future, they might come in handy. These little orange pills here relieve pain from the inside out, small dose aspirin. I believe you have this remedy in a leaf you brew; this is just easier to take and not quite so bitter. Just swallow them, don't chew, and in about 20 minutes you should feel some relief from the aching."

Linda gently shook the box of Epsom salts.

"These salts work if you place them in hot water and soak your feet. They're called Epsom salts and can be quite handy for those days when you've trekked too far. I'd be more than happy to get a tub so you could start the healing now."

Ailidh looked at Kayne's worried face and the concern on the Librarian's face. She pushed out a sigh.

"All right. If it will make both of you happy..." She watched relief flood the faces of the two people she cared about the most. If this would stop her feet from throbbing… she'd try anything.

"I'll get Chrissy to give you a hand." Linda took a step and hesitated. Turning, she asked, "Is that all right with you?"

Ailidh nodded.

Linda trod lightly on the old oaken floor. As she came close to the kitchen, she stopped, waiting until all her clothing had stopped rustling. She cleared her throat and closed her eyes. She'd made an agreement with the small ones to ask permission before peering directly at them--it was considered polite in their realm.

"Chrissy?" Linda whispered.

"Yes, Librarian?"

"May I speak with you?"

"Of, course, Librarian. Let me dry my hands and I'll join you."

Linda sighed quietly. These wee ones had taught her to slow her world down. It was a lesson she greatly valued.

The whirl of wings wisped past her face and she scrunched her eyes tight.

"Please, Librarian. I thought we had agreed we would not stand on the formalities. Open your eyes. I wish to see your storm-cloud colored eyes."

Chrissy maneuvered herself to sit on the hand railing that separated the kitchen from the main floor.

Linda relaxed her features and allowed her eyes to open; before her sat the tiny nymph. She had clad herself in a fifties-style, carhop uniform, ingeniously made from the petals of daisies and roses.

Linda allowed a smile to touch her lips. "You're looking very... official today. Any particular reason?"

Chrissy shifted her position. "Yes, I was reading on the Internet that servers used to get something called tips. Every server I saw had a uniform so I decided I like this style best and put it together. Maybe I'll get some tips."

Linda was finding it very hard not to laugh aloud. "Well, Chrissy, I don't really think you have a need for tips."

Chrissy pushed her lower lip out and furrowed her brow into a thunderous frown. "Why?"

Linda caught herself before a grin covered her face. "Because tips are paper money customers leave if they think the server has done a good job. Since you live here in the forest and most of your housing, food, and needs are met without having to buy anything, paper money doesn't really have any value, does it?"

Chrissy's lip pulled in and she smoothed her brow. Her face took on a quizzical look and she tilted her head. "I think you're right. Well, this uniform would be wilted by the end of the day, anyway. I'll just wear my regular clothes tomorrow. Was there something you needed, Librarian?"

Linda allowed herself a small chuckle. "Yes. Ailidh has injured her feet, and I wish to get a pan large enough for her to fit in both her feet. I'll need to have water warm enough to melt these salt crystals and then a towel available for her to dry her feet."

The little nymph narrowed her eyes and puzzled the situation. "I know there are some large pans in the very back of the cupboard. Will you come in and pull them out?"

Linda hid her surprise. She never entered the kitchen when Chrissy was working. Her size terrified the little nymph and it was, again, one of the agreements they had made. Moving very slowly, Linda entered the tiny room. She crouched on her knees and opened a very tiny door. In the back was a small, quart size, sauté pan which she was sure was the pot the little nymph meant. Using two fingers to slide out the pan, she pulled it from cupboard and placed it on the top.

"Is this the one you meant?"

Chrissy buzzed into the room and looked at the pan. "Yes. I'll warm some water in it in the microwave…"

"Uh, don't do that. The one thing that won't work in the microwave is metal. If you'll allow me, I'll find something plastic…"

Chrissy smacked her forehead. "Librarian, don't worry. I'll just have to use my magic. How silly of me to forget heating water is one of the first things we're taught. So, if you'll leave?"

Linda rose slowly from the floor and feeling somewhat like a pretzel, backed out of the small space. She rolled up to her full 4 ft. 8 in. height. It felt good to stretch her cramped muscles.

"I'll leave this to you, Chrissy."

Turning she noted Ailidh and Kayne deep in conversation. Something about the body language of the two wee ones was very wrong. It made Linda think. These two were not the only faeries to come into the library and whisper in frightened, muted tones. Linda was determined to find out what was causing such consternation among the Fae community. From the trembling of their wings, she needed to move fast or her tiny folk would be gone, and Linda would be alone with her library full of books.

Chapter Two

Linda crept toward the huddled bodies of Kayne and Ailidh. She stopped, her eyes cast down, and cleared her throat. Her ears picked up the rustle of wings.

"Yes, Librarian?" It was the melodic voice of Ailidh.

"I was wondering if I might speak with Kayne privately for a moment."

Frantic whispering ensued. Linda was hoping the two would decide soon as her neck was beginning to pain her.

"Please look up, Librarian."

Linda brought her eyes up to face the piercing forest green orbs of the tiny faerie.

"What do you want with my mate?" A tiny eyebrow slowly arched upward.

"There has been some unrest within the…" she hesitated.

Calling the faeries by that name could bring a world of problems on herself and the library. She frantically searched for the proper terminology.

"…the Hidden Ones' community."

Ailidh and Kayne smirked at each other.

"It's okay to call us faeries, Librarian. You have our permission." They saw her shoulders relax and she breathed a sigh of relief.

"I've noticed many of my patrons whispering in hushed tones and frowns have replaced the happy smiles once exhibited. I'm very worried and hoped Kayne might enlighten me as to how I might assist."

Chrissy arrived, carrying a towel-wrapped, steaming pan of water. She placed the pan on top of the towel on the floor in front of Ailidh.

"There. I've brought some of the salts to sprinkle in the water once you've slipped your feet in the pan, Ailidh."

Kayne turned toward his mate. "I'm going to talk with the Librarian outside. I'll be back shortly." He kissed Ailidh lightly on her forehead and winged his way out through the open window.

Linda moved carefully toward the door listening to Chrissy fuss over Ailidh and her sore feet.

"What were you doing to get your feet so swollen? Oh, Ailidh, they must really hurt. Here, slip them into the water. See, isn't that better? Now, I'm supposed to sprinkle these crystals in… Ooohhh, look! They fizz!"

Linda allowed a smile to touch her lips. Chrissy had been a godsend in the small community. Unlike most forest nymphs, she was determined to be successful in a businesslike way and had welcomed the opportunity to work and be around an Other. Linda couldn't understand the little nymph's need to be human. She would've given her right arm to be a fae of the forest. Oh, well, seemed no one was happy with their lot right now.

Linda slipped out the door and quietly sat on the second step. Kayne had drawn up one of the chairs to the edge of the top step and was tipping the legs back.

"What is it you want to know, Librarian?"

"Kayne?"

"Yes?"

"Can you read?"

"Yes, Librarian. Quite well. As the first son, my parents made sure I was well educated. They felt having the ability to read the Others' language would help me to keep the community safe. I've tried to keep up with the news by reading the daily papers when I can find them."

Linda nodded. An old mystery had now been solved. When she and Donald had first moved here, their paper was tossed on the front porch. Out of seven days of a week, four of those days the paper would go missing. They never could figure out why. So Donald constructed a paper holder and set it at the end of the driveway. Toward the end of his life, the only exercise he got was to walk to the newspaper box and get the daily paper. They never lost a paper again.

"Good. It will make my request a little easier then. I've noted my patrons are very upset. They gather in clusters in the coffee shop and start discussing--something. I'm not sure what it is because if I venture out to get a book, all conversation ceases. I'm beginning to get hostile looks. From what few snatches of conversation I gather, there is construction machinery damaging your homes?"

Kayne turned his head and looked at this Other. Should he let her know what was happening? Would he be betraying his kind? What if she could help?

He weighed the options and decided.

"The machines, you call them bulldozers, are moving swiftly through our forest and homes. They seem to strike without a pattern. We're terrified and unable to do anything. We don't know how to make them stop." Kayne sighed. "I'm afraid we're all going to have to move to Faetown."

Linda blanched. Her faeries were going to leave the forest. She couldn't have it.

"Has anyone come close enough to read the name of the company on the side of the machine?"

Kayne flinched and pulled back. His eyes were wide, his jaw had dropped open and his wings began to beat furiously against the chair.

"Get close! Are you mad? Those machines would crunch us in a minute, and no one would know!" He shook his head. "No, no one has been close and I wouldn't ask anyone to try."

Linda waited for his wings to stop churning. When Kayne folded them against his back, she knew he'd settled down enough to broach him with her idea.

"I asked because if we could get the name of the company off the door of the bulldozer , then we might be able to check on the computer to see who owns the construction company. I'd be able to check official records to see what the project is requiring them to work so haphazardly.

From that point, we might be able to formulate a plan to stop the destruction of the Ancient Ones."

Kayne's eyes popped open. "You know of the Ancient Ones?"

Linda nodded. "I had many years to study before you wee ones showed yourselves to me. I know of the Ancients. It angers me to see them systematically destroyed for no reason."

Kayne shook his head. The librarian was amazing him with her revelations. She seemed so in touch with his kind, and he knew... well, nothing about her. He turned his deep brown eyes her direction.

"Why would you aid us? You're one of... them?"

He watched anger flash across the face of this Other. As quickly as it had surfaced, he saw it replaced by a kindly smile.

"I always knew of you wee ones. Before I married the Mr. and took his name as my own, my family name was O'Rourke. The little folk have long been welcomed in my family's homes.

"The cups and saucers, plates and silverware you use in the coffee shop were all forged and molded by my great, great, grandfather. Our hearth always featured food for the fae. I grew up with faerie..." she glanced quickly to Kayne at her slip of the tongue.

He smiled and nodded forgiveness.

Linda cleared her throat and continued "...friends. They didn't change--I did. As I got older, they seemed to disappear, and I began to believe seeing them had all happened in my head.

"Then we moved here. Chrissy was the first to show herself."

Linda smiled. The day she arrived had been a particularly tough one. Donald, her husband, had been so sick; Linda knew he wasn't long for this world. She'd had to make a decision to like living in the woods or sell everything and move back to San Francisco.

She had sat on the front porch--Donald having finally fallen asleep--and stared into the woods surrounding their home.

Suddenly, there she was standing on the top step, her wings poised elegantly.

Linda remembered holding her breath not sure the sight before her was real.

~ * ~

The two stared at each other.

The Librarian not daring to move.

The nymph not sure if she should speak, and when she did ,where to start.

Chrissy spoke first.

"Might I have a cup of coffee?"

Linda blinked and released the breath she'd been holding.

"Black?"

"Sugar and milk if you have it."

Linda nodded. "I'll bring it out. Have a seat."

She backed slowly toward her front door. Ever so gently, she opened the door and sprinted to the kitchen. She put a cup of coffee in the microwave warming the brown liquid. As she waited, she looked around for a container small enough to fit the nymph's hands. As she was beginning to panic, she remembered the tea set, forged by an O'Rourke hundreds of years earlier and passed from one generation to the next.

Moving quietly through the house, she went into the second bedroom and grabbed the set. She washed everything in the kitchen sink then filled the small coffee pot, sugar bowl, and creamer. Adding a cup next to her own porcelain teacup, she balanced the tray as she measured her steps to the outside.

She wasn't certain she would find the tiny wood nymph on her porch. She *had* been up for the previous 24 hours taking care of Donald. She could have hallucinated the tiny mite.

Upon opening the door, she spotted the miniscule visitor still seated on the porch. Noiselessly, she placed the tray on the top step, sat, and poured a cup of coffee for her guest, nodding her head to the sugar and creamer containers.

"Please… help yourself."

She poised her cup while the nymph doctored her drink. It wasn't until the little creature had taken a sip of her coffee that Linda spoke.

"I don't want to seem ungrateful but... what brings you to my home?"

She brought the cup to her lips and pulled a sipful of the warm liquid into her mouth.

"Because I need your help."

The liquid seemed lodged in her throat. Linda swallowed hard and looked at the tiny beauty. She cleared her throat.

"You need *my* help?"

Golden brown eyes reminding Linda of the bark of the oak trees surrounding her small home stared up at her.

The wood nymph nodded her head.

"One of the machines that the Oth... your kind uses came and tore my oak tree, my home, from the ground. I was down by the stream enjoying the day and dipping my feet in the coolness when I heard the screams of the yellow machinery. I hid myself behind a boulder near the edge of the trail running past my tree. If I would have been inside..."

The tiny nymph shuddered, her wings rustling to the very tips.

"...anyway--I was wondering if I might stay in the old oak behind your dwelling. I've checked and it appears vacant."

The tiny visitor looked so lost, Linda felt her heart melt.

"Of course."

The little visitor's shoulders dropped. "Thank you. And thank you for the coffee."

"I'll try not to disturb you. Do you need help moving in?"

"No. I'm carrying everything I now own."

The two sat drinking their coffee. When they had finished the pot, the nymph rose, her wings working lazily, and turned to Linda.

"You're different than most of the Others..."

"Linda."

"How is it you can see me?"

Linda watched the effort the nymph was exerting to keep herself aloft.

"Well..."

"Chrissy."

"Chrissy, as you appear to be very tired..."

The visitor bobbed her head in agreement.

"…why don't we save that discussion for another time?"

A slow nod of the tiny head, bobbing of the body, and the nymph winged to the end of the porch disappearing around the side of the house.

Several years and many cups of coffee later, the two had formed an unusual friendship.

Chrissy's home destruction was the first Linda had heard of the decimation of the Ancient forest and the homes of the fae folk. It was not, unfortunately, the last.

As the fae started to trust Linda, thanks to Chrissy's concerted efforts, and had begun to use the Lending Library, she picked up on the whisperings and saw the trembling wings more often.

~ * ~

Now she sat with Kayne hearing yet again another tale of unprovoked, wanton destruction of the ancient forest and fae folk homes.

Linda looked at Kayne. "If you can remember the name on the side of the dozers, we could use the Internet to track the owners. There has got to be a way to stop the devastation."

Kayne shifted on the step.

"I was trying to stay away from the machines."

Linda watched the color rise to his cheeks.

"I understand and I would have done the same thing. However, anything you can recall will help us to halt this killing."

Kayne thought for a moment. He closed his eyes and scrunched them tightly.

"I think I recall a triangular shield with a long sword crossing from the top left through the bottom right. There was also a name… black… black catco. That's it. It was black catco."

Linda rose. "Great. Let's see if we can find some information about the company on the Internet."

"Excellent idea. A chill has begun to descend on my wings."

Kayne winged his way inside.

The librarian waited until the faerie had disappeared into the building.

Maybe, just maybe they'd get somewhere now. She hoped so. The daily razing of the forest was moving dangerously close to her home.

Like the wee folk, Linda feared the bulldozers... and like the fae folk, she had nowhere else to go.

Chapter Three

The setting sun spiked light off the gray circular tower of the multi-storied, river rock building covering two acres of the mountaintop. Wrought iron gates set in stone walls protected the summit fortress known as Citadel Saun from the rest of the world. The castle had overlooked the valley for as long as the residents could recall. Very few recognized the design as a direct copy of the Bothwell Castle in Strathclyde, Scotland.

Gitty stood in her dining hall at the long oak table. Chandeliers hanging on cast-iron chains from the 25-foot ceilings shed light around the long narrow dining hall. A crackling blaze in the man-sized fireplace emitted enough heat to warm the cavernous room. Strewn across the 16-foot tabletop covering the slab's magnificent wood swirls bordered in gold leaf, lay a topographical map of the eastern 25 miles of the valley closest to Faetown. The tall, muscular night elf leaned over and drew large red x's on areas noted to be home to groves of oak trees.

"There's one less bunch of trees to search."

A sneer marred the fair face. Ice blue eyes pored over wavy lines showing mountains, rivers, valleys, and acres upon acres of wooded lands.

"That wretched little raisin of a leprechaun better not have lied to me, or I'll let Lancelot have him for dinner."

A 40-pound cat with glowing yellow eyes prowled its way around the leather clad legs of the elf. She reached down and pulled her pointed nails along the thick black fur of the animal's back.

"Soon, my love, soon."

Leaning closer to the paper, Gitty noted she was nearing the edge of the Ancient One's land and had yet to find what she sought.

"If we don't come across something soon..." She let the thought die.

The cat growled deep in its throat; the hair down the center of its back standing on end.

Gitty tried to ignore the cat's warning, but the sound of soft leather on flagstone disrupted her concentration and she looked up to see who dared to interrupt her.

"Oh, it's you." Gitty shrugged and turned back to view the map.

"Wow. Don't let your sisterly love overwhelm you at my return." Morgan strode his way to his sister's side and the map that seemed to have ensnared her constant attention.

"I just can't figure out the little raisin's rhyme.

'A stand of oaks
That all can see,
Hides the fortune
You seek from me.'

"I've bulldozed nearly all the oak groves in this valley and have yet to find the miserable little beggar's fortune. If I don't come up with it soon, I'll put him on the rack and torture the information out of his leathery hide. Then Lancelot can have him for dinner."

The cat yeowed at the mention of its name.

"That's right, my sweet, leprechaun for dinner."

Gitty traced a road with her fingernail. In her own writing, she'd drawn a house and noted, *Lending Library*. Directly behind the structure, per notes she'd written herself, was an enormous oak tree shading the building. The towering perennial housed several forest creatures and covered the building with shade in the summer. Gitty had dismissed it as inconsequential. She was beginning to reconsider.

"Maybe the leprechaun was playing with his words."

Morgan leaned over her shoulder and peered at the squiggly lines and circles on the paper.

"I think, sister, you need to get a hobby. This looks to be a child's attempt at art."

Gitty huffed her impatience. "It's a topography map, you idiot. If you weren't so busy trying to enchant every female that passes by you, you'd realize our time will be coming to an end very quickly if we don't find some sort of gold to purchase the land."

Morgan straightened and looked at the hunched back of his sister. "What in the world for? We're elves; we have no need for the things humans consider so important."

Gitty dropped her head to her chest and pushed out a sigh. "You fool. Of course, we don't *need* money. If we want to continue to live in this castle and keep the grounds human-free, we need to be able to purchase the land around it to stave them from our fortress."

Morgan's brow furrowed. "Why? No one *owns* the land. The land belongs to all who live in the forest."

Gitty whipped around, fisted her hands on her hips, and glared at her younger brother.

"You, mushroom brain, have been thinking with your sexual organ and not your head. If you'd taken the time within the last 100 years to notice, man has begun *buying* all the forest. Somehow they have found a way to own what was not ownable. If we don't use their paper money to purchase what was ours by rights, we will be thrown off our family's land.

"Are you going to go and get one of their jobs to bring in some of their paper money?"

Morgan pulled himself to his full 6' 5" of height. "I don't need a job. I'm elfkind."

"Well, elfkind, help me locate the leprechaun's fortune or you'll be elfkind living in a cave and bathing in the river."

Gitty resumed her position at the table studying the map.

Morgan looked at his older sister. She was not one to mince words. He thought about his latest ventures into the nightclubs of the humans. The females were drawn to him as bees congregated around the hive, but the moment they learned his looks were not attached to money, they disappeared. He'd spent more than one night in the company of some troll of a woman due to the lack of this paper money of which Gitty spoke.

Morgan moved next to his sister and looked at the map.

"The only thing I see is this place here."

Morgan's finger rested under the simple drawing Gitty had made of the Lending Library.

Chapter Four

Linda dragged her hand through her hair, scrunched her eyes shut, and tilted her head back. She'd been sitting in front of the computer for hours trying to track the business name Kayne had said he spotted on the side of the excavation machinery. What she located was a maze of business organizations bleeding into other organizations all circling back to Black Catco. No one seemed to own the company, and there was no paper trail on the county site indicating a permit issued to bulldoze the woods surrounding her home.

She sighed deeply and brought her head forward squinting at the stream of light spiking her eyes. Glancing at the clock on the computer, she moaned.

"God, I didn't realize how late... make that early... it was. I need sleep, or I'll be as grouchy as Simon Stockington on a good day."

Linda emitted a tired giggle. No one could be as grouchy as the ancient mailman. Feeling woozy and lightheaded, she left a note for Chrissy asking her to watch the library while she got some sleep. The destruction of the Ancient Woods and faeries homes would have to wait. Otherwise, her thinking capacity would be worthless.

~ * ~

Chrissy opened the door to a dark interior.

"This isn't good."

The bluish hue of the computer screen caught her attention and, after flicking the switch to lighten the room, she allowed her curiosity to guide her. Taped above the computer display was a note from the Librarian.

Please watch the library today. Up all night researching. Need to sleep.

Chrissy moved the cordless mouse and watched the screen flicker to life.

"Oh no."

She sharply sucked in a breath at the image on the screen. Centered on the computer monitor was a triangular-shaped shield. From one upper corner across the face of the shield to the lower corner, a long blade was pictured. Above the sword and shield was the heavily printed word, *Black*, and under the image was one other word, *Catco*.

"Not again. I thought she'd left the area. Damn!" Chrissy muttered. "Tiamoon, you'd better be close by. We really need you now."

Turning off the computer, the little nymph trudged to the kitchen to start her day. She was going to have to call on the mice to get a message to the warrior gnome, Tiamoon. If Black Catco was in the area, the Lending Library was in trouble... as was everyone who lived in the surrounding woods.

Chapter Five

Ailidh tittered nervously as Kayne placed their luggage in the wagon. The dog pulling the vehicle shuffled in place, his actions bobbling the bed.

"Silas! Hold still!" Bram huffed.

"I'm anxious to get going. I'm only doing this as a favor to Ailidh, you know." The terrier mix turned to look at his business partner.

"I know, I know," Bram arranged the suitcases in the bed of the wagon. He fluffed the pillow on the seat and pulled out a blanket to cover the slender shoulders of his dainty passenger and her mate.

Ailidh winged to the front of the wagon and settled herself in front of the dog, Silas. She looked into his dark brown eyes and smiled. Resting her hands on his furry muzzle, she placed a tender kiss between his eyes.

"Thank you, so much, Silas. This is a tough move for us but knowing you care enough to take us there helps. Really, it does."

Kayne watched his mate work her wonder on the dog. If dogs could blush, he was sure Silas would be red to the roots of his fur. He figured to get things moving before it got too late.

"I think we should be moving before it gets dark. We have a long way to go my love."

Ailidh nodded but didn't move until she'd wrapped her arms around the dog's neck and squeezed gently. "Thank you."

She winged to the wagon and hovered over the seat next to Kayne.

He laid the blanket on the wooden bench and when she had set herself down, he wrapped the woolen spread around her body.

She shivered and leaned into him. "Let's get started. We have one stop to make before we leave the woods."

Bram clucked his tongue and Silas took off at a trot.

Ailidh and Kayne turned to catch one last look at their home.

"I sure hope this works out," she whispered to him.

"Me too."

~ * ~

Chrissy sat cradling the hot cup of liquid in her hands. It had been a long time since the *Black Cat* name had appeared. The last time the name had been uttered, the fae community was nearly wiped out. She couldn't--wouldn't--let that happen again. Tiamoon needed to be contacted; but how?

No one had heard from the warrior gnome in several years. After the last debacle, she'd left the glen swearing never to return.

Chrissy rolled her eyes. Kayne's brother, Keegan, had rejected every command the warrior had issued. His insubordination came close to undermining the defense of the woods and the inhabitants. Only after Kayne had thrashed him soundly had Keegan agreed to pitch in with the others and fight for their homes.

She felt the rise of panic. How was she going to find the warrior? Her reverie and questions were interrupted by the squeaking of the front door.

"Going to have to get that hinge oiled." She put her cup on the table. Standing, she blinked in surprise at the visitors.

"Ailidh, Kayne. You're here awfully early today. What brings you in?"

Kayne stepped toward Chrissy and extended a hand. "We're leaving the forest and wanted to stop by to thank you for helping Ailidh the other day. Will you let the Librarian know we've gone?"

Chrissy's mouth hung open. "Leaving, why?"

Ailidh looked at her feet, a shy smile touching the corners of her mouth.

"My sister invited us to live in Faetown with her. I've always told her no, but the other day when the huge yellow machine the Others drive nearly destroyed our home, well… " Ailidh lifted her chin, crossed her arms, and stood straight. "…I just made up my mind I'd had enough. I'm tired of living in fear. At least in Faetown my home won't be torn down."

She gave a nod of her head. "That's what my sister says."

Kayne shrugged his shoulders. "Where Ailidh goes, so go I. Thanks again, Chrissy, and please let the Librarian know how much we appreciate her help."

Chrissy pushed out a sigh. "Best of luck to you both. Send me news when you settle. I'll keep watch on your home--just in case things don't work out and you decide to come back to us."

Ailidh straightened her shoulders. "They will work out. I'm determined."

Chrissy cast a glance at Kayne. He was shaking his head slightly. She knew he would support Ailidh no matter the cause but recalled many an argument where he had been vocal about not wanting to live in the city. This change of heart meant Ailidh was very, very frightened.

The two faeries walked to the porch and down the steps to the wagon bearing their belongings.

Chrissy watched with a feeling of hopelessness as the pair departed.

I have to contact Tiamoon. Somehow, someway. The forest is in grave danger and we need a champion… the sooner, the better.

Chapter Six

Tiamoon paced the floor of her hut, the sound of her pliable leather boots whispering over the river stones. She couldn't sit still. She wasn't sure what the problem was, but she *just* couldn't sit still. This feeling of... restless dread permeated every pore in her body. She found herself whipping around at every creaking branch outside her window, jumping with every snap of wood in the fireplace, and in general, trying to escape her own skin.

Something was wrong in the forest; something was terribly wrong in *her* forest. She could sense it. A high keening carried on the drift of clouds pushed by the winds of the south filtered through the evergreens. The last time the woods spoke to each other in such worried tones, Mt. St. Helens exploded and killed many old friends. The feeling in the forest was taking on the same trepidation as it had in May 1980.

She stepped out her hut door and stood in front of her home listening. Restless trees swished their branches through the air, groaning in fear and expectation. The bushes rustled nervously and the only other sound was the throaty hooting of an owl searching for dinner. All else was silent--too silent.

Inside, she reclaimed her chair facing the fire. She bent forward and stirred the stew simmering in the pot hanging over the fire. The fragrant smell of cooked vegetables curled around her nose and her stomach grumbled at her.

"Yeah, yeah. Soon."

A quick dip of the wooden spoon in the pot and she brought the steaming liquid to her mouth receiving more complaints from her stomach. The hot tangy liquid burned the edges of her lips, and she blew across the top of the spoon to cool it. A second test proved the cooling to be a success, and she gulped the food down.

"It's cooked long enough. I'm hungry."

Tiamoon dipped her bowl into the mixture pulling the dripping wooden container toward her. As she was about to tuck into the stew, a scratching at her hut's door halted her progress. She dropped the spoon into the filled bowl, precious liquid splashing over the side. Rising from her stool, Tiamoon set her dinner down and stomped to the door.

"This had better be damned good."

She flung open the door and stared out at the dark night. As she was about to roar her anger at the wind, a tapping on her boot directed her attention downward. Standing before her was a mouse with a note clutched between its teeth.

Tia snatched the document from the creature's mouth.

"Thank you. My jaws were beginning to ache."

Tia nodded.

"I'm to wait for a reply."

Tiamoon stepped out of her warm home and glanced around the nearby woods. There was no unusual movement, nothing out of the ordinary; just an early spring wind blustering through the tree branches.

Stepping inside she motioned the mouse to enter.

"Sit next to the fire. I'll bring water and some food."

"That would be lovely. It's very chilly this evening."

Tia humphed an answer as she fetched a container in which to dip water from the pail. She pulled a small bowl from her cupboard and filled it with the soup which still bubbled in the cooking cauldron on the fire.

Her hostess duties fulfilled, Tiamoon sat in her chair and opened the message.

Forest facing destruction from unknown assailant. Need your help, again. Please come as soon as possible.
C.

Tiamoon crumpled the note in her hands.

"Why should I? The last time I helped they ignored my advice and exiled me off the land. I don't care if they all get pushed into Faetown and never have a home again."

"Beg pardon?" The mouse pushed aside its empty bowl.

"Nothing. It may take me some time to come up with an answer."

Settling itself next to the warmth of the hearth, the mouse replied. "Take your time. My bones need warming, and this fire is very inviting."

Tia finished her soup and dipped out another bowl as she tried to formulate an answer to the message that wasn't as bitter as she felt. She realized much time had slipped away as the mouse began to snore gently.

She threw several large logs on the fire, washed out the bowls, and crawled under the covers on her bed. The goose down comforter gifted her by the Valley geese held her body warmth, causing her eyelids to flutter and close. She still had no response for the mouse to take back but maybe a good night's sleep would bring the right words to her mind. Tiamoon sighed deeply and drifted into a restless slumber.

~ * ~

She rose from her bed and rubbed her eyes. There was something dark gray in front of her fireplace.

"What the..." she furrowed her brow as she tried to place the strange apparition on her hearth. Grabbing her boots, she pulled the supple leather over one foot then the other. She leaned to grab her sword from it resting place next to her bed and stalked silently on leathered feet toward the intruder. Her journey to the hearth halted at the piece of crumpled paper on the floor.

The sword slid quietly into its sheath on her belt, the events of the previous evening replaying in her mind.

"Oh, yeah... an answer."

Tiamoon grabbed her fur cloak from the hook by the front entry and braced herself for the chill and probable rain of the morning. She pulled open the door and found herself squinting at the brightness assaulting her.

"Wonders never cease."

She trod around the side of the hut and gathered wood to start the morning fire. Above her a formation of geese headed north squawking noisily as they left the approaching summer.

Hoisting the wood in her arms, she muttered, "Looks to be a hot summer."

She bobbled the load to the front of the hut and pushed the door open with her foot shoving it closed behind her. Padding to the hearth, Tia dropped the cut logs on the flagstones.

The gray lump stirred. From the mountain of fur a furiously moving nose and twitching whiskers appeared. Tiny, bloodshot eyes blinked rapidly and peered at Tiamoon.

"Ah, yes. I really can't thank you enough for allowing me to share the warmth of your fire and dryness of your hearth. Have you an answer to send back?"

Tia sighed. She'd like to tell them to handle their own problems; they were so certain they didn't need her the last time, but Fae Forest was her home. She was as tied to it as if the land had born her. Last night's message had put understanding to her restlessness of the last few weeks.

She watched Mouse stretch. Tia moved forward arranging the logs in the fire pit and set flame to the wood. The night's chill began to subside from the hut's interior.

"I have fresh bread baked by one of the local lasses in payment for a favor I did for her. Let's have some bread and water. After that, I'll give you a reply."

Mouse's ears perked up and his pink tongue slipped out around his lips.

"You know, you're not obliged…"

Tiamoon held up a hand. "I know. I also know it's better to work with a full stomach."

"That's true." Mouse wiggled himself as close to the fire as he

32

could without singeing his fur. "Ah, but this feels good."

Tia had gone to her pantry to retrieve the bread and returned with a full bowl of water and thick slice of bread. "You'll be pleased to know the sun shines today. No rain to soak your fur."

Mouse's eyes brightened. "How wonderful! My senses tell me we are to have a long, hot summer."

Tia nodded. "The geese fly north as we speak."

As the two ate in silence, Tiamoon intently watched Mouse. He shifted and cleaned his whiskers.

"Have I dropped crumbs on my coat?"

Tiamoon stood. "No, no, that's not it. I think I may have a solution to you having to carry the message back in your mouth."

Mouse smiled. "That would be welcomed. I get so tired I have to stop more often than I should. Any help would be appreciated."

He watched her rummaging under her sleeping spot. All sorts of curious items emerged from beneath her bed until he heard her exclaim, "Aha! This is just what I wanted."

She turned and held up some kind of log-shaped item with a long string attached.

Mouse's eyebrows came together. "What is it?"

Tiamoon explained as she walked toward him. "This is an old quiver I haven't used for a very long time."

Mouse's frown deepened. "A what?"

"Quiver. It's used to store arrows when you are hunting and need to carry more than one with you. That's why it has a securing strap."

"Oh."

"I think if I extend the strap as far as it will go we'll be able to strap it to your back. Once that's done, we can put a message inside, create a cover for the end and you'll be able to travel without holding the message in your mouth."

Mouse sat on his haunches and smiled. "When do we start?"

"Let me reply to the note you brought me and we'll get things set."

Tiamoon padded to the cupboard where she stored her dishes and pulled open a drawer. Lifting out a pad of paper and a pen, she stood at the counter and formulated a reply to the note. She rolled the answer into a cylinder and placed it inside the quiver. Opening the second drawer of the stand-up cupboard, she located a knife. Kneeling down on the floor, she pulled the quiver to her and punched a hole in the very end of the leather holding strap. Next she got up and started toeing through the items on the floor she'd pulled from under her bed.

"There."

She bent down and pulled two items from the floor using her foot to shove the rest of the stuff back under the bed.

Mouse watched as she placed a piece of tanned leather over the opening of the quiver and secured it with a leather thong.

"That should hold everything inside. Now, mouse," Tiamoon turned to the messenger, "I need you to allow me to put this around you."

Mouse looked at the contraption, thought of his aching jaws the previous night, and nodded.

Tia slid the cylinder up his arm, over his head, and settled it between his shoulder blades. Noting it slipped easily, she moved back to her bed and got on her hands and knees.

"I know it's here somewhere." She reached beneath and pulled a long strand of leather to her as she sat on her knees. She looked at the strand then at the mouse with the quiver hanging off its side.

"I must make an adjustment."

The mouse sat back on its haunches.

Tia took the leather strand in hand and walked around the mouse. She stopped behind him and a smile began to slowly emerge on her lips. "Bingo."

"What?"

"I'll be just a moment. Don't worry if you feel tugging. I'm not doing anything that will harm you."

"I guess I just have to trust you." Mouse felt a tugging and heard a soft zipping sound.

Tiamoon stood in front of him with a leather end in hand. "Hold this please."

He grabbed the end and waited.

She had the other piece of the leather strand and standing in front of Mouse, grabbed the end she'd handed him and tied the two together. She adjusted the quiver until the cylinder was positioned squarely in the middle then she cinched the strand to a comfortable tightness.

Mouse patted the leather at his waist. "The missus says I need to lose some weight. Guess she's right."

Tia smiled. "Well, I'll never tell. If I had more time, I'd fashion this to fit more comfortably. For now... this will do."

Mouse wiggled back and forth, the cylinder on his back staying in place.

"I think this is great. I'll be able to move faster, keep up my pace, and get home sooner. I've no complaints."

Tia threw her cape over her shoulders, opened the door, and walked outside with Mouse.

"How long will it take you to get back to Fae Forest?"

Mouse considered for a moment, sniffed the air, and narrowed his eyes against the light.

"If I can find Grizelda's Flight Service, two days. If I'm on foot, a fortnight."

She nodded. "Well, be careful. All sorts of creatures are waking from winter's sleep right now."

Mouse hopped into the field, his gray fur disappearing within the tall grass.

Tiamoon strode to the back of her hut. She untied the cape and slung it over the top rail of the fence. Drawing her sword, she crept toward the first outcropping in the field behind her hut. Tia's senses tingled. The skin on her arms prickled and her ears tuned to the sounds of the land.

"It's been a long time, my friend, but your sleep time is over. Ha!"

She jumped up and jabbed a well-used straw dummy. The arms swung around wildly, a flail at each end with the ability to deliver painful, bleeding wounds. Tiamoon dropped to the ground under the swinging arms her sword clutched tightly in her hand. She crawled on her stomach until she was beyond the dummy then ran the obstacle course twice until her undershirt lay soaked against her skin. Pushing aside wet strands of her hair, she plodded back to her hut. She divested herself of her sword and heavy cloak. The wall at the back of the hut sported a heavy velvet curtain which Tia pulled back, to reveal a modern bathroom: shower, toilet, sink, and storage for towels and linen. She turned on the faucet in the shower until steam roiled to the ceiling. Dropping the last of her sweat and dirt-covered clothing to the tiled floor, Tia slipped under the scalding liquid allowing the water to soothe her aching muscles.

"I will not be run from my forest again. I may ache and pain now, but in a fortnight my body will be the weapon it once was. I can only hope you are the cause of this, Gitty..."

The mention of the name caused Tiamoon to shudder, even within the scalding cascade of her shower.

"...this time, you'll face eviction. I'll see to it."

Chapter Seven

Ailidh's head swiveled from side to side and up and down. She'd never seen such wonders as there were at this city at the edge of the forest where her sister resided.

"Kayne, will you look at how tall those buildings are. They must be the size of the old oak in the middle of the forest. I thought the Lending Library was big but compared to these... " Her green eyes resembled the saucers the librarian placed under her teacups.

Kayne narrowed his eyes. All he could see was the dirty concrete streets filled with trash floating in the light breeze which seemed to push them into town. There were strange vehicles parked near the concrete pathways and people seemed to be rushing around, their heads staring down as they quickly walked to and fro. The gray colored buildings *were* the height of the old oak, probably 50 to 100 feet tall in Others measurements. Unlike the oak, these monstrosities were dead, lifeless, and gritty.

"Yes, Ailidh, it's very different from the forest."

"I know. I think I'm going to love it here. There's so much happening and the town feels... alive!"

Kayne snapped his head to look at his mate. Her face glowed and she smiled as she hadn't in many a month. He couldn't remember her smiling like this since the Other's machines started tearing up the forest.

A pain touched his chest. He'd been gone less than a week, and he missed the smell of the meadow near their dwelling, the damp of the moss-covered streambed nearby, and the rustle of leaves in the branches of the tree above their home. He was here in Faetown because he loved

Ailidh. That was the only reason. Plucking up courage he didn't feel, he answered.

"I think this is going to be… an experience." He slipped her hand into his and gritted his teeth in to a smile. *For Ailidh.*

The dog and cart drew up to a curb in front of a tall brick building. Kayne counted ten sets of glass above extra large windows at ground level. The façade of the building was plain red brick with light gray accents. He noted the panes looked like eyes peering out at the world. In the center of the building at the top of the ten-step staircase was a set of double doors featuring etched glass casements. Kayne looked up in time to see one of the doors swing open and a faerie with blue-tinted dark hair fly down the steps.

"Ailidh!"

"Cadhla!"

Ailidh jumped from the cart tearing her hand from Kayne's and ran to hug her sister. They were a contrast in color. Cadhla was dressed in a black long-sleeve shirt, black jeans, and black high heels on her feet; her blue-tinted, short-cropped, dark spiky hair shimmering in the light streaming between the buildings. Ailidh was attired in her forest clothing of grass green diaphanous skirt, buttercup yellow blouse, and bare feet, her blonde hair billowing in the breeze.

Kayne shook his head. How could two such opposite people have the same parents? The answer was beyond him.

The two girls jumped up and down hugging as they danced in the street.

"Come inside and see my place. We have about three hours before I have to go to work so we can catch up." Cadhla linked her arm through her sister's and led her up the apartment steps.

Kayne looked at Bram and Silas and shrugged his shoulders.

"I guess we get to unload the cart."

"Better you two than me," Silas said. "Soon as you're done taking stuff out of the back, I'm taking a nap. My pads are sore."

Bram started to grumble about good-for-nothing, lazy help as he moved suitcases from the cart to the sidewalk. He frowned deeply as Silas lay down when he and Kayne were finished.

"Useless mutt. If he didn't own sixty percent of the business, I'd fire him."

Kayne smirked, knowing Bram wouldn't know what to do without his business partner and best friend.

"I know what you mean."

The two men hurried up the steps dragging suitcases hoping to find the giggling faerie sisters. They barged through the doors and stood inside a lobby with ceilings as tall as an oak tree. Both men gawked at the ornate paintings on the walls and ceiling, gold accents glistening in the light of the day.

"Wow!"

"You can say that again," Kayne said.

"Hello?" Cadhla called to them from a square hole in the wall. She motioned them over and pushed her hand against the side of the opening until they'd dragged all the suitcases inside. Once she removed her hand, the wall slammed shut on them.

Kayne, Bram, and Ailidh started pounding on the wall.

"Open up!"

They stopped and gulped air as the floor started shaking and the walls groaned. Each one clutched their stomach.

"I feel like I'm going to be ill," Ailidh turned to Cadhla.

She smiled. "It's an elevator. Sort of a moving room. This is a faster way to get to my apartment than walking up ten flights of stairs."

She could see the confusion in their eyes. "I'll show you when we get to the top. I live in the pent… in the top of the building; similar to the top of the tree--the highest branch on the tallest tree in the forest. You'll see when we get there."

The floor shuttered and bounced and the feeling of movement stopped. The wall opened into a hallway with rugs all across the floor. The three forest faeries stepped tentatively on the carpet. When the floor proved stable, they pulled the suitcases out of the moving room and turned to watch the wall shut again.

Cadhla motioned them to follow her. She walked to the end of the hallway and opened a large door. The trio followed her inside, Kayne and Bram bumping into Ailidh who'd stopped in the entry.

Before her was floor to ceiling glass showcasing the top of the city and the woods beyond.

"It's, it's so beautiful!" Ailidh dropped her suitcase and darted to the window. Her eyes swept the rooftops of Faetown and caught sight of the forest leading to the mountain. She could just make out the castle of the night elves. The sight made her quiver.

Cadhla had eased up next to her sister. "I know. If I could block out the castle, this view would be perfect--the tallest branch on the tallest tree, don't you think?"

Kayne cleared his throat. "Cadhla?"

She turned to see Kayne and Bram still clutching suitcases. "Sorry, boys. The room over there." She pointed to a doorway leading off the main area. "You'll have your own bathroom and there is a tiny kitchenette inside if you want to make coffee and snacks. I have a maid who cleans and a cook. I gave them the week off so you could settle in and get comfortable. Just put your things in there."

Ailidh hadn't moved from her spot. "Sister?"

Cadhla moved to her side again. "Yes?"

"How can you afford such a place? In the forest, there is no need for gold, but I imagine you must need it here." Ailidh turned to her sister, the mirth gone from the forest green orbs.

Cadhla cleared her throat and avoided Ailidh's gaze. "Don't worry about that. It's handled."

Ailidh dropped her voice. "We can't stay without helping you somehow. I don't know what I can do if you already have someone to cook. Do you want me to clean?"

"No! That's what the maid does. Don't worry about it right now, okay? Just get settled in and we'll talk about it later."

Kayne had walked up behind Ailidh and wrapped his hands around her waist. "This view is magnificent."

Cadhla forced gaiety to her voice. "Isn't it? See, over there is the city hall and there is the oldest church in town…"

Ailidh watched as her sister rattled on about the buildings, streets, and history of Faetown.

Bram stood at the front door, his hand on the knob and cleared his throat. "Well, I'll be on my way."

Kayne and Ailidh trotted across the large room to the door where she hugged him and Kayne shook his hand.

"Give Silas our thanks for the great care and smooth ride he took in transporting us. Do drive carefully, Bram."

Ailidh watched as Kayne reached into his pouch for coins to pay Bram.

Bram held up a hand. "I will take payment when I have returned you to the woods. Let's just say this trip is only half over. I will convey your thanks to Silas. We'll wait for you to contact us about the return trip." He leaned closer to the two. "After all, you are Fae of the woods and that's where you belong." Nodding, he slipped out the door.

Kayne grabbed the handle, jerked the door open, and looked in the hallway for his friend. He was nowhere to be seen. A smile touched Kayne's lips. "Been a long time since Bram used his magic. Guess he wasn't too fond of that moving room."

He closed the door and drew Ailidh to him. "I will take care of you, my love. I promise."

He placed a gentle kiss on her forehead. "I'm very tired and the bed in the other room beckons to me. I'm going to lie down. You and your sister can catch up without me."

Kayne slogged across the living area and disappeared into the room gently closing the door behind him.

Ailidh turned to find Cadhla gazing out the windows.

"I'm glad you took my offer to come to Faetown. The forest isn't safe any longer, Ailidh. I've heard rumblings about the destruction of the Ancients. I wanted to be sure you were okay and having you here with me is the best way."

"How can you know what is happening there when you live here?"

Cadhla turned to face her sister. "I have my ways."

"Oh, you're magicing."

"No. It's not allowed in most of the common areas of Faetown. I have... sources who kept me aware of the situation in the Fae Forest."

"Then you know just how frightening it has become. I don't

41

know why someone would want to dig up and destroy the Ancients."

"It's more frightening than you can imagine, Ailidh."

Ailidh looked at the lines around the eyes of her sister. Something was not right about this place where Cadhla lived. Faeries did not show age and this human quality about her sister frightened Ailidh.

I must find out what is going on… but not tonight.

"There is much we need to discuss, and I urge you to take heed of my words. However, I suspect you are as tired as Kayne."

Cadhla moved to her sister's side and picked up the forest faerie's hand.

"Sleep well, Ailidh, for tomorrow, your world will change."

Chapter Eight

Gitty stood tall, pulling her shoulders back and holding her head high. She knew the human construction workers talked behind her back, but she paid them well enough that while she intimidated most of them, they stayed for the wages.

She'd learned from her grubbing gnome stepmother the value of money. While the faeries had no use for money and its power, the humans who were slowly taking over the fae forests put a high value on their paper with funny looking men's pictures on it.

Gitty had lived to see her stepmother try, and fail, to bleed her father of all his possessions. At the end of the last war when the fae and gnomes had succeeded in keeping the forest from the night elves, she swore she would get revenge. She'd gotten her half sister run out of the forest, but Gitty wasn't happy with that small victory.

Her father's wealth of lands and gold had been dwindling over the years, thanks in part to her narcissistic, spendthrift brother Morgan. The other culprits were these pestilent humans. Their belief that everything they saw belonged to them had eaten through the family's gold as Gitty had to buy back ancestral lands. She'd taken over the family wealth, sent her stepmother back to the underground hovel where her father had discovered her, and pulled the purse strings closed on her brother. The silence of her missing stepmother was filled by the constant whining of her brother.

If she had not stumbled across Thomas, *that obnoxious little leprechaun*, drinking himself to an early grave over the loss of some wayward faerie, Gitty might have been forced to sell the family's massive castle and surrounding lands.

But the gods had smiled on her. With a bit of the old leprechaun's magic turned on himself, she had been one drink from getting the *exact* location of his fortune. As it was, she was working from a poem muttered by a drunk, mere moments before his kin burst into the inn and rescued him.

She was nearing the end of her search. There stood only twenty more stands of oak between the treasure she sought and the titanium safe in her basement.

Gitty ran her hand along the brilliant, yellow earthmover. She trembled at the power the machine exuded as it sat rumbling, eager to start its path of destruction.

"What the hell is taking so long?" Speaking more to herself than anyone else, she stomped her work boots on the ground. Time was wasting while they waited for the inspector's go-ahead. And everybody knows--time is money.

She turned to give her crew the thumbs up when her messenger came running and yelling with each step.

"DON'T START THE EARTHMOVERS! DON'T START DIGGING!"

He stopped in front of Gitty, panting and holding his side.

She crossed her arms and glared down at the underling.

"What do you mean, don't start digging?"

He had his hands planted on his knees, head down, gulping in great drafts of air.

"Like I said... don't start excavating."

Gitty bent over and locked her ice blue eyes onto his.

"Why the hell not?"

The young man gasped at the face before him. "Be... be... because there's been a 'cease work' order put on this site... on all this company's sites."

He straightened up and took a step back.

Gitty mirrored his actions. She watched his face drain of color.

"A cease-work order?"

The runner's mouth moved wordlessly reminding her of a fish on the riverbank. She pulled up to her full height and towered over him.

"Uh, uh. Somebody's filed a protest against this company. According to the inspector, until there's a hearing, nothing moves."

"Great!" Gitty smacked the side of the earthmover.

The young man jumped and started moving backwards.

"Ahhhh! Everybody go home!" She slammed both hands against the machine. The resulting boom echoed around the small valley. The human crew bolted to the four-door crew cab, the vehicle tires scattering rocks as they sped away. She checked the equipment, securing those machines left unlocked by fleeing workers, and trudged to her Hummer kicking pinecones with her boots as she walked.

How could anybody know who owned the company? She'd done her best to bury her name under layers of fake corporations just as she'd been shown. She was not going to let these human interlopers run her off land that had been in her family for centuries.

Gitty piloted the back road to her driveway and turned up the winding lane maneuvering the switchbacks until she drove through the gated entrance.

Looking through wrought iron bars into the valley below as she closed and secured the gate, she spotted the roof of the building the faeries called the Lending Library. She parked the Hummer in the converted stables and strolled to the front lawn. Standing in front of the massive stone castle on top of the hill, she planted her booted feet and fisted her hands on her hips glaring at the nondescript rooftop. Her self-centered brother Morgan had pointed out the obvious--the only structure left in her search area was the Lending Library.

"Those little faerie pains wouldn't know how to use the Internet, would they? What of the woman they call the Librarian? Does she have some human magic?" Gitty glared trying her best to magic an answer determined to elude her.

She started when the thought struck her. "It can't be, can it? Is it possible my dear stepsister is behind this?"

A wicked sneer marred the flawless face and lit the ice blue eyes. "I can only hope."

45

Chapter Nine

Linda woke with a start. The work she'd done ferreting out the owner of the construction company, who seemed hell bent on tearing down the forest, haunted her sleep. Every labored step had led down one convoluted quagmire to another false lead. It was a labyrinth designed by an expert--but not as expert as Linda at getting to the center of the maze.

She'd found Black Catco was owned by someone named Gitty Saun. More research had provided her with another entity named Morgan Saun and a Lancelot Saun. Land ownership records of the early settlers showed vast chunks of acreage in the area had belonged to the Saun family. Recently plots seemed to have been sold off at an alarming rate. Linda could only guess at the reason for the sales.

This latest flurry of movement on the owner's part was haphazard and sloppy. Her search had turned up evidence the Sauns were carrying on covert negotiations and buying the land surrounding the castle on the hill overlooking the small valley. Battlements were rising around the fortress at an alarming rate. Meadows shared by the community were being fenced with razor wire and charged with electricity.

Linda shuddered. Why was no one asking questions? Had the family bought off, or worse, eliminated their detractors?

She was glad her husband Donald had forced her to learn the ins and outs of the legal system. When he knew his health was failing, he'd pushed her to take over their business affairs. She'd hated the endless paperwork bog at the time and with his passing swore she'd never touch another form again. However…

Maneuvering the legal alleyways, Linda had been able to get a sitting judge to issue a cease-work order to the Black Catco construction company effectively stopping the forest destruction--temporarily. She, too, had been forced to hide her identity under blankets of deception, but the final results had been to waylay the earthmovers for a couple months. After the hearing... Linda shook her head.

I'm not going to worry until the time comes.

She dragged herself from her quarters, her slippered feet hissing quietly through the empty rooms of her Lending Library. She looked around. The book-lined walls felt strangely cool and foreboding. Linda realized there was no sound coming from the kitchen. She tread lightly so as not to scare Chrissy and announced herself before peeking around the kitchen door.

The room was empty.

That's strange. Chrissy is always up before me.

Linda decided to check on the nymph. Maybe she was ill and unable to leave her home in the oak tree. She grabbed a jacket from her room and headed to the front door. A quick survey out the window revealed no waiting patrons so she opted not to lock her door. She pulled open the windowed entry, turned left, and stopped in her tracks.

Beating her wings frantically against the wall of the house near the eaves was Chrissy. The expression of horror frozen on her delicate features stabbed Linda's heart. Reaching up as far as its black body would allow was a monstrous cat. At least that was what Linda figured it to be; whether it be wild or tame she wasn't sure. The creature was enormous and about to dig its claws into the aging wood siding on Linda's home.

"HEY! GET OUT OF HERE!" She stomped her foot on the wooden porch.

The creature turned slitted yellow eyes her direction and dropped front paws to the deck. It began to stalk toward Linda, a guttural growl growing louder with each padded step. As it approached, the animal barred gleaming, long white teeth as it wrinkled its nose and quickened its pace.

Linda kicked a foot in the animal's direction and, as the creature crouched to pounce, deftly sidestepped the subsequent attack.

The cat tumbled to the edge of the porch and, with her foot Linda shoved it over the edge, barely escaping the extended claws swiped at her.

"Chrissy! Quick!"

She opened the door and the tiny nymph shot into the house. Linda slammed the door shut and locked it. She peered to the front where the cat had fallen from the porch and noted the beast was sitting on its hindquarters licking the spot where her slipper had connected with its fur.

"What in the name of all faedom is that thing?"

Chrissy had fluttered to the nearest tabletop and was panting heavily. She pulled in deep draughts of air and closed her eyes. When her breathing had slowed, she opened eyes wide with terror and spoke.

"That is Lancelot Saun, the pet of Gitty Saun. "

Linda stared out the glass at the animal currently curling up in a sunspot on the driveway.

"That's a pet?!"

Chrissy nodded. "That's Gitty's cat. Gitty passes herself off as human but she is elfkind. Her family used to act as though they owned all the land between here and the mountains."

"According to the records at the courthouse, they did." Linda checked the whereabouts of the black cat again. It had not moved from the warmth of the sunny spot.

"Well, whatever, they demanded payment from all of the forest folk for living on their lands. We've been here longer. When the Fae council convened and decided they would no longer pay the ransom, the Sauns hired rogue elves to make trouble in the valley."

Wrinkles creased Linda's forehead. "When was this? I don't recall reading about it in the news."

"You wouldn't have heard of this. Humans were so busy with something you called a world war that our small grievances were of no consequence to you." Chrissy stood on the tabletop. She crept to the window and observed the napping cat.

"My father and brother were killed in the ensuing battles. Many fae folk lost family. The treaty the two sides signed held a clause exiling

Gitty's stepsister, Tiamoon. Gitty was furious the gnome warrior had taken up the cause of the fae folk. She made the demand mandatory, stating if it was not carried out, the elfkind would slaughter all but their living within one hundred miles."

Chrissy sighed and brushed unseen wrinkles from her clothing.

"I really miss Tia. She was a good friend and a ferocious fighter. I would feel much safer with her here and not off in some distant land. I've sent word with the mouse network to the last place I knew she lived. I can only hope she still lives there and cares enough for some of us to come back home."

The little nymph's shoulders sagged.

Linda felt her heart ache for the little fae. She knew the loneliness of losing your best friend. Movement from the driveway captured her attention. The monstrous black cat was stretching all four limbs and looking as if he were going to settle in for the day. Something about his actions felt--wrong--to Linda. She could see his body quivering slightly, muscles ready to leap at a moment's notice. His head rested on his front right leg, eyes appearing closed, but she could sense they were opened ever so slightly and focusing on the Lending Library's front deck.

She watched the constant movement of his ears twitching back and forth. Linda had been so intently watching the cat, she'd closed out all action except the movements of the black animal in her driveway jumping when the loud clang of metal rent the air. She clutched the table the little wood nymph stood on.

"What the…?"

Lancelot jumped from his resting spot and arched his back, setting his hair on end, hissing loudly and baring his teeth.

Linda followed the line of his angry gaze to a small figure in full battle gear, a gleaming sword held high and to the right of its head in advance stance.

The cat hissed, crouched, and feigned attack.

The figure stepped forward switching the blade to the other side and advancing on the feline. The animal ruffled its fur to appear fuller, stood on the tips of its paws, and commenced growling.

The small warrior figure, body tensed, soft booted feet moving steadily forward, continued toward the creature.

Sensing the figure was not backing down, the enormous cat turned on its paws and fled across the driveway and through the meadow. The figure gave chase ,sheathing its sword behind it and pulled out a throwing knife.

Linda stared at the spot where the confrontation had just taken place. She couldn't wrap her mind around what she had just seen.

Chrissy strained forward trying to look sideways out the glass.

A face popped into the center of the window. Chrissy threw her hands over her face and screamed, the sound creating goose skin down Linda's back. Moving her fingers slightly from her eyes, Chrissy dropped her hands and screamed again.

"TIAMOON!"

Chapter Ten

Linda flung open the door and stepped back as Chrissy streaked past her to the figure on the porch.

The wood nymph threw her arms around a grim looking small person who grudgingly returned the hug.

"Tia! You came!"

Linda looked at her small friend. She'd never seen Chrissy smile so widely or beam so much as she was at this moment.

"Yeah, I came."

The voice from the small warrior was surprisingly soft, and Linda chose to stay where she was standing inside the doorway of the Lending Library.

"Come in, come in. You must be tired, hungry, and probably thirsty too."

Chrissy slipped her arm through the warrior's and led her through the portal to just inside the building.

Tiamoon stopped and gawked at the walls filled with books. Floor to ceiling on every surface were books; small books, large books, picture books, books of all shapes and sizes.

"When did this happen?"

Chrissy took Tia's arm and steered her toward a chair at one of the tables.

"Uhmmm, about 15..." she turned to look at Linda, her eyebrows raised in question.

Linda nodded.

"...years ago. The librarian and her husband lived here before that time but when he passed away, she started this." Chrissy waved a hand around indicating the shelving. "I've only been here for a year and a half in Other's time. My home was destroyed by the Other's machinery. They've destroyed homes of most of the forest fae and the meadow fae are finding themselves having a difficult time keeping their dwellings from being damaged. Kayne remembered the design on the yellow machine that tore up my tree and told the Librarian. She looked up the logo and discovered all the machinery belongs to a company Gitty and Morgan own."

Tia released the strap holding her sword and scabbard to her back and placed the gleaming weapon on the table. She divulged herself of two throwing knives and a hatchet she had worn on the belt of her hauberk. She hooked her thumbs on the collar of the protective shirt and pulled it over her head and off her body. Once divested of the warm, heavy gear she placed on a chair beside her, she sat at the table and looked around the room. After she had made a thorough reconnaissance of the room, she turned to the librarian still standing up by the door.

"This abode is yours?"

Linda nodded. "It is."

"How is it you can see us?"

Chrissy grinned. "She believes."

"Let me get you some water and a sandwich. Get comfortable and after you've eaten, we'll take your gear to my tree behind the house. It's probably the only oak still standing in the valley."

Chrissy winged to the kitchen and the sounds of water running and the refrigerator door opening and closing echoed in the empty library.

Tia watched the librarian.

"Why do you stand there?"

"I've learned to move carefully. I wait until invited before sitting with the forest folk."

"I've got a lot of questions. It's been many years since I left the forest and much has changed. Sit with me." Tiamoon nodded to a chair across from her. "My first question is why should I or any of the forest creatures trust you?'

"Tia!"

Chrissy flew to the table and alighting deftly near her friend, placed a container of clear water in front of the warrior. The gnome grasped the glass with both hands and gulped the contents in one swig. Chrissy raised her eyebrows. "Another?

"Please."

Tia looked at Linda who sat examining her fingernails. "My question remains. Why should I trust you? Have you bewitched my friend into believing what you say?"

Chrissy returned with the refilled glass and a plate with a sandwich she slammed on the table in front of the gnome.

"Labhoise Tiamoon Saun!"

Linda watched the face of the warrior darken. Eyebrows knit together and eyes narrowed.

"What did you call me?" She stood slowly, the chair legs scraping against the wooden floor.

"You heard me." Chrissy fisted her tiny hands on her waist and tapped a foot on the floor as she faced the warrior. "You know how careful I am. Do you think I would live anywhere near someone who would harm me?"

Tiamoon stood with her hands at her side, clenching and unclenching her fists.

"How am I to know? I've been away a very long time. Who knows what these Others have learned to do?"

Chrissy glared at Tiamoon who was glaring back at her.

Linda could see neither of them was going to give an inch.

"Ladies?"

"What?" They answered in unison.

"I'm very tired so I think I'll take a nap. Why don't you take some time and work out this problem together?" She rose from her chair and made her way to her room at the back of the library. She really *was* tired. The confrontation with the monster cat had drained all her energy. A nap would feel good, and the two friends could discuss her at their leisure.

Chrissy crossed her arms, frowning at the gnome warrior standing across the banister from her. When the Librarian's door clicked shut, she huffed. "I would have thought you knew me better."

Tiamoon pulled a chair out and dropped into it. "Chrissy, how could you put trust into an Other?"

Chrissy rolled her violet eyes, flipped her light brown hair over one shoulder, and winged her way to the chair across from Tiamoon.

"You idiot. If the Librarian were a 'normal' Other she wouldn't be able to see us!"

Tia considered the nymph's comment. "Okay, so she can see us. That doesn't necessarily make her trustworthy, does it?"

"No it does *not*. But I've been living here for a nearly a year, ever since my Ancient oak was destroyed. She lets me live in the one behind the building. Tia, she knows the customs."

Tiamoon found two deep violet eyes peering earnestly at her. Huffing impatience, she acquiesced. "Alright. If you trust her, Chrissy, I'll keep my mouth shut."

The nymph smiled.

"I didn't say I would trust her--just keep my mouth shut about her. Now, what's going on here?"

Chrissy shook her head.

"Tia, it's been a nightmare. After you left, things were quiet--lonely but quiet. Gitty and Morgan kept to themselves, adding to that enormous house on the hill where they live. Time passed, and all those machine inventions starting appearing everywhere. Our forest started shrinking when the Others moved in and built homes. For the most part, we've kept to ourselves and life has gone smoothly. That is until about eleven moons, sorry, months ago.

"Huge machines started coming into the forest and killing the Ancients. Just tearing them up for no reason. They weren't even cut up for firewood!"

"My tree was the first to go. I gathered what belongings I could find and came here. I'd heard via the fae this human was different, trustworthy, and I needed to see for myself. She was able to see me; extended me kindness and understanding. Never said anything about my size or try to talk stupid to me like so many of the regular humans do. I asked if I could live in her tree out back and she said yes."

Tia watched her friend's facial expressions change with the story she told.

"So why are you working here, Chrissy?"

"Keeps me busy, and I like the Librarian's company. She's smart and helps everyone who comes through her doors. She's a good person, Tia."

Tiamoon scowled. "No Other is good, Chrissy. Don't ever forget that. So what happened to cause you to contact me?"

"Remember Ailidh and Kayne?"

Tia nodded.

"Kayne's brother's home was torn down about four months ago. When their home was facing destruction, Ailidh and Kayne started coming to the Lending Library to learn about city life; Ailidh's sister lives in Faetown. About three weeks ago, they moved away. They're not the first, and I'm afraid probably won't be the last to leave the forest to the Others and…"

Tia looked up to see the hesitation on Chrissy's face. "And what?"

Chrissy slowly blew out a deep breath. "…Gitty and Morgan. "

Tia raised her eyebrows high on her forehead. "The night elves? My dear stepsister and brother?"

Chrissy nodded her head. "The Librarian got Kayne to remember the picture and name of the company on the side of the huge digging machine. It was Black Catco. She got on the Internet and researched the company finally finding the main stockholders and owners to be Gitty, Morgan, and Lancelot."

"Mangy creature."

"That's when I knew I had to get hold of you. If anyone can stop Gitty, it's you, Tia."

The warrior gnome smirked. "Thanks for the confidence, but I think I'll need as much help as I can get. Any reason for them destroying the forest?"

Chrissy shook her head. "No one has been able to figure it out. There is no pattern to the damage they do, but they're only tearing down the oak stands. Only a few remain. It was the Librarian who used the

Other's laws to stop the digging up of the trees. She says this is just a temporary hold. If we can't do something quickly, Gitty will be able to continue digging up the Ancients."

Tia sat looking up at the ceiling and tapping a finger on the table. Finally, she looked at Chrissy.

"We need to convene the Fae Council."

Chrissy nodded her agreement.

"I'll use the mouse network to get the elders here then we can decide what to do from there." Tia nodded in agreement with herself. "I'll whistle for a messenger to deliver my requests."

She smiled at Chrissy. "Right after I eat."

Chapter Eleven

Kayne walked from the bedroom to the living area searching for Ailidh. He hated the long pants he was forced to wear and the leather shoes were causing blisters on his feet. However, he had promised Ailidh he'd try town living for three months. No more. If he hated it as much in three months as he did now, she had given her word they would return to the forest. He had to admit this penthouse, as Cadhla called it, did have advantages over the oak tree in the woods. He was getting used to warm showers and hot food on demand. Truth be told, he was also becoming quite fond of silk sheets. He felt himself stir with the thought of Ailidh naked on the soft sheets, her wings spread, hair cascading down the pillow…

Stop! We have to get to the job. He stopped on the step of the entry and turned to the windows.

There stood his mate facing the glass. Her shoulders drooped toward the floor. He noticed her beautiful, flowing hair seemed to hang limply and the sparkle from her wings was gone. In fact, she now kept her wings closed tightly against her body except at the job. Her delicate hand touched the glass and he heard a shuddered sigh leave her lips. He'd watched the fire leave her green eyes and her eyes had dark circles beneath them.

"Ailidh?" He spoke her name quietly.

The little faerie jumped.

Kayne watched her flutter her wings, lift her shoulders, and fluff her hair. She turned to face him.

"Kayne. How long have you been standing there?" she cocked

her head to one side.

Danger old man. Don't push. "Not long my love. I think we need to get to the club. It's almost time for your first set. Are you ready?" He hoped the lie would go unnoticed.

Ailidh narrowed her eyes and pursed her lips. "Are you sure?"

He crossed the floor and gathered her into his arms. Placing a hungry kiss on her delicate lips, he tried to relay the love he felt for her through this action. Finally, he pulled back and stared directly into her face. "I'm sure. Are you ready?"

The two turned to take a last look toward the forest they loved so much. A sigh escaped Ailidh's lips.

"Yes. Let's get going."

~ * ~

Kayne pushed open the entrance to the cabaret, halting as smoke roiled out the door. He coughed, pulled in a deep draught of fresh air, and plunged into the dark, stale smelling interior. He hated having to work. He especially hated the way the fae men of the city leered at Ailidh while she sang.

Gareth, the owner, made sure the lighting on the stage highlighted her tantalizing figure through her diaphanous forest dress. When her sister had brought Ailidh in to meet him, as she had promised, Gareth's eyes glittered greedily at the nearly transparent garment and had made Ailidh promise to wear the dress solely for performing. He knew his clientele would pay to see innocence and beauty in such a package. He'd been proven correct. In the three weeks since Ailidh had been featured at the cabaret, business had tripled.

Tonight was putting Kayne's patience to the test. Twice he'd had to pull men from the performing stage as they lunged at his mate during her performance. Ailidh was in tears the last time.

"Kayne, please," she'd wept into his shoulder.

He'd just tossed a drunken, swearing gnome out the door as the creature had gotten close enough to lay his grasping hands on his mate's delicate breast.

"Take me back to the apartment. I'll talk with Cadhla, and we'll find another way to make money to give to her. Please!"

Kayne had helped her from the stage, protectively holding her trembling shoulders, down the hallway to the performer's area when they encountered a furious Gareth, arms crossed over his muscled chest, feet wide and planted, blocking access to the rooms.

"Where the hell do you think you're going?" The faerie's face was crimson, puckered, and glistening with sweat.

"I'm taking my mate home. She's too delicate to put up with the rude actions of your customers. Aren't there other places for the things they insinuate to Ailidh? I've heard you and Cadhla speak of such abominations."

Ailidh quivered beneath Kayne's grasp, a suppressed sob escaping her lips.

Gareth sneered at Kayne. "The only reason Ailidh is not working there is because her sister garnered my promise, on a 5-year contract, she wouldn't. How the hell do you think you and your 'mate' are able to stay in such luxury? Most forest fae who show up in the city eventually wind up living down by the river in hovels that make their oak trees look like castles. You are lucky your mate has a beautiful and willing, sister."

"Get Ailidh back on the stage before those blighters out there tear the place apart. Getting groped is part of her job, and she needs to act like she likes it!"

Gareth dropped his arms to his side and clenched his fists.

Kayne glared at his opponent. Gareth's three-foot form towered over him and he was not in the position to take on the larger man. His mouth pulled to a single, angry slash, his jaw setting tightly. He felt his wings flush red. He drew himself to his full height and pulled a trembling Ailidh closer to his body.

"I'll not expose her to that humiliation."

"Oh, yes you will," Gareth walked up and placed his hands on the tiny faerie's breasts.

Ailidh gasped and stepped backwards, Gareth keeping pace with her. Kayne's arm was wretched from her shoulders.

"I own these and everything else that goes with them. I'll touch them, the customers will touch them, and if someone pays me enough…" he let the suggestion die.

Gareth fondled Ailidh as Kayne watched all color leave her face. Her wings quivered and several emotions crossed her pale face.

The tall faerie then placed his hands on her shoulders and propelled her down the hallway and back to the stage.

The crowd applauded and yelled lewd suggestions. The microphone crackled as Kayne heard Gareth's coarse laugh. His stomach rolled with the realization he'd been unable to stop Gareth and protect his mate.

"Isn't she something boys?"

There was thunderous applause.

"And look as these perfect domes of womanhood…" The floor shook with the beating of shoes on wood. "Why don't we get this little beauty into our spotlight and have her sing us a tune?"

Applause drowned out anything else the owner may have said.

Kayne felt the heat of anger flush his face. He strode to the wings of the stage and watched as Gareth's large hands stroked from shoulders down to the buttocks of his beloved. As he started to charge the stage, two pair of strong hands restrained him.

"Don't."

Kayne turned to glare at his mate's sister on one side and a muscular dwarf holding him on the other side.

"She'll get over it and neither of you wants to live in the hovels down by the river. Gareth is crude but generous with his money when you understand he is the boss and his word is law. Once you resign yourself to that fact, everything gets easier."

Kayne strained against the hands.

"Please don't. He'll turn her over to the hospitality house owner." Cadhla shuddered. "She WON'T survive… the worst sort of lowlifes go there. Do you have any idea what they do to the likes of a faerie as beautiful as she?"

Kayne jerked his arms from the two as the breathy, whispering voice of Ailidh drifted through the microphone over the smoky room.

The cacophony subdued and the sweet voice continued to strengthen with each sung note. He watched his delicate mate pull her shoulders back, lift and spread her wings wide, and stand straight, her chin held high. A strength he'd never seen in the forest seemed to fill her. By the end of the song, she'd stepped full into the spotlight, her diaphanous clothing disappearing in the strong glare.

A fae man weaving and sneering lopsidedly made his way to the stage. He reached a hand up to place it on the thigh of Ailidh. Kayne sensed rather than saw the shiver run through her but she leaned over, looked directly in the eyes of the drunk fae and spoke very quietly, her lips barely moving.

Kayne watched the drunk leer then, without warning or a visible move on Ailidh's part, he staggered backward.

Gareth scurried over to the customer. He frowned, nodded, and pointed a finger at Ailidh.

She stood tall, smoothing the fabric of her dress and tossing her hair over one shoulder.

Kayne, Cadlha, and the dwarf watched as the customer back stepped to the bar shaking his head and pushing Gareth away from him.

Cadlha turned to Kayne. "She is stronger than you can know. Someday I will tell you just how strong but not today. I told you she would do fine." She turned to her companion. "Turner, we have work to do."

Kayne watched his mate glide from the spotlight to the stage wings, a spark of fire dancing in her eyes as she caught sight of him.

Uh oh. I think someone is in trouble and I don't think it's me.

Ailidh strode with surety past him.

"Come on. We've got packing to do. I won't be treated like this. It's high time I started behaving as my true self."

Kayne found himself scurrying to keep up with his mate. Something about the set of her mouth and forward thrust of her step kept him from asking the thousand questions in his mind.

Ailidh grabbed her few belongings in the dressing area. She burst from the door and marched to the adjoining room barreling her way through the portal.

Cadhla's started at the intrusion. "What…"

Ailidh held up her hand.

Kayne noted there was no quivering, no shaking visible.

"I need you to call the person in your building who will let us in the apartment."

Cadhla leaned back in her chair and cocked her head. "Now why would I do that?"

Ailidh placed her hands on the desk and moved to within inches of her sister's face. "Because if you don't, I'll invoke the ancient spell."

Kayne watch all the smug leave Cadhla's face. She picked up the phone and called someone at the building where they'd been staying. Hanging up the phone, he watched her eyes as they swept over his mate.

"If you leave, I'll be locked into this contract with Gareth for five long years, Ailidh. You don't want me to suffer, do you?" Cadhlas' eyes darkened with the question. She unconsciously twirled a wayward strand of dark curls around a finger.

Ailidh straightened and stared down at the only living sister she had.

"You chose this path not I. Nowhere in your flowering invitation to visit the city was there a mention of the degrading job you arranged for me." Stealing a glance at Kayne, she lowered her voice. "I'm a warrior, Cadhla, not a trollop. That was a role you chose during the wars, not I."

Cadhla rose so quickly from her chair it tumbled to the ground.

"How dare you! I chose not to fight because I didn't wish to die! I was never any good with a sword, and you know that. I was good at… at… making things run smoothly." Steel gray eyes flashed dangerously, the ceiling light highlighting her blue streaked hair now flying freely about her face.

Ailidh planted her feet and crossed arms in a stance Kayne had not seen since he'd come into the tiny fae's life.

"I've been listening to the gossip from the customers these last three weeks. There is trouble in the forest and many fae are fleeing in fear of their lives. I will not stand by idly singing to drunken dwarves, city fae men, and what-all else while some outside force takes over my homeland. This life is yours, Cadhla, not mine. I belong in the forest--not this squalid mud bog you call the city. Don't get in my way, sister, or you will regret the day I arrived."

The tension in the room crackled, each sister squared off ready to battle the other.

Cadhla made the first concession. "I'll not stop you. I also won't stop Gareth if he seeks to find and bring you back."

Ailidh humphed at the suggestion. "You know of what I'm capable. Do you really think that gargantuan, lusting fool can capture me?"

"No. I'm just warning you he might try."

"Let him." Ailidh turned to find Kayne a step away from the door.

"We're leaving."

Ailidh blew past Kayne and strode out the side door to the street, Kayne hurrying to match her strides.

Getting in the apartment proved no problem, and the couple thanked the doorman for his assistance. Once inside they moved to the bedroom closet.

"Is there anything here you need?" Ailidh stood with the door open gazing at the clothing they'd needed for town living.

"The sooner I'm done with these city clothes the better."

She looked at the clothes hanging in the closet and the shoes she'd learned to walk in and nodded her head. "Me, too."

Kayne had moved to the balcony off the bedroom and leaned on the rail gazing at the view from this vantage point. He glanced down at the street.

"Ailidh!"

"What?"

"Are we ready to go?"

"Yes, why?"

"Gareth just walked in the front door in a hurry."

Ailidh dashed to the balcony and peered down. Glaring up at her was Turner, the dwarf.

She pulled back and looked at Kayne.

"We're going to have to use our wings."

Kayne took a deep breath and nodded.

Ailidh closed the sliding glass door, grabbed Kayne's hand and they jumped from the balcony spreading their wings and heading in the direction they had come from three weeks earlier.

Chapter Twelve

Gitty paced in front of the living room windows that overlooked the valley. Since Lancelot had come streaking back to their home several days ago, she couldn't get him to sit still long enough to magic what had made him so agitated. Seeing him on edge and not knowing why made her jumpy... and testy. All she could do was walk off the feeling until the wretched animal would allow her to see what had spooked him so badly.

Morgan breezed through the living area toward the front door his evening cape fluttering behind him.

"I'm going to use the Hummer today. I'll see you when I get back... whenever that is." He flipped a hand over his shoulder in a weak wave and made to grab the keys sitting in the crystal dish centered on the oak sideboard in the entry.

Gitty reached the bowl before Morgan had uttered the last word.

"No. You're not taking the Hummer, or the truck, or the Corvette, or any of the vehicles in the garage. You haven't earned the right to drive any of them."

He pulled himself to his full height and glowered down at his sister.

"I'm part owner of the company and because of that fact, I can drive any vehicle I choose. Move away from the sideboard."

Gitty distributed her weight evenly on her feet, ice blue eyes locked onto her brother's and fisted her hands on her hips.

"Our father was stupid enough to think you would actually learn to like working. He may have forced me to list your name as part owner of the business, but he can't force me to share the rewards of my hard work. When you put in a full forty hour week working, real work, not wooing some bimbo in a bar to take you home, then you'll get the privilege of driving. Not until then."

The siblings stood face-to-face, daring the other to make the first move. Morgan finally tossed his head, turned, and started toward the game room.

"By the way, I heard a rumor our stepsister is in the valley."

Gitty sucked in a breath. She bolted after him and, grabbing his arm, turned him to face her.

"What did you say?"

Morgan smirked at her. "What? I know something you don't? Well, well."

She punched his shoulder. "Tell me what you heard."

He rubbed the spot where her fist had met his muscles. "Ow! That hurt. I'm not sure I want to tell you now." He feigned a pout until he saw the smoldering fire in Gitty's eyes.

"Oh, all right. I was at one of the taverns in town…"

Gitty rolled her eyes. "Morgan, just bottom line it for me."

He stopped, narrowed his eyes and stared at her. "This is my story. I'll tell it my way. Clear?"

Gitty huffed out an impatient breath. "Fine. Just get to the point sometime today."

"Anyway, as I was saying," he shot her a veiled glare, "at the tavern nearest the forest edge, I think it's called Dew Drop Inn or something stupid like that…"

Gitty closed her eyes and shook her head.

"…I wasn't having much luck finding a friend for the evening so I decided to move on from there. I stepped outside and nearly crushed one of those mice who work the message network they have. I wouldn't have known he was anything more than a common field mouse except he spoke to me. I wonder how he knew I'd understand?" Morgan frowned slightly.

Gitty stood looking at her 6'5" brother; his white hair glistening in the light from the front window, blue eyes framed by white eyebrows and lashes knitted together and shook her head.

He's such an idiot.

"Morgan?"

"Oh, yes. Well, he told me they were being kept very busy since Monday…"

Gitty whipped her head in the direction of the sleeping Lancelot. The cat opened one eye and turned his head from her.

"…running all over the valley delivering messages. I asked him if it was something I might be interested in, and he shook his head. Told me some gnome had just arrived in the valley and was in contact with family members, that's all. I mean; we know how they multiply like rabbits. After all, remember the family gathering when I was…"

"MORGAN!"

He jumped at the shouting of his name.

"No need to get all huffy. I asked if he knew the name of the gnome and the mouse nodded, saying it was something about a moon. I deduced the rest. Tiamoon is in the valley and contacting her family." Morgan nodded his head and smiled.

Gitty pushed a big sigh through her lips. "You're an idiot but a useful one. Here."

She tossed him the keys to the Corvette. "Don't scratch it."

He allowed a sly smile to cover his lips as he walked toward the garages. "I wouldn't dream of it."

Gitty wandered back into the living room to stand looking out the picture window. She took in the view of the valley below and let her mind travel back to a time when the woods were full of fae folk. Her family had been generous enough to let them live in the woods they owned and what had it gotten them? Whining, gripping tenants who complained about a little rent. They'd even had the nerve to threaten a war!

On top of all that fuss, her father had moved a wretched gnome woman and her daughter in with Gitty and Morgan. Gitty never understood his fascination with the little creature. She was certain the blasphemous being had bewitched him at some gathering they were always having. Served him right when she left. Never trust a gnome.

So Tiamoon is back in the valley and networking with her family.

Hmmm.

Gitty voiced her thoughts. "Thinking of starting another fracas, my sister? Feel free to try; it won't do you any good but please go ahead and try. It's been many a year since I was able to wade into the middle of a good fight. I'm actually missing the action."

Her hand ached to hold the sleek weighted blade, fingers wrapped around the handled designed specifically for her. Maybe, just maybe, she could rid herself of this stunted blight once and for all.

Gitty smiled. She rolled her head and shoulders trying to ease the tension that seemed to build daily. While the eflkind were superior to any other beings living in the area, the treaty which bore her signature along with her father and brother's signatures still restricted all the night elf community from using their magic to take over the humans. Tiamoon had just broken part of the original agreement by showing up in the valley. Gitty allowed a smirk to touch her lips.

"You set the ground rules, Tia. Only this time, I'm finishing the battle. You won't live to be banished. Once you're dead, the old treaty will only be good as fodder to start a fire. It's time for the night elves to move out of the shadows of the mountains and forests and take our rightful place in the world."

Gitty gave the valley one last look before heading to the basement. She followed the steps down to a hallway that ended in a large room featuring three walls lined in mirrors, a floor with rubberized matting as covering, and the fourth wall of floor to ceiling windows allowing natural light to stream in and bounce off the silver and black gym equipment.

"The fools who idled my construction company may think they have beaten me, but I will make use of this time and turn their foolish decision against them." She glanced around the room surprised at the cleanliness of the area. Morgan was not known for picking up after himself. She wrinkled her nose at the faint aroma of stale sweat and wandered to the changing area. Once attired in workout togs, she moved toward the free weights. She lifted a 20-pound barbell in each hand and began curling them to her biceps. Physical labor always improved her thinking. At the moment, she was faced with two major challenges; one-finding out what her stepsister was up to and stopping her; and two-finding the leprechaun's treasure.

"If I dispose of Tiamoon, I might not need the leprechaun's treasure."

Gitty clunked the hand weights down on the stand and stared at her image in the mirror.

"Of course! With Tia out of the picture, the agreement is void releasing me from peaceful behavior toward non-elfkind. I won't need the leprechaun's treasure. I can grab all the property in the valley, and no one will be able to stop me."

She smiled at her reflection.

"Some days I amaze myself."

Chapter Thirteen

Kayne dropped to the ground on the balls of his feet then fell to his hands and knees. Ailidh floated down beside him.

"What's the matter?"

He panted heavily, his head bobbing with each breath.

"I--haven't--flown--that--much--in--several--years."

He pulled up to rest his weight on his knees and heels, toes tucked under his bottom. Forcing himself to pull in deep draughts, Kayne slowed his breathing and heart rate. "I'm so out of shape. I've gotten lazy."

Ailidh looked at her mate resting on the ground. "We've both gotten lazy. I allowed you to make all the decisions and think I was…fragile. I'm done with that. My home is in danger, and I'll not trust anyone else to protect the forest but myself."

Kayne peered sideways at his mate. Her arms were crossed defiantly, legs planted on the ground as she rested her wings against her shapely back. Her alluring figure was barely covered by her diaphanous dress. Even with the intimate knowledge of what lay beneath the flimsy fabric, Kayne realized his fragile flower of the forest was gone for good and the temptation to suggest a quick interlude withered in his mind. The creature that had pushed him from the balcony in Faetown wouldn't succumb to his male vanity with fluttering eyelashes and a shy smile. This Ailidh was one he'd never known. The strength she had exhibited in the crisis surprised him considering her timid reaction not but an hour earlier. Something about the drunken male fae staggering to the stage had triggered a power from deep within his mate.

He considered her profile. He was going to enjoy this strong female. But would it last?

"What about your sister, Cadhla?" Kayne rose from the ground and approached Ailidh.

Ailidh pushed out a humphing sound. "I have no sister."

Kayne raised an eyebrow. To this point, Ailidh had spoken continuously about the older sister who had succeeded in the city; how smart, bright, and wonderful she was. This turnabout was... unexpected.

"Any being who would sell another doesn't deserve respect or a family. As of this morning, my sister ceased to exist." Ailidh looked around and pulled in a deep breath. "The forest smells so clean." She looked at Kayne. "Let's go to the Lending Library. I'm sure the Librarian can help us find a new home."

She started down the road, Kayne trotting to keep up.

Within the half hour, the two faeries spotted the familiar lane leading to the Lending Library. Ailidh stopped and gazed at the building, a mixture of elation and concern filling her.

"Do you notice anything?"

Kayne narrowed his eyes. "Not really. Why?"

"Where is everybody?"

He looked again at the front porch of the white building. Ailidh was right. Normally, on a day like today when the sun opted to appear from beneath the clouds, there were several fae outside sipping those coffee drinks Chrissy made, and the door was opened allowing fresh air to dissipate the closed-up smell. He couldn't sense his kind anywhere within a quarter mile radius. There was movement within the building and the essence of the Librarian and Chrissy wafted on the air. There was also another essence. One that was familiar but...

Ailidh snapped her head his direction. Her eyes were wide, sparkling with joy.

"Tiamoon! I sense Tiamoon."

She started to run then spread her wings and flew to the front door. Kayne followed, groaning with the ache his wing muscles produced. He touched down on the porch a mere seconds behind Ailidh. Her hand was already pushing open the Library door.

~ * ~

Tiamoon sat, her chin resting in the palm of her hand, staring out the window down the lane. Chrissy had made up a spot in the oak tree for her that she appreciated, but the inactivity of sitting around was irritating her. She really needed to practice her skills if she was to have a chance when facing Gitty. The thought put a smile on the warrior's face. She was sure she could convince the council to allow her the opportunity to face her detractor.

Movement at the end of the lane derailed her daydream. She strained her eyes to see if she could spot the movement again. At the beginning of the turnoff to the Library were two small figures trudging toward the building. Tia noted the two appeared to be fae in stature. She wondered if it were someone she might know. The figure wearing a flowing garment stopped then was suddenly flying up the road.

"Chrissy! Someone's coming up the driveway."

Tia stood up, feeling the rush of adrenalin pumping through her veins. Her fingers twitched over her knife blades, and she flexed her legs in anticipation of a confrontation. She could hear faint shouting from the flying figure. Her mouth went dry and she waited for the right moment to jerk open the door and meet the intruder head on.

She peeked out the window and saw two figures flying directly toward the Library.

As the two neared, Tia realized she was looking at Ailidh and Kayne. A gentle thudding indicated the fae had landed on the porch. Tiamoon opened the library door to find herself enveloped in the slender arms of Ailidh. Kayne dropped into the nearest chair on the porch, his wings quivering with exhaustion.

"TIAMOON!" Ailidh hugged the tiny gnome warrior tightly.

"Ailidh," Tia gasped for air. The little fae's small size belied her strength.

"Oh, I'm so sorry." Ailidh let go of the warrior and danced around her. "You're here, you're really here."

She clapped her hands in glee. "I'm so glad. Now everything will be just like it was before Gitty sent you away."

Tiamoon straightened her tunic and cleared her throat. "No, Ailidh, things won't be the same. Gitty has more knowledge of the magic and has had years to practice its use. She is more dangerous and cunning than before the war. I can only offer my help but will do my best to save our land. However, I have sent word for all the clans to gather. The decision to proceed must be made by everyone who has something to lose in the valley."

Tia turned to Chrissy. "Would the Librarian represent the Others?"

Chrissy thought for a moment. "I believe she would."

"Then what we must do now is wait for the mouse messengers to bring back replies to my requests for a council meeting. The decision for action will be made at that time."

~ * ~

Gitty stood at the front window staring down at the roof of the Lending Library. It seemed she spent a great deal of time in this spot contemplating her fate since the court had closed her work sites. The atmosphere of magic was building; she could sense it in the air, a light buzzing that tickled her ears.

"Tiamoon is back. Lancelot has finally allowed me to see his confrontation with her. But there is more to this than just her presence. This sensation feels more and more like the forest before the war."

"What are you muttering about, dear sister?" Morgan sluffed into the living room and flopped on the couch, throwing one leg over the couch's arm. He bit into an apple. The pungent sweet aroma of the fruit combined with the loud crunch disrupted Gitty's attention.

She turned in time to witness juice running down her brother's cleft chin. He swiped at it with a sleeve and crunched away. His lackluster eyes and drawn expression along with the listless position he took on the couch grated Gitty's nerves. At the best of times, she could barely tolerate his presence but now, with the company shut down, she was ready to kill him.

"Don't you have some young thing to impress?"

"Naw. All the local girls know I don't have any money, and if I want to go out of town, I'll need to borrow some cash from you."

He shot her a lazy grin then bit into the apple again.

"When you put in a decent day's work, you'll get a decent day's pay. Since my construction sites have been closed down, you're just out of luck." She pushed him out of the way and sat on the end of the couch. "Have you noticed, brother, the magic level has spiked in the last few days?"

Morgan laid his head on the back of the couch and stared at the ceiling. "And this would interest me because…?"

"Because, you oaf, our dear stepsister is in the valley and must be gathering some of her little friends together. Can't you feel the difference?"

Morgan pushed out a sigh as he pulled himself to his feet. He turned to his sister.

"I've noticed, but why should we care? They can gather a thousand of those stunted, miniscule creatures and still not have the power we have. So what's your point? Are you afraid of Tiamoon?"

Gitty looked into the smirked face of Morgan. "Get real. That midget of a sister has as much chance of defeating me as you do of convincing the local tavern wenches you're wealthy without using magic."

She watched the sneer on his face morph into a scowl. *Point for me.*

She magicked a hundred dollar bill that she handed to Morgan. "Go play with your little friends but keep your inner ears open. I may call on you. Don't ignore me or you'll live to regret it."

He raised an eyebrow in question, gave Gitty a nod of the head then bolted to his room to shower and get ready for an evening out.

"It's very strange how much magic is pooling around the Lending Library. The air is rippling with waves of enchantments. There is something going on and I need to know what it is. How…?"

Lancelot tread lightly across the floor and undulated around Gitty's legs. She started to scold him and stopped herself. Scooping up the large creature in one hand, she moved to the window at the front of the living room.

"Lancelot, my love," she cooed.

A rumbled purr was her answer. The cat had blanked its mind of all thought.

"Now, now, lovey. I want you to do a task for me. Capture one of the messenger mice."

The mind picture the cat projected was of a mutilated mouse disappearing down his throat.

"No, my love, not for eating."

Lancelot huffed his unhappiness.

"I need information from the creature. Once I have what I need, I don't care what you do with it as long as you don't do it in my house."

"Rrrrooowwww."

Gitty watched the magic dwindle around the Library to small sparkles of light.

"I *will* find out what's happening, Tia. Then you'll regret leaving your safe, comfortable exile."

Chapter Fourteen

Linda slid quietly from her room to a chair she'd set against the back wall. Since the arrival of the small warrior and return of Ailidh and Kayne, life in the Lending Library had been anything but sedate. There were daily arrivals of faeries, wood nymphs, gnomes, sprites, and more wood creatures than she knew existed in this region.

On top of the daily arrivals, the sweet, shy, timid Ailidh who had left clinging to Kayne's arm had returned brandishing an attitude that rivaled the warrior gnome's own brashness. They had taken up sword practice behind the library and the clanging of metal against metal had become routine background noise. Kayne wandered around the first day or two looking lost but soon realized if he were to keep his ladylove, he'd just have to accept the change. Within a short period, he was offering his services as sparing partner for the two female warriors so one or the other of them could rest between practice sessions.

Linda realized her home, her library, had the feel of a base camp of operations during war. The thought frightened her a bit, but she wouldn't turn away any of the fae community. She was now, and always had been, a guest in their world.

The front door opened and several fae men wearing the trappings of clan chiefs entered the premises jostling for lead position.

"Innkeep!" The tallest fae thumped his sword on the wooden floor. "Innkeep! I need a room, a pint, and a willing wench!"

Raucous laughter rolled through the room.

Linda watched Chrissy dart from the kitchen to the front door, her wings a blur of movement.

"Behave yourself, you uncouth, loudmouthed, brute of a creature or I'll throw you out." The little wood nymph plunked herself in front of the two foot tall fae outfitted in chainmail and fawn leather shirt and leggings. His unruly flowing black hair fell loosely down his back. He placed his sword into the scabbard and faced the nymph.

Chrissy straightened to her full height, fisted her hands on her waist, and glared at the interloper, her violet eyes sparking wildly at the warrior.

Linda rose from her spot against the wall not sure how quickly she could cover the distance between her chair and the front door, but determined nothing would harm her friend. She edged along the bookshelves until she noted the sparkle in the deep brown weathered eyes of the fae chieftain.

"Will you now, Crystal of the Glen?"

Chrissy was trying hard but losing the battle to maintain her frightful frown. She giggled then hurled herself into the arms of the faerie.

"Oh, Raghnall! Where have you been? I've missed you so much." She pulled the warrior's face to hers and locked him in a tender kiss that pulled a low moan from deep in his throat.

Breaking the kiss, he sighed and offered a tender, sweet smile to the little nymph.

"When the treaty was signed all those years ago, Tiamoon was not the only one to be exiled. I had to put my mark on the paper and promise never to return to the valley if I wanted my family and," he ran his forefinger down her velvety cheek, "my love to remain healthy and alive. I've missed you so much, my sweet."

Ignoring the pandemonium that was quickly becoming the norm for the Lending Library, the two lovers gazed into each other's eyes. Linda eased her way back to her chair and felt the ache of loss as the sight of the two reunited lovers tugged thoughts of her husband from the recesses of her memory.

I do miss him so.

"What is all the turmoil I'm hearing? Someone is destroying the ancients?" Raghnall nodded at the troupe of men around him. "Rest.

We'll camp in the meadow beyond the house tonight. I have business."

A few of the men snickered.

Raghnall turned an icy glare their direction. The sniggering stopped. As the clan chiefs fanned out around the room, he grasped Chrissy's hand and led her to a table.

"I have to get back to the kitchen."

"You what?"

"I work here, Raghnall."

"Why? You're faefolk. We don't need to work."

The corners of Chrissy's mouth tipped up. "I know but I needed something to keep me busy. Most of the other nymphs left after the war and the faeries tend to stick together." She looked at him, water pooling in her eyes, threatening to spill down her cheeks. "I had no one and when they destroyed my tree... well, the Librarian kindly offered the oak behind her house to me. She can see us, Raghnall."

"Who is this Librarian? And what difference does it make if she can see us? I can see you."

"She's an Other?"

His eyes widened. "She's an Other?" He rose hurriedly from his chair knocking it over in his haste. He started toward the door. "I need to get out of here. I don't want anything to do with Others. The night elves..."

"AHA! That proves it!" Chrissy smacked the tabletop.

The noise in the room abated for a moment as all eyes centered on the furious wood nymph.

"It has been the Saun family and night elves all along! This is the first I've heard of you being exiled. Why did you feel you couldn't trust me with the knowledge of their treachery?"

Raghnall swung around, pulling his shoulders back and raising his head high.

"Because it was my choice and my burden to bear. I made the sacrifice for my family, friends, and the woman I love."

Chrissy narrowed her eyes at him. "You were the only family I had, Raghnall. Mine was all killed in the war. Remember?"

He opened his mouth to respond but was drowned out by the

shouts of the other fae warriors.

"Food! Where does a man get some food around here?"

Chrissy looked at him. "We'll continue this discussion later. I have to work now."

She bustled over to a table of rowdy warriors and, dodging grasping hands and leering grins, took their orders.

Raghnall exited to the front porch. He stood, reconnoitering the surrounding meadow and woods. There was a sense of unease in the air that set his nerves to twitching. He felt certain someone was watching. *But who?*

~ * ~

Linda observed the increasing bustle in her home. There were fae of all sizes and shapes. She didn't know why but the realization the fae were as different in form as humans took her by surprise. Then she felt guilty she had presupposed what appearance faeries would take.

"Guess prejudice comes in all forms." She muttered more to herself than anyone else.

The cacophony took on a pattern and Linda sensed liaisons were being formed throughout the room. The conversation around the tables appeared serious in nature. When the speaking ceased, each clan representative would look to the others sharing the table and, with a nod of the head, end the meeting. There would be back slapping and hand shaking then the appearance of little flasks let Linda know the faeries were magicking while she was present.

It was an honor she had never expected to happen. As the day wore on the seriousness of the meetings abated and soon the fae were relating tales of their time away. The atmosphere lost the seriousness of the morning and a relaxing joviality expanded around the room.

Linda noted Chrissy wander to the front porch where she siddled up to Raghnall. He slipped an arm around her waist and the two engaged in quiet conversation. Chrissy's face glowed as she looked up at the faerie warrior and Linda, feeling ever the voyeur, found herself wishing for one more time of feeling the same way. She got up and slipped into the kitchen to clean so Chrissy could spend time with her beau only to find the counters and workspaces spotless.

"You could've asked my help, my little friend…"

Turning on her heel, Linda stopped at the doorway then tiptoed back to her room. She was tired of sitting quietly away from the action. The need to feel fresh air on her face overwhelmed her. Slipping on her tennis shoes, Linda exited through a back door she seldom used anymore. She stood on her small back porch taking in the view of the valley. It had been many months since she gazed at the meadow and surrounding peaks. The mountains still rose majestically from the basin floor and groves of evergreens blanketed their sides. But all was not right with the valley. There was something… missing. Linda squinted at the expanse, narrowing her eyes to focus on the vast terrain in front of her. In the distance among all the green grass of the meadow and surrounding trees, sat a brilliant yellow machine. She started looking at the stands of trees more carefully and realized the oaks were missing in large numbers.

The recognition of this truth chilled her to the bone. If she had not stopped the dozers, they would soon have demolished every stand of oaks in the valley. *But why? What is so important about the oak tress?*

Linda strolled the back of her property until dusk darkened her path. She watched in amazement as the air around her home wavered wildly. *Must be more tired than I thought.* With each step toward her domicile, Linda's tiredness abated. When she stepped on the back porch, she experienced a lightness in her step she'd been missing lately.

The room hummed with activity and laughter smattered around the area. No one noticed her enter nor did her presence interrupt conversation.

They must be getting used to me. She smiled and nodded at a couple fae chieftains who acknowledged her. She changed her sneakers and moved from her bedroom to the kitchen intent on fixing herself a snack when the metallic ringing of multiple swords being drawn stopped her. She snapped around to face the front door and sucked in a deep breath at the sight she beheld.

Looming in the doorway, a figure attired in a floor length, tan duster ducked under the doorframe standing erect once he entered. Short white hair, tanned skin, and eyes so blue they stood out across the room completed the image standing on her landing.

"If he stays, we go!" A warrior attired in all red stood, his sword pointed toward the figure at the door.

"Aye! We'll not stay in the same building as he!" Several others chimed brandishing swords and knocking over chairs in their haste to rise.

Raghnall stepped from behind the tall stranger and lifted his sword.

"This man was invited."

"Who would be foolish enough to invite a night elf to our gathering?"

The group muttered their agreement.

"I would."

All eyes turned to Chrissy.

Macartan, a river fae, walked to the nymph and hissed in her face. "And why would you do something so stupid?"

Raghnall sped to Chrissy's side. She looked at him and shook her head.

"Because this is a problem faced by all of us... including the night elves."

Macartan puckered his mouth to spit then thought better of it. He stomped to his table and began gathering his belongings. Many in the room followed suit.

Linda watched as the handsome, extremely tall, stranger stepped toward the center of the room.

"If I may..."

She felt her heart race and unconsciously ran a hand through her hair.

The stranger put up a hand. "I know all of you feel we night elves were the cause of the last war between our races..."

The gathered crowd in the room bellowed agreement.

"...but I'm here to tell you the fighting was initiated and continued by the clan Saun. By the time the rest of our world heard of the war, the Saun's had secured the lands using rogue elves as soldiers and secured treaties signed by many of your clansmen. The use of brute force on another race is forbidden by elvan law. It's not our way."

"Tell that to my dead uncle!"

Chrissy faced the sea of angry warriors. "We *all* experienced loss from the war. It scarred every family represented in this room. I don't think anyone wants to experience the pain of loss again. That's why I asked Uther to join us. Maybe he can help find a solution to our problem that won't involve fighting."

Raghnall stepped next to her. "We have nothing to lose and Uther has taken the fae oath of silence. If he breaks that silence the penalty is…"

"DEATH!" The room roared.

Uther tipped his head in agreement. "Death. Frankly, I have many years left to live in my life. I don't wish to end it too soon."

Macartan dropped his belongings on the floor. "Then you will agree to anything we decide?"

Uther shook his head. "No."

Swords rattled and warriors snarled.

"I won't agree to anything that will end in the loss of life. I do think, however, I may have a solution to benefit us all."

Chrissy cast Raghnall a sideways look.

"If I might request a chair and something to drink? It has been a long journey this day."

Chrissy winged her way to Linda who stood in the doorway of the kitchen gazing Uther's direction. The little nymph smirked at Linda. "Is he not the most beautiful man you have ever seen?"

Linda felt heat flame her cheeks. "I, uh, guess so."

"Would you help me get him a chair and some water?"

"Of course. How rude I am."

Chrissy giggled. "Uther has that effect on people."

Linda dragged the chair she normally used toward the front door. As she neared the night elf, her senses began to work overtime. She licked her lips and cursed the moisture forming in her palms. Her mouth felt dry and she knew she must look a sight. *Why didn't I run a comb through my hair after my walk?* She sighed in resignation.

A pitcher of water and a glass had been set on a table near the elf. Linda brought the chair and set it on the floor. As she was about to make her escape, a gentle hand on her arm stopped her. She turned to see who was holding up her progress from fleeing the room and long forgotten sensations.

"Thank you." Uther's deep silky voice vibrated the air around him.

"You're... you're welcome." She knew her cheeks were blazing red and she moved her gaze to the floor.

Chrissy flitted over to the table. "Uther? This is the Other I was telling you about. She's opened her home to us, given me a place to live, and agreed to help if there is anything she might do. This is Linda."

"Pleased to meet you Linda. I find it fascinating there is an Other who believes in our existence."

Linda squirmed. "My family is from Ireland, and I grew up with the tales of faeries and elves. I'm just luckier than most; I can see everyone."

An unseen force drew her gaze to the eyes she'd noted from the other side of the building. She looked into the cool blue orbs and found herself ensnared in their kindness. The hand resting on her arm halting her attempt to flee was strong. Well-formed fingers with calluses showing a practiced work ethic detained her escape but didn't clutch her in force.

"Your name is spoken throughout the magic community with respect. There are some in my clan who could afford to take a lesson from your actions."

Her lips moved but no sound emerged. Her cheeks flared hotly.

He smiled; a slow enveloping movement that lit the room with brilliance. His hand dropped from her arm to his side.

"You give no thought to personal gain. That's unusual in both our worlds. I hope to learn much from you during this meeting of clans."

Linda cleared her throat. "I believe it is I who has much to learn. I hope I'm worthy of the privilege."

Chrissy smiled and winked at Uther. "I think so, Librarian, but then I know you."

Linda quickly escaped to the back of the library and disappeared into her room.

~ * ~

Uther gazed at the wood nymph. "Do you really believe she is worthy of standing for the Others in this meeting?"

Chrissy snapped around and stared at the night elf.

He watched her tiny body shake with anger, her wings rustling with the effort she was making not to explode into a tirade.

"I had to ask. Your reaction tells me what I need to know."

"Ahhh!" Chrissy streaked to the kitchen, the sounds of metal against metal letting all know of her anger.

Uther turned to look at Raghnall who'd been standing quietly back and observing the conversation. "She's quite outspoken, is she not?"

Raghnall shook his head. "You have no idea *how* outspoken. Had the Others' women not taken up the cause of equality first; our own would have demanded such rights a long time ago."

Uther flashed a wide grin. "Ah, but it puts spice in to life."

Dragging sounds of metal on wood interrupted the conversation. Tiamoon pushed through a throng of fae warriors congregating at the door.

"Where is he? I heard he actually had the nerve to show his face in these woods. Where is that devil Uther?"

She swung around to find herself facing the very soul she sought.

"Uther!"

"Tiamoon."

"So have you come back to try and finish what your kind started all those years ago? We're better armed now, and many of us have been practicing for just this occasion."

"No, my fierce little warrior. I came to clear up some myths about the night elves in the last war and to make sure there is no war this time."

Tia narrowed her eyes at the creature whose kind had forsaken her to live near her family and friends. "Do *not* make assumptions based upon the size of a thing, elf. The sharpness of my blade doesn't judge the size of the thing it cuts."

Raghnall stepped between the two. "Tia, Uther. Let's not start on bitter ground. It's time for the clans to sit, discuss, and decide how we will handle the problem we all face. Uther says he may have a solution. Let's hear him out before we throw him out. What do you say, Tia?"

The gnome glowered at the elf. A barely perceptible nod signaled the beginning of the first meeting of the clans in nearly 80 years. Raghnall stepped outside to the porch and pulling a horn from his side, blew three short blasts. An hour later, the fae warrior called the meeting to order.

~ * ~

Linda peeked out at the roomful of clan chieftains and warriors of all sizes. The gleam of silver blades in the light set goose bumps on her skin.

Several of the higher clan chiefs spoke and were well received. Points were made about what was happening in the valley; homes being damaged, innocents nearly being killed, and Ancients being completely destroyed. The atmosphere was heading toward heated when the night elf stood and cleared his throat.

"I've heard enough to know what I'm about to propose is the best solution to rid this valley of the threat… permanently."

Chapter Fifteen

Gitty pulled the barbell up for one more curl before dropping it on the stand. She grabbed the nearby towel and wiped the sweat from her forehead. *I'm done.*

She'd found herself in the basement gym more often these last few weeks since the construction company had been closed down. *Temporarily, only temporarily.* She headed for the shower. Letting the hot liquid sluice down her pumped muscles, Gitty relaxed until the water ran lukewarm. A change of clothing and the growling of her stomach demanded an immediate response.

As she stood waiting for the microwave to finish heating her meal, Lancelot trotted across the flagstone floor.

"Where've you been, you mangy beast? I thought I told you to grab one of the messenger mice so we could find out what's going on in the valley. Well? What happened?"

Lancelot turned his back to her as he drank from his water bowl. Gitty, unable to see into his mind unless she looked directly in his eyes, walked over and picked up the cat. She held him in her arms and stared into his golden orbs. Once connection had been made she got the pictures she was seeking.

"What? No mice *anywhere*?" She unceremoniously dropped the cat to the floor. "Vermin infested monsters are in hiding. I can sense something big is happening, and I aim to find out what. Better to be one step ahead than one step behind."

The microwave dinged in response and Gitty retrieved her food. She sat at the kitchen table, microwave food container on a heating pad, fork held mid-air, staring morosely out at the woods below. She could see the glow of lights from the Lending Library and all day long she'd been feeling the light fingers of magic dancing across her arms. The warmth of the room and heat from food in her belly began to lull Gitty's eyelids downward. The muscles of her neck relaxed and her shoulders slumped. *A quick nap would feel so good.*

Leather boots thudding on the stone flooring interrupted the pleasant moment. The harsh sound drew closer, preceded by a wave of unpleasantness dispelling the magic's warmth. Gitty pushed her food away and looked up at the sour expression on the face of her brother as he stomped into the kitchen area.

"What's the matter, Morgan? Won't anyone come out and play with you?"

He growled at her. "What would you know about playing? No one can stand to be near you."

"My but we're touchy this evening. Did some gnome steal your best girl?"

Morgan strode to the window and peered toward the valley, arms clasped behind his back.

Gitty began to worry. Morgan never let a chance go by to try and outdo her insults. His silence was unnerving.

"Morgan? What happened out there tonight? You're home entirely too early."

Gitty watched the broad back of her brother rise and fall with a deep sigh.

"We have a *very* large problem, Gitty."

She rolled her eyes. "For elves sake, Morgan, don't go drama king on me. What in the name of dragons and unicorns are you talking about?"

The tall night elf dropped his hands to his side and shook his head. He turned to face his sister.

"I hit a couple of my local haunts to see if any of my favorites were out with no luck. It was pretty quiet so I made my way north. There are a couple clubs near the university I've avoided because young Others are so--so…"

"Human?" Gitty raised an eyebrow.

Morgan narrowed his eyes and pushed out an exasperated sigh. "No. So unbelieving. The younger women still believe they're attractive to any and all men. They're harder to convince than the older ones who've had their hearts broken. Anyway, I strolled into several clubs and found myself welcomed for about an hour until the young girls got tired of buying my drinks.

"They informed me I wasn't anything like the 'other tall, white-haired guy with really cool icy blue eyes'."

"Like this is news?" She held her chin in the palm of her hand, her elbow resting on the tabletop. "So?"

Morgan glared at his sister.

"I decided to push a little and see who this guy was. I asked around to see if anyone could remember his name. A couple of the girls giggled and nodded their heads. They said he had an unusual name; something really medieval, like Geoffrey or Arthur or something like that."

"Morgan? Is there a point to all of this rambling?"

"Gitty!"

"What?!"

"Quit being such an ass."

Gitty dropped her hand to the table and raised her eyebrows at her brother. "What did you call me?"

Morgan puffed out his cheeks in frustration. "Think! What tall, white-haired guy with blue eyes and a medieval name do we know?"

Gitty stood, the chair scraping the floor. "I'm done. This is a guessing game for children, and I haven't been a child in over 100 years. Why don't you go online and tell your tall tales to some of your Internet lovers? You can still magic over distances, can't you?"

She trudged from the kitchen toward the hallway and her bedroom.

"Uther."

The name, spoken softly, stopped all movement in the household; even Lancelot stopped eating, flattened his ears against his head, and growled.

Gitty stopped in the middle of the hallway and turned. Her face had drained of all color and her eyes were the size of the tea saucers in the cupboard.

"What did you say?" She whispered.

"Uther."

She walked back to the living room and fell on to the couch. "It--it just can't be."

"Why not? Because he fears the Sauns and the house of Saun? I doubt it."

"No, because I was sure I'd seen our father put a blade to him. He was sprawled on the ground; blood everywhere, not breathing. I was certain of it!"

Morgan moved to the wingback chair and lowered himself into the plush upholstery.

"Well, sister dear, apparently you were wrong. There is an elvan man in these parts calling himself Uther and being kind to everything and everyone.

"If he is the same Uther... we're in trouble." Morgan turned to his sister. "We need to find out what's happening in that library place before it gets out of hand and we lose everything."

Gitty snapped her head his direction. "You *think*? I've been trying to get you to see what's been going on for the last month, but you've been too busy leeching off your girlfriends to see beyond your next free drink.

"Closing down our company was just the beginning," Gitty got up from the couch and paced back and forth. "The longer we're closed, the more chance there is someone will find the treasure Thomas talked about. If he told me in a drunken stupor, you can be sure he told someone else too."

She shuddered, stopping to cross her arms over her chest.

"I can't swear to it but it feels as if the magic level of the surrounding area has risen one hundred fold. I continually feel the buzzing of cast spells. Before, when it was just the two of us, the air was still until we used our own magic. Now, there's constant movement. The key to all of this lies inside the Lending Library."

The siblings turned and stared at the small rooftop. Light shown from the windows and the meadow moved with activity.

Gitty nodded her head. "I think it's time to make a neighborly visit."

Morgan frowned at his sister. "Why would we want to do that? You don't read."

She huffed out a breath, rolled her eyes, and shook her head. "You are such an idiot."

"What?"

"Think. What is the best way to find out what is happening?"

"I don't know."

Gitty dropped her head and let her hands drop to her side. Looking up at her sibling with eyes blazing, she gritted her teeth as she answered.

"How have you lived so long without being killed? The best way to find out what is happening is to *be* there when it happens. If we make a friendly visit to the Library, should Tiamoon or some of her pathetic little friends show up, we'd know about it because…"

"…we'd be there." Morgan brightened as he finished his sister's sentence.

"Uhhgg." Gitty shook her had and headed down the hallway. "I'm going to bed."

Morgan turned his attention to the light in the valley. "Maybe there'll be some women who don't know me there." The reflection in the window showed a lecherous smile spreading over his face.

Chapter Sixteen

Tiamoon sat in the child-sized chair and propped her legs, crossed at the ankle, on the lower slat of the porch railing. She made a visual reconnoiter of the surrounding area. There were a few spots of wavering air consistent with magic being used, but beyond that nothing was happening. The calmness made her uncomfortable. With her step-siblings so close, she didn't trust the serenity. She sensed the presence before noting his fawn colored boots standing next to her.

"Tiamoon."

"Uther."

"May I join you?"

"Still a free country."

The elf sat on the top step his long legs stretched languidly in front of him.

"Do you sense Gitty and Morgan nearby?"

Tia shifted her weight and recrossed her feet. "No. There's nothing here for them to gain. I know elvan magic is stronger than fae magic, one on one, but with so many fae present, the two would have to be out of their minds to attempt any confrontation. I also suspect they've felt your presence. Gitty may be bold, but she's not stupid. Everyone in the fae kingdom knows how powerful you are."

Uther smiled at the compliment. "Thank you, I think. I'm powerful but no more than any other night elf. I've just learned to utilize what's been given me. Two night elves in tandem against me could easily defeat me. I hope circumstances don't take that turn."

Tia snorted. "I can't see Gitty and Morgan *ever* doing anything in tandem. The only reason they live in the same house without killing each other is our father demanded it."

Uther raised an eyebrow and shot the gnome a side look.

"Yeah. We share a father, nothing more. When he was killed in the war, those two sent my mother away and exiled me. They wanted to make sure no one knew we were related. Hence, the stepbrother, stepsister verbage. It was as if anyone knowing we shared the same blood would taint them in your community. I couldn't have cared but it brought an early end to my mother's life. She idolized my father and willingly accepted his children. The feelings were not mutual.

"Anyway, I hope you know what you're doing with this party idea."

Uther leaned himself back on his elbows stretching to his full length. "I've sensed them watching the building."

Tia's eyebrows shot up.

"Yes. They're keeping an eye on the unusual amount of fae traffic in and out of the house. They, too, can feel the spike of magic around the Library. If, as you say, control and power is foremost in their minds, they'll want to make sure they're prepared to protect what they have. Any attempt to overtake them will be met with brutal, deadly force.

"The party tonight will peak their curiosity. I'm surprised they haven't shown before now."

Tiamoon humphed. "Gitty likes to sneak up and ambush people. Walking up to the front door and knocking is not her style."

The two warriors sat quietly for a moment soaking in the smells and sights of a spring day in the forest. Sun filtered between the trees exposing new life on the forest floor. A gentle breeze wafted the sweet scent of early flowers celebrating the break from the constant rain and cold of winter.

"Has anyone figured out why the Sauns are killing the Ancients?" Uther sat up, placed his elbows on his knees, and stared down the driveway.

"No. That's the strangest thing of all. About ten to eleven months ago, seemingly out of the blue, they started tearing up the oak groves;

nothing else, just oaks. The construction equipment appeared and a sign went up announcing a new subdivision of houses according to the Librarian. However, nothing was built, just the destruction of the oaks."

"Then our mission is twofold; stop the Sauns wanton destruction of the Ancients and finding out *why* they're killing the forest."

~ * ~

Ailidh and Kayne slowed their trek as they neared home. The tree still stood and she turned to him, a smile touching her lips.

"We may still have a place to live!"

Kayne looked around the meadow. He felt exposed and vulnerable walking in the open.

"Ailidh? Let's just check out the tree and get back to the library. Something is not right about this place."

"Oh, don't be silly." Ailidh pushed open the door. Dust covered every item in the living area, but nothing had been taken or moved. It was as they had left it nearly two months earlier. She pushed a sigh through her lips, her shoulders relaxing, and smiled widely.

"We're home, Kayne. We're home."

Kayne had been backing into the trunk of the oak that served as home to the fae pair, watching the horizon for trouble. His magic sense tingled with danger warnings. He'd turned, gripped the door, and was pushing it closed when a large black paw clutched the side and shoved.

"Ailidh! Run!"

Enormous gold eyes gleamed dangerously as the cat tried to push its way into the hole. It swiped the air with one paw, pushing the door inward with the other.

Kayne tried to push back but the creature's size and weight made the battle an uneven match.

"Kayne! The incantation!" Ailidh drew her sword, closed her eyes, and pointed toward the door. She began chanting.

"I command you, I compel you, creature of Gitty, get out of my house now!"

Kayne added his voice raising it until he was shouting at the black intruder.

Chanting the incantation, Ailidh opened her eyes, glared at the enormous yellow-eyed monster, and pushed toward the door. A high-pitched keening began to rent the air. The cat dug its heels in pushing backwards from the tree and, yeowling in pain, fled. The two faeries watched the monster streak from their home in the oak.

Ailidh looked at Kayne a smug smile on her face.

"Welcome home."

~ * ~

Linda watched the activity in her lending library. The building was humming. She couldn't believe how many of the small magical folk were inside the walls of her home. Childhood dreams never included this many faeries in one place. The hub of activity was Chrissy's kitchen. The little wood nymph had taken control of the celebration planning and was barking out orders like a general planning a campaign.

"No, Rory, not there; near the doorway."

"What difference does it make? They're not gonna notice it anyway."

"No, but I am."

Throwing up his hands, the warrior-turned-unwilling-room-decorator moved the floral display.

"Women!"

Linda couldn't stop the giggle that escaped her. Chrissy was a force to be reckoned with.

She'd been so busy watching the decorating, she'd not taken notice of where she was walking. Bumping into a muscular, wide chest, Linda felt the heat flood her cheeks. She immediately looked to the ground and apologized.

"I'm so sorry. My mistake."

A hand gently cupped her chin and brought her head up. She found herself looking directly into the stunning blue eyes of the night elf Uther. Again, her cheeks flooded with heat.

"Please don't apologize to me. The fae folk are notorious for not trusting anything they haven't invented or been around in the last 200 years. Frankly, I think they owe you a debt of gratitude for offering your home as a refuge."

"I agree." Chrissy interjected as she sped past her wings churning furiously. "Laughlin! Not there! *Why* didn't they bring their mates? Aaahhhh!"

Uther chuckled.

Linda felt the sound roll over her skin and tickle her ears. This beautiful man was reminding her of sensations she'd long put away. It made her uncomfortable on the one hand and happy on the other that she could still feel.

"I'm happy to have my house full of life again."

Uther smiled. "Yes, Chrissy told me of your brave fight to help your husband in his last days. He was a lucky man."

"I miss him." Linda looked horrified she had confided something so personal to a virtual stranger. "I'm sorry. That was very... rude. If you'll excuse me?"

She fled out to her backyard. Tiamoon was practicing her sword moves alone. Linda slipped past the gnome warrior and walked the fence line to the back of the property. A small creek served as the demarcation of the end of her property. Linda found her favorite stump and sat staring at the rippling water.

"Are you okay?"

She jumped at the sound of the deep voice.

"No. I'm flustered, confused, overwhelmed... you name it. I had my life all planned out then my husband got sick and died. So--I changed my plans. I indulged my love of books and surrounded myself with items I knew wouldn't die or require me to do more than love them.

"Then Chrissy showed up. I couldn't believe all the tales my relatives told me were true and standing in front of me in the form of a wood nymph. I guess I got carried away thinking they would ever accept me.

"Then you showed up..."

Uther nodded. "And I stirred feelings you thought long dead."

Linda's mouth dropped. She put a hand over it and nodded her agreement.

He smiled. "No ,I don't read minds but you *are* fairly see-through. You don't hide your feelings very well."

She shrugged. "Yeah, Donald always did say I was an open book."

Uther knelt to the side of the stump and gently placed Linda's hand in his.

"If I may say… you are still a magnificent looking woman, Librarian…"

"Linda."

He tipped his head. "Linda. I would be honored if you would allow me to become a friend."

She turned her head and peered into his face. "I'd like that."

A grin touched his lips. "We can see where it goes from there."

Linda blushed. "Darn this blushing stuff."

Uther chuckled. "I find it attractive and honest. Would you like me to leave you to your thoughts?"

"Maybe for a little bit. Chrissy has everything so under control I feel in the way in my own home. I sure hope this works out for everyone."

Uther stood, kissed the hand he held and placed it in her lap. "So do I."

~ * ~

Gitty walked the perimeter of her property noting the increasing activity at the Lending Library. She felt a pressing, unrelenting need to be there; so much so the need wretched her senses to the point of restlessness. Uther was there--she could *feel* his presence. *Before this night is over, Uther, there will be a shift in power in this valley.*

Gitty strode to the house and, upon entering, called for her brother.

"Morgan! It's time we met our neighborhood librarian. Get down here!"

She heard the laconic shuffle of feet and looked up to see

Morgan dressed in a running suit and shoes ambling his way toward her.

"Oh, no, little brother. Get back upstairs and put on your best dress-to-impress outfit. For the most part you're useless, but unsettling the ladies with your first impression is what I need to give us the advantage. Move it!"

Morgan stuck out his lower lip and pouted as he turned around and trudged back to his room to change.

When he returned and received Gitty's approval, the pair climbed into the Hummer and drove to the Lending Library. The closer they got to the building the more agitated Gitty felt.

"There is a lot of magic being performed in this vicinity." She parked the car out front and exited her side. Morgan followed suit, allowing Gitty to take the lead. She walked up the steps of the quaint building and read the sign on the door--Open. Just walk in.

~ * ~

Uther shushed the noisy crowd as he watched the night elf pair ascend the steps.

"They're here. Shhhh!"

~ * ~

She pushed the door open slowly, unsure of what she would find on the other side. Once in the building there was a festive atmosphere, floral arrangements adorned walls and the tables had tablecloths and centerpieces. An older woman in a stunning blue dress came from the back room and jumped when she saw the pair.

"Oh! I'm sorry. You startled me. Welcome to the Lending Library. We're celebrating our 10th anniversary with a party. You're welcome to stay if you like."

Her smile was bright and Gitty returned the gesture.

"Hello. I'm Gitty Saun and this is my brother Morgan." She turned around and grabbed him by the coat muttering under her breath. "Get over here, you idiot."

From behind the tall, white-haired woman's back, stepped a man with waist-length white hair and deep blue eyes. Linda sucked in a breath, smiling to cover her surprise. Uther had warned her Morgan was handsome, but his warning paled in comparison to the reality. The man smiled, showing a set of dazzling white teeth, but Linda noted the smile didn't reach his eyes.

"Pleased to meet you."

Linda subtly stepped back and slightly to the side. "I'm Linda and this is…"

"UTHER!"

The brother and sister spoke in unison. Their faces were locked in an expression of shock when Uther pulled his staff and pointed it their direction.

"FREEZE!"

The two forms were trapped in the positions they had been standing when the night elf had cast a stunning spell on them. Linda watched as their eyes blinked.

Uther lifted each of the night elves separately and carried them to the center of the room standing them side-by-side. Once in place, the room filled with fae warriors, wood nymphs, gnomes, and forest creatures.

Tiamoon walked from the back porch to face the elvan pair.

"Gitty and Morgan Saun."

Linda swore she could see hatred radiate from the pair's eyes.

"You have terrorized this valley for many decades; killing many of our relatives, stealing from those who remained, and banishing others as you saw fit. Your actions have indicted you. The fae clans, along with Uther representing the Night Elves and the Librarian representing the Others, have decreed that as long as you wish to act like the humans, you will live like the humans and die like the humans."

Tiamoon nodded and the elvan pair watched as clan chieftains came from various parts of the room and stood in front of them. Uther and the person they called the Librarian moved to the back of the fae. The group looked directly into the eyes of the two rogue night elves while Tiamoon spoke.

"Guardians of magic, your hearts have strayed,
You seek wealth and power and have chosen the dark way.
This council has voted to speak as one,
We withhold your powers from this day on.
No longer will you use the Old Magic ways,
A human life you'll live for the rest of your days.
All the room pointed at the elves and spoke in unison.
Gitty and Morgan Saun: It is over, it is done.
Gitty and Morgan Saun: It is over, it is done.
Gitty and Morgan Saun: It is over, it is done."

Uther moved to face the elves and lifted his staff pointing it their direction.

"FREE!"

The startled expression on the two faces turned to frowning snarls, and the two began to flex muscles and move around.

"Don't think this is over, you little freaks. You've just made the biggest enemy you could have in your lifetimes." Gitty lifted a hand toward Tiamoon. "Destroy!"

Silence filled the room.

Tiamoon stood tall, her right hand clutching the handle of her sword. She looked at the woman who'd exiled her and smiled.

"Like to try that again?"

"MORGAN! Help me!"

The two elves stood pointing at the gnome and yelled together. "Destroy!"

A ripple of laughter passed through the room when nothing happened.

Gitty's face blossomed to a bright red. "AAAAHHHHH! I still have the construction company and I'll bulldoze every stand of trees in this valley!"

"I don't think so." Uther moved to face Gitty.

She glared at him, her fists clenching and unclenching. "Oh? Do you really think I care what you think? My crews will make matchsticks of this building then I'll dig until I find the blasted treasure that drunken leprechaun babbled on about."

Linda stepped forward. "Treasure? There's a treasure in my house?"

Morgan had slinked to the door and attempted to leave. Several fae chieftains held him at sword point inside the room as Tiamoon walked up to face him.

"You're not going anywhere, brother dearest."

She watched him flinch at her use of the word brother.

Gitty narrowed her eyes and spit her words out through clenched teeth. "Yes, treasure, as if you didn't know."

Linda looked at her. "What leprechaun?"

Gitty rolled her eyes. "Others. You're all so stupid."

Uther moved toward Gitty. "Watch your mouth."

"Or you'll do what?"

Linda stood, finger tapping on her chin. She looked at Uther and a smile spread to cover her whole face. "Is he a short man with an Irish accent and bright green eyes?"

Gitty shook her head. "That describes three quarters of the men in this valley."

"A little man who speaks of enough gold bricks to build a mansion?"

Gitty stopped and turned to Linda. "That's the one."

Linda bit her lip to keep from laughing but gave into the urge. Soon she was holding her sides and guffawing.

The effect soon had the room responding the same way.

"WHAT IS SO DAMN FUNNY?"

Linda stopped laughing long enough to look directly into the eyes of the angry female night elf.

"Thomas always told me my books were worth more than any monetary fortune. In fact, he made up a little ditty just for me.

A stand of oaks
That all can see,
Hides the fortune
Most seek from me.

Linda watched the vein in the elf's neck throb. Her face turned purple and she screamed as she ran from the room grabbing her brother

100

in her escape. Linda looked at Uther.

"She's quite upset. Are my forest folk really safe from them?"

He nodded. "Yes. They've lost their magic. Right now, they don't understand what that means, but next time they try to magic something away, nothing will happen. They wanted the power and life of humans, now they have it until they die."

Linda shook her head. "How sad. For something as fleeting as power, they gave up the most important thing of all--they sold their heritage."

Uther slipped her hand into his. "It's their loss. Now, let's not worry about them and celebrate. This week has resulted in a gathering of clans that hasn't been seen in many decades. The valley now has its rightful owners back, and I have a new friend I intend to visit often.

"Is there any cake?"

Linda felt her cheeks flush. "I believe I can arrange that."

~The End~

Chasing Rainbows

Genie Gabriel

Dedication

To the other Rogue's Angels,
Christine Young and C. L. Kraemer.

To Linda Hamer, who makes a fictional cameo appearance in this story,
and to her daughters, who honored their mother by sponsoring this
appearance.

To all the animals who have passed through the doors at
Willamette Humane Society--
may you always know the joy of chasing rainbows.

Chapter One

Ka-boom! The blast shattered the settling peace of dusk as Marissa Madison pulled into the circular drive. Rissa threw open the car door and sprinted toward the gray stone house.

"Please, no blood this time," she whispered as her feet hit the rough-hewn steps leading up to the broad double doors.

A bespectacled man stepped through the doorway amid a confetti shower of envelopes and leaflets. His silvery hair stood in startled spikes around a balding pate as if it too had been a victim of the explosion.

"Too much torque in the mail conveyor," he muttered with a frown.

"Please turn it off, Uncle Horace!"

"Right." The old man disappeared back into the house. Within moments, the clanking stopped and silence fell over the rolling hills once again.

Just another normal day, Rissa thought, as she surveyed the day's mail scattered in gay abandon across the landscape.

The sullen gray sky rumbled ominously and tossed a few raindrops against her face. Rissa grabbed a check out of the privet hedge, an overdue bill off the bird bath, a shampoo sample from the branches of the azaleas, and a plain brown envelope from the lawn.

I hope I didn't miss anything important. Rissa scanned the inner courtyard once more. Lightening crackled across the sky, hurrying her steps back to the navy blue sedan to grab her briefcase and a bag of groceries. She closed the heavy wooden door behind her as a gust of wind pushed fat, sloppy raindrops against the mullioned windows.

Maybe Uncle Horace should invent a mail dryer instead of a mail conveyer. Rissa dropped the soggy mail on a cherry wood table as she stepped out of her shoes. With the bag of groceries balanced on one hip, she padded barefoot toward the kitchen. A tall figure in a sweeping lavender print dress stood at the sink.

"I couldn't tell if the grocery list said chips or cheese, so I got both." As Rissa moved closer, the person she thought was her aunt turned toward her. She shrieked and dropped the groceries. "Ryan!"

Rissa's twin brother grinned at her from beneath the purple feathers of one of her aunt's collection of hats.

"Do I want to know what's going on?" Rissa asked warily.

"I'm going to a Valentine's party tonight," Ryan replied.

"Dressed as Aunt Madelaine?" Rissa retrieved a head of lettuce and a package of marshmallow pinwheel cookies from the marbled tiles.

"It's a great way to pick up women." Ryan bent down and caught an escaping tomato. "You'd be amazed at what they tell dear Aunt Mads."

"You've done this before?"

"Sure. Madelaine thinks it's a hoot."

"Where is Madelaine anyway?" Rissa pushed aside a stack of unwashed dishes to set the tattered grocery bag on the counter.

Ryan shrugged. "She's been gone all day. By the way, I left your food in the microwave since I knew you'd be late."

Rissa opened the microwave and poked at the still-warm entree.

"It's beef tips over rice--one of your favorites."

"Thanks." Rissa glanced over her shoulder. With the hat pulled low across his face, Ryan bore an uncanny resemblance to their tall, raw-boned aunt. She couldn't resist one jibe. "You'll make someone a wonderful wife some day."

Ryan fisted a hand on one hip and struck a pose until Rissa chuckled.

"Come with me," Ryan urged. "When was the last time you went out?"

"Thanks, but I'm tired."

"You work too hard."

The truth of her brother's statement stirred a wistfulness in Rissa, which she quickly pushed away.

"I think Madelaine might have a special surprise planned for tonight." Ryan grinned wickedly.

"What are you scheming now?" Rissa frowned at her brother.

"Guess you'll have to come with me to find out."

"Oh, no. I'm not falling for that trick. I'm going to eat this gourmet dinner you so thoughtfully prepared and go to bed."

Ryan shrugged, and Madelaine's lavender feather boa slid off his shoulder. "Well, you can read about it in the morning paper anyway."

Rissa's fingers gripped the plate holding her dinner. Ryan was baiting her. That was all. He wouldn't really do anything too foolish.

The muffled thud of the front door echoed her brother's departure.

He'll go to the Pink Flamingo, have a few drinks, pick up another blonde, and come home just before my alarm clock goes off, Rissa told herself. *Nothing out of the ordinary.*

Of course, she never would have guessed that Ryan dressed up as their aunt, either--and apparently got away with it.

"No, I am not going to follow him." Rissa marched to the kitchen table, pulled out a chair, and spread a napkin across her lap. She even lifted a bite of food to her mouth.

"Oh, bother and damnation." She set her fork carefully back on her plate. What if her brother really did something spectacularly stupid? Rissa would have to pick up the pieces anyway. She might as well stop the disaster before it got started.

~ * ~

"Come on, you bucket of bolts, just another couple miles." Ian MacGregor was determined he could motivate the sputtering 1972 Pinto station wagon through sheer iron will as he did raw army recruits. In spite of his command, the car belched a cloud of black smoke and the engine died. Ian managed to steer the well-used vehicle onto the shoulder of the road before it stopped moving completely. Then he cranked the engine until the battery groaned weakly in protest.

Cursing under his breath, Ian climbed out and stared at the disabled vehicle. If it hadn't belonged to his recently deceased father, Ian would have kicked the tire. An unexpected lump formed in his throat. He should have been enjoying a roaring drunk to grieve his father, not selling every piece of personal property so his mother didn't have to live on the street.

A raindrop spattered against his face, followed quickly by another and yet another. Ian scowled at the darkened sky. Not a star was visible through the thick blanket of clouds and no headlights brightened the gloomy evening. In fact, he hadn't seen anyone else on the road for the last half hour. He punched a button on his cell phone, but got only a "no service available" message.

With another muttered oath, Ian swung his duffle bag out of the back seat, took one last look at the tired auto and set off down the road. As he walked, his thoughts turned as bleak as the driving rain and cold wind that jabbed at the upturned collar of his battered leather jacket. The two thousand dollars offered by a collector for the Pinto wouldn't go far toward paying off the debts racked up by his father's business partner. However, his mother insisted on paying what they could.

Ironic that his mother was the strong one in the family when a crisis hit. Soft-spoken in the way of the librarian she had been for years, no one argued twice with Linda MacGregor when that steely glint flashed in her eyes and her jaw took on a stubborn tilt. Ian remembered the first and last time he had made that mistake. His teenaged social life shrank to the size of his bedroom and his father just laughed when Ian begged him to intercede.

So he marched down a deserted midnight road, gaze focused forward, until flashes of neon green and pink began to dance in the misty sky. His steps slowed cautiously as a square concrete building appeared and the neon colors took on the shapes of palm trees and flamingoes.

Ian scrubbed a hand across his eyes, thinking the illusion would disappear. But when he looked again, the neon still winked at him. What

4

the hell. As long as it was warm and dry with a phone to call a tow truck.

Once under the portico, Ian brushed the rain out of his short-cropped hair and pushed open the door. Shades of pink engulfed him, rather like falling into a bottle of stomach antacid. Pink hearts suspended from the ceiling. Pink stencils around the mirrors. Pink napkins and pink drinks with pink straws. Even the waitresses wore pink and carried heart-shaped trays.

Oh-kay, Ian thought. *The hallucinations inside were even stranger.*

He touched the arm of a waitress passing by, wondering if he could order something that wasn't pink with hearts.

But the moment her startled gray eyes met his, Ian's voice disappeared. *I knew I would marry your mother the first time I saw her.* His father's awed statement echoed in Ian's mind. Many times he had heard the story of how his parents met on Valentine's Day and were married on that day a year later. Ian always smiled and nodded when they retold their tale.

However, he hadn't actually believed them until this moment.

The woman he knew would be his future wife lifted a pink heart-shaped plastic tray in front of her like a shield, calling attention to a bosom barely contained in a rose-colored tube top. Then she backed away a few steps, spun and sprinted toward the bar.

Hovering at the far end of the bar, Rissa rubbed her arm where That Man's fingers had rested. Dressing as a waitress had seemed like the perfect solution to keep an eye on her brother. Put on a wig and some selected endowments, then circulate through the bar and smile. Unfortunately, because she looked like a waitress, she was expected to act like one also. Except that she didn't know a Black Russian from a Bloody Mary, and her feet hurt. She supposed that her backside would have been black and blue from pinches too if it hadn't been artificially padded.

However, Rissa quickly figured out a simple system. Wine in the tall glasses; hard liquor in the short, squatty ones. Match the color of the umbrellas or what was left of the drink. If she mixed up the orders, she just smiled and apologized profusely. Her system had worked fine.

Until That Man touched her arm.

Rissa couldn't even look into his mesmerizing green eyes without growing dizzy. A dimple appeared briefly in his left cheek as he flashed a smile.

Lowering her gaze was another mistake. His worn-soft bomber jacket and faded-on jeans conveyed a dangerously intimate message. A message her body picked up loud and clear.

Ceiling fans moved languidly, shifting the air but not cooling her heated flesh. Perspiration dampened her palms, her upper lip, the valley between her glued-on, enhanced breasts.

For the first time in her life, Rissa was confronted with the raw sexual power between a man and a woman. It startled and intrigued her; made her want to draw back even as it pulled her under its spell.

The physical impact of someone stumbling against her brought Rissa back to reality--and a commotion by the bar. Rex Foxworth stood alone beside a three-foot-tall cake, his face covered with a stunned expression and clumps of pink frosting.

Where's Ryan? Rissa thought. *What happened?*

She took a step and her padded breasts slid downward. "Oh, bother and damnation."

The glue must have been loosened by the perspiration generated from close proximity to the tempting stranger. Rissa placed a hand under her sagging bosom and nudged it upward.

The emerald-eyed stranger reappeared, regarding her curiously.

"Are you feeling alright?" the man asked.

Rissa nodded vigorously, which started her bosom sliding once more. She crossed her arms and hugged her waist.

"Are you sure you're not in pain?"

"No!" she whispered as her phony breasts continued their downward slide. *If I can just get out of here without the entire bar noticing my escaping body parts.*

6

Rissa edged along the bar. The door seemed miles away, but she could make it. She knew she could.

"Wait!" That Man touched her arm again.

The contact caught Rissa by surprise. As she spun around to face the stranger, her arms dropped their frantic hold across her midsection. She felt a shifting and realized her borrowed bosoms were now at her waist. Horrified, she watched the slow motion descent of her faux breasts as they fell at the stranger's feet.

"I'm sorry," Rissa whispered. She snatched the padding from atop the man's spit-shined shoes and double-timed it out of the Pink Flamingo.

Chapter Two

Ryan was in the kitchen, picking blue moons out of the cereal when Rissa stumbled downstairs the next morning, hung over from dreams of mesmerizing green eyes and sliding fake body parts. "Hey, sis, you're up late this morning."

At least he was wearing jeans and not lavender chiffon. "Where is everyone?"

"Horace is in the basement working on holograms, Mother is in her suite, and Madelaine hasn't shown up yet," Ryan recited dutifully, then added, "She's probably off chasing rainbows."

Rissa poured a cup of coffee then slid into a chair across from her brother. The mid-morning sunshine spilled through the leaded glass window, casting rainbows of color on the oaken table, which she traced with her finger. "Do you remember how Madelaine used to take us to look for the pot of gold at the end of the rainbow?"

"Yeah. She would drive for miles and miles and you'd jump up and down shrieking 'go faster'. Your hair stuck out all over--just like it is now." Ryan crossed his eyes and waved his hands around his head in imitation of his sister's hair.

Rissa smoothed a hand over the corkscrew tangle of her curls. "I don't think I'd survive one of her adventures any more."

"You're not as boring as you try to pretend."

"Gee, thanks--I think."

Ryan took a bite of his cereal. "Did you have a good time last night?"

Rissa's coffee cup stopped halfway to her mouth. Dear heavens!

8

Had her brother recognized her at the Pink Flamingo? Surely not, or he would be mimicking her frantic movements to keep her borrowed bosoms in place. She decided to brazen this one out. "Your idea of a good time differs from mine."

"Jeez, did you go back to the office last night? If you're going to stay out later than me, you should at least be doing something almost fun."

Rissa sipped her coffee and remained quiet.

"That's good, though," Ryan continued. "If you went to the office last night, you shouldn't have to work today, right?"

"I didn't say that. It's tax season. We're busy."

Ryan leaned closer to Rissa. "I need a favor."

"I'm not going on a blind date with any of your buddies."

"No, it's not that. Besides, you've got all of them convinced that you're boring."

Rissa pointed a spoon at her brother in warning.

"Hey, that's what you wanted," Ryan defended himself. "But listen, I invited Tiffany over today and I want you to keep Mother busy."

"Who's Tiffany?"

"I met her last night." Ryan grinned. "Blonde, great body--"

"Sounds like your kind of girl. Why spoil it and bring her home?"

"You wound me," Ryan protested as he put his hand over his heart.

Rissa fixed her brother with a you-can't-fool-me look.

After another quick glance over his shoulder, Ryan confessed, "She thinks she's coming to see Madelaine."

"Madelaine's not--" Rissa stopped mid-sentence as she remembered that Ryan had been dressed as Madelaine last night. "You lied to her."

"Well, not exactly. She said she really liked the neon flamingoes Madelaine made for Rex's restaurant and I asked her if she wanted to see some other art work."

"You used the come-and-see-my-etchings line on her? Ryan, anyone dumb enough to fall for that line should be pitied, not taken

9

advantage of."

"Tiffany's not dumb. She's also a very nice person."

"That's never stopped you before."

"She was really upset that Rex pinched me."

"Is that why you pushed his face in the cake?"

"You were there!" Ryan exclaimed triumphantly. "You must have come up with a great disguise. I didn't even see you."

"You could at least be nice to Rex at his own party." Rissa tried to sidetrack her brother. She did not want to tell him about her night out. The only one in at least six months and it had been a disaster.

"Madelaine would have decked him."

Rissa's smile almost escaped. "I suppose you're right."

"You were there, huh?" Ryan grinned at her. "I knew you still had a spark of fun in you. So keep Mother occupied, okay?"

"On one condition. That you don't masquerade as Madelaine any more."

"Hey, I hardly ever do that any way."

Rissa scowled at her brother. "Justice will find you some day."

"As long as she's blonde and beautiful." Ryan stood and pushed his chair back, ruffling Rissa's hair. "Maybe Mother can do something with your frizzies too."

He dodged her right jab and bounded out of the room.

~ * ~

Ian gazed at the gray stone building perched regally on the hillside. Its lofty stone turrets seemed to disappear high into the clouds above, bringing to mind the castles he had seen in Scotland on his last trip across the Atlantic.

As he crossed a stone bridge, he expected to glimpse a long, scaly tail in the water. He drove slowly across the cobbled courtyard, envisioning oxen, prancing stallions, and a princess with gray eyes.

Ian hadn't fantasized about a woman in a long time. Now he couldn't get the woman he met last night out of his mind. One minute she was standing in front of him, all seductive curves and wild hair; then

10

her fake breasts slid out from under her tube top. Most women would have died on the spot, but she picked the things up, apologized as if she had bumped his arm on the sidewalk, and sailed out of the bar.

Ian wondered what he would have done if he had caught up with her. Maybe he would be tired as a new recruit at boot camp, but not so restless this morning. He parked beside a Volvo and a Ford sedan, reminders that this wasn't a castle from the days of knights and rogues; this was the twenty-first century. He didn't have time to dally with a princess. His mother needed the money from selling the Pinto station wagon to Madelaine Ainsworth, an antique car collector with an eccentric reputation.

Deliver the car and go home, Ian reminded himself.

He stepped up to the castle door and rapped the cast iron doorknocker against its base. A shrill whistle pierced the air, followed by two clanks and a thud. The whistle shrieked again, then pieces of paper spewed out of a slot beside the door.

Ian jumped aside as a staunch man with spiky white hair burst through the door. Within seconds, another person tumbled out the door.

"Uncle Horace, what's happening?"

"Mail conveyor. Still too much torque."

"Please--"

"I know, I know. Turn it off." The older man shot a bewildered smile toward Ian then disappeared back inside.

The other person was definitely a woman, Ian thought, eying her shapely legs outlined in slim fitting pants. And damned if her baggy sweatshirt didn't have the same effect as the hot pink top that last night's waitress wore.

Ian forced his gaze to the woman's face and realized she had been staring at him too. She quickly ducked her head and bent to pick up the papers that had drifted to rest on the porch. He squatted to help her. They worked side by side to gather the debris as clanking, thudding and an occasional whistle echoed across the hills.

The sudden silence jolted Ian's attention back to the woman. She stood gracefully, papers clutched in her hands. He rose also and handed her a fistful of envelopes. Their gazes locked for a moment and recognition jolted Ian in the groin. She was the waitress from last night's Valentine's party.

The woman he was going to marry.

"I'm sorry." She stepped away from him. "We don't always greet visitors with a confetti shower."

Her voice wafted over him. "No problem."

Ian waited for her to say more. *I knew you were the one the moment I saw you. May I touch your hand? Kiss your lips? Spend my life with you?*

But she remained silent.

What if she didn't feel the same way he did? To hear his parents tell their story, his mother took some convincing that Calvin MacGregor was the man she should marry. That was okay. Ian was no stranger to challenges. If this slender woman was Madelaine Ainsworth, he would certainly find other items she might like to collect.

"I'm Ian MacGregor." He smiled and held out his hand, anticipating the pleasure of her touch, if only briefly. "I'm looking for Madelaine Ainsworth."

The woman opened her mouth to speak, but was interrupted by another voice. "Yoo-hoo, Marissa, is that you out there?"

"You're not Madelaine?" Ian asked.

Rissa shook her head. "Madelaine isn't here."

She stepped inside and started to close the door.

The thought of losing both the money his mother needed and the woman he had been fantasizing about stirred Ian to action. He kicked his foot forward, effectively stopping the heavy wooden door from closing. "When will Madelaine be back?"

"It's hard to tell. Try later in the week."

"Wait a minute--"

"Marissa, do we have company?" The door opened wide once again, framing a woman who could have stepped straight out of the 1950's, wearing a poodle skirt and sweater, with her shoulder-length blonde hair teased and sprayed into a turned-up curl at the ends.

"Mother, he's looking for Madelaine."

"Oh, she'll be back any minute. Do come in and have some tea with us."

Triumph flashed through Ian as the older woman motioned him inside and led the way down the hall, chattering.

~ * ~

After her mother and Ian were settled in the sitting room and engrossed in conversation, Rissa sat into a caged wicker chair off to one side. The chair's woven sides curved to a peak above her head, leaving a modest open circle in front through which she could watch her mother charm their unexpected visitor, but he could see little of her.

Simply looking at the man sent a shivery tingle through Rissa's body. She wondered if his lips would be warm with the taste of the Earl Grey tea her mother had poured into the delicate white china cups. Or if his fingers would be as gentle as his care in selecting a petit four from the silver tray Daphne offered.

Perhaps only Rissa felt the lightning flash of recognition as their eyes met. She didn't want to relive the total humiliation she felt last night when her faux breasts landed at his feet. The best hope of keeping her secret was to stay quiet.

Unfortunately, her mother had different ideas. "What do you know of Scotland, Mr. MacGregor?"

"Please call me Ian. I've been there a few times."

"Wonderful!" Daphne clapped her hands together. "Rissa has been dying to go but needs a traveling companion. Traveling is so much more exciting with someone you love. When my Charles and I went on safari in Africa, he simply adored it. I hated the bugs and the dust, but it was worth it just to be with my darling husband."

Ian murmured a polite response and surreptitiously glanced at his watch. "Do you have any idea when Madelaine will be back?"

Daphne waved a hand dismissively. "Madelaine didn't go with us. She couldn't bear the thought of those animals being killed."

"No, I mean tonight," Ian said.

"Tonight? Madelaine can't be gone tonight. She wanted me to do her hair." Daphne jumped to her feet. "Now I'm cross with her. If she

13

disappears without telling me, she can just wait until next week. I'm going to my room."

Without a backward glance, Daphne flounced out of the room, her petticoats rustling indignantly.

Rissa hurried after her mother then remembered their guest. She turned back to Ian. "Let me show you out."

Ian didn't move. "Uh-uh."

The breath caught in Rissa's throat as she stared at the tall, broad-shouldered stranger. He hadn't seemed dangerous, except to her heightened libido. Could she have been wrong? "Would you like another cup of tea while I make sure my mother is settled?"

Ian shook his head. He was watching her. Too intently. Perhaps being found out as the waitress with the drop-away bosom might be less dangerous than the intense scrutiny that created a yearning heat in her belly.

"A scone? Jelly tart?" Rissa's heart beat louder as Ian shook his head at each of her offerings.

"An explanation."

An explanation? Ian's demand echoed in her head. How she was going to explain dropping phony body parts at his feet without seeming like a total idiot?

"Is Madelaine Ainsworth here or not?" Ian demanded.

Rissa blinked in surprise. Could it be he didn't recognize her?

"You say she's gone. Your mother says she will be back at any time, then changes her mind and decides that Madelaine is indeed gone. What's going on?"

"Madelaine."

"Yes. That's who I came here to see."

Relief and disappointment flowed through Rissa, dousing the heat that had engulfed her body. Her secret was safe, but part of her longed to think that Ian had been so enamored that he had tracked her down.

She pulled on her familiar façade of responsibility to protect her heart. "Madelaine isn't here right now."

"When will she be back?"

"As I said, I'm not sure." With another deep breath, Rissa's posture became charm school perfect. "Madelaine keeps her own schedule. Sometimes she disappears for several days or a week at a time."

Ian frowned. "Don't you worry about her?"

"She's been doing it for years. She always comes home with a new adventure to tell."

Scowling, Ian pulled a card from his jacket pocket and scribbled on it. "Ask her to call me when she returns."

Their fingers brushed as Rissa took the card. She struggled valiantly to hold onto her composure as Ian stared at her with startled intensity.

"I'll be available any time--day or night."

Rissa held her breath as Ian paused on the threshold. He stared at her once more then left without saying another word.

~ * ~

The next day, Ian stood once more in front of the massive plank door of Rissa's castle home and rapped the doorknocker, hoping Madelaine was home today. When he had returned to his mother's home last night, she was close to tears. Though she tried valiantly not to show her distress, another creditor had presented her with an unpaid bill. Ian needed to generate some money quickly.

The door swung open slowly, but no one stood on the other side. Ian cautiously stepped inside. "Is anyone here?"

A vision of the white-haired man Ian had seen briefly yesterday materialized in front of him. The image beckoned for him to follow and moved down the long hallway. Definitely another unusual way to greet a guest, but nothing about this family seemed ordinary. He followed the shimmering hologram until it disappeared at the top of a set of stairs.

"Come on down," a muffled voice called out. This one Ian judged to be human.

Ian picked his way down the stone staircase, staring with interest as more and more of the cavernous room became visible. Long plank tables crisscrossed the room, covered with metal tubing, engines, wire, and lights--a stockpile of mechanical creations in various stages of completion.

When Ian reached the foot of the stairs, the old man glanced up from a beeping metal box he had been poking with a screwdriver. "What can I do for you, son?"

"I'm looking for Madelaine Ainsworth." Ian raised his voice to be heard over the noise.

"What did you say your name was?" The older man poked at the buzzing machine, and it threw sparks at him.

"MacGregor. Ian MacGregor." He wondered if there was a fire extinguisher nearby in case the contraption burst into flames.

"MacGregor, eh? I'm Horace Ainsworth."

"So you're related to Madelaine?"

Horace nodded as he tightened several bolts and rearranged a coil of wire on the side of the box. Abruptly, the buzzing stopped.

"Aha!" Horace cried triumphantly. He patted the little machine fondly and turned his attention to Ian. "So, Mr. MacGregor, what can I do for you?"

"I'm delivering an automobile to Madelaine. Is she here?"

Horace leaned closer and lowered his voice to an intense whisper. "She's gone again."

"Do you know when she'll be back?"

Horace shook his head and frowned, then picked up a wrench and began fiddling with the bolts on the machine again.

"Perhaps you can take delivery of the car for her?"

Horace shook his head. "Rissa takes care of finances. As soon as Maddie is back, Rissa will write you a check."

"But--" The sudden whirs and beeps of the little machine drowned out Ian's protest, but not the frustration building in his chest. His mother had tried to keep the worry out of her voice when they talked last night, but she admitted that the most recent bill collector was rather insistent.

Ian watched the older man for several minutes, but Horace seemed to have forgotten he existed. How much longer before Madelaine returned? Or until Rissa came home?

Perhaps someone else could answer Ian's questions. He walked up the stairs then paused at the top to look back at Horace. The older man still tinkered intently with the machine on the workbench.

Ian continued down the hallway and called out a greeting but received no response, not even a hologram. Thanks to manners drilled into him in his childhood, discomfort edged up his backbone at the thought of snooping through someone else's house. But, damn, his mother needed the money from selling that Pinto.

After one quick look around the inside of the house, Ian decided to wait outside. He closed the front door quietly and surveyed the grounds. The only person walking in the gardens was Rissa's mother, today dressed in a different color skirt and blouse but of the same style she had worn yesterday. Ian guessed some traumatic incident had caused her mind to seek refuge in a happier time. He didn't want to upset her by asking too many questions, so he followed the curving cobblestone driveway in the opposite direction, which led behind the main house.

As soon as he rounded the corner, Ian was confronted with a number of large archways at the back of the building. Curiosity nudged away the manners his mother had instilled and he stepped closer to investigate. A moment later he regretted that decision as a hissing sound like a giant snake echoed around him and a heavy net dropped over his body. Before he could react, a loop of rope closed over his ankles and lifted him off the ground, where he dangled like the crabs his father used to haul out of the ocean on their beach vacations.

Chapter Three

Anticipation hurried Rissa out of the office at five o'clock for the first time in weeks. It was just as well, she reasoned, since all her thoughts were on Ian MacGregor and she wasn't getting much work done.

Accelerating her sedan as the hill sloped upward, anticipation flowed through her bloodstream. If Madelaine had returned, she would have an excuse to call Ian MacGregor. The man had disturbed her routine since she had met him and she wasn't quite sure what to do about it.

Once on the castle grounds, she pulled around the main house to the garages--then slammed on the brakes. A body was hanging in the net in front of her.

Rissa rummaged through her purse for the can of pepper spray then slowly emerged from the car. She approached the net carefully, unsure if one of the neighborhood boys had been playing again or if they had actually captured someone up to no good.

"I'd like to get down," the captive called out.

"Ian? What are you doing up there?" Rissa circled beneath her fantasy man. How could he have set off Horace's booby trap? It was only supposed to activate if someone tried to break into the garages.

"Rissa, watch out!" Horace puffed around the side of the building, carrying a metal rod with a cone-shaped sphere on one end, which he pointed at the net.

"Whoa! Careful with that thing!" Ian yelled.

"Mr. MacGregor?" Horace peered upward. "What are you doing

18

up there?"

Rissa and Horace stared up at Ian, waiting for an answer.

"If you let me down, I'll explain."

Rissa glanced at her uncle, then ducked under one of the archways and pushed a red button. The net slowly moved downward until it touched the ground.

Horace hurried forward to free Ian. "I'm so sorry, Mr. MacGegor. I don't know how this could have happened."

"No harm done," Ian assured Horace as he stepped out of the criss-crossed lengths of rope.

"Well, as long as you're not hurt." With an absent wave, Horace meandered back toward the house, leaving Ian to confront a scowling Rissa.

"Why exactly were you by the garages?" Rissa crossed her arms over her chest.

"Waiting for you or Madelaine to show up. Horace said you could write me a check for the Pinto station wagon."

Truth or cover-up? Rissa wondered. "I'll need to confirm the price with Madelaine."

A muscle tightened in Ian's jaw as he drew a deep breath. He stared hard at Rissa for a moment then executed an abrupt about-face, tossing a retreating comment over his shoulder. "Fine. Call me when Madelaine shows up."

Rissa followed Ian back around the garages to the front of the castle. His long strides carried him quickly to the Pinto, where he jerked open the door. Before he slid inside, he paused and looked once again at her. The sun broke through the clouds for a moment, shining through the droplets of rain, casting a rainbow across the sky, its bow coming to rest behind Ian.

"Your dreams lie at the end of the rainbow." Madelaine's whispered advice niggled at Rissa through years of memories. She squeezed her eyes closed. When she opened them, both Ian and the rainbow were gone.

~ * ~

19

The man glanced around suspiciously before he tucked the Beretta in his belt and pulled a mud-spattered flak jacket down to cover the bulge of the gun. He slipped inside the red brick building and scanned the rows of brass-fronted boxes.

Limping slowly, he paused in front of one of them and traced his fingers across the number--293.

His narrowed gaze darted around the room once more as he rubbed the aching in his side. Then he reached up and spun the lock quickly--to the right, to the left, and back to the right--then swung the door open.

"Damn!" He slammed the box shut and limped away. A gray-haired lady cried out in alarm as he pushed open the glass door and bumped her off balance. The postal clerk shouted futilely at the old green sedan as it fishtailed on the wet pavement out of the parking lot.

The man ignored all the commotion behind him. He had one question on his mind: Why hadn't the ransom money come? He'd take care of that with a phone call.

~ * ~

Ian stood in front of Madelaine Ainsworth's castle home with his arms crossed and legs spread wide as the wind tossed strands of copper hair over his brow. Behind him, the morning sun fought a losing battle with the clouds roiling dark and low on the horizon. He had waited as long as he could for Madelaine to return. He had to get payment for the Pinto or find another buyer.

Horace yanked open the door before Ian pulled his hand away from the knocker. His white lab coat flapped around him as wildly as the gestures of his arms. "MacGregor! Thank God you're here!"

"What's going on?" Ian asked.

"Maddie's in trouble. They want money or they're going to hurt her. Find her--please find my Maddie." Horace clutched at the lapels of Ian's trenchcoat.

"What happened?" Ian looked to Rissa for an explanation.

"Someone called and said they were holding Madelaine for ransom. They said don't call the police--"

"No police or they'll hurt my Maddie." Horace looked quickly up and down the driveway, pulled Ian inside and closed the door. "Scotland Yard isn't exactly the police, but we've got to keep your involvement quiet."

"Scotland Yard?" Ian asked.

Horace held a finger to his lips. "I won't tell a soul that you're on U.S. soil."

"Why do you think I'm with Scotland Yard?" Ian asked.

"Why, it's obvious," Horace stated.

I can figure out enemy strategies. Surely one old man's thinking can't be that convoluted, Ian thought. "A kidnapping needs to be handled by experts--"

"Exactly. That's why I'm putting my Maddie's life in your hands." Horace slapped Ian's back confidently, then hustled down the hallway.

"Wait--" Ian turned to Rissa. "How did I go from being an Army MP to an inspector with Scotland Yard?"

"Because your name is Scottish and you're wearing a trenchcoat?"

"And?"

Rissa shrugged. "That's enough for Horace."

With a shake of his head, Ian followed Horace down the stairs into his workroom. "Horace, listen to me. I'm not with Scotland Yard."

Horace stared at Ian for a long moment, his eyes wide with fright. "What am I going to do? The police won't listen. No one will listen. Can't you help? Just this once?"

The pleading in Horace's eyes stabbed at the soft spot in Ian's heart--or his head, he thought derisively. As an MP, he had more law enforcement training than most police officers, but his specialty wasn't finding missing persons. However, he told himself the sooner he found Madelaine Ainsworth, the sooner he could get his money for the Pinto. "I'll see what I can do."

"Thank you, son, you won't regret this." Horace gripped Ian's hand in gratitude for a moment, then turned back to shoving an assortment of mechanical items into a duffel bag.

Ian marched up the stairs to where Rissa waited. "I need a rundown of anywhere your aunt might have gone the day she disappeared."

"Have you ever dealt with kidnappings?"

Ian tightened his jaw to keep from snapping out an abrupt upbraiding. Dealing with someone not used to taking orders could slow down the process of finding Madelaine. Explaining the reasons for his methods would make things even slower. "Military police units are trained in the most advanced law enforcement techniques available."

"But have you ever dealt with kidnappings?"

"I spent two years in Iraq flushing out enemy strongholds."

Rissa considered him for a moment then said, "I'll go with you."

Irritation tempered with anticipation zinged through Ian's body. His mind did not want a civilian--especially an attractive female one-- tagging along. On the other hand, his body very much wanted this particular female in close quarters.

~ * ~

The owner of the Ova Easy Café greeted Ian and Rissa with a cup of coffee. While Ian questioned him about Madelaine, Rissa sipped her coffee and watched this man who had taken on the task of finding her aunt--something she and her brother had tried many times with no luck.

Sure, Madelaine had been in, the café's owner said. They talked about the mural she was painting for him, then Beatrice Winters had come in. She was complaining, as usual, about no one taking her seriously as an artist. So he quit listening. About fifteen minutes later, Madelaine said she had some errands to run and would be back to work on the mural. She never returned, which was really odd, the owner stated. Once she committed to something, she stuck with it until it was done.

As she and Ian left the café, Rissa wondered why hadn't she

noticed Madelaine's commitment to her art. She didn't think about the long hours of work her aunt put into a project. The completed artwork just seemed to appear. She knew that couldn't be true, but why had she only noticed Madelaine's free-spirited side and not seen the hard-working artist?

"Let's stop at the art store," Rissa suggested. "If Madelaine was working on a mural, she would need supplies."

Once again, the owner of the store greeted Rissa warmly as she and Ian stepped inside. He told them Madelaine had been there over a week ago for paint and brushes for the Ova Easy mural. While she was there, she "convinced" him to donate some paint to the homeless shelter. However, she hadn't been back to pick it up, so would Rissa please deliver the paint to the shelter?

As Rissa agreed to deliver the paint, she puzzled over the fact she had no idea Madelaine was involved with the homeless shelter; and obviously dedicated enough to wrangle help from others. Why didn't Madelaine include her contributions on the tax return Rissa prepared for her each year?

"While we're downtown, let's talk to Beatrice Winters."

Ian and Rissa walked the short distance to Tassie's Gallery, stepped inside and paused to glance around.

"There she is." Rissa indicated a woman arguing loudly with two other people. The woman's upper body was big enough for a football player. In contrast, two spindly legs poked from under the flowered tent of a dress.

"Any reason why she would want Madelaine out of the way?"

"Beatrice may be bossy, but Madelaine has helped her out of a lot of jams when she offended everyone else. It wouldn't be to her advantage for Madelaine to disappear."

"Does Beatrice own the gallery?"

"It's owned by two sisters named Tammie and Cassandra. Tassie is a combination of their names."

Ian turned his attention to the sparsely populated gallery. The display in front of them seemed to be made up of castoffs from someone's garage sale, welded together to form precarious towers.

"What is this supposed to be?" Ian whispered as they stopped in front of a six-foot tall stack of pots and pans.

"Isn't this just awful?" A braying voice exploded behind them. Beatrice Winters' lionine head sat squarely on her shoulders with only an extra chin where her neck should have been. A frizz of gray and black curls was pulled so tightly at the top of her head that the smattering of hairs across her top lip moved like a whiskbroom when she talked.

"I think it captures the spirit of the homeless beautifully," Rissa commented.

Beatrice snorted. "It's supposed to be a statement on women's independence from housework. However, your aunt never returned with my pans."

Ian glanced at the pans prominently featured in the display and back to Beatrice.

"I know what you're thinking." Beatrice sighed. "Any old pans will do. But I wanted the ones Nathan Peters has had stashed in the room over his garage for thirty-five years. He promised to sell them to me too--for an outrageous price, of course. That man never did appreciate true art. However, your aunt ruined that."

"What do you mean?" Rissa angled a puzzled frown at Beatrice.

"Your aunt kept the pans. Tell you what." Beatrice lowered her voice conspiratorially. "If you get my pans back from your aunt, I'll pay you double what Nathan was asking for them."

"But I don't know where your pans are," Rissa said.

Beatrice sighed dramatically and turned her attention to Ian. "She is as bad as her aunt. First Madelaine offered to pick up the pans for me. Then she never returned. Now her niece refuses to give me what is rightfully mine."

With one last glare at Rissa, Beatrice stalked away.

Silently, Ian reminded himself he was dealing with civilians. "No torture techniques allowed."

"Pardon me?" Rissa asked.

"Military humor," Ian muttered. "I'll see if I can talk to her."

Rissa held up her hands in a be-my-guest gesture as Ian strode after the indignant woman. "Mrs. Winters, wait!"

With an exaggerated sigh, Beatrice stopped and waited for Ian to catch up to her.

"Let me make sure I have this right. Madelaine was supposed to pick up some pans for you from a man named Nathan Peters, but she never came back."

"Days ago." Beatrice stated. "I haven't seen her since."

"Was anyone else with her?" Ian asked.

"Oh, Madelaine always has someone following her around."

At last, Ian thought, *a solid lead.*" Do you remember who was with her that day?"

Beatrice looked at Ian closely. "Have I seen you before?"

Ian extended his hand to Beatrice. "Ian MacGregor."

Beatrice smiled as she clasped his hand and winked at him. "I've always had a soft spot for Scotsmen. There's something about a kilt on a handsome man."

Oh-kay, Ian thought. *Perhaps an uncooperative civilian was better than an older one flirting with him.* He extricated his hand from hers and forced a polite smile. "I've never worn a kilt, ma'am. Now, you were saying there was someone with Madelaine when she went to get your pans?"

Beatrice sniffed, not so friendly now the conversation was back to Madelaine. "I don't know why it would matter."

She won't talk unless it benefits her. And Ian knew the right angle. "It might help us find your pans."

The older woman thought about that for a moment. "Well, there was Rex, of course."

"Rex?" Ian asked.

"Rex Foxworth," Beatrice clarified. "He owns the Pink Flamingo and thinks Madelaine secretly pines for him."

"Anyone else? Anyone who might tell us where your pans are?"

"I'm not certain..." Beatrice frowned. "You might try her new friends at the country club. Now, I really must get to work."

As Beatrice marched away, Ian returned to Rissa.

"Anything helpful?"

"She said a Rex Foxworth was following your aunt and maybe her friends at the country club could provide more information."

"Rex always follows Madelaine," Rissa said. "But my aunt got into a fight with the mayor and town council about displacing the homeless shelter to build the club and refuses to go near it."

"That's what Beatrice said. It's worth checking out."

"Okay," Rissa agreed. "To the country club it is."

Once again, Ian took the lead in questioning the mayor about Madelaine's last visit to the country club. As the mayor started to recite the names of the younger female members Madelaine had taken an interest in, Rissa thanked the mayor and said they had another appointment and would be happy to talk to the mayor later.

Irritated, Ian followed Rissa back to the Pinto. "Why did you interrupt him? He was giving us more leads to follow."

"Only if we want to know which blondes my brother has been flirting with."

"What are you talking about?" Ian fastened his seat belt with a smart click.

"I think my brother has been at the country club masquerading as our aunt," Rissa stated. "Which means all the names from the mayor would have been false leads."

"Your brother dresses up like a woman?"

"Only rarely--so he says. But perhaps that's only what he wants me to think."

Ian started the car and kept his comments to himself. *So maybe this search would be more challenging than he first thought.*

The gravel road they followed for several miles ended outside a crumbling brick building flanked by a sagging gray board fence on one side and a tangle of blackberry bushes on the other.

"I think the town council should have extended their efforts at urban renewal a little farther north of town," Rissa said.

Ian nodded as he climbed out of the car and looked around. He didn't want to alarm Rissa, but he hoped her aunt had an escort when she visited this part of town.

"What are we looking for?" Rissa asked as she joined Ian.

"Anything out of the ordinary or any signs of a struggle."

"I think every day is a struggle here." Rissa inched closer to Ian.

"I agree, but a woman's footprints shouldn't be hard to pick out."

"My aunt is six feet tall and wears size 11 shoes."

Ian frowned. "Is there anything else I should know about Madelaine?"

"She wouldn't be caught dead in public without a hat."

She's kidding, right? Ian watched Rissa for a moment, then merely nodded. Maybe it was time to try a different tack than questioning the town's unusual citizens.

"I'm going to see if Horace's gadgets work." Ian hauled a squarish metal box out of the car. "This is supposed to track auto exhaust. Horace calibrated it for the fumes from Madelaine's car."

"Must be a new invention." Rissa considered the box skeptically. "While you do that, I'm going to see if anyone has seen Madelaine lately."

Ian gave a half-salute as the little machine hummed to life. However, it emitted no beeps and blips that might indicate Madelaine's car had been nearby.

Ian patiently wheeled the machine around the perimeter of the building, ignoring the occasional raindrop that splattered against his face and the interested group that began to follow him. However, when the drops grew larger and fell faster, he remembered Horace's caution that rain dissipated the particles of exhaust and rendered the machine useless.

Ian turned off the machine and looked around for Rissa. What he saw instead were the gazes of a half dozen men with scruffy beards and rumpled clothing. The smell of stale wine and old cigars surrounded him as the men moved closer.

"Nice night, isn't it?" Ian played for time as he tried to determine if the intent of the group was threatening or merely curious.

"Whatcha doin' here?" A snaggle-toothed man asked.

"Testing this machine. It tracks cars by their exhaust fumes."

The group moved closer and someone snickered. "Think it could track people fumes too?"

"Hey, Gasser, leave us a trail around the building," someone else stated.

The group laughed and knotted around Ian, and he realized the mellow approach wouldn't work here. "Just back off and nobody will get hurt."

The group only laughed louder, and someone lobbed a muddy missile that splatted against Ian's chest. Anger spurted through him at his own carelessness. He was separated from Rissa by a group of clowns who thought they were funny. He figured using the little machine as a battering ram was his best bet of getting out of this situation and finding Rissa.

So he grabbed the handle, lowered his head and charged forward.

"Ian!"

He looked up at the sound of Rissa's cry. The group of men parted--enough for Ian to realize he was going to plow right into her!

Chapter Four

With a muttered oath, Ian yanked the handle sideways. The machine faltered and fell directly in his path. He tripped over the hunk of metal and tumbled to a stop at Rissa's feet.

As Ian slowly opened his eyes, he saw Rissa peering over him, her mouth a frightened "O." A priest stood beside her.

"Am I dead?" Ian asked.

Chuckles and murmuring swept through the group gathered around.

"Ian, are you hurt?" Rissa knelt beside him.

Ian groaned as he shoved to his feet, knowing he would have some bruises in the morning. More irritating was the mud covering most of his clothing. Four years in deserts and swamps and every place in between should have cured him of his desire for a shower and clean bed every night, but it only strengthened the need for cleanliness he had endured from the time he was a small child. "Is there a place where I can clean up?"

A barely contained smile tugged at the corners of the priest's mouth. "Perhaps we should go inside."

The inside of the building was as warm and homey as the outside was rundown. A fire crackled in the red brick fireplace, its warmth reflected in the muted shine of the polished wood floors.

In a sparse but clean bathroom, Ian changed into the faded jeans and well-worn flannel shirt offered by the priest. He looked at the neatly stacked towels and shining fixtures with approval. At least someone else at the shelter shared his desire for order and polish.

Ian rejoined Rissa and the priest by the fireplace and gratefully accepted a cup of coffee.

"I'm Father Jacobs." The priest shook Ian's hand. "I'm sorry if the men seemed threatening. Usually a stranger poking around means someone sent by the mayor or town council to try to shut down work on the new shelter."

Ian waved away the priest's apology.

"I was telling Father Jacobs we brought some paint from the art store," Rissa said.

The priest smiled broadly. "Madelaine came through for us again. She stops by regularly on Wednesday to see how we're progressing on the new shelter. She won't let the council forget their trade-off for all those fancy buildings at the country club--although they'd like to see us move out of existence altogether."

"We're looking for Madelaine," Ian said. "She's disappeared."

"Ah, yes. Marissa explained the situation to me." Father Jacobs leaned back and laced his fingers over his slightly paunchy stomach, frowning thoughtfully. "I haven't seen her for nearly a week and a half."

Father Jacobs settled his chair back on all its legs. "Let's talk to the men. Perhaps someone has seen her since then."

The priest moved among the neatly made cots that filled the main room of the building. As he explained to the men that Ian and Rissa were connected to Madelaine, the suspicion in the men's eyes faded to concern.

No one had seen Madelaine since the last time she had been at the shelter.

"But we'll look for her and help any way we can," a red-bearded man said.

Murmurs of agreement rose from the rest of the group. "Maddie's always been good us."

"Thank you," Rissa said. "I don't know how to repay you."

"Friends don't ask for payment." The man squared his jaw. "They just do what needs to be done."

"We'll all pray for Madelaine's safety," the priest said as the men left to spread the word to others.

"Thank you." Rissa hesitated. "Father, how long has Madelaine been...helping out?"

"Since we opened our doors when you were just a young girl." Father Jacobs smiled. "Madelaine didn't want a big fuss. Said it was an agreement between her and God."

~ * ~

Madelaine listened carefully. That was all she could do, considering she had been tied up, gagged and blindfolded for most of the past several days. She wiggled her fingers, trying to bring some feeling back to them. She was becoming annoyed. It was one thing to snatch her from her errands. It was quite another to leave her trussed up like a Thanksgiving turkey.

Madelaine grunted loudly and jiggled the chair she was bound to.

"Boss, I think she wants something." The man's voice was slightly nasal, as if he had a chronic sinus infection.

"Yeah, yeah, yeah. Everybody wants something," a harsh voice replied, the one Madelaine figured belonged to the "brains" behind this incident.

"What if she's hungry?"

"Let her eat that old grease rag in her mouth." The rude comment was accompanied by a snort.

Reflexively, Madelaine spit at the cloth in her mouth. *Just the reaction they want,* she thought, forcing herself to remain still.

Footsteps clattered closer, then stopped beside her. Light burst across her face as the blindfold was jerked away.

Madelaine blinked, then stared disdainfully at her two captors. If it wasn't for the nasty-looking piece of hardware clutched in the bald one's fist, she would have knocked their heads together. The camouflage uniform and bullet belts criss-crossed over his barrel chest made him look like an aging commando. The scraggly whiskbroom moustache on his upper lip lifted in a snarl as he addressed his partner. "Take off the gag."

A quiet, pointy-faced man who looked like a ferret Madelaine had as a child cautiously approached her. His watery blue eyes met her steely glare and flinched. He gulped as he looked back at the gun-waver.

"Go on. She ain't gonna hurt you."

The little man slowly took a few steps closer, gently removed the gag and stepped back, slicking a hand nervously over his thinning dishwater blond hair.

"Get back over here," the gun-waver ordered, drawing Madelaine's attention once more.

"What do you intend to do with me?" Madelaine asked sharply.

The gun-waver sneered. "We'll decide that after your old man brings the money."

"You're wasting your time," Madelaine stated. "He's too smart to give money to the likes of you."

"Why, you--" The gun-waver raised the arm holding the gun, then groaned in pain. He doubled over, clutching his belly, then bellowed at his partner, "Put her gag back on."

The quiet one looked at Madelaine, then back to his partner. "You better take it easy, boss. You haven't been feeling well."

The gun-waver did indeed look quite pale; but hung onto his bluster. "Yeah, you're right. Don't let her get away with no funny stuff while I'm gone."

His partner nodded. Apparently satisfied, the gun-waver stumbled out the door of the tiny, musty cabin.

The point-faced man carefully set Madelaine's purple-feathered hat back on her head and shrugged in apology. She was still tied up, but at least that horrid gag was out of her mouth and she could see.

One step at a time, Madelaine reminded herself. *One step at a time.*

~ * ~

"Ten o'clock. Dump box by the mall. Be there."

Rissa listened in horrified silence as Horace played back the call that had come in while she and Ian were out looking for clues.

"We missed them," she whispered. "How could we miss them?"

"He didn't stay on the line long enough to trace where he was calling from," Horace said with a sigh.

"Was this the same guy?" Ian asked.

"Same wheezy voice as the first call," Rissa confirmed.

"What happened to the cell phone?" Horace's spikes of hair quivered in agitation. "I tried to call you."

"The battery must be dead." Rissa took the phone out her pocket and shook it in disgust.

"That might be just as well," Ian said. "If they listened in on our cell phone conversation, it might have put Madelaine's life in more danger."

The corners of Horace's mouth turned down at the thought. "What do we do now?"

"Do you have money for the ransom?" Ian asked.

Horace nodded.

"Then I suggest we prepare for the drop," Ian stated. "Horace, we're going to need all the surveillance equipment you can come up with and a van for tomorrow morning."

Rissa managed to sleep a few hours before nervous energy roused her. She took a quick shower and was descending the stairs when the doorbell rang.

A short time later, Ian and Rissa were sitting in a van surrounded by a half dozen closed circuit monitors and myriad technological gadgets. As Ian adjusted the dials on the monitors, Rissa wondered if his fingers would just as efficiently attune her body to pleasure. Trying to ignore the man was about as effective as telling Madelaine to stay home.

"How much longer do you think they will be?" Rissa glanced at her watch.

"They might not come right at ten. They might be a little nervous and want to be sure they aren't being watched."

"But they are being watched. What if all this technology scares them away?"

"This looks like any other van from the outside."

Rissa forced her attention to the monitors in the van. The rain had stopped, although clouds still hung low in the sky. An easy-going Sunday afternoon crowd took advantage of the break in the weather and created a steady flow in and out of the shopping center.

The kidnappers had chosen well, Ian had said earlier. A very public place in broad daylight. It would be easy to move in with the crowd, pick up the brown paper bag beside the trash dumpster, and move away again without arousing any suspicion.

"How will we know it's the real kidnappers?" Rissa asked.

"If they pick up the sack, it's them."

A mother with a baby on one hip and a toddler in a stroller warned her third rambunctious preschooler away from what Rissa had come to think of as The Bag. "What if someone is just curious?"

"Then they'll put it back down." Ian had placed empty food wrappers on top of the money to discourage casual passersby from looking too closely.

"What if the kidnappers dig through and find out there's only one layer of money?"

"By then, we'll have them." Ian flashed a smile at her before turning his attention back to the monitors. The stiffening of his shoulders drew Rissa's attention. "There's movement at the bag. You stay here."

Rissa made herself sit still as Ian slipped out of the van. She stared at the monitor, watching a scruffy old man poke at the food wrappers. Her pulse jumped with concern as she saw Ian moving toward him. *What if the old man was armed? He might look harmless, but what if he attacked Ian?*

Too late, Rissa decided this was not a good trick to try alone. She looked around the van for something to use as a weapon. Air freshener, garbage bag--then her eyes fell on the tire iron.

Clutching her makeshift weapon tightly in both hands, she slipped out the door of the van. She peered around the corner of the vehicle in time to see Ian hand the old man a twenty-dollar bill.

"What is he doing?" she muttered under her breath as the old guy grinned, dropped the bag and moved away.

Ian sauntered back toward the van, almost stumbling over her crouched beside the vehicle. "What are you doing?"

"Checking the air in the tires," Rissa snapped. Her silent message said, *Do not laugh. Do not even smile.*

Wisely, Ian chose not to pursue that particular topic. "He wasn't our man."

"If he wasn't the right guy, where are they?" Churlishness battled with worry in Rissa's belly. "It's 10:30. The pick-up time was ten."

~ * ~

"Where is that damn kid?" Gunner muttered. He slammed his fist against the hood of the car. "Ouch. Damn car."

"Cars don't usually run without gas," Madelaine said reasonably.

"Shaddup," Gunner snarled. He leaned against the car, clutching his abdomen.

"You really should see a doctor," she said."

"I...said...shut...up." Gunner slid down until he sat on the ground with his back against the vehicle. That left Madelaine tied to her chair on the porch far above him, a fact that seemed to anger Gunner even more.

"Get down here where I can keep an eye on you."

"That would be a little difficult to do since I'm tied up, don't you think?"

"Argh!" Gunner doubled over.

Madelaine couldn't tell whether it was in pain or anger--not that she could have done anything about it, bound up as she was. But at least they hadn't replaced the loathsome gag."

"I got gas!" Weasel panted as he jogged into the clearing by the cabin. "Where's Gunner?"

"On the ground," Madelaine stated.

Weasel dropped the gas can and hurried over to his pal, now crumpled in an awkward heap. Weasel looked accusingly at her. "What did you do to him?"

Madelaine rolled her eyes skyward and ignored the question. "Your friend needs a doctor. And if you don't pick up that gas can that's leaking all over the ground, we won't be able to get him to one."

Weasel gasped as gas trickled against his foot. He quickly righted the can, then turned his attention back to his cohort. "Come on, Gunner. Tell me what to do."

Gunner's reply was unintelligible.

Weasel grabbed Gunner's shirt and shook him. "Talk to me! What do I do now?"

"Stop shaking him," Madelaine stated. "If the pain doesn't kill him, you will."

Weasel dropped his hands and leaped back. "You can't die on me, Gunner. Don't die!"

Madelaine shook her head. Wouldn't it figure she would get kidnapped by two bozos who didn't know what they were doing. "Untie me."

Weasel swiveled to look at Madelaine then shook his head.

"Look, Weasel, your friend is very ill. You know that, don't you?"

Weasel's head bobbed in the affirmative.

"He needs a doctor, right?"

Again, Weasel nodded.

"Someone needs to ride in the back with your friend."

Another nod.

"Then who is going to drive the car?"

Weasel stared at Madelaine uncomprehendingly, and she wondered if she should have stuck to yes or no questions.

"You drive." Weasel grinned and nodded his head once more.

"Yes." Madelaine sighed; relieved Weasel had come up with the answer she wanted to hear.

"Come on, Miz Mads, we have to hurry."

"You'll have to untie me."

"Oh, sorry."

Weasel loosened Madelaine's bonds, then hurried back to the fallen Gunner. She rubbed the circulation back into her hands and feet, then stood and stretched.

"I put Gunner in the back seat. Can we go to the doctor now?"

Weasel's voice beside her made her jump.

Madelaine wondered briefly how the small man had managed to wrestle an inert body larger than himself into the car. However, she didn't ponder that question long. She just wanted to get out of here. "We have to put gas in the car first."

The little man's eagerness to help slowed their progress in getting gas in the car, but she didn't have the heart to discourage Weasel's enthusiasm in his quest to get his friend to a doctor.

Finally, they got most of the gas in the tank and got the car started. Before she climbed into the car, Madelaine took a look around, intending to say a not-so-fond good-bye. She would be glad to be out of this place she had seen only from the inside of a ramshackle cabin. Just a few sticks perched on a hillside, she could see now. The guest quarters left a lot to be desired, but the beauty of the surrounding countryside tugged at her to pick up her paintbrushes and niggled at her memory. She knew this place--

"Miz Mads, we gotta go." Weasel tugged at his earlobe. "Gunner--he's getting worse."

Madelaine climbed behind the wheel of the old green Buick and revved the engine. Then she slipped the car into gear and pointed its nose down the mountain. As they passed a rusted hulk of a boxcar overgrown with blackberries, she realized where she was. The old Hockley place, across the ravine from where she had lived as a girl.

"Can't you go any faster, Miz Mads?" Weasel asked from the back seat. "Gunner don't look so good."

Indeed, Madelaine could hear Gunner moaning. Remembering the many races down the mountain when she was a teenager, she pushed the gas pedal to the floor. After a surprised spurt, the old vehicle responded with a powerful purr, settling into a breakneck pace like an old pro. Despite the roads being soaked by recent rains, the old car skidded only on the worst of the corners as she zigzagged toward town.

It wasn't until she pulled up to the emergency entrance of the hospital that Madelaine realized she might have two patients. Weasel looked almost as pale as his moaning friend. "I didn't mean that fast, Miz Mads."

Chapter Five

Madelaine shrugged in apology, then turned her attention to the white-coated attendants who had hustled to the side of the old Buick.

Within minutes, Gunner was whisked behind a curtained alcove and Madelaine was sitting in the waiting room with a cup of coffee. Soon, she would call Horace and let him know she was safe. Then she could go back to her own house with her own paints and her own canvasses, with the comforting sound of her loved ones around her. But for now, she just wanted to enjoy the heady taste of freedom.

She closed her eyes and drew a deep breath.

"Let's go, Miz Mads." Weasel's urgent voice roused her. She opened her eyes and stared at the little man. He was waving a thermometer in her face while his jaw worked spasmodically.

"Is your friend going to be alright?" Madelaine asked.

"We have to go." Weasel pointed the thermometer at her and jerked his head toward the exit door.

"Is the car in the way?" Madelaine walked leisurely toward the door. Weasel pranced behind her, swiveling his head from side to side to look around them.

"I can move the car if you want to stay with your friend."

"No. We have to go," Weasel repeated.

"Look, we're in no hurry. Your friend is going to be here awhile."

"More bills. Can't afford them. Have to go now." Weasel's thermometer wobbled and jittered once more as they reached the car. "Get in."

Madelaine hadn't seen this side of mild-mannered Weasel. All during this adventure, he had been the one who was concerned with her welfare and had tempered Gunner's nasty streak.

"Back to the cabin," Weasel stated as he slid in the passenger side. "Gotta pay. Gotta pay."

Madelaine wondered what had gotten into the little man. Could she have totally misjudged the situation? Was Weasel really the brains behind this caper? She glanced at the man sitting beside her, mumbling under his breath and waving the thermometer.

Naw, Madelaine thought. *He's just a mixed-up, overgrown kid. I'll get him straightened around and go home.*

~ * ~

"Why haven't they come?" Rissa asked.

Ian glanced at his watch. Eleven-thirty. Yet the bag still sat by the dumpster, as forlorn as the look in Rissa's eyes. Ian couldn't break her heart. Not if there was still a chance. "Let's give it another half an hour."

The hands of the clock crept to 11:45, then noon, then 12:30.

"They're not coming, are they." Rissa stared straight ahead, a slight quiver in her chin.

The flatness in her voice alarmed Ian. What had happened to the spitfire who was ready to save him with only a tire iron for a weapon?

Ian got out of the van once more and moved toward the bag. Two teenagers jostled by him, eager to join their friends on the sidewalk. An elderly woman gingerly stepped off the curb, wobbling slightly against her cane before shuffling toward a beige sedan. None of them showed any interest in the bag.

Ian stopped by the dumpster and looked around once more. His eyes locked on Rissa for a moment before he leaned over to pick up the bag.

When he returned to the van, she continued to stare at the spot where the bag had been. Ian frowned, then started the engine and set the vehicle in motion. Rain began to fall, slickening the pavement beneath the swish of the tires. The sound blurred against the darkening gloom of storm clouds rolling across the sky.

As they approached the castle, its gray stone turrets stretched upward to blend with the clouds casting raindrops on the earth.

Ian helped Rissa out of the van, settling an arm around her shoulders as he tented a jacket over her head as protection from the rain. He paused in the entryway to talk to an anxious-looking Horace as Rissa moved down the hall. Somewhere she walked out of her damp shoes and now padded barefoot on the cool tile.

She was slowly circling the turret when Ian rejoined her, fingers tracing the life-sized mural that wrapped around the room. "Aunt Madelaine painted this the first summer we were here--after Daddy died. I got to help her."

The mural was painted from the perspective of a princess surveying her domain out the window of the castle. The picture featured muscled oxen pulling wooden carts while sturdy peasants in rough clothing toiled just beyond the courtyard. A knight in silver armor galloped across the drawbridge on a white charger. And above it all, a multi-colored rainbow stretched across the sky, its bow coming to rest inside the castle walls.

Rissa's hand lingered on the rainbow as she smiled wistfully. "She said rainbows are everywhere, you just have to look for them. So we did. Up in the hills, over at the coast--even at night. Auntie would open the sun roof in the pouring rain and ask if we could see the rainbows across the moon."

"And did you see them?"

"We pretended to. She said it was okay to pretend sometimes. But Mother didn't quit pretending and Aunt Madelaine stayed." Rissa leaned her forehead against the grill in the tiny rounded window. "She changed her whole life for us, and I don't think I once said thank you."

Ian gently touched her arm. "Rissa--"

"I thought she was a kooky old lady like everyone else said. I tried to be the opposite of her: Ms. Responsibility." Rissa's laughter cracked on a sob. "But she fooled us all. She was the responsible one. She was the one who paid for this house and refused to put Mother in a home and took care of six-year-old twins."

Rissa's voice trailed off into tears as Ian gathered her in his arms. Her body shuddered against him, wracked with sobs. Ian set aside his own frustration at not finding Madelaine and rocked Rissa gently, murmuring nonsense words of comfort.

What had gone wrong? Did the caller have Madelaine or was this a hoax? Whatever the situation, the effect on Rissa was the same. The protector who loved her family so fiercely had dissolved into a shattered little girl who huddled in his arms.

Ian stroked her hair. Her tears had lessened to occasional hiccups and her body relaxed in limp exhaustion against him. He settled more comfortably on the cushions scattered around the floor and pulled a gold-fringed blanket around them.

Let her family think what they would. Ian was damned if he would leave Rissa alone tonight.

~ * ~

"You'll have to marry her now, that's for sure." The voice above Ian pulled him from the last vestiges of a restless night.

Ian blinked against the brightness of the morning sun and eased to a sitting position. "If you were wearing a dress and high heels, I'd say you were Rissa's brother."

Ryan grinned. "You just might make it in this family after all. What's wrong with her?"

"The kidnappers didn't show up to collect the ransom money yesterday."

"I told her this was a scam." Ryan shook his head. "Madelaine probably planned this herself. But Rissa thinks she has to take care of everyone."

Rissa stirred beside Ian, reminding him the noble gesture not to leave her alone last night could be construed as something else entirely in the light of day and in the eyes of her family. Especially when she rolled over and threw her arm across his lap.

"Watch out. She's always grumpy in the morning," Ryan

commented. "I'll lock the door on the way out."

Through the remnants of sleep, Rissa heard the latch click. She snuggled deeper against her pillow and hugged it closer to her body. Except this pillow didn't feel like the eyelet-covered goose down on her bed. It felt rougher, more solid, more--

Rissa opened one eye.

An expanse of denim with a zipper centered over a bulge brought the night's events flooding back. Her tears, Ian comforting her, drifting off to sleep in her arms...which meant waking up with her face pressed intimately close to--

"Oh, bother and damnation." Rissa tried to sit upright. Another mistake, since her hand pressed dangerously close to--

"Oh, hell." She glanced up, at a definite disadvantage from her position on the floor. Fragments of dreams swirled in her head. They had seemed especially vivid last night.

Rissa squeezed her eyes tightly together, then opened them again. However, Ian's tousled, very male image didn't disappear. Surely she could tell the difference between fantasy and reality, couldn't she?

Then her fantastic reality--or was it her real fantasy--lifted her upward until she lay sprawled on his chest.

"How are you doing this morning?" Ian's voice rumbled against her breasts, which meant he could surely feel the quickening cadence of her heartbeat and her nipples pebbling with desire.

Embarrassment reddened her face. She had never spent the night with a man, and had been especially careful not to allow a man into her family's home. Yet she had curled like a trusting child into Ian's arms last night.

Any one of her family could have walked in and thought the worst. With shaky palms against his chest, Rissa pushed away, then turned her back to him as she straightened her clothing.

"I couldn't leave you alone while you were so upset about your aunt." Ian's gentle voice wrapped around her like the cashmere blanket Aunt Madelaine had brought back from a trip to Scotland.

"I can follow our leads by myself today if you'd rather stay home or if you have to work."

Rissa shook her head. Aunt Madelaine had given up so much for all of them. "My boss will just have to understand I'm going to keep looking for my aunt until I find her."

~ * ~

Madelaine watched Weasel pace the cabin until it made her seasick. Finally she could take the movement no longer. "Come now. Let's have something to eat."

Weasel sat down at the table in one of the rickety chairs as Madelaine slid a peanut butter sandwich and a scoop of baked beans in front of him.

They ate in silence, broken only Weasel's muttered, "Drat it all!" when the last bite of his sandwich dropped onto the floor.

"I'll fix you another one."

"No, I'd just drop it again," Weasel muttered. "I can't do anything right. I got kicked out of kindergarten. My dog hated me. My mother told everyone I was adopted..."

Weasel's litany ended with a heartfelt sigh.

Madelaine's maternal heartstrings quivered as she stared at the little man's bowed head. "It can't be all that bad. You've been very kind to me."

"Tying you up against your will isn't kind."

"Well, the ropes weren't fun. But you stood up for me. I think your friend might have shot me if you hadn't come to my rescue."

Weasel flushed at the praise. "Gunner's not really bad."

Madelaine snorted in disbelief.

"Lately he's been kind of cranky," Weasel conceded.

"Well, you seem to be a very good friend to Gunner."

"He says I'm stupid. He says he'll get another partner if I mess up this job." Weasel blew out a heavy sigh. "I'm sorry, Miz Mads, but I gotta make this kidnapping work."

Madelaine patted Weasel's hand. "I understand completely. And I'm going to help you."

The little man looked at her warily. "Why would you want to

help me?"

"I think you're a fine young man who just needs the right guidance to find your true vocation."

Weasel looked as if he wasn't quite sure what she meant.

"Now, first of all, we have to send a ransom note." Madelaine cleared a space on the table.

"We did that. It didn't work."

"Then we'll just make a better one."

Weasel frowned. "I don't write too good."

"We won't write it because we don't want anyone to recognize your handwriting. Now, do you have any old newspapers or magazines around?"

Weasel scurried to the cot in the corner and pulled a magazine out from under the blanket.

Madelaine frowned her displeasure at the buxom nude on the front. "I certainly hope that isn't yours."

"Oh, no, ma'am." Weasel's eyes grew round. "I only read the interviews."

One lesson at a time, Madelaine reminded herself. "Very well."

A half an hour later, Madelaine and Weasel examined their handiwork with satisfaction. "Send MonEy oR yoU will nOt sEe mAdelAinE again."

"How do we get it there?" Weasel asked.

"We mail it," Madelaine replied. And she knew just the place: the Village Green Motel with its unique Spruce Goose steam train postmark. That should lead Horace right to them.

~ * ~

"Good accountants can always find another job," Ian said as he and Rissa descended the steps of the castle.

Rissa walked with head held high, shoulders stiffened with hurt pride. "Maybe I'm not a good accountant."

"You were being honest with your boss."

"For all the good that did." Rissa yanked open the door of an ancient green Land Rover borrowed from Madelaine's collection of automobiles. Her boss wouldn't even listen. He just demanded that she come in to the office immediately or not bother coming back at all. If she dug past her smarting pride, Rissa was glad to be free of the stifling atmosphere of Burns, Kenyon and Burns, Certified Public Accountants. She would worry about another job after they found Aunt Madelaine.

In silence, Ian and Rissa wound through the foothills above Watermark toward Nathan Peters' property. Far up the mountain they found what they had been looking for: a barely-graveled driveway posted with signs that screamed NO TRESPASSING.

"He doesn't seem very welcoming," Ian said.

"He may have been the last person to see Aunt Madelaine."

With a nod, Ian once again nosed the Land Rover forward. Rissa turned her attention to the overgrown drive grudgingly unfolding before them. Trees pressed in close overhead, casting a gloomy half-darkness to the already cloudy day, while branches scraped along the windows as if trying to reach inside. Their route was occasionally marked with red-lettered signs warning KEEP OUT.

"We should almost be there." Ian steered over a large rock in the road. "Beatrice said it was only a half mile past the main road."

Rissa nodded and braced her hands on either side of the seat beside her as they bounced over yet another boulder jutting out of the slippery track that passed for a road.

Then abruptly the trees gave way to a small clearing. Ian stomped hard on the brakes and the Land Rover slid to a halt, its nose almost touching Nathan Peters' front porch.

Nathan Peters himself came out to greet them. He put one booted foot on the bumper of the Land Rover and leveled a double-barreled shotgun at the windshield. "Get out--nice and easy."

Chapter Six

The old man's mouth barely moved beneath a droopy salt-and-pepper moustache, but Rissa heard the words loud and clear.

Ian eased open the driver's door and stepped to the ground. Rissa stumbled to her feet behind him.

"Step over here where I can see you."

Ian moved slowly away from the vehicle, maneuvering her behind him so he stood between her and the man with the gun.

"Any particular reason I shouldn't shoot you?"

"I'm Madelaine Ainsworth's niece." Rissa stepped away from Ian so the old man could see her clearly.

Peters spit a stream of tobacco juice out of the side of his mouth as he studied her. "So?"

"You may be the last person who saw Madelaine before she disappeared."

"Ain't seen no one for weeks. Most folks is smart enough to read the signs."

"Madelaine was coming to get some pans from you when she disappeared."

The man cackled with laughter. "I wondered who Beatrice would send to do her dirty work."

Hope flared through Rissa. "Then Madelaine was here?"

"Nope." Another stream of brown liquid shot from between Nathan Peters' teeth.

"But you said--"

Peters raised the shotgun in warning. "I said she wasn't here."

46

Ian tugged Rissa behind the shield of his body and edged them both toward the Land Rover. "Thanks for your time, Mr. Peters. If Madelaine shows up, let her know we're worried about her."

Peters watched them intently as Ian boosted Rissa into the Land Rover. "Hold on now."

They both froze in place.

"You tell Beatrice Winters to come get her own darn pans." The old man cackled with mirth again, as if someone had told an immensely funny joke.

As Ian hastily backed the Land Rover out of the clearing and reversed their route out of the gloomy canopy of trees, Rissa hunched low in the seat, not arguing with Ian's terse command to keep her head down.

Finally, they pulled to a stop under the shelter of a copse of trees just before they reached the main road.

Rissa dared a look back toward Nathan Peters' place. "What do we do now?"

~ * ~

Horace watched listlessly as the mail rode along the conveyor belt and dropped into the waiting bins. What did he care if the mail conveyor was finally working flawlessly? Maddie was gone--kidnapped by some heartless fiend. It wasn't likely the kidnappers would drop him a letter telling where they were. Still, puttering with his machines gave Horace something to do besides worry.

The mail floated by: a magazine, an advertisement, a yellowed envelope with funny-looking letters pasted on it--Horace slammed the conveyor belt into reverse, unmindful of the grinding of gears as he snatched the envelope out of the bin. He fingers shook as he tore it open.

"No!" Horace cried. He hurried down the hallway toward the study, where he knew Ian and Rissa were planning the next move to find Madelaine.

"This is it! This is it!" Horace shouted as he burst through the double doors. "I know where Maddie is!"

47

He shoved a paper at Rissa. She scanned it quickly while Ian read over her shoulder. Ian frowned as he read the missive. "Was there an envelope?"

He carefully took the stained envelope that Horace handed him. "It would have been easier if they had given us a return address."

"They almost did." Horace pointed to the postmark. "The Spruce Goose."

Rissa eyes shone with excitement. "The steam train that runs just south of here. I remember Madelaine taking us there when we were kids."

Her uncle nodded vigorously, setting the white spikes of his hair into a wild dance. "Maddie grew up in the Bohemia mining area near there."

"Why would a kidnapper take Madelaine somewhere she knows?" Ian wondered out loud. "Then mail a ransom note that would give away their location? That doesn't make sense."

Rissa slid a frown at Ian that smoothed into comfort as she patted her uncle's hand. "We'll check it out."

Ian scowled, but didn't contradict Rissa's statement. "The sooner we get moving, the better."

~ * ~

Rissa stared at the gleaming silver engine of the Spruce Goose, as fascinated as she had been when she was seven years old.

She stood barely taller than the red and black painted wheels when Madelaine took her and Ryan for their first ride on the train. As she looked up at the polished silver body gleaming in the sunlight, it distorted her reflection like a fun-house mirror. Rissa made faces and laughed--for perhaps the first time since her father died.

The chug and whoosh of the steam building in the boiler grew faster and louder, drawing her up in its rhythm.

"Whoosh." Rissa moved her arms up and down like pistons. "Whoosh!"

"All aboard!" the conductor shouted.

48

"Got our tickets and some information." Ian took Rissa's arm and helped her up the steps and into one of the cars.

They found a seat and settled in while the rest of the passengers boarded. When the train rumbled out of the station, Ian leaned closer to her and spoke softly. "The clerk at the ticket booth remembers a tall woman wearing a feathered hat coming in several days ago."

Instantly, Rissa was on the edge of her seat. "Did they talk at all?"

"The woman insisted her letter be postmarked while she watched."

"Sounds like Madelaine. Was anyone with her? Did she seem upset?"

"A smallish man with a pointed chin. The clerk said it sounded like the woman was telling the man what to do."

Rissa frowned. Sure, Madelaine liked being in charge. But if she had been kidnapped and was now telling her abductor what to do, why didn't she just come home? She had to know Horace would be worried, especially when he received the ransom note. "That doesn't make sense."

"No, it doesn't. Do you have any theories?"

What could Rissa say without making her family seem any more unusual than they were? So she shook her head and focused her attention out the window.

The train passed the manicured lawns of the Village Green complex and started to climb into the foothills. The buildings became farther apart, until only an occasional house intruded upon the lush green of the wooded hills.

As their guide recited the history of the area over the public address system, Ian tried to ignore the woman beside him. Rather than be a hindrance as he had feared when they started this venture, Rissa had brought insight and common sense to the search.

He caught her gaze and smiled as his thigh bumped against hers. The ride on the train with its smallish seats was an excellent lousy idea. He pretended an inordinate interest in the passing scenery and, in doing so, leaned in front of Rissa, occasionally brushing her arm or her breast, which swamped his senses with the sunshine scent of her.

Unfortunately, acting on his fantasies was severely restricted by their public surroundings.

Ian tried to rein in his licentious thoughts by actually concentrating on the countryside passing leisurely by the window. He used a pair of binoculars to scan the gaping holes in the side of the mountains and the rusting ore cars beside the track that hinted at the gold mines that had once riddled these hills. If he hadn't been staring so intently, he would have missed the bounce of purple feathers inside an old green sedan as it pulled into a tiny grocery store.

"There's your aunt!" Ian grabbed Rissa's hand and pulled her toward the engine.

"Where are we going?"

"To get the engineer to stop the train." Ian hustled along the narrow aisle with Rissa in tow.

However, the engineer saw no reason to stop the entire train just so they could investigate purple feathers.

"Let's go." Ian tugged at Rissa's hand.

"But Madelaine--"

"Come on." Ian led Rissa out of earshot of the engineer. "I'm going to jump off."

"Are you crazy?"

"The train is only going about ten miles an hour. Not as bad as hitting the ground after parachuting out of a plane. It will be a cinch."

"I'm going with you," Rissa stated.

"No way. It's too dangerous."

"You said it would be a cinch."

"For me, not for a girl--"

Rissa glared at him. "I used to jump off the McKenzie Bridge into the river."

"The bridge wasn't moving."

"I'll go by myself."

"Okay," Ian agreed reluctantly. "Just remember to tuck and roll."

They strolled casually toward the door at the end of the car, then bolted through. A rumble of astonishment went up from the other passengers as Ian and Rissa jumped.

Her gasp as they hit the ground jolted in Ian's gut. *Damn, I should have made her stay on the train.*

"Are you alright?" As he expected, Rissa nodded in response to his question. However, he figured she wouldn't admit she was hurt even if her leg fell off. "Let's get out of here before the engineer comes back."

On their dash toward a group of trees, they slipped and almost fell several times on the rain-slick ground. When they reached the sheltering branches, they paused to catch their breath. "Are you sure you're okay?"

"I'm getting my wind back now. Let's go find Madelaine."

They snaked through the brush and trees that clustered along the side of the tracks, then jumped across a small stream to arrive at the back of the store where they had spotted Madelaine's hat. Cautiously, they paused at the corner of the building and peered toward the parking lot.

"The car is gone." Rissa's voice sagged with disappointment.

"They may still be around. Wait here."

Unfortunately, Ian's quick survey of the tiny grocery store confirmed Rissa's fears. If they had been a little faster getting off the train or if the kidnappers had lingered a few minutes longer...

"We missed them, didn't we?" Rissa asked.

Ian nodded. "But at least we know we're on the right track."

"Speaking of tracks, how are we going to get back to train station?"

"And the van." Ian looked down the empty train tracks. "Well, there must be another way back to the station. I'll call to see if there's any taxi service..."

"I'm going inside to get some coffee."

A few minutes later, Rissa emerged from the store carrying two cups. She handed one to Ian. "Any luck?"

"It would be three hours for a taxi to get here and no busses come through any more." Ian turned up his collar against the increasing rain. "Right now I'd rent a donkey to get back to town."

"How about a livestock truck?"

"Did you find us a ride?"

"Well, sort of. I told the man I'd have to check with you first."

"Just tell him yes," Ian stated. "And let's get moving before he changes his mind."

"Um, there's only room for one person in the cab."

"You can sit on my lap." Ian couldn't resist a wolfish grin at that thought.

"I don't think Mr. Jones would approve."

"Jones? As in Farmer Jones?"

"He seems like a very nice man," Rissa said.

The stoop-shouldered old man glared at Ian suspiciously when Rissa introduced them. The farmer shuffled all around Ian, examining him from head to toe.

"In the back, but don't be upsettin' Bessie," the old man said at last. He spit on the ground near Ian's feet and hobbled toward his pick-up truck.

"We can still say no," Rissa whispered.

"Let's just get this over with." Ian wiped the worst of the rain out of his hair and climbed into the back of the truck with Bessie, Mr. Jones' milk cow. Bessie glanced at Ian, then went back to chewing her cud.

A quick look told Ian there wasn't much of anywhere to sit that wasn't covered with old hay and post-digested animal droppings. He considered standing up all the way back to town, but discarded that idea when Mr. Jones bolted away from the store like a bucking bronco out of a chute. He quickly sat down in the cleanest corner of the hay.

During the ride, Ian's eyes strayed toward the cab where Rissa rode in relative luxury next to a shepherd mix dog.

The truck lurched suddenly, causing the cow to stumble sideways and moo in protest. Ian stood up to see what the problem was. As he looked out the rear of the cattle rack, he heard a plop, plop and felt something oozing over his foot. The odor struck his nostrils at the same time he spotted the growing brown glob spilling over his shoe.

"Oh, sh--"

"We're here," Rissa called. She swung open the rear gate of the cattle rack. "How was the ride?"

She glanced from the look of pure disgust on Ian's face to the cow pile on his shoe. To her credit, she didn't laugh.

"I expect hazardous duty pay for this." Ian hopped out of the truck on his unsullied foot and hobbled toward the water hose at the back of the train station.

Rissa hastily thanked Mr. Jones for the ride and trailed after Ian. "Is there anything I can do?"

Ian directed a spray of water toward his offended foot. "Don't laugh. Don't say a word."

She stood in the rain and watched soundlessly as Ian cleaned the goop off his shoe.

"I smell like a cattle barn." Ian turned off the water and glanced at Rissa. "You can talk, just not about this. I want to forget that ride ever happened."

Rissa nodded.

Ian grimaced. "I suppose I'll look back on this and laugh someday."

Rissa smiled.

"But not today," Ian warned.

~ * ~

Ian and Rissa paused at the castle only long enough to change clothes--or rather, to change into what Ian referred to as disguises. Rissa considered it torture. "Tell me again why we're dressed in these ugly uniforms?"

"We don't want the kidnappers to recognize us before we get Madelaine safely away. So we're going to be birdwatchers."

She wrinkled her nose at the khaki shirt and slacks Ian had insisted she wear. "I didn't join Girl Scouts because I hated uniforms."

"You look lovely. And don't forget the matching scarf and cap."

Rissa didn't smile. "Are your disguises always this...um..."

"Birdwatchers really do wear this kind of stuff."

"Why do you get the binoculars?"

"Because it was my idea," Ian said.

The rest of their drive up the narrow, twisting mountain road passed mostly in silence. Rissa thought about her aunt, while Ian scanned the mountains with the binoculars.

"Do you see anything that could be a hide-out?" Rissa asked.

"Not so far--stop! That may be--"

Rissa stomped on the brakes and Ian jerked forward against the shoulder harness.

"Sorry." Rissa set the brake on the van. "What did you see?"

Ian climbed out of the vehicle to stand at the edge of the road, pointing the binoculars toward a nearby ridge of land. "Come take a look."

Rissa squinted through the binoculars. "I don't see anything."

"Here, let me help." Ian reached over her shoulders and turned the binoculars so the sun glinted off something shiny--the window of a cabin.

"I see it!" Rissa spun around, grinning at Ian. Then her breath caught. She was wrapped in his arms and he was staring at her mouth.

He's going to kiss me, Rissa thought, as Ian dipped his head toward her. *And I'm going to let him.*

She braced her feet and her mind as her eyes drifted shut. *It's just a kiss.*

Yet as Ian's lips claimed hers, the earth trembled. The rushing wind lifted her high above the earth and his arms tightened around her.

His whispered curse brought her back to reality a moment before they jarred against the ground, tumbling over and over down the hillside.

Rissa grabbed at shrubs and protruding rocks--anything that came within her grasp. This was no sensual fantasy. They were crashing--perhaps to their deaths--and she wasn't through with life yet. There were so many things she wanted to do--

Chapter Seven

Just when Rissa thought they would fall forever, she landed with an abrupt thud against his chest. For several moments, they both lay stunned and silent.

Too silent.

"Are you alright?" she ran her hands over Ian's chest and arms, although she wasn't sure just what she was supposed to find.

"Uuh," Ian moaned. "Landed on a rock."

"I'm sorry." Rissa tried to wiggle her weight off of him.

"Don't move."

She froze. "Am I hurting you?"

In an instant, their positions were reversed, and Rissa found her back pressed against the mossy ground. "I can rise above the pain."

By the wicked twinkle in Ian's eyes, she knew he was going to kiss her again. She should have resisted. Instead, she anticipated the sensual caress and reveled in the devastating assault on her senses as Ian's mouth plundered hers.

Until Ian's body stiffened--all of it, not just certain parts. "We have company," he whispered.

As her mind tumbled back to reality, a stranger's voice demanded, "What are you doing here?"

"Birds. We're looking for birds." With facial expressions, Ian urged Rissa to follow his lead in the conversation. "Dear, wasn't that a foggy-billed finchbeak?"

"No, darling, I believe it was a ruby-throated sapsucker."

As they struggled to their feet, Ian stayed between Rissa and the stranger. "Perhaps we should go back to camp and check our field guide."

"Not so fast." They froze at the man's command. He took a step closer, then another, and peered at them intently. The man, though small, was armed with a baseball bat-sized limb he occasionally waggled in their direction. Did he also have a gun? A knife?

"I'd really like to get my wife back to camp. We had a bit of a tumble--" Ian waved toward the hillside they had fallen down. "And we don't have our first aid kit."

"You could clean up here--" The man's face softened in sympathy, then slid into a frown. "No, that wouldn't be a good idea. You'd better go."

He waved the branch for emphasis.

Ian and Rissa took several steps backward.

"Wait!" the little man cried.

Once more, they abruptly stopped their retreat as the little man hurried toward them. With a quick glance over his shoulder, the man whispered, "Do you have any marshmallow pinwheel cookies?"

"Just some sunflower seeds," Ian said.

Rissa held her breath as the man's face dropped in disappointment. *What would he do now? Would he bludgeon them to death because they didn't have cookies?*

"Thanks anyway," the man mumbled and turned away.

Ian and Rissa didn't move until the man was some yards distant.

"Let's get out of here." Ian steered her at a fast trot away from the cabin.

They couldn't go back up the crumbling rock slope, so were forced to find a more gradual ascent, which placed them on the far side of the ridge, farther away from their vehicle. At the top of the ridge, they crouched behind a thicket of shrubs to catch their breath.

"He has Madelaine," Rissa declared.

"How do you know that?"

"Marshmallow pinwheel cookies are Madelaine's favorite."

"It could be coincidence," Ian said. Rissa lifted an eyebrow. "Okay, let's go with that theory for a moment. Once we get to the van,

I'll come back here and find a way into the cabin."

"You're not going to dump me miles away to worry about you--I mean, about Madelaine. I'm staying with you."

Ian frowned. "I don't think that's a good idea."

"Why not?"

"This guy could be dangerous."

"What makes you think I'd be any safer at the van than with you? If I stay with you, you won't have to worry about me being all alone and helpless."

Ian's expression showed he clearly didn't believe Rissa was helpless. "Fine. But you have to do exactly as I say. Is that clear?"

Rissa nodded.

They circled the ridge once more until they found a shrubby stand of vine maple where they could hide yet easily watch the activity below. Both Madelaine and the little man were outside the cabin as they settled down to watch.

"She's alright!" Rissa exclaimed as she spotted Madelaine standing behind an easel painting.

"Shh. Keep your voice down," Ian whispered.

Rissa focused the binoculars on Madelaine, looking closely for signs her aunt had been mistreated. She saw no such signs. In fact, Madelaine seemed quite content.

"I wish I could hear what they're saying," Rissa whispered.

"If you'd quit talking, I could tell you that."

"How?"

Ian pointed to a gadget that looked like a hearing aid attached to his ear. "Horace's magic ear."

"Is it working?"

"If there aren't any noises close by."

"Sorry." Rissa subsided into silence for a moment, but it was hard to be so close to her aunt and not hear what she was saying. "What are they talking about?"

"The sad story of his life so far."

Reluctantly, Rissa lapsed into silence once again. However, she watched Ian closely for some sign of what her aunt could be saying to the stranger below.

At one point he looked at her oddly, as if to ask a question. Then he shook his head and returned his concentration to the couple below.

"Here, listen for a while." Ian handed Rissa the magic ear.

Delighted, she fitted the transmitter over her own ear and settled down to listen. What she heard startled her. She looked at Ian and shook her head. "This can't be."

"Tell me what you heard." Ian's mouth set in a grim line.

"Madelaine is giving the man tips on kidnapping."

"How does your aunt know about kidnapping?" Ian asked.

Rissa shrugged. "She's probably trying to gain his confidence so she can escape."

Ian thought Madelaine looked much too calm to be planning an escape, but he didn't tell Rissa that. Instead, he looked through the binoculars at the tableau just a short distance away. He had heard of victims bonding with their captors, but not after such a short time. Besides, considering Madelaine's reputation, she wouldn't buckle under so easily. Something was definitely amiss. This was no ordinary kidnapping.

"We have to let Madelaine know we're here," Rissa whispered.

"OK. The little guy has gone inside. Maybe we can get close enough to talk to her without him knowing. You stay here," Ian ordered. Before she could protest, he added, "You said you would do exactly as you were told."

"I never actually agreed to that."

Ian scowled at her and she pressed her lips together, consoling herself by watching him carefully as he slipped down the hillside toward the cabin.

Ian followed Madelaine around the corner of the cabin and toward the outhouse. *Should he wait outside like a gentleman and hope the kidnapper didn't show up? Or should he approach Madelaine before she reached her destination?*

His decision was made for him when Madelaine spotted him. He grabbed her arm and whispered they had come to take her back with them. Her reply was a sharp right jab to Ian's jaw.

Momentarily stunned, he staggered backward as Madelaine disappeared into the cabin. Then he hustled back up the hill, before she could re-appear with the little man and a firearm.

"Where's Madelaine?" Rissa asked as he tumbled back to their hideout behind the bushes.

"Back there." Ian flipped his thumb toward the cabin.

"But why? What happened?"

Ian rubbed his jaw. "She slugged me."

"She slugged you?" Rissa repeated in disbelief.

"She's got quite a wallop."

"I can't believe you were close enough to touch her and you blew this."

"I didn't touch her--she slugged me."

"Then we'll just march down there and bring her back."

"I don't think that's a good idea," Ian cautioned.

"Maybe she didn't know you were one of the good guys." Rissa indicated Ian's stained and rumpled clothing.

"Or maybe your aunt doesn't want to be rescued."

"How can you say that?"

"Well, there's only one kidnapper. With the right cross your aunt has," Ian rubbed his jaw again, "She could easily overpower him and get away."

"Are you saying this is just another adventure for Madelaine?"

Ian shrugged. "Does she...ah, step out on your uncle?"

Rissa glared at Ian.

"We have to look at all the angles. I've seen it many times before. A couple may seen happy to outsiders--"

"I'm not an outsider. Horace and Madelaine are perfectly happy," Rissa stated.

"Okay." But Ian wasn't convinced. Even if Rissa wouldn't believe it, he wasn't going to dismiss the possibility completely.

~ * ~

The clouds that had been threatening all day sprinkled their first

59

warning drops less than an hour into Ian and Rissa's vigil. Rissa ignored them at first. She was intently watching the door of the cabin, willing Madelaine to appear once more. However, her aunt and her kidnapper stayed snugly inside as the rain fell in ever-larger drops.

"We need to find some shelter." Ian pulled his saturated shirt away from his skin.

In spite of wanting to stay, Rissa had to agree with Ian. Only a fool with no choice would be out in today's downpour.

The rain had cut a jagged stream in the already mud-slickened path as they started down a trail away from the cabin. Through the gray haze of the rain, they spotted a white structure. Ian clasped Rissa's hand and ran toward it.

As they drew closer, the structure became recognizable as a covered bridge--old and in disrepair--but shelter nonetheless.

Once inside, Rissa shook the water out of her hair and glanced around. Huge support beams crisscrossed above them in the muted gray shadows. A diamond-shaped window midway on either side of the structure allowed a shaft of light and, on this day, a good measure of raindrops inside. Still, it was a definite improvement over the deluge outside.

Suddenly, Rissa was too aware of Ian. Was it her imagination that fancied him staring at her nipples beaded against the chill? She wrapped her arms over her chest and moved as close to the arched entryway as she could without becoming further drenched in the rainstorm. Perhaps the open space of the out of doors could somehow lessen Ian's effect on her.

But the silence pulsed between them until she could stand it no longer. "You said you had been to Scotland?"

"Yes." Ian's gaze lingered on Rissa's profile.

She looked out over the jagged hills. The rain had turned to mist and now shrouded the nearby hills, deepening the robe of the trees to emerald green. Under the protection of the old covered bridge, she could appreciate the beauty of the coming evening, something that had escaped her notice in the downpour of a short time ago.

"I've always imagined Scotland would look like this," she said.

"Emerald green hills with the mists rising off the lochs."

"Hmm." Ian had moved closer, until his breath stirred against her face. "Are you warmer now?"

His focused gaze made Rissa tremble with uncomfortable emotions. Still, she fought the attraction. "I've always wanted to go to Scotland."

Ian reached toward her, his fingertips brushing her cheek. "I'll take you there."

Her skin tingled where Ian touched her, making it difficult for her to remember what she was saying.

"I'll take you anywhere..." The rest of his words were lost to Rissa as his lips moved against hers and the world exploded in a kaleidoscope of colors.

Sensations whirled through her, energizing her body yet draining her of any will to do more than hold tight to this man who had somehow scaled the walls protecting her heart.

A gust of wind whipped around them, chasing a chill over her skin.

"You're freezing," Ian whispered. "We'd better go back to the van and get out of these wet clothes."

Darkness had settled over the hills by the time they reached the van, and the rain had started again in earnest. Rissa tumbled inside as soon as Ian opened the back door and gratefully sank onto the carpeted floor.

"Get out of those wet clothes and wrap a blanket around you. I'll wait outside." He slid the side panel door shut, leaving her enclosed in darkness.

Feeling guilty that Ian stood out in the rain, Rissa quickly scrambled out of the soaked khaki uniform, then fumbled behind the seat for a blanket. She wrapped it securely around her and opened the door. "All done."

Ian grinned at her, his teeth a flash of white in the darkness.

"My turn to wait outside." Rissa started to step out of the van.

He caught her arm. "You'll be drenched in an instant. Then I'd have to wait outside and get wet and have to change again while you waited outside getting wet and--"

"Okay, I get the picture." Her mind conjured up delicious images of Ian stripping off his clothes and standing gloriously naked just a heartbeat away.

"You can turn your back," Ian said softly. "Or not."

The last words were said so quietly that Rissa wasn't sure she had heard right. However, the slow, sexy smile on his face told her she had heard correctly. Rissa swallowed hard and clamped her blanketed arms across her chest, facing deliberately forward.

Ian chuckled as he climbed into the van. The swish of a wet shirt dragged across her nerve endings as he peeled off the soaked garment. His shoes and socks came next, bringing images of Ian's legs entwined with hers, his toes caressing her ankles, her calves...

The scrape of his zipper skittered goosebumps along Rissa's spine. She kept her gaze resolutely looking out the windshield at the darkness.

"Will you hand me that bag under the seat?" The velvet softness of his voice slid across her skin as smoothly as the darkness crept down the mountains.

Rissa groped for the bag, then handed it to Ian, carefully not looking.

"Thanks." His husky voice stroked across her tautened nerves as his fingers tightened for a moment on her hand.

With a will of its own, Rissa's gaze was drawn to Ian. She could make out a half smile on his lips but little else in the murky darkness.

The silence lengthened. Was it hours or only minutes before they drew together, kneeling face to face on the nubby carpet in the back of the van, while the patter of raindrops against the rooftop provided a counterpoint to their quickened breathing.

Ian's fingers stroked across Rissa's cheek in a whisper of desire, causing her to tremble. The hand she extended to steady herself met the soft mat of curls on his chest. His heartbeat pulsed desire through her fingertips. Her fingers strayed over his chest; then lower, where she realized with a jolt of sensual awareness that Ian wore nothing at all.

His fingers grasped Rissa's hand and lifted it to his lips. The rasp of whiskers rubbed erotically over her palm as he traced a path to each fingertip with his tongue.

She shivered and swayed toward him. His fingers eased open the blanket she clutched to her chest as his tongue teased her mouth to open beneath his.

Lightning flashed, briefly illuminating the darkness and the desire in Ian's eyes. Rissa sighed, giving herself up to the emotional storm that raged between them.

~ * ~

Ian watched Rissa sleep. Her half-moon lashes brushed a shadow across her cheeks. Her lips parted slightly, inviting another kiss.

She was even more perfect than he imagined when he first met her. Only a couple minor hurdles stood between them and happiness. One was he had a hitch in the military to finish and Rissa had responsibilities to her family she took very seriously. That hurdle required they be in different states and perhaps different countries.

Convincing Rissa she was madly in love with him was another hurdle. She moaned and shifted against him. Would she hate him this morning or cling to him?

Making sleepy noises, Rissa struggled to a sitting position against the wheel well of the van and rubbed at her eyes. She blinked, stared owlishly at Ian, and closed her eyes again.

When she reopened her eyes, she seemed startled to see Ian. "Omigosh. I have to go."

On her hands and knees, she searched through the piles of discarded clothing.

"Try these." Ian handed her a sweatshirt and pants. "Don't forget your shoes. It's probably cold out there."

She mumbled something that resembled "thanks" as she groped for the door handle.

"Better take these too." He handed her a wad of tissues.

Deciding discretion would be appreciated, Ian stayed in the van while Rissa took care of her immediate needs. The damp morning chill soon chased her back inside.

She closed the door behind her and stared wordlessly at Ian.

"Good morning." Ian had never considered himself a coward, but he had never faced rejection by the woman he knew he wanted to marry either. He broke eye contact first and rummaged in the duffel bag. "We have granola bars or granola bars for breakfast."

"Just what I would have requested." Rissa took one of the proffered packages and tore it open.

Ian considered it a good sign she neither threw the food in his face nor burst into tears. Now he just had to convince her they would be perfect together.

After breakfast, they discovered the van was stuck in the mud where they had pulled off the road.

A good opportunity to show Rissa how resourceful he would be as a husband, Ian thought. They moved everything they could find--including Rissa--over the back tires to add weight and hopefully provide more traction.

Then Ian shifted the van into gear. The vehicle jerked forward, then rocked back into its muddy nest. A change of gears into reverse brought the same result, but in the opposite direction.

The van lurched again as he shifted forward and pressed on the accelerator. The wheels spun ferociously, shooting an arc of mud against the back window in furious brown splotches.

Ian frowned as the van jolted backward once more and slid ominously closer to the ravine. Forward, then backward; its wheels shrieked in frustration as they churned, firing one last volley of sloppy brown mud before settling hub-deep in the muck.

He climbed out of the van and surveyed the situation. "We should have brought the Land Rover."

"I'm sorry. I should have stayed on the graveled part of the road."

"You could have ordered sunny weather too." Ian's gentle teasing brought a slight smile from Rissa, which pleased him more than a unit of new recruits finishing their first week in boot camp. "Maybe we can jack up the wheels enough to slip something under them for traction."

Rissa stared doubtfully at the half sunken tires, but held her tongue. In a van filled with the latest technology, surely there was something that could get them out of this muddy mess. "I'll look through the boxes Uncle Horace put in the back to see if anything might be useful."

While Ian fussed with the tire jack, Rissa dug through boxes of "stuff" stashed in the rear of the van. The tops of the boxes were filled with wires and gauges similar to the ones connected to the video monitors inside the van. Deeper down was a hubcap that concealed a camera and a clock that hid a radio transmitter.

The answer to their dilemma was so simple she almost missed a folded rubber object with an air pump attached. "Ian! This is it."

From his position ankle deep in the mud, Ian scowled at the tire jack mired as deep as the tires. "You found a tow truck?"

Rissa held up the rubber object. "Almost as good."

"A whoopee cushion is going to get this van out of the mud?"

"It's not exactly a whoopee cushion." She shoved the rubber gadget under the bumper and flipped the switch on the air pump.

As air flowed into the rubber bag, the van floated up out of the mud.

Damn. Upstaged by a giant whoopee cushion. Ian shook his head. "So some of your uncle's inventions really do work."

Soon they had the van back on the gravel road, mud-spattered but otherwise in good shape. When they parked closer to the cabin, they made sure the van was sitting on solid ground.

"We need to approach them cautiously," Ian warned as they got out of the vehicle. "The man might be armed, so remember to stay close to the cover of the woods and away from the pond in the clearing."

Rissa nodded. She didn't want to think of her aunt at the mercy of a crazed criminal. But soon Madelaine would be free. She fell in silently behind Ian as they made their way toward the cabin.

At the edge of the wooded area, Ian motioned for Rissa to wait. As she watched him crab-walk across the clearing to the rear of the cabin, her heart thumped loudly in her chest.

When he at last reached the cabin and crept around the corner, Rissa slowly counted to fifteen, just as he had instructed, giving him time to reach the door. Then, on trembling legs, she scurried across the clearing.

Rissa dashed through the door of the cabin and stopped abruptly. "There's no one here."

Ian stood in the middle of the room, hand on his hips. "Looks like we're back to square one."

Rissa wrapped her arms around her waist as guilt squeezed her belly. This was her fault. She should have insisted they keep watch over the cabin. Instead, she had taken selfish pleasure with Ian. And Madelaine was gone again.

Chapter Eight

Rissa walked slowly down the hallway of the castle. She had been with her mother much longer than she planned. Daphne was inordinately curious about where Rissa had been the last few days. She didn't want to lie to her mother, but she didn't know what the truth was. Had Madelaine been kidnapped or was this just another adventure? Did Ian want to find Madelaine only to get the money for a car or did he really care what happened to her?

Rissa was supposed to be the responsible one. Yet within the past week, she had lost her job and fallen in love--two decidedly irresponsible actions. Why wasn't she begging for her job back? Why wasn't she running as fast as she could away from Ian?

It seemed as if an impish child had taken possession of her. One that shook off responsibility and chased after rainbows.

She settled in the study and stared at the fire crackling in the fireplace. Ian had gone to bring Horace up to date on their latest search for Madelaine. They had agreed to meet in the study and decide the next step.

However, when Ian entered the room, Rissa's body stirred with interest, pushing away thoughts of her aunt. Her senses focused on this man who had quickly become too important in her life. The smell of raindrops in his hair. The taste of his kisses guiding her toward heaven. The ripple of his muscles beneath her fingertips.

Ian caught her gaze as he approached. "How did you explain Madelaine's disappearance to your mother?"

"I let Mother assume Madelaine was off on another adventure."

What Rissa didn't tell Ian was Daphne asked a lot of questions about "that handsome Scotsman."

"Do you think this is just another adventure for your aunt?"

"I don't know. I can't believe Madelaine would intentionally put us through this worry, but things don't add up."

"You said you've discovered things about your aunt you never knew."

"True. But all those things just reinforce how generous she is. It makes her more responsible and less likely to treat something like this as another adventure."

"Could someone be blackmailing Madelaine by threatening to hurt your family?"

"I hadn't thought of that." A frown settled across Rissa's brow. "Mother is so vulnerable, and Horace is far too gullible."

"I was thinking about you."

"Me?"

Ian fingered a strand of Rissa's hair. "You work long hours, often alone."

"Not any more."

"Did your job mean so very much to you?" His direct gaze demanded an honest answer.

"My pride is hurt about being fired. It was a good job-- respectable." Rissa shrugged. "But my aunt is more important right now."

The slight pressure of Ian hand over hers warmed Rissa's heart. "I had another thought. What if the blond man has an accomplice? Say, the man with the raspy voice."

"Or more than one accomplice," Ian added. "Nathan Peters could hide someone on that mountain for days or even weeks. And any one of the men at the homeless shelter could be involved. Or even Beatrice at the gallery."

"I don't want to think someone local--"

"You will never believe what happened to me tonight." Ryan burst into the study, the hem of the lavender dress he wore nearly dragging the floor on one side.

"You made a pass at the wrong blonde," Rissa said.

Ryan scowled at her. "This is serious. I was assaulted by a man."

"Not one of your friends, I hope." Rissa tried to hide a smile.

"You're not taking me seriously at all." Ryan complained.

"You have to admit that's a little difficult while you're standing here in a dress." Ian commented.

"Fine. Neither one of you want to hear this. But the police believed me."

"Okay, Ryan, sit down and tell us what happened." Rissa scooted over on the couch to make room for her brother. She figured the sooner she heard about Ryan's latest drama, the sooner they could get back to searching for Madelaine.

Ryan settled onto the couch and rubbed his hands enthusiastically in preparation for telling his story. "I was in front of Tassie's Gallery waiting for Tiffany to show up. All of a sudden, this guy in a hospital gown--you know, one without a back--grabbed my arm and started yelling at me.

"Well, I could see Tiffany coming, and I really didn't have time to mess with the guy. So I shook him off and started walking toward Tiffany. But he didn't get the hint. He jumped on my back and started choking me. Tiffany was so upset her hands were all fluttery. I was not going to let this guy ruin our evening.

"So I shoved my elbow into his side. He must have hit his head when he fell because he just groaned and lay there. Tiffany insisted on calling the police even though I told her I was fine. I would have been too, except I caught my damn heel in the hem when I stood up from checking on this guy and tore this dress.

"The police seemed to know this guy, though. Said he had escaped from the hospital after waving a pair of scissors at a doctor. They've been watching for him.

"Well, I have to get changed and meet Tiffany back at Tassie's." Ryan walked to the doorway and paused. "Funny thing--at first I thought this guy was Beatrice Winters--but younger."

"Why is that?" Ian asked.

"Same pigeon-body shape. Same whiskbroom moustache." Ryan

shrugged. "Gotta go. Don't want to keep Tiffany waiting."

Rissa stared at Ryan's rumpled lavender backside as he hurried down the hallway. "I guess if my brother dresses as a woman and gets away with it, why couldn't Beatrice Winters dress as a man."

"Or maybe she has a close relative who looks a lot like her," Ian said.

"No one who lives nearby," Rissa responded. "But I think she has a brother and maybe a nephew who live out of town."

"Maybe we should keep an eye on our abrasive friend to see if she's had any recent visitors."

~ * ~

Shortly after midnight, Beatrice Winters turned out the lights of the gallery and slowly made her way toward an ancient Chevy. The old car protested as Beatrice turned the key in the ignition, then reluctantly started.

She drove to the outskirts of town and parked in front of a shabby little house whose white picket fence tried valiantly to impart a note of cheer and welcome. However, its gate hung crookedly on one hinge, looking as tired as its owner as she lumbered up the walk.

Beatrice called to a cat as she unlocked the door. Ian and Rissa watched her shadowy form move around inside the house for a few moments, then darkness settled over the tiny house. Gradually, the muted night sounds crept closer. Ian suggested Rissa get some sleep. It would likely be a long night.

A long and quiet night, Ian thought, as the sun peeked between the horizon and a low bank of clouds several hours later. He gently woke Rissa and told her he was going to walk over to a nearby coffee kiosk.

Rissa yawned and stretched as Ian slipped back into the van.

"Anything suspicious?" He handed her a cup of coffee.

"Heaven." She sipped the liquid gratefully. "Nothing so far. Beatrice Winters seems to be a lonely old lady who lives with her cat."

Tousled and still sleepy in the gray dawn light, Ian wished Rissa was lying on his bed instead of huddled in a vehicle at the break of dawn. He needed to do something to get his mind off the lower part of his anatomy.

"Do you think our friend Beatrice is an early riser?" Ian asked.

"Probably. It takes an early start to run other people's lives."

He grinned and shoved a pink box at Rissa. "It's a good thing I brought donuts to sweeten your disposition."

With another sigh, she selected a cream-filled pastry and bit into it. "You do know how to please a woman."

Ian stared at the smudge of powdered sugar on her chin. If he was a gentleman, he would hand her a napkin instead of fantasizing about licking off the smudged sugar.

As Rissa took another bite, chocolate filling clung to her lip for a moment before her tongue darted out and flicked it away. She closed her eyes, savoring each bite. "Mmm."

The sound reminded Ian of another sigh on a darkened night with the storm crashing around them. He had become part of the storm-- turbulent and powerful--when he made love with Rissa. Afterward, he seemed connected to her in some primitive, elemental way.

When Ian brushed his thumb lightly across Rissa's chin, she stopped in mid-bite and stared at him, awareness and remembering in her eyes. He leaned forward and nibbled at the donut she held in her hand. As he explored the ridges of her fingertips with his tongue, he tasted sugar and woman, softness and energy.

And remembered why they were once more sitting in a vehicle on surveillance.

Drawing a deep breath, Ian slowly straightened. "Time to stir up some action."

"What are you going to do?"

"Plant a bug on her car." Ian pasted on a false brown moustache, eyeglasses and pulled a cap low over his brow. "I'll be right back."

With a casual glance around, Ian strolled toward Beatrice Winters' old car. He reached the rear fender just as the front door swung open and Beatrice bent to pick up the newspaper. She straightened and looked directly at him.

"Say there, young man, what do you think you're doing?" Beatrice advanced on him, waving the newspaper like a nightstick.

Ian stepped away from the car and dazzled a smile in the older woman's direction. "Just admiring this lovely classic automobile. Almost as beautiful as its owner."

Beatrice giggled as she paused at the gate. Ian was sure the old woman's eyelashes fluttered and wondered if he was laying the flattery on too thick.

She's just a lonely old lady, Rissa had said.

Or was she? Even better than a bug on her car would be one on Beatrice herself.

As they chatted, Ian sidled closer to the older woman. The car had been a gift, she said. An engagement present--she stopped in mid-sentence and frowned. "I have to go now."

Now or never, Ian thought.

"Thank you for talking with me." Ian gallantly lifted Beatrice's hand to his lips as he dropped a transmitting device into the pocket of her flowered dress. Beatrice flushed and hurried back inside her house.

"What was that all about?" Rissa asked as Ian climbed back into the van.

"I planted a tap on Beatrice. Not only will we know where she goes, we'll be able to hear anything she says."

Ian bent to adjust the receiver for the bug.

"Who's that?" Rissa pointed toward a shadowy figure creeping around the corner of Beatrice's house.

Ian swung the binoculars toward the stealthy figure. "Looks like a male version of Beatrice Winters."

Ian and Rissa hunkered down in the seats of the van as Beatrice's visitor rang the doorbell and glanced suspiciously behind him.

Beatrice threw open the door and greeted him with a smile. "Hello, Louis...out...hospital?"

The answer was an unintelligible mumble as the man pushed his way inside.

"Static." Ian fussed with the dials on the receiver.

"Don't need no damn doctor telling me what to do."

The raspy voice came through clearly now.

"It's him," Rissa whispered. "The voice on the phone."

"Now where's the old woman with the funny hat?" the raspy voiced man demanded.

"I haven't seen Madelaine for days." Beatrice stated. *"She just disappeared with my pans."*

The man cackled evilly. *"She didn't just disappear. I snatched her."*

"What do you mean?"

"I'm gonna make some money off the rich old bag and take care of your problem too."

"No! Madelaine is my friend."

"You ain't got no friends, old lady," the man snarled. *"But you and me are family. We got to stick together. I promised my pa."*

"What did you do with her?" Beatrice demanded.

"I'll show you when I find her again." Louis cackled...

...and their conversation stopped.

Ian and Rissa peered over the edge of the window. A moment later, Louis limped out of the house, hustling Beatrice along in front of him. "We're gonna go find your friend."

The man shoved Beatrice into her car and cranked the engine. As they squealed away, Ian pulled the van in behind them, following at a discreet distance.

Louis headed--erratically--into the hills above Watermark. He drove very fast at times, then slowed to almost a crawl, swerved to the shoulder of the road, then stepped on the gas again.

As the road narrowed and grew bumpier, Ian dropped further behind. "This is the way to Nathan Peters' place."

"I guess Peters is involved too."

"So it would seem. Watch for him through the binoculars. I don't want any more surprises."

Ian drove cautiously, following the serpentine route up the mountain. "At least they won't get back down without running into us."

"I'm not sure that's a good thing."

A response froze in Ian's throat as they rounded a sharp corner.

He tromped on the brakes and brought the van to an abrupt halt. Beatrice's car sat in front of them, mired up to the hubcaps on the muddy shoulder of the road, with Beatrice huddled beside it.

"Stay down," Ian warned. "There may be someone else close by."

Rissa crouched beside the van until Ian gave the all-clear signal. As he led Beatrice toward her, Rissa stood up and fetched a blanket out of the back to wrap around the older woman's shaking shoulders.

"I've been such a fool." Beatrice moaned as Ian helped her to sit down.

"I never thought I'd hear you admit that. " A chuckle accompanied the voice that rang out behind them.

Not again, Ian thought. He slowly turned around to find Nathan Peters' shotgun aimed at their heads.

"Oh, Nathan, put that silly thing down." Beatrice smoothed a hand over her hair.

"You know this man?" Rissa asked.

"Unfortunately, yes," Beatrice admitted with a haughty sniff.

"That's not what you thought twenty years ago." Peters shifted the gun across his arm.

"Can we talk about this without the gun pointed at us?" Ian asked.

Peters--and the gun--swung toward Ian. "I've seen you before."

"Yes, looking for Madelaine Ainsworth." Rissa stepped in front of Ian, drawing Peters' attention.

Ian pulled her behind him. "Are you trying to get shot?"

"I'm trying to keep you from getting shot." Rissa stepped in front of Ian once more.

"I don't need protection," Ian said.

"And I do?" Rissa fisted her hands on her hips.

"Well, obviously. You're standing right in front of a man with a gun."

Rissa glared first at Ian, then at Nathan Peters. "Would you shoot a woman?"

"I've been tempted a time or two," Peters replied.

Rissa took a step backward--right against Ian's chest.

"Look, we just want to take Madelaine home," Ian said.

"Madelaine is up here too?" Peters spat. "Now I won't get a moment's peace. Take her with you and go, all of you."

Ian and Rissa stood waiting while Peters glared at them. "Well, what are you waiting for?"

"For you to tell us where Madelaine is," Rissa said.

"How would I know?" Peters shouted. "You're the one who said she's up here."

"But we thought since Louis came this way--" A puzzled frown wrinkled Rissa's brow.

"What is Louis is doing up here?" Peters addressed Beatrice.

Beatrice hung her head sadly. "He said that he kidnapped Madelaine, but now he doesn't know where she is."

Peters laughed. "That boy never could do anything right."

"He's my nephew." Beatrice squared her jaw and shoulders.

"I wouldn't be braggin' about that," Peters said.

"So you don't know where Madelaine is?" Ian asked.

"I told you that the other day, son."

"And you didn't work with Beatrice's nephew to kidnap Madelaine?"

Peters hooted with laughter. "If I wanted to be around people, I wouldn't live up on this mountain. And I'm gettin' might tired of all this company. So I suggest you skee-daddle out of here."

"My car is stuck in the mud," Beatrice stated. "We shall have to get it unstuck first."

Peters grinned. "You'll have to ask me real nice."

Beatrice sniffed and turned her back toward the older man.

Peters shrugged. "Suit yourself. If it rains, that old rattletrap will be here 'til July."

"It's not a rattletrap. And Mr. MacGregor will assist me," Beatrice declared.

"I told him to leave." Peters leveled the shotgun at Ian and Rissa and winked--just enough to lift his salt-and-pepper moustache slightly, but not so Beatrice could see.

Ian took Rissa's arm and tugged her toward the van.

"You're not going to leave me with this-this uncouth boor." Beatrice's gaze darted from Peters to Ian and back again.

Ian shrugged as he helped Rissa into the van. "You heard what the man said."

"Will she be alright?" Rissa glanced in the mirror as Ian started the engine.

"They seem to have unfinished business that would be better settled in private," Ian said.

Rissa glanced back once more. Beatrice stood with feet braced apart and arms akimbo. Nathan Peters circled the mired-down car, a satisfied smile on his face.

As they drove back toward the cabin, Rissa snuck glances at Ian. In twenty years, would she regret making love with him? Or would she wish she had taken a chance on love?

The cabin was empty when they arrived, but the door hung open, indicating someone had recently been there.

"Let's take a look around," Ian said quietly. He circled the cabin, then squatted down to study the muddy ground. "Fresh tire tracks."

"And green paint on this rock," Rissa added.

Ian wiped at the liquid on the ground and sniffed it. "Oil. Looks like they scraped the oil pan."

"Madelaine must be driving."

"Let's see what Horace's exhaust tracking machine can do." Ian lifted the little machine out of the van and set it beside the tracks. As soon as he flipped the power switch, its dials quivered and hummed. "Okay, we've got a reading. Let's see if this baby really works."

Ian and Rissa stopped at each intersection, rolled out the little machine and let it point out Madelaine's trail. They were exuberant over the results: the machine worked faultlessly.

However, as they drew closer to the city, a flaw became obvious in their plan. Rissa stopped at a red light and Ian jumped out with the exhaust tracer. However, the light turned green before the little machine got a fix on the car Madelaine was driving. Angry horns blared behind them as Ian stood in the middle of the intersection urging the machine to work faster.

Rissa accelerated into traffic as Ian jumped back into the van. "That guy in the BMW almost hit you."

"Pull in at this service station. We need gas and it will give us time to rethink this plan."

"What can I get for you folks?" the attendant asked as he wiped his hands on a red shop rag.

"You fix cars." Ian stared at a vehicle up on a rack.

The attendant shrugged. "Yeah. Maybe the only service station in town that still does."

"Has a tall woman wearing a purple hat stopped by to get an oil leak fixed?"

"Sorry, no." The attendant shook his head.

But they may have stopped somewhere else. Rissa quickly caught Ian's line of thinking. As she stretched her legs and bought a soda, a phone book swinging on a silver wire by a pay telephone caught her eye. The yellow pages boasted several ads for auto repair shops.

Rissa felt a twinge of guilt as she ripped the page out of the phone book, but promised her conscience she would somehow make up for this one small sin after Madelaine was home. She folded the page and tucked it in her jeans pocket, then sauntered back to the van. She waited until they were several blocks away from the service station before she shared her treasured page with Ian.

He grinned as she smoothed the paper out on her lap. "Good job. What's our next stop?"

Ian and Rissa drove to repair shops until they found a mechanic who remembered Madelaine well.

"What a character," the mechanic declared. "Came sliding in here on two wheels and almost took out my carburetor display."

"That sounds like Madelaine," Rissa said.

"She strode into the auto bay like she was royalty and looked all around, then promised me a bonus if I could fix the car right away."

"How long ago was that?" Ian asked.

"About an hour," the mechanic said. "She said they were going over to the festival for awhile. Crazy thing to do--I told them it was going to rain."

"They?"

"Yeah. There was a little guy with her. Seemed awed by the woman. Hell, I was awed." The mechanic chuckled.

"How do you get to the festival?" Rissa asked.

"Couple miles down the road and turn left. You can't miss it."

"How did they get to the festival without a car?"

"Aw, I loaned her my mother-in-law's car. She said she'd take real good care of it." The mechanic's laughter echoed around the auto bay as Ian and Rissa climbed back into the van and headed toward the festival.

In spite of the off-and-on rain, the crowd was lined up umbrella to umbrella along the festival's parade route. Ian and Rissa huddled together under the edge of an oversized stadium umbrella offered by a sympathetic college student.

"A lot of people are wearing hats with feathers," Rissa said as antique cars and kids on bicycles rolled past.

"Let's get closer." Ian grabbed Rissa's hand and snaked through the crowd.

Their progress was slowed by the scores of people leaning forward to catch the candy thrown from the vehicles in the parade. Twice Ian stopped to retrieve candy from the street and drop it into the waiting hands of delighted youngsters.

He would make a good father, Rissa thought, then stumbled as images of sweat-slickened bodies and tangled legs filled her mind.

"We'd make more progress if we were part of the parade," Ian said. For a moment, he watched a teenager on a scooter weave circles among the floats. "Come on, I have an idea."

Ian broke through the crowd and onto the street. He caught up with the teenager, exchanged a few brief comments, and soon appeared in front of Rissa astride a scooter.

"How did you do that?" Rissa asked.

"A little persuasion." Ian grinned. "Hop on."

Rissa slid her arms around Ian's waist as the motorcycle jumped forward. Her senses reeled from pleasurable shock as the sway of the scooter molded her body against Ian in a sensual embrace. Madelaine could have waved her feathered hat in Rissa's face and she probably wouldn't have noticed.

She did notice when the scooter took another jump forward, bringing them a hairs-breadth from a set of ponies pulling a cart of ladies from the women's auxiliary. The startled little horses snorted and sidestepped in the traces, which set the wagon rocking side to side. The ladies shrieked and scrambled for a steady seat as the driver tried to calm the beasts.

Ian muttered a curse as he swung the scooter away from the horses. The scooter jerked and slid around, face to face with an oncoming cavalcade of cub scouts on bicycles. The boys scattered as Ian aimed the scooter toward a stack of hay bales at the side of the road.

"Hang on!" Ian shouted over the frenzied whine of the little engine. He killed the engine and braced his heels just before impact.

Chapter Nine

Rissa tumbled off the bike and landed with a thump against a bale of straw. Dazed, she lay still for a moment to regain her breath and her bearings.

"Are you hurt?" Ian squatted beside her, his fingers gingerly touching her face and body in search of injury.

"What would a real date be like?" Rissa shoved her hair out of her eyes.

"I'm sorry." Ian extended a hand to help her to her feet. "There was something wrong with the scooter--"

"Hey, you wrecked my scooter!" the teenaged boy cried as he raced to the scene of the accident.

"You didn't tell me the throttle stuck or the brakes grabbed when you took my twenty dollars." Ian scowled at the kid.

"You didn't ask." The kid picked up the scooter and pointed toward the front fender. "This dent wasn't there."

"That fender was dented when you ran into Mrs. O'Gerlehay's gate," a stern voice stated.

Rissa's first glimpse of the stranger revealed a tan shirt with the word "sheriff" stitched across the pocket. She tilted her head back and connected with solemn eyes shadowed under a Smokey-the-Bear hat pulled low across his forehead.

The teenager shoved his hands into his pockets. "I was just giving him a bad time. All in fun."

"Take your bike and scram, Ronnie, before I keep it as evidence," the sheriff stated.

"Jeez," Ronnie muttered, pushing his scooter away from the crowd that had gathered in a loose circle around them.

"Thanks, sheriff, we appreciate your help." Ian took Rissa's elbow and started to move away.

"Where do you think you're going?" The sheriff's stern voice stopped them in mid-step.

"Back to the festival. We're looking for, ah, somebody."

"Are you now?"

Ian and Rissa nodded in unison.

"Well, I'm afraid that will have to wait," the sheriff said. "I need you folks to come down to the office with me."

"But we have to find my aunt," Rissa protested.

"You folks have busted up our parade pretty bad here. Not to mention unauthorized use of a motor vehicle."

"I paid for the use of that vehicle," Ian said.

The sheriff shrugged. "We'll straighten this all out if you'll just come with me."

"But--"

One scowl from the bulky sheriff silenced any further protests from Rissa. She swore she could see a glint of humor in his eyes, but his Smokey hat was set at an uncompromising angle. She reasoned it would be better to straighten this out away from the curious eyes of the onlookers.

Under the watchful eyes of the parade-goers, Ian and Rissa walked toward the small building the sheriff indicated. Once inside, the sheriff pulled the blinds over the wide glass window.

"You folks want a cup of coffee?" the sheriff asked.

Rissa shook her head, but Ian accepted the brew gratefully.

"Sit down. Make yourselves comfortable." The sheriff eased into a swivel chair and propped his feet onto the battered wooden desk. He took a sip of the coffee and grimaced. "I swear Sally adds axle grease to this stuff."

He set the cup on the desk and turned his full attention back to Ian and Rissa. "What brings you folks out this way?"

Rissa glanced at Ian before answering, then responded with a slight shrug. "We're looking for my aunt."

"Meeting her at the festival, were you?"

"Not exactly."

The sheriff lowered an eyebrow in a partial scowl.

"We thought we saw her hat during the parade."

"You raised all this ruckus over a hat?"

"The hat is how we've traced her so far--well that and Uncle Horace's machine. She's been missing over two weeks."

"Have you talked to the local police?" The sheriff shuffled through a stack of papers.

"Well, they don't take Madelaine's disappearances too seriously."

"You wouldn't happen to mean Madelaine Ainsworth?" The sheriff's feet hit the floor.

"Have you heard of her?"

"I went to school with her. You say she's your aunt?"

Rissa breathed a sigh of relief. Maybe this man would listen to them. She briefly told him the story of Madelaine's disappearance.

"Same old crazy Maddie," the sheriff remarked.

Was he no different than the police in Watermark? But Rissa held onto a glimmer of hope. "Can you help us?"

"I can pick up Winters for questioning, and I'll make sure he doesn't get near Madelaine as long as she's in our county. But knowing Maddie, she can take care of herself."

"Thank you so much! And I'll pay for any damages to the parade."

The sheriff waved away Rissa's offer. "That's the most excitement we've had since Ronnie tossed a firecracker under the ambulance. But I have to keep up appearances of law and order. Just make sure you look properly chastised when you leave."

Ian and Rissa grinned at each other. For the first time since they started the search for Madelaine, Rissa felt like they had an ally.

~ * ~

Madelaine slipped away from the others while they swarmed the grocery store. Weasel was caught up in the midst of the new friends they had made during the festival. He wouldn't notice her absence for now.

With a cell phone borrowed from one of the group, she punched in the numbers for home, hoping Horace would answer. She really didn't have time to get into a discussion of responsibility with Rissa or have Ryan hang up on her, thinking this was all a joke. She loved her niece and nephew, but Rissa really needed to lighten up and Ryan could use a strong dose of maturity.

Madelaine needed to hear Horace's voice and know all was well at home.

"Hello?"

The tenseness in her husband's voice flooded remorse through Madelaine. "It's me."

"Maddie! Where are you? Are you alright?"

"I'm fine. Listen, I don't have much time." Madelaine glanced over her shoulder.

"Have they hurt you? I swear, I'll--"

"I really am fine, Horace. I knew you would be worried--"

"You were kidnapped. Of course I'm worried," Horace declared.

"Well, yes, at first I was kidnapped. But now--look, it's a long story."

"Did you escape? Rissa and MacGregor from Scotland Yard are looking for you."

"Rissa and who?"

"Ian MacGregor from Scotland Yard. It was quite extraordinary how he came to be here. He came to sell you a car of some kind, but I think that was just a cover. Then he claimed he wasn't really from the Yard, but I knew he was because you were missing and someone had to find you."

Madelaine tried to make sense of Horace's convoluted logic and gave up. His tale was almost as unbelievable as hers. They would have to sort this out when they had more time. "Where are they now?"

"Following you. Please come home, Maddie. I'm worried about you."

Madelaine heard shouts of laughter coming nearby and knew her friends had finished their junk food shopping spree. "I have to go. I'll call you soon."

"Wait--"

"I love you, Horace." She pushed the end call button and was straightening her hat when the others came around the corner.

"I wondered where you got off to. Just wanted to get out of paying the bill, huh?" one of them teased.

Madelaine laughed with the others and handed the phone back to its owner. "And now I'm going to leave you on your own again. Hoist a brew for me."

The group protested as she grabbed Weasel's arm and pulled him along behind her. However, she ignored them as she flagged down a passing motorist and jumped inside the car with Weasel. Soon, they had left the group behind.

Madelaine knew if Rissa and her friend had tailed her this far, they must have found the car. It also stood to reason they would return to the car when they couldn't find her. She had to get back to the auto repair shop before she was discovered. She had the driver drop them off a block away from the shop, then zigzagged through an alley, and crouched behind a stack of tires near the shop.

"Why are we hiding here?" Weasel asked.

"Shhh!" Madelaine held a finger to her lips. "A good kidnapper always knows what their pursuers are up to."

"I don't think I want to be a kidnapper, Miz Mads," Weasel lamented. "It's too much work."

A good sign, Madelaine thought. But right now, she had more important things to worry about, such as figuring out what that gorgeous hunk with Rissa was really up to.

~ * ~

"They should have come back for the car by now," Ian said. The lights inside the repair shop flickered off, leaving the old green car huddled forlornly outside in the dark.

"Unless Madelaine has figured out we're watching them." Rissa wiggled her shoulders to ease the stiffness of slumping down in the seat. "Look, there's someone by the car."

Ian's gaze swung toward the old green Buick. "It's Beatrice's nephew."

"What's he doing?"

The pigeon-bodied man popped the lock on the driver's door and slid inside. The old car grumbled and sputtered, then roared to life. It jerked once, then accelerated out onto the street.

Ian started the van and pulled into traffic at a discreet distance behind the Buick. They followed the old car back up the mountain and to the cabin where Madelaine and the thin blond man had been earlier.

The sounds of Louis' anger reverberated across the hills, punctuated by the slamming of the door.

"I think we should talk to Horace," Rissa stated.

"We don't have anything to tell him."

"But he may have something to tell us."

"What do you mean?"

"From what we know, Beatrice's nephew really did kidnap Madelaine, probably with the help of the blond man who's still with her. I'm not sure why she stuck with the little guy--she probably thinks she can save him from a life of crime. But she would contact Horace so he didn't worry."

Ian frowned skeptically. "And if your aunt is having an affair?"

"At some point, you just have to trust the people you love."

Horace was on the telephone when Ian and Rissa arrived at the castle, talking with whispered urgency and obviously unaware the intercom to the study was still turned on from listening to an earlier call from the kidnappers.

"When are you coming home?" Horace asked.

"As soon as this works out," a voice answered.

"That's Madelaine," Rissa mouthed to Ian.

"Perhaps we shouldn't interfere," Horace suggested.

"Nonsense," Madelaine stated. "The man is perfect. The sooner Rissa realizes that, the sooner I can come home."

"Are you sure, Maddie?" Horace signed.

"Of course, my darling. We'll do this for Rissa then I'll be home."

Ian stared at Rissa's averted profile for several moments after Horace's conversation with Madelaine had ended. Though he had suspected something didn't ring true with this kidnapping, having that fact confirmed triggered his anger at wasting time that could have been spent ensuring his mother had enough money to keep the creditors from camping on her doorstep.

"Your aunt supposed to be kidnapped," Ian said. "Why is she worried about setting you up if her life is in danger?"

Rissa drew a deep breath, but didn't look at Ian. "I'd say Madelaine thinks she has control of the kidnapping and has gone on to run someone else's life--mine."

Ian strode across the room, tamping down his anger, then returned to where Rissa stood. "Every day we've wasted has brought my mother closer to financial disaster. When my father died, I discovered he had mortgaged all they owned to cover debts his business partner had run up. Now my mother insists on selling everything she can to pay off the creditors who are hounding her."

The stunned expression on her face twisted like a knife in Ian's belly.

"I'm so sorry," she whispered. "I'll cut a check for the Pinto right away."

"Wait." Ian laid his hand on Rissa's arm as she stood up. "I shouldn't take my frustration out on you."

"I should have done it days ago. I've been so focused on finding Madelaine--I didn't realize the sale of the Pinto was urgent. And of course we'll cover your expenses and the time you've spent searching for her."

"No. I told Horace I'd find his wife and I will."

"And your mother?"

"We'll be fine." *I hope,* Ian silently added. This time, it was Ian who didn't meet Rissa's gaze.

"I'll print a check right now." She moved to the computer in the corner of the study.

As the machine whirred to life, Ian didn't move from the spot where Rissa left him. Frustration and shame gnawed at him. He should be able to take care of his mother. He should have the money to pay her bills.

But these weren't her bills, he reminded himself.

He nodded his thanks as Rissa handed him a piece of paper. "We still need to find Madelaine before Beatrice Winters' nephew does."

"Or let her find us."

"What do you mean?"

"Madelaine is a master at disappearing," Rissa said. "Ryan and I couldn't find her when we were younger. You and I have been chasing glimpses of feathers for over a week with only scrapes and bruises to show for our efforts."

Ian conceded this point with a short nod of his head.

"If we convince Madelaine her matchmaking is working, maybe she'll come home on her own."

A thoughtful expression settled on Ian's face as he stared at Rissa. "So we convince Madelaine we've fallen madly in love and the only thing holding up the wedding is for her to come home."

"Yes. We should be together in places where Madelaine would be likely to see us. Sunrise breakfast at the café, sitting in the town square reading poetry to each other, window shopping at the jewelry store."

Ian couldn't believe his luck. The check he held in his hand would pay off another creditor and, thanks to this crazy situation that may or may not be a kidnapping, Rissa was telling him how to court her. He could just follow her instructions, add a few touches of his own, and be assured of capturing the heart of the woman he intended to marry.

The next morning, Ian and Rissa sat snuggled together at the Ova Easy Café.

Ian smiled his thanks to the waitress as she delivered plates of steaming hotcakes, eggs, and bacon. Then he carefully adjusted the placement of his sunglasses on the table so their darkened lenses mirrored the room and anyone--including Madelaine--who might be watching them.

"These hotcakes are delicious. Here, try this." Ian speared a bite of pancake on his fork and leaned toward Rissa.

As her gaze locked with Ian's mesmerizing green gaze, Rissa's appetite for anything but the man beside her disappeared. She took a deep breath and, as her lips parted, Ian moved the fork forward. The bite of food hit the side of her mouth and crumbled down her chin.

"Sorry." Rissa tried to catch the food with her hand as Ian grabbed a napkin.

"My fault." In the process of dabbing at syrup on her chin, Ian knocked over his glass of orange juice. He cursed under his breath as Rissa stifled a giggle and mopped at the spreading orange puddle. He pulled several napkins from the holder and bent over to wipe the liquid that spattered to the floor.

"Feathers!" The whispered word came from under the table as Rissa felt Ian's hand around her ankle. A tingling sensation traveled from her ankle up her leg to where his hand now rested on her knee.

"I think Madelaine is here," Ian whispered.

Rissa stared down at Ian kneeling on the floor and realized his words were trying to give her a message much different than the one her body was receiving from the touch of his hand. "Madelaine?"

"Over by the restrooms."

"Let me talk to her this time." Shaking off the effects of Ian's touch, she slid out of the chair and moved with what she hoped was casualness toward the back of the building. As a flash of purple slipped through the bathroom door, she gave up all pretense of casualness and hurried after the woman.

Inside the room, Rissa stared at the closed stall door. What should she say first? *I'm glad you're safe* or *why did you worry us? Let's go home* or *we have to put your kidnapper in jail?* She was still contemplating what words to say when the stall door opened.

The woman stared at her for a moment, then looked pointedly at the three other empty stalls.

"Sorry." Rissa took several hurried steps backward, then turned and ran out of the room. She paused in the main restaurant and looked around.

"Was it Madelaine?" Ian appeared at her side.

She shook her head as a matronly woman in a dark purple dress walked past them and glared.

"We'll just keep looking." Ian took Rissa's arm and steered her toward the cash register. Once outside, He curled his arm over her shoulders. "We need to stick with our plan to make Madelaine think we're madly in love."

As Ian's teeth nipped at Rissa's earlobe and pleasure shivered down her spine, she could believe just that, especially since they were standing in front of a large plate-glass window stenciled with the word "silversmith." A bed of black velvet cushioned its treasure of silver filigree designs accented with stones of onyx and turquoise and amber cats eye. One setting cradled a smoky agate swirled with shades of gray ranging from dark charcoal to the pale slate.

"Like your eyes." Ian murmured as he tugged Rissa inside the shop.

The silversmith agreed the ring was made for her. "It fits perfectly. It was only waiting for you to discover its beauty."

From under her lashes, Rissa glanced at Ian. He quirked a smile at her, causing an odd catch in her breast. When she slipped the ring off her finger and handed it back to the silversmith, her hand felt strangely empty without the curved ornament.

To regain her composure, she stared out the window--and noticed purple feathers poised just outside. "Madelaine."

"Save this ring for us." They hustled out of the shop and stood once more looking in both directions. Instead of feathers, they spotted the jerky movements of a man bumping into pedestrians as he stumbled along the sidewalk.

"Beatrice's nephew," Rissa whispered.

They dodged into a nearby doorway, feigning intense interest in the window display until the man careened by. "Time's running out."

Rissa nodded. "If Madelaine is following us, maybe she'll follow us home."

They went straight to Horace's workshop as soon as they arrived at the castle and confronted him.

"Uncle Horace, do you know where Madelaine is?"

"I almost have repairs made to the projector." Horace's gaze bounced only briefly toward Rissa before he focused once more on the holographic projector, concentrating on screwing a new circuit board in place. "We'll now have a flawless butler."

"Horace, we know this kidnapping is a fake," Ian said. The older man's shoulders stiffened, but he didn't reply. "It didn't start out that way. Madelaine really was kidnapped. Then one of the kidnappers ended up in the hospital. But he's out now and looking to finish what he started."

"She just wanted you to be happy." Horace clasped Rissa's hands in both of his.

"I know. But things are different now. This man is dangerous. He could hurt Madelaine. Do you know where she is?"

"She said she would come home after she did this for you, but I don't know where she is--" Horace's voice cracked.

"If she calls again, tell her Louis is after her," Ian said. "She needs to come home or go to the police."

Horace nodded. "What are you going to do?"

"Enlist some help from my brother," Rissa stated.

~ * ~

Madelaine crouched on the side of the gray concrete building with Weasel, flanked on either side by a pair of pink flamingoes. She had seen Rissa kissing Ian after they pulled up. That should mean her plan was moving along nicely, but she wanted one final piece of proof: an engagement ring on her niece's finger. After that, she could go home.

"Are you ready to go home yet, Miz Mads?" Weasel asked.

Madelaine turned to answer Weasel at the same time as an arm snaked around Weasel's neck.

"Yes, Aunt Madelaine, are you ready to go home?" Rissa asked.

Madelaine smiled. "Horace was supposed to be my hero. But you and your brother will do."

"We were worried about you."

"Oh, pooh. You know I can take care of myself. Now introduce me to your young man."

Madelaine sized up Ian as he reached around Weasel's nearly inert body and shook her hand. Firm handshake. Direct eye contact. That was good. "Have you had sex with my niece?"

"That's none of your business," Rissa stated.

However, other than a slight upward flick of an eyebrow, Ian showed no sign that Madelaine's question was anything more than normal conversation. "When a gentleman makes love with a lady, he doesn't discuss it with others."

Madelaine smiled. "Let's drink a toast to love. Then I want to go home."

"There's one other thing you should know--"

"You can confess after the toast, young man."

Once inside, Ian propped Weasel at a corner table with a ginger ale while Madelaine ordered champagne all around.

"To the happy couple." Madelaine raised her glass toward Ian and Rissa. "Have you set a date yet?"

Ian glanced at Rissa.

"Come on, Aunt Mads, leave them alone or you'll scare this one off too." Ryan's comment earned guffaws around the bar.

"Why are you wearing my pearls?" Madelaine frowned as she stared at her nephew dressed in a green satin evening gown.

"You always wear your pearls with this dress," Ryan replied.

"I wear them. You don't."

"Yes, ma'am. Tiffany thought emeralds would look better anyway."

Madelaine's attention focused briefly on the slender blonde with Ryan. "I assume this is Tiffany. Now let's finish this bubbly and go home."

Someone put a dollar in the player piano, and soon a ragtime tune echoed around the room. The jazzy music was almost loud enough to cover the squeal of tires near the front door.

It was not loud enough to hide the loud, raspy voice of the man who pushed inside. "What is that racket?"

The man glared at the piano. With three shots from the piece of

hardware slung over his torso, Beatrice's nephew brought stunned
silence to the Pink Flamingo.

Chapter Ten

"Gunner," Weasel whispered from his corner table.

"Get the old woman," Gunner demanded.

"I'll go peacefully." Still dressed in a green satin gown, Ryan stood up.

"Oh, no, you don't. I started this and I'll finish it." Madelaine pushed in front of Ryan.

Gunner glared from one 'Madelaine' to the other. "Which one of you is the real dame?"

"I am," both Ryan and Madelaine stated.

Gunner leveled the gun at them. "I can take you both out. Now, who's for real?"

"I am," Ryan and Madelaine once again replied in unison.

Gunner's mouth worked furiously. As the man's finger twitched on the trigger, Ryan pushed his aunt to the floor. More shots rang out as patrons scrambled to get out of the way.

Ian dodged toward the gunman, hoping to disarm him in the chaos. He collided with Rex Foxworth in a clatter of glassware and complimentary peanuts. Gunner turned on them, his face twisted with rage, and sighted down the steel-blue barrel.

"No!" Rissa threw herself at Gunner.

Gunner caught her arm and cursed as sirens wailed in the distance. He tossed one last look at the two 'Madelaines' and barked at Weasel. "Take this one."

He shoved Rissa toward Weasel. With an apologetic shrug, Weasel backed toward the door, Rissa in tow. Gunner followed, his gun trained on the bar patrons. "Don't anybody try to follow."

He showered a round of ammo around the bar to emphasize his point.

Ian waited only until Gunner's shiny black boots disappeared out the door before he scuttled to the doorway and peered around the jamb.

"I'm going with you," Madelaine stated.

"No. You stay here and fill the cops in," Ian answered. "And your nephew may need a doctor."

Madelaine glanced toward Ryan, now tended by the blonde fluttering around him. "He'll be just fine. He was only grazed, but it should serve his purposes well."

Ian barely glanced at Ryan, now leaning heavily against the beautiful young lady kneeling beside him. "If the cops doubt your story, just go to Sheriff Conchobar."

"I haven't seen Concho in years."

"He remembers you well. Horace rigged your car with a tracking device, so they can follow me easily." Ian took one last look around the doorway to see if it was clear, dashed to the red Cadillac, and sped after the fleeing kidnappers.

Ian muttered a combination of prayers and curses as he followed the erratic trail of the old green Buick. He pleaded with whatever deity would listen to keep Rissa safe, and cursed his clumsiness for not capturing Gunner at the Pink Flamingo.

"I love you, Rissa. When this is over, I'm going to convince you to marry me. Your aunt doesn't have to matchmake. This is for us."

Ian focused on the spiraling trail of taillights up the mountain. He didn't dare turn on the headlights in the gathering dusk for fear of alerting Gunner he was being followed. But at least the evening twilight helped disguise the shiny Cadillac in tucks carved in the side of the mountain.

Ian hoped Madelaine had been able to explain the situation to the police quickly. Neither the thin blond man nor the aging commando seemed particularly stable. He would feel much more comfortable with reinforcements on the way.

~ * ~

Rissa studied Gunner covertly out of the corner of her eye. From the back seat, the gun he pointed in her direction bounced erratically as Weasel followed the zigzag road past the scars of old logging operations and tracts replanted with trees. Higher on the mountain, the trees thinned to occasional lonely fir sentinels then boulders took the place of stumps. A steep switchback in the road brought them briefly face to face with the sky, then flattened out to offer a panoramic view of the valley below.

Weasel slowed the tired old Buick as the sun disappeared behind the shale face of the mountain. Several boulders the size of small cars littered the road in front of them, as if they had been tossed there by a giant hand irritated with traffic. Weasel turned the wheel sharply to avoid one of them but nicked the edge of another with the right front tire.

An explosive bang rocked the old vehicle and Rissa ducked reflexively, thinking Gunner had finally pulled the trigger. However, no burning jolt of lead tore through her body. Just the whiplash jerk of stopping abruptly.

Gunner loudly cursed Weasel's lack of driving skills and kicked the back door open. He nearly yanked the passenger door off its hinges and pulled Rissa out of the car. "Let's go."

"But the car--" Weasel protested.

"Leave it." Gunner shoved Rissa in front of him up the road toward a gaping hole in the side of the mountain. Weasel stumbled along behind, glancing back occasionally.

"Come on," Gunner snapped. "We need that light up here."

Weasel moved uneasily to the mouth of the mine. The anemic light from the metal flashlight trembled in his hand. "It's really dark in there."

Gunner cackled. "The better to hide in. Now get inside."

He prodded Rissa's back with the cold barrel of the gun. Inside, the darkness intensified the dank smell of cold, wet earth. Rissa shivered. She could see little of the planks on which they walked, but knew from the occasional hollow echo of their footsteps they passed over areas where nothing but emptiness lay below them.

"Stop here," Gunner ordered. Weasel flashed the weak light over the reinforced beams carved into the rock surrounding them. "You keep an eye on the girl. I'm going to look around."

Gunner shoved a silver pistol at Weasel in exchange for the light, and walked deeper into the mine.

Soon even the pale halo of light disappeared, leaving Rissa alone in the obsidian blackness with the thin blond man. She wrapped her arms around her waist to try to conserve body heat. The temperature in the mine reminded her of a walk-in freezer, although she knew from the constant drip of water it wasn't that cold.

"I don't want to be a kidnapper," Weasel whispered.

Rissa looked in the direction of his voice. "Then why are you doing this?"

The man didn't respond for some moments. "I'll try to help you get home."

Silence settled over them once again, but the little man's words gave Rissa hope. If he did nothing more than stay out of the way, that gave her a better chance of surviving until Ian arrived. The stricken look on his face when Gunner hustled her out of the Pink Flamingo was etched permanently in her mind.

When--not if--she got out of here, they were definitely going to have a serious conversation. Or maybe she would just let her body do the talking.

A glow from the mineshaft alerted Rissa that Gunner was returning. She shifted toward the opening, wondering how far she would get if she made a run for it. She feared it wouldn't be far enough in the darkness. If she stalled for time until Ian got here, she could escape and not get lost on the mountain.

"Ain't nobody gonna get to us here." Gunner waved the flashlight beam over Rissa. "We'll just wait here for the money."

Gunner doused the light, plunging them all into utter darkness and silence once again. Rissa felt strangely comforted in the darkness. She couldn't see the kidnappers and, if she closed her eyes, she could let her imagination take her out of the cold, dank mine. Even the drip, drip of the water off the walls was soothing.

"Somebody shut off that damn drip, drip, drip!" Gunner exploded. The light flashed on and stabbed accusingly at the walls.

"Sponges," Rissa murmured.

"What'd you say?" Gunner swung the light into her eyes.

"Sponges," Rissa repeated. "Imagine giant sponges soaking up the water."

Gunner snorted. "Stupidest thing I ever heard of."

But he fell silent again, and Rissa knew from the vague frown on his face he was thinking about her comment.

"Maybe we could imagine some heat too." The light flashed across the blond man's face in response to his comment.

"A fire would give away our position," Gunner snapped.

Weasel shrugged. "Maybe a blanket out of the car?"

"Someone'd spot you in a minute," Gunner jeered. "Anyways, a real man can take the cold."

Rissa rubbed her hands up and down her arms. She needed to do something to keep her mind off the cold. "Do you mind if I sit down?"

The light flashed across her face once more.

"It's going to be a long night. No one would dare come up the mountain in the dark, so you won't have your money until morning."

Gunner scowled at her, then nodded. "Right. Morning."

~ * ~

"Mighty tall tale you're spinnin'." Nathan Peters spat at the ground by Ian's feet.

"We want your promise not to shoot us before we can get Rissa out safely."

"You say they're in a cave?"

"One of the old mines," Sheriff Conchobar stated. "We figure Louis is holed up in the safe house. It was built to keep the miners safe in a cave-in, which unfortunately means it also going to be the toughest place to get into without warning Louis we're coming."

Peters stroked his moustache thoughtfully. "So what did you

have in mind?"

"Look for another way in," Ian said. "And provide a distraction while we get Rissa out."

"Maybe the airshaft," Peters said. "I'll show you. Then I want you all to clear off my mountain."

Soon Ian was standing with several other men rigging a pulley to a teepee-like structure Horace had fashioned over the opening of the airshaft.

"As I recollect, it drops straight down for about twenty feet, then levels off to a more gradual slope before it empties into the safe house," Peters said.

"Is the holographic projector working, Horace?" Ian asked.

"I can't guarantee what it will do without more time to make repairs."

"The kidnappers are unpredictable. Each minute we waste puts Rissa's life in more danger," Ian stated.

"Weasel will help," Madelaine said.

Ian looked at Rissa's aunt. She had barely uttered a word since arriving on the mountain with Sheriff Conchobar, Horace and Nathan Peters. The purple feathers on her hat sagged dejectedly to one side, underscoring the worry etched in her face.

"I'm not sure we can count on a kidnapper to help, Maddie," the sheriff stated.

"Yes, you can," Madelaine insisted. "He told me he didn't want to be a kidnapper any more."

The sheriff shook his head and Horace looked distressed, but Ian simply stated, "I'll remember that when I get inside."

"Okay, let's get rolling." The sheriff looped a rope around Ian's ankle. "Ready?"

Ian slid on a pair of infrared goggles and nodded.

Madelaine laid a hand on Ian's arm. "This is my fault. Tell Rissa I'm sorry for being a foolish old woman."

"You can tell her yourself," Ian said. "She's going to be fine."

Clutching the projector, Ian dropped head first into the shaft. As Nathan Peters described, the first twenty feet or so were a straight drop downward. When the shaft eased to a slope, Ian was able to crawl rather than dangle like a spider on a thread. For a time, the journey through the earth was almost comfortable.

Then shortly ahead, the opening of the shaft narrowed. At first, Ian thought it was just the perspective of distance. However, as he crawled closer, Ian could see a pile of rock all but obscured the opening. A hollowed-out pocket just in front of the rockslide allowed him to sit up, cradling the holographic projector on his lap. As he looked at the walls, it seemed the rocks now blocking the opening came from the space where he was sitting.

Ian had two choices: he could go back and hope there was another way in somewhere or he could dig out and move forward. If he dug out, the rocks he removed would block his passage back the way he came in, and there was no guarantee the passage ahead would be clear.

Images of Rissa flooded his mind. Running through the rain hand in hand. Standing inside the covered bridge, her drenched form silhouetted in the fading evening light. Making love while the storm crashed around them.

Going back was not an option.

Ian untied the rope--his lifeline to the outside--from his ankle. Then, one stone at a time, he slowly refilled the hollow with rocks. Occasionally they creaked and shifted and Ian paused, praying the mass didn't roll down and crush him.

Gradually, the opening grew wider. Just a few more inches and his shoulders would fit through. He moved faster, transferring the last few stones that blocked his way to Rissa.

The ground rumbled a protest behind him and Ian realized his carefully replaced rocks were very unstable. He felt a nudge against his shoe, followed by a thump against his leg; and he knew the rocks were starting to slide again.

He clutched the projector under one arm and scrambled through the opening. As his body jolted forward, Ian grabbed at nothing but air. He heard a rumble behind him just before he slammed to a stop against a rock wall.

Chapter Eleven

Rissa heard the rumble echo above them.

"What was that?" Weasel squeaked.

"A few rocks shifting," Gunner answered, pointing his gun in the direction of the noise as if to scare it away with the weapon.

Or a rescue attempt, Rissa thought. Ian would be counting on her to prepare the kidnappers. "I understand a lot of men died in these mines."

The light from the almost spent flashlight wobbled across her face and onto the walls behind her.

"Who told you that?" Gunner's voice was a growl.

"Why would there be this reinforced area with an air vent if they didn't need it?"

"Maybe we should get out of here." Weasel glanced at the heavy beams above them.

"I'll bet their ghosts still haunt the mines," Rissa said casually. "I heard a pickaxe earlier--"

"I don't wanna be here," Weasel stated.

"Shaddup and sit down, the both of ya." Gunner pointed the weapon at Rissa. "Not another word, girlie. We're stayin' here until we get that ransom money--one way or another."

~ * ~

Ian heard voices below him--Rissa's and two men. Right on cue, she was distracting the kidnappers. They would be jumpy as hell by the time he got the holographic projector set up and running. If it worked, especially after the bruising it got coming down the airshaft.

If not, he would have to go to Plan B--whatever that was.

He scooted as close to the opening as he dared, cradling the projector in both arms. Horace had said to set it on a flat surface and push the button.

Nothing.

Ian picked up the machine and patted the metal sides. Dust puffed out the side vents. He jiggled the battery pack and set the machine down with one final pat.

Ian crossed his fingers for luck and pushed the button again. The projector belched a mini-cloud of smoke and started humming.

"Oh, no! That one's been cut in half." Rissa's voice drifted up to Ian. "Ugh, Decapitated."

The projector must be working, at least partially. But now was not the time to be concerned with perfection. Ian had to put the rest of the plan in motion.

"I'd like to leave now." Rissa moved away from the airshaft and toward the front of the mine.

"I said we ain't goin' nowhere." Gunner aimed the gun at her head.

"Aw, she's right." Weasel hurried to hover beside her. "I don't like ghosts."

"They ain't ghosts. It's a trick. Wait a minute--"

"And Louis, you know I told you never to play with guns." A diagonally challenged image of Beatrice Winters appeared by the back wall, shaking her finger and scolding.

"Who's there? I know somebody's there." Gunner spun around, pointing his gun at first one distorted image and then another.

"Let's get down," Rissa whispered to Weasel. "That thing might go off."

Weasel nodded as they crouched low and edged away.

"Where d'ya think you're goin'?" Gunner shouted.

The light went out and someone grabbed Rissa's hand.

"Horace's infrared goggles work pretty good in the dark." Ian's whisper flowed over Rissa with the sweetness of a Celtic song.

"Thank the graces." She held tight to Ian with one hand and reached out to Weasel with the other. "Weasel, take my hand and let's get out of here."

Crouched low, the three stumbled toward the entrance of the mine, leaving Gunner shouting at the images from the holographic projector. They were nearly out of the mine when a shot rang out from deep inside. The trio landed on their hands and knees and scrambled toward the opening.

They met the sheriff on his way in. "What happened?

"Gunner's the only one left in there." Rissa huddled against Ian.

Ian put his arm around her shoulders. "And some very distorted holograms."

"I hope he's not dumb enough to shoot inside this mine," the sheriff said. "There's no telling where a ricochet bullet might hit."

More shots rang out, followed by an enraged yelp.

"Well, he just might be that stupid," the sheriff said. "I'm going in. Ian, you get Rissa to safety. Weasel, consider yourself under arrest. Report to Madelaine until I get your partner taken care of."

"Yes, sir." Weasel hung his head and skulked in the direction the sheriff pointed.

"You're not going in alone," Ian stated.

"You've done enough, but I'm not going to argue with someone to watch my back."

Ian pressed a hard kiss on Rissa's lips. "Stay where you're told to for a change. I want a real kiss when I get back."

Following the sheriff, Ian descended once more into the mine, this time upright on his feet rather than head first. They cautiously sidled against the slippery wall as they neared the safe house where Gunner had holed up. At first they heard nothing but the hum of the holographic projector and a strident voice stating, "I told you not to play with guns...with guns...with guns..."

Then they heard another noise: a low whimpering came from one corner. The sheriff nodded toward Ian. They aligned themselves on either side of the mineshaft.

"Put your hands up and come on out," the sheriff ordered.

"Please make her shut up," Gunner pleaded.

The sheriff turned his search light toward the whispery voice. Gunner huddled against the wall, holding his hands out beseechingly toward the sheriff.

"Push your weapon out here," the sheriff ordered.

Gunner shoved the gun toward them.

"Now get up slow."

"I can't," Gunner whimpered. He leaned to one side so the dark stain on the back of his trousers was clearly visible. "Bullet got me."

Ian could see the sheriff was fighting back laughter as he scooted the weapon toward Ian and told him to be sure it was unloaded. It was-- probably emptied at the holographic image of his aunt. She was still shaking her finger at them, slower and slower as the battery pack wore down.

"I can't walk," Gunner whined.

"If you want to get away from her, you have to walk out of here under your own steam." The sheriff hefted Gunner to his feet.

Gunner hobbled a few steps. With assistance from Ian and the sheriff, he made it out of the mine almost as quickly as Ian and Rissa had stumbled to freedom.

A cadre of police in full SWAT gear arrived soon afterward.

The sheriff removed his hat and dusted it against his leg. "As usual, the cavalry shows up after the action is over."

"I'll take over now." A stiff-necked corporal presented himself in front of Sheriff Conchobar.

"The hell you say." Conchobar settled his Smokey hat back on his head.

"Special orders from the mayor."

"Well, neither the mayor nor you has any jurisdiction up here, so I'll just have to take care of the prisoner myself." The sheriff steered Gunner toward a patrol car. "I do appreciate the loan of the vehicle, though."

"Sir, you can't--that is--"

Conchobar paused as he opened the back door for Gunner. "You know, there is one very important thing--nah, too dangerous."

The sheriff turned and tucked a grumbling Gunner into the back seat.

The corporal scurried over to the car. "Danger is my middle name."

Conchobar dropped his voice. "It's not just anyone I'd trust with this information, but I think there's a top secret weapon still in the mine."

The corporal nodded eagerly.

"You have to go in through the airshaft up above. Now, there's a small rock slide in the way--not something a man like yourself can't handle, of course." The sheriff looked cautiously over his shoulder before continuing. "It's a metal box about a foot square. Had this guy cowering."

The corporal glanced at the scowling Gunner. "He looks pretty tough."

"Caterwaulin' like a baby."

The corporal nodded solemnly.

"I want you to bring it in so we can take a look at it."

"Yes, sir!"

"Not a word to anyone you don't trust, understand? You might want to take on this mission yourself."

"I think that's a wise choice, sir." The corporal saluted smartly and hurried back to the men milling around the SWAT truck. Soon they were swarming up the hill toward the pulley Horace had set up over the airshaft.

"What got into him?" Ian asked.

"Just the hint of a top secret weapon still hidden in the mine."

"You sent him after Horace's holographic projector?" Rissa asked.

The sheriff nodded.

"But they could have walked right in..."

The sheriff grinned. "Exactly."

"I suppose you didn't warn him about Nathan Peters either."

~ * ~

Ian checked once more to be sure the silver filigreed ring was in his pocket, then lifted the knocker on the castle door. The door swung open and a voice intoned, "Welcome to our castle, Inspector MacGregor."

Horace's projector is working again, Ian thought with a smile.

Instead of following the holographic image, Ian detoured to the study where Rissa waited for him. A fire crackled in the grate, but it was the desire in her eyes that warmed him.

She rose from the chair where she had been sitting and slid into Ian's arms. "I've missed you."

Ian chuckled. "It's been a long hour for me too."

After a lengthy embrace and kiss, Ian took Rissa's hand and tugged her to sit down while he knelt on one knee in front of her. He took the ring box from his pocket and looked into her eyes. "I love you. Will you marry me?"

Tears sparkled in her eyes. "I love you too. And yes."

Relief flooded through Ian. So simple! Just like his parents' story so many years ago. He pulled her into his arms and nearly wept with joy--until a voice over the intercom interrupted their embrace. "Inspector MacGregor, you have a visitor."

Ian frowned. Only one person would interrupt him here and for one reason: he was being called back to the MPs to deal with an emergency situation. The timing couldn't be worse. Not only was there work left to do to get his mother settled, Ian wanted firm plans for his marriage to Rissa before he left again.

He took both of Rissa's hands in his. "This is not the way I wanted this, but will you marry me now?"

"Now? As in right this minute?"

"Within the next twenty-four hours."

The look in her eyes searched Ian's soul. "Is this the better or the worse part?"

"I knew the first time I saw you that you were the woman I wanted to marry. But an Army wife has some rough times. Sometimes

I'll have to leave you and not be able to tell you where I'm going or when I'll be back. Sometimes I'll bring my work home and be nearly impossible to live with until I vanquish the demons. Sometimes I'll love you better than any man ever could and bring you flowers and sing off-key love songs just for you."

Ian had never felt so exposed and vulnerable in his life. Rissa could destroy him with just one word.

The gentle caress of her fingertips on his cheek and the touch of her lips against his provided his answer. "We have a lot of work to do in the next twenty-four hours, partner."

Ian swept Rissa into a hug and twirled her around in circles. "Let's get busy."

While his MP friend was dispatched to pick up Ian's mother, Rissa's family mobilized the town with wedding preparations. The priest from the homeless shelter to perform the ceremony. Ova Easy's baker to prepare the cake. Flowers specially ordered by Rex Foxworth. A bit of tailoring to slightly alter Daphne's wedding gown to fit Rissa. A license and special waiver of the waiting period so Ian and Rissa could be married the next day.

With barely any sleep, the next day passed in a haze for Rissa. The last memory she had of Ian was a look of regret and the whispered words, "I love you. Please take care of my mother."

Then he was gone.

Rissa sat among the flowers and gifts and wondered if her wedding had been a dream. But the filigree ring on her finger gleamed with the love of the man who had placed it there, and his kiss still lingered on her lips. Already she missed Ian!

Her brother walked by and patted her head. Uncle Horace kissed her cheek and beamed at her. Her mother stared at the wedding gown she had worn some thirty years before and seemed baffled, but let Ian's mother lead her away with the promise of dinner.

"So you've found your prince at the end of the rainbow." Aunt Madelaine settled on a chair beside Rissa.

Rissa's eyes filled with tears as she nodded.

"Don't you worry. I saw the determination in that boy's eyes when he looked at you. He'll be back."

Rissa allowed herself a few moments in Madelaine's comforting embrace before she wiped the tears out of her eyes and stood. "And I have a lot to do before he comes home."

Epilogue

VALENTINE'S DAY, the next year

Ka-boom! An explosion rocked the night sky as Ian MacGregor pulled into the circular drive, followed by another and another as rainbow-colored fireworks arced across the sky.

Rissa had warned him the entire family had a hand in planning his welcome home reception. The warning faded like the spent fireworks as Rissa launched herself into his embrace and clung to him.

Eleven long months had passed since he had kissed his bride good-bye. An eternity of nightly fantasies that ended in frustration and empty arms. Now that he held her, he would never let go. Ian buried his face in her hair, remembering the sunshine woman scent of her. The soft curves of her body against his brought an instant memory of making love with her. He whispered, "I love you," over and over, between claiming her mouth in vivid caresses that left him shivering with need.

"How long before the rest of the welcoming committee shows up?" his panted question brought a quiver of anticipation from Rissa.

"Eighteen-hundred hours tomorrow."

"Let's not waste a second of that precious time." Ian swung her up into his arms.

"Welcome home, Inspector MacGregor." A hologram of Rissa in a form-hugging satin dress shimmied to life as they stepped across the threshold of the castle. Her voice purred, "Want to come up and see my balance sheets?"

Laughing, Ian carried his real bride to her bedroom. Once the door closed behind them, he tried to go slow, but Rissa yanked up his shirt and tunneled her hands across his chest and back while her hips rocked against his erection.

A low, rumbling groan escaped from Ian's throat as he pushed up her skirt and unzipped his pants in one motion. Their first coupling exploded as quickly as the intensity of the fireworks that had lit up the sky when he arrived.

"Now for a change of tempo, my beautiful wife." Ian laid Rissa across the sturdy four-poster bed and slowly stripped off the rest of her clothing, kissing and caressing as he exposed bare skin. His fantasies all the previous long months simply served as foreplay to this exquisite night.

We have the rest of our lives, Ian reminded himself. But his body refused to be sated. One bout of lovemaking led to another and another and another.

Rissa dozed off as the gray fingers of dawn crept over the eastern horizon. Ian cradled her in his arms and watched her sleep, releasing the horrors of the past months in the joy of being home. Of loving Rissa.

Thanks to a well-stocked mini-refrigerator in her suite, they didn't even have to leave the room for food and drink. They dined naked in the middle of the bed, then pushed aside the bread and grapes to make love again.

As eighteen hundred hours drew closer and their time alone ran out, Ian led Rissa to the whirlpool tub in the bathroom. Once the tub was filled with water and bubbles, they sank into the steaming water and made love once again. He could easily imagine her as a sea siren who had captured his soul, though he had no desire to escape.

Watching her dress seemed as sexy to Ian as removing her clothing had been hours earlier.

"Your mother said dinner would be at exactly eighteen-hundred hours." Rissa buttoned Ian's shirt, stopping several times to plant kisses on his chest.

"How is it working out to have my mother living here?"

"She's done a great job of organizing us."

"Does that mean she's been overbearing and bossy?"

"Finish getting dressed and come see for yourself." Rissa's smile reminded Ian of a Cheshire cat--like she knew something he didn't.

Curious now, he fastened his slacks and belt, gave his already spit-shined dress shoes another quick dusting, and offered his arm to his wife.

The rest of the family engulfed Ian with hugs and joyful greetings when he and Rissa entered the dining room. Immediately apparent was the exuberance of this family, but without the chaos Ian had witnessed when he left almost a year ago.

"Let's sit down and eat," Linda MacGregor suggested. Ian clasped his mother's hand and gave it a lingering squeeze. "Kudos to Daphne for this wonderful meal."

"Thanks to your suggestion that I take cooking classes." Gone was the fifties woman that Rissa's mother had been when Ian shipped out. Her haircut was as modern as the other women and her clothing echoed the classic fashions currently in upscale stores.

"What happened?" Ian whispered in Rissa's ear as he held her chair.

"Your mother's influence," she replied sotto voce.

Light conversation continued as a conveyor belt began moving delicious-smelling food toward the table. Ryan held a chair for his mother and then for the blonde who had been introduced as his fiancé, Tiffany. Ian recognized her as the same woman Ryan had tried to woo by dressing as Madelaine. Tonight, Ryan wore jeans and a button-down shirt--no sign of satin and pearls.

"Have you set a wedding date?" Ian asked.

"We want a June wedding." Contentment shone in Ryan's face as he lifted a large bowl from the conveyor belt and set it on the table. "Most of the planning is done and the invitations are ready to go out."

"That's great. Congratulations." Odd as it seemed to Ian, his brother-in-law's playboy leanings seemed to have disappeared along with his penchant for dressing as a woman.

"Sorry I'm late." A small man with thinning blonde hair arrived in the dining room, his breath coming in short gasps. "The auto shop was running late."

Linda frowned slightly. "They promised the car would be ready at seventeen-hundred hours."

"I-I'm sorry, Ms. Linda. One of their workers went home sick, so they were short-handed."

Linda patted the little man's hand. "Not to worry, David. I'm sure you came as quickly as possible while still driving safely."

"Yes' ma'am."

Ian leaned toward Rissa and whispered, "Isn't that one of Madelaine's kidnappers?"

"Now reformed. Could you resist the combined forces of both Madelaine and your mother?"

"I see what you mean."

"David, would you please help Ryan serve dinner." Linda smiled as she reached for her glass of water.

"I have a challenge to issue." Madelaine stood at the head of the table and tapped her water glass.

"We sisters--" she glanced at Daphne and Linda. "Have decided we need babies in our lives. Since we now have two happy and healthy young couples in this house, we are adding an incentive. Whoever produces a child first--after Ryan and Tiffany's wedding in June, of course--will have their pick of my collection of classic autos."

"I'm up for that," Ian agreed.

A gleam of challenge shone in Ryan's eyes as he smirked at Ian. "I think we should count from the wedding date. So you're already a year behind, my Scottish friend."

"We can make up for lost time," Ian stated. "Hand those oysters this way, would you?"

"Or maybe we should set a moratorium on practicing until after June." Ryan passed a bowl to Ian.

"Do you want a camera in your bedroom?" Ian asked. "Watch out for those potatoes behind you."

"Isn't that conveyor belt moving faster?" Rissa asked.

"I-I can handle this." David shuffled bowls and platters off the conveyor belt as fast as he could, yet more serving dishes came his way, faster and faster.

"It's been working just fine," Horace muttered as he ambled toward the conveyor belt.

The serving dishes were now rushing out, with David and Ryan trying to transfer them two and three at a time. Ian hurried over to lend a hand, but not soon enough to prevent a plate of biscuits from crashing to the floor. Ryan saved the bowl of gravy, but missed catching the beans as the food sped faster and faster.

The squash landed on top of the beans, followed quickly by the Brussels sprouts and a Jell-O salad.

"Uncle Horace--" Rissa joined the group trying to save the food.

"I know, I know," Horace muttered as he hurried from the room. "Turn it off!"

Outside, the sun smiled through the raindrops, arching a rainbow of iridescent colors across the sky, coming to rest on the steps leading inside the gray stone castle.

~The End~

The Gift

Christine Young

Dedication

To my niece Lucy, who was born on Valentine's Day

Chapter One

"Get in the house, now!"

"Mama?"

Elice Weld shielded her eyes and watched the ground fog rising in the distance. She didn't know what was coming her way, but she could guess. The rumors that a Union cavalry unit was in the vicinity had spread like a wildfire on a Kansas prairie.

Rain had fallen all morning. Now the clouds had separated, and the sun heated the earth, causing the evaporation of the water-soaked ground. The cavalry rode through the mist like dark, avenging wraiths bent on the destruction of all mankind. She could see seven men silhouetted on the horizon.

"Izzy, go." Elice didn't want to frighten her daughter but the urgency of the moment could not be denied.

"But mama?"

"Go to the cellar. Now."

"It's dark."

Izzy's voice echoed in Elice's head, filling her with a wild panic she didn't know how to stop. Every time soldiers approached she was terrified. The last four years had been the longest years of her life. "Do as I say, quickly." Elice hugged her daughter, turning her at the same moment and with a gentle shove sent her through the open door of her house.

"Izzy."

Elice knew the panic in her voice would mobilize her young daughter. She despised the fear and the terror. She loathed the war. She looked up. The fog was dissipating, and she could see the dark blue of the Union coats. She didn't have anything left for the soldiers to take. Good God, they'd taken everything already--everything save her daughter and her hope for the future.

She inhaled a quick breath then stood on the steps, hands folded together in front of her, watching the dark wraiths inch closer. She knew from experience she couldn't fight these men. She would do as they said and when they left, she would put the pieces of her life back together.

Until the next time...

"Mama," Elice jumped when her daughter tugged on her skirt before looking at her with sorrow-filled eyes. "Are the soldiers going to take my doll?"

"No," Elice ruffled her little girl's hair. "Go back inside. Go to the cellar and don't come out until I tell you it's safe."

"What about you?"

"I'll be fine." But Elice knew she might be lying to her child. She wasn't always fine when the soldiers invaded their home. "Now go and don't make me say it again. Stay there until I come for you."

Izzy nodded before she turned and walked through the parlor to the stairs leading to the cellar.

For a brief moment Elice smiled. The second was whimsical and fleeting. She had not wanted her daughter's life filled with this terror. She had not wished for the war. Although in the beginning she had joined the other Confederate women in sewing uniforms for the troops. It had all seemed so honorable and romantic.

What had she known about war? There was nothing romantic about the missing limbs of the returning soldiers, the letters telling of the deaths of young men and husbands, or the raping of the land and the women by the Union soldiers as well as the deserters from both armies. All she wanted was for this to be over.

Elice couldn't hear the orders from so far away, but in unison the men along with the commander dismounted. After taking the saddles from their horses and hobbling their own horse, each man seemed to have his own chores. Some put up tents, one man started a cook-fire, and others stood guard as if waiting for some rag-tag confederate army to invade the territory they had claimed as their own.

From the distance she felt the commander's gaze rest on her. Shivers traveled up her spine, and a cold sweat broke out on her forehead and between her breasts. She clenched her fists, willing her nerves not to betray her now.

The sun rested half way between its zenith and the top of the black birch trees on the horizon. She swallowed the lump in her throat and closed her eyes as she watched the commander of the Union cavalry unit take his hat from his head and slap the ride's dust from his trousers.

He paused for a moment as if he were having second thoughts about walking the distance between his troops and the house. Terror knifed through her when he finally made his decision and strode with measured strides her way.

He was too slender for his tall build. She guessed that at one time he'd filled out the uniform he wore with perfection. His hair was long, dark, and shaggy. He wore a mustache that curled downward in the fashion of the times. She had the uncanny thought she knew this man. But that wasn't possible. There was only one man she knew that had joined the Union, and she'd heard he died in some battle after Chancellorsville.

Her heart skittered to a stop before it started beating again. She didn't dare glance inside toward her daughter's hiding place in the cellar for fear she would give away her biggest secret. Oh, she knew he'd find out soon enough, and she prayed the commander was a gentleman and wouldn't stoop to hurt a child.

Every other time a unit had been in the vicinity her neighbors had given her warning. Not this time. There were too few of them left to give anyone warning.

Squaring her shoulders, she waited for the man. He would take the master bedroom and for the time he stayed, he would take over the house as his command center. She didn't know what battles were about to be fought near here. She wasn't sure she wanted to know.

She and her servants had taken shelter in the cellar several times when there had been small skirmishes.

"Mam," Bertha stood beside her. "You want me to check on

Izzy?"

"I wondered when you would get here," Elice sighed. "Yes, go inside and don't leave her alone. I'll take care of this man. Is your man out back?"

Bertha nodded. "He's going to stay safe unless you need him."

Elice smiled. "Good."

"You give him everything he wants. 'Cept you." Bertha turned then and walked to the door.

Elice heard the door squeak. It needed repair just as everything else on her farm did. Bertha and her man, Henry, had stayed with her through these long years. They'd earned their freedom long before Mr. Lincoln had declared all the Negroes were free. They had stayed and worked the farm even though she'd been unable to pay them.

A breeze sweeping down from the hills brought the scent of horses and men to her. She choked back the panic welling within.

"No," she whispered and the sound floated away on the breeze as the commander closed the distance between them. She backed up a step, wishing she could turn and run into the woods, wishing too she could bring out the rifle the last men here had confiscated and shoot a hole right through his black heart.

Her hands loosened and fluttered by her sides. She inhaled a sharp breath before raising her hands to rest at her throat. She shook her head, closing her eyes and opening them as if she could erase the sight walking towards her from her memories. She felt as if she were watching a ghost walk toward her.

"Not you. Not again," she said on such a low note that only the cat swishing its tail while he sat on the railing of her porch could have heard. "I guess the rumors were wrong. You didn't die."

Her bottom lip trembled and the words she wanted so much to say clung to her throat. *Go away. Please, go away.*

"Hello, Elice," the voice she'd dreaded floated around her, echoed inside her chest, hiding the erratic beat of her heart.

"What do you want?" she gasped out. She moved next to the cat and clung to the railing, holding on as best she could so her knees wouldn't buckle.

"A place to stay," he said and the timbre of his voice resonated in her soul. "A meal."

She shook her head and moistened her lips, daring herself to tell him what was on her mind. *You can go to hell.* She didn't dare. She didn't want to end up in a Yankee prison. Did he know what she'd done? Did he know she had left messages in the hollowed out trunk of an old oak tree when he'd been through these parts two years ago? If he'd been captured, she would not have felt happiness, but she'd done it to protect herself and her daughter.

"Your…" she brought her hand to her mouth, biting her knuckles to keep from telling him what she didn't want him to know.

"My?" he prompted her.

"You're not welcome here."

~ * ~

"I'm not going anywhere," he told her, smiling inside but not daring to show the young woman standing in front of him what he felt. He was damn glad to be alive and to be here, welcome or not.

Memories brought him back to another time and place--a place that existed at a different moment, almost as if it had never been. He watched the flush creep up her face--watched her lips thin and curl inward then her eyes narrow, small frown lines forming across her brow. He knew what a look like that meant. She wanted to tell him to go to hell. The words were bubbling inside her hot and steamy, like a potion in a witch's cauldron. Oh, and he was sure she'd love to give him a potion that would send him back from where he came.

"What do you want?" her question crisp and precise.

"Ah, but that isn't what you would like to say, is it?" he queried softly, the warm smile growing in his heart. He wanted to reach out and touch her cheek, brush the soft strawberry blond tendrils from her face.

"I'm sure that to the likes of you it doesn't matter what I think." She stood a bit straighter with those words as if the weight of what was happening here wasn't an emotional drain. All the while her blue eyes shimmered with fire and passion.

"You have too much courage for one so little," he told her, realizing the implications of the words and how true it was. With all that courage and so little rational thought, she was lucky to survive the war.

"Sir," one of his men approached.

His attention turned to the soldier addressing him. "Take one of the privates and set up a command unit in the den. Any incoming messages I want to see as soon as they arrive."

He heard her sharp indrawn breath. "You plan on staying?"

"I'll be here a couple of months." He turned in a full circle, looking at the landscape and for a moment his hand shielding his eyes. He searched for something, he wasn't sure what. But he had the uncanny feeling she was hiding something.

"You have servants still here?" he asked, wondering if anyone had stayed. He suspected the two older ones--what were their names? Bertha and Henry--would probably be here. They had always been loyal.

"You mean my blacks?" she asked her voice curt and laced with reprisals.

It was his turn to sigh. "Yes."

"They are free to come and go as they please. They don't have to wait on you even though I'm sure you expect them too. They don't have to do anything, because I don't have money to pay them."

"I won't be asking them to do anything. I was just curious."

Bertha strode from the door her arms spread wide. "Michajah Brooks, give me a hug. It's been so long and we've all been so worried about you."

Micha wrapped Bertha in his arms and hugged her then set her away from him, studying her for the longest second. "Why, you're just as pretty as the day I left." He grinned shamefully.

"You quit your flirtin'. Now you don't have to be telling me no lies. You best get inside and get washed up. I've got a pot of soup on the stove. It's not the best but it will fill your insides."

Micha gave a bow that would have done any southern gentleman proud. "Thank you. But I have to see to my men first. You, Henry, and Elice, need to eat first. Henry is still with you?"

Bertha beamed. "Yes, he is. He's hiding out in the backwoods to make sure you weren't deserters. He was going to show up with our rifle the minute there was trouble, if'n there was."

"There won't be any problems." He looked at Elice. *Unless she decides to go into a wild panic and do something crazy.* "You should all be safe--at least for the time being."

Elice stiffened but didn't retaliate with words that were about to burst from her.

"Bertha, would you go on into the house and see to that soup you said you have cooking?" Micha asked.

Bertha nodded and backed into the house her coloring slightly rosier than it had been when she first made her appearance.

Elice's chin jutted out. "We don't have enough soup to feed your men."

"We have rations. But is that fresh baked bread I smell?"

"Yes, but we only have enough for ourselves," she said pointedly.

"I'm sure Bertha won't mind cooking some more." He wasn't sure why he goaded her when all he wanted was to make amends. She had a crazy way of making him angry. She always had.

"We don't have flour." Elice shrugged for a moment, turning her back to him.

Elice was too thin yet her curves were still abundant beneath the dress he knew had once molded every curve exquisitely. "Check your cellar."

"The Union cavalry unit through here last summer took everything they didn't trample. There is nothing in the cellar or the pantry, sir." With that said she strode into the house. She looked up the stairs and around the room as if she searched for some elusive thread that might keep her from reacting to him more strongly than she already had. Not finding what it seemed she sought within herself, she marched up the stairs.

He heard a door shut with just a whisper. Every part of him tensed as if he waited for the tornado he was sure would follow. He knew the storm brewed. He just didn't know when she would unleash it on him. Yet he looked forward to it, hurricane or tornado, whatever blew his way.

He peeked into the kitchen. "Is it safe?" he asked.

Bertha plastered a huge smile on her aging cheeks and cackled happily. "Never you mind her, Micha. She's been through a lot since the war started and everyone she loved marched off to serve in the Confederate Army as if it was the grandest thing that ever happened to them."

"Everyone save me."

"We don't talk about that around here. She don't talk about you at all. But I hear her crying at night sometimes."

"Well?"

"Never you mind. There are some things a fellow can't be told. You're just going to have to figure this one out all on your own. You hurt her good when you left the first time. And then when you showed up the second time and left without even a goodbye…"

"I didn't have a choice," he said in self-defense.

"Pshaw, we've always got a choice. It's how we choose to use our time. I never took you for a coward, Michajah Brooks, but when you rode out of here in the dark of the night…"

He knew he wasn't going to convince Bertha of anything. He knew he wouldn't convince Elice of anything either. Where Elice was concerned, he was a coward.

"A fellow can't win," he said.

"There's nothing to be won or lost around here. The way I figure, everything already gone."

Micha didn't know how to answer. His stomach rumbled and for the moment there was a slice of warm bread sitting on a cracked and chipped blue plate he wasn't going to let get cold. "Much obliged," he said.

"There's no butter, jam, or honey. The last ones through here…"

"Smashed the hives?"

"Didn't leave…"

"Enough, Bertha, Mr. Brooks doesn't want to know how things have been or about our troubles. He's just come here to make things worse. You can go now. Go find Henry and make sure he gets enough to eat." Elice walked up to the kitchen table.

Truth told he hadn't come with that in mind at all. He'd asked for this house and this assignment, knowing that when the war was over and General Lee signed the papers of surrender, all hell would break loose. No matter what had gone on before and during the war between them, he meant to be here to protect her or at least pick up the pieces when things fell apart.

Micha knew Elice didn't think anything could get worse. He hoped he was wrong but when he thought about what was about to come sweeping over the horizon like a hoard of locusts, the hairs on the back of his neck stood on end.

He watched Elice look to Bertha then downward toward the cellar steps. He'd bet his last dollar Miss Elice Weld lied about something. Puzzles were always something he had enjoyed. He prayed this puzzle wasn't someone who would slit his throat in the middle of the night.

A bowl sat on a cutting board by the soup. He ladled a small portion into the bowl then sat down and enjoyed the soup. He watched Elice. She sat across from him, her hands folded in her lap, glaring at him. Appreciation for her courage and her convictions had always been something he'd admired in her. But now her fight was lost. She needed to figure out how she was going to survive this new situation--a new war for her if he guessed right.

As if reading his mind, she cleared her throat and spoke. "We've survived a lot more than you can dish out, Mr. Brooks."

"Micha," he reminded her.

She ignored him. "You'll be here and then you'll leave again. When you leave this time, don't come back."

"Is that an order?" he smiled while he chewed. The soup was delicious. But then Bertha had always been a great cook.

"You going to eat?"

She nodded. "When you're done and leave the room. I won't share meals with Yankees."

He grinned and sat back in the chair, crossing his arms in front of him. "Is that so? What if I decide to stay here until you eat?"

"I've always had more willpower than you."

His smile was broad. He leaned forward on his forearms. "I let you think you were more stubborn. And more times than I can count, I let you have the last word."

She turned from him as if his gaze was so hot it burned. He felt her hatred as well as her despair and fear. He needed to erase those feelings, but he'd long ago discovered the task was daunting.

He pushed back from the table and stood. "Private."

In less than a second, the soldier was in the kitchen. "Sir."

"Prepare the master bedroom."

He heard the sharp hiss of disapproval as well as resignation coming from Elice.

Chapter Two

"What are you hiding, Miss Elice?" Micha asked when she appeared in the kitchen for breakfast the next morning.

Elice's hand flew to her throat, surprised yet displeased at the same time. Despite all the obstacles the war had created, she had always prided herself in her ability to provide for her family. She smelled the real coffee, not the hickory stuff. A stack of flapjacks graced the once fine blue dinner plates her family had owned.

"Where did all this come from?" she asked, making a sweeping motion with her hands. "I can still put a meal on the table."

"You didn't answer my question."

She ignored him. "Mr. Michajah Brooks, you tell me right now where the food came from, or I'm going to toss it all out back for the pigs."

She heard Bertha's gasp of outrage. "Never you mind, missy. You don't throw God's work in his face for stubborn pride. Besides, we don't own any pigs."

Elice sat down, defeated again, yet hearing her stomach rumble. Her first thoughts went to Izzy. She glanced quickly at Bertha. Seeing the woman nod, her heart stopped pounding quite so hard. Bertha had seen to Izzy first.

"My company's mess wagon showed up early this morning. Bertha was more than willing to make breakfast for everyone."

Elice looked at Bertha and she sent her a knowing smile with a cock of her head toward the cellar.

"I'm going to have to visit that cellar of yours," Micha said, looking pointedly at the two women.

"No," both Elice and Bertha chimed in unison.

Micha smiled and let the fingers of one hand drum on the kitchen table. He forked a bite of flapjacks and chewed slowly, watching Elice with a feral gleam in his eyes. She found herself nauseous with fear.

"After I finish my breakfast, I'm thinking I'll take a look for myself." He sipped his coffee, a luxury to Elice in these hard times.

Elice felt the color drain from her face. She didn't want Micha of all people to discover Izzy. But she couldn't keep the little girl hidden away much longer. Sooner or later, she would have to introduce the two. But she didn't have to tell him the truth about the child. He could believe what he wanted to believe.

"Sir," his second in command poked his head inside the door. "I have something for you."

"I'll see to it in the den. How important is it?" he asked.

"I think this one can wait for your attention. The messenger said it wasn't urgent."

"Good," Micha finished his plate then his coffee. He leaned toward Elice. "It's not hickory."

"No, and I'm supposed to thank you for that? Thank you," Elice said with a note of sarcasm in her voice. She reminded herself she should be a bit sweeter to this man. He had the power of life or death over her. He could determine if she would stay in her home or languish in a Union prison camp. She needed to keep her horrible temper in check. She'd done so often enough in the last few years. With this man it was different. It was personal.

"You're welcome," he said with a grin that had a way of infuriating her. "Now about the cellar, am I supposed to guess what is down there or can the two of you come up with a plausible answer?"

Bertha cleared her throat and looked from Elice to Micha, "All of the armies that have come through here have raided our cellar. We were just hoping you wouldn't do the same. And from the looks of it, you have enough food."

"I do," he stared at Elice long enough to make her squirm.

"You've never been a very good liar, Elice, or you Bertha. If you will swear an oath you don't have a Confederate spy hiding down there, I'll let it go for now."

She let out a long breath, stiffening her shoulders and scowling at him. "I've learned a lot since you deserted us, one of them is how to lie."

"Elice," Bertha said.

"Well, I wanted to tell him we aren't lying. And there is no spy in our midst--that I know of." Lord, how she wanted to end this battle between them. But she couldn't let it go. When he found out about Izzy, he'd never forgive her. She had been married. Charles Tickner had been her husband for about three hours before he rode off and was killed in the first battle of Bull Run. But she didn't think Micha knew about any of that.

"No, you still can't lie at least not to anyone who knows you," he said smoothly. He leaned forward again, "And I think I probably know you better than anyone else."

She stared at her food, no longer able to eat or make eye contact with him. There were times she'd been so hungry she wanted to cry-- times when she'd given all her food to Izzy. Micha wouldn't understand any of that.

"I've changed more than you could ever guess."

"Haven't we all," he said. "Now, I've inches of trail dirt on me, and I would dearly like a bath and perhaps a shave."

"I'll get…"

"No you won't, Bertha. He has men to bring him hot water. That's not your job." She blushed slightly, thinking of Micha naked in her tub. She remembered other times…happier times.

"You could join me," he said, a smile quirking the corners of his mouth.

"Don't taunt me."

"Well then, I would like your gentle ministrations when I'm done. I need a haircut and a shave. My men don't have gentle fingers, and I'm looking for something with a little more style than what the soldiers I ride with can give me."

13

"Do I have a choice?" she asked sweetly, smiling at him as if they were in a southern parlor and he was courting her. The courting had taken place a long time ago. Then he'd left her alone and terrified.

"There is always a choice," he told her. "Are you afraid?" He sent out a challenge to her.

"I'm not afraid of you," she told him. *I'm terrified of what you make me feel. I didn't think I'd ever be able to feel again.*

"Then I'll see you in the bathing room in about ten minutes," he told her, leveling his gaze at her. His steel blue eyes sending shivers of heat down her spine, making her remember when she had longed to touch him--a time when she would have jumped at this chance.

"You're not afraid of me? I'll be holding the razor."

"I'm not afraid. You couldn't kill a flea, let alone a person." She wondered if she should tell him she'd already killed two men, two deserters whose uniforms were so tattered you could barely make out which army they were from. They were two men who had threatened her and Izzy. Henry had killed the third soldier.

"You two had best behave yourselves. I won't be accountable for cleaning up any blood," Bertha shot out at them.

Micha let out a whoop of laughter. Elice looked the other way to hide her reaction from the discerning gaze of the soldier sitting so confidently in her kitchen. A man who had just walked into her life as if nothing had happened between them--as if five years hadn't passed since he'd left her alone and frightened.

Before she knew what had happened, Micha stood behind her, keeping her from escaping. She couldn't move her chair and she didn't dare show her fear by trying to escape out the one thin space he'd left her. He touched the back of her neck, ran his finger across her shoulder until it rested next to the fabric of her dress. She shivered from the heat of the touch.

"I'm glad you're not indifferent to me," he whispered, bending low and letting his breath whisper across her cheek.

"I'm not sleeping with you, Michajah Brooks."

"I don't recall asking," he told her. "And by the way, he warned as he moved away from her, "I'm going to discover all your secrets."

~ * ~

He listened to the soft sound of slippered feet at the door. Then a hesitant knock before he heard her enter the tiny room. He let his head rest on the back of the tub, planning the next steps to winning over Elice Weld.

"I have bath sheets for you." Her voice was unsure and Micha didn't like the vulnerability he heard.

"Come in," he said. *If you have the courage to confront the man you love.*

The silence that followed unnerved him. He'd wanted so badly to pick up the pieces from where they'd left off five long years ago. He'd been a fool to think picking up the pieces would be remotely possible. A long campaign would only wear her down. The skirmishes would not make her love him, nor would it regain her trust in him.

The door creaked open. The creak was one of a long list of things to do to help Elice with the upkeep of her home. He'd already set his men repairing fences as well as the land for spring planting. He'd talked to them for a long time about the work, and the men he'd brought with him were all willing to help out before they traveled home. Some said it was a hell of a lot better than fighting.

"I'll put them on the shelves here. Don't let me bother you." She stared openly at him for a half-second before flushing crimson and turning her back on him. But she didn't leave the room.

Do you like what you see? he wanted to ask. "You would never bother me. You can stay," he told her. "Wash my back."

"When pigs fly."

He grinned. That held shades of the woman he loved. "You don't have any," he said. "So that's hardly fair."

Her shoulders stiffened and the steel rod in her spine couldn't get any straighter. He needed to find a way to bring back the woman he once knew without changing the indomitable courage that seemed to have become her calling card.

Buck naked he rose from the bath, water sluicing from his skin.

He heard her slight gasp, and he wondered if he had just made a huge mistake. She'd seen him naked before. Inwardly, he sighed. One step backward and two steps forwards sometimes worked. He stepped from the tub. He wondered if the wounds on his body upset her. She didn't look upset just curious.

"Could you hand me a bath sheet," he asked nonchalantly.

Her beautiful azure eyes were huge. He watched her swallow then lift her chin a notch. She unfolded a sheet and walked to him, holding it out. He didn't mean to make this too easy for her. But he also didn't want to scare her away. He let her get within a few inches before taking the sheet from her. He wrapped it around his waist and grabbed another sheet from the counter where she'd set the rest of them. He towel dried his hair and chest then sat down on a chair near the tub.

"I'm ready anytime you are. Do you want to change your mind?"

"I'm not afraid of a Yankee soldier, if that's what you're asking," she said as she put the scissors and the razor on a table near the chair where he sat.

"Maybe you should be."

She ignored him. "Scoot the chair out so I can get around the back," she said, the tone in her voice told him her courage returned full force.

He obliged with a smile and a nod. At the moment, teasing her didn't seem like a great idea so he rested his hands in his lap and let her work her magic. When she ran her fingers through his hair, he closed his eyes and clenched his fists, wishing for things that couldn't be right now. Beneath his ribs his heart thundered as loud as stampeding horses. When she smoothed the soap across his jaw and upper lip, he hardened. When she moved in front of him, his legs spread wide to let her stand between them. He understood a need so great he'd do everything in his power to convince Elice Weld he deserved another chance.

He groaned.

She paused, the razor hovering near his upper lip. "Are you all right?" she asked.

"Just dandy," he said, wondering why he'd wanted to torture himself. One of his men could have done this.

Ah, but not as well as Elice and not with her breasts an inch away from his mouth, not with the scent of vanilla lingering and swirling around him, enticing every sense he possessed.

"Do you want me to take off the mustache?"

"Yes," he choked out. When he made love to her, he wanted to feel every soft and gentle touch of her finger tips.

Thinking about making love brought an unconscious reaction from him. Without giving it a second thought, he brought his hands to her hips. His fingers tightened, his thumbs and hands exploring while he still had the chance.

Startled, the razor nicked his cheek. "That's probably not such a good idea," she whispered.

"What?" he asked, knowing full well of what she spoke.

"Touch me," she whispered raggedly.

"I thought you would never ask," he said smoothly but let his hands drop to lap once again.

"Michajah!"

"Sorry," he said a bit sheepish. *I'm not sorry one little bit.*

Elice caught her lip with her upper teeth, watching him. Micha knew she was wary, but her response to him wasn't all negative. Hope was all he wanted. She wiped the spots of soap from his face. He watched her every move, wishing he could read her mind and praying perhaps she would soften toward him.

A din rose from outside the bathing room, growing with each passing moment. Micha could make out Bertha's voice and one of his men's. The shouting grew louder.

"What the devil?"

"Stop."

"You're hurting me." The paper thin wail sent shivers down Micha's spine.

Elice's face turned ashen. She dropped the razor in the sink and turned to the door.

"No," he said, "let me see what's happening."

She shook her head, a wild panic shimmering in her eyes. "No," she said.

He wasn't used to anyone disobeying his orders, and he'd thought he'd made it clear what he wanted her to do. "Don't be foolish. Stay put."

The sound of a smaller voice came through the door--then a roar of pain from one of his men and swearing. The cursing grew louder.

"Izzy," the whispered word stopped him.

He turned but the loud din sent him bolting through the door without a thought to his safety.

Bertha was wrestling on the floor with his second in command. A little girl was on top pummeling his officer who had his hands around his head, shielding the blows raining down on him. And Elice stumbled into him when he stopped, totally awed by the ludicrous scene.

"Sergeant!" he said. "Stop."

"I would if they'd get off me," he said weakly, hiding his head again from the little girl's punishing blows.

"Yankee, get away from her. I hate you, all of you." the little girl cried out.

Elice rushed past him. "Izzy, stop. You're going to hurt someone." Rushing past Micha, Elice scooped the little girl into her arms.

"But they're the enemy," she cried out, clearly appalled at finding Union soldiers in her home.

Elice snuggled the little girl in her arms, tears running down her cheeks. Micha felt a moment of reality. So, this is what Elice had been afraid of him discovering. But he'd never been cruel. He would never hurt the child. He wondered who's child Izzy was. So many families had lost mothers and fathers.

He strode closer to the pair and knelt down so he was eye level with the little girl. The child glared at him with azure blue eyes and pushed back into Elice's body, hiding her face.

"Who do we have here?" he asked in the gentlest and softest voice he'd ever used.

Chapter Three

"Are you going to take my mama away?" Izzy blurted out, tears of anger sliding down her cheeks.

Still kneeling in front of the little girl, Elice watched Micha console her little girl. "No," he said, "I would never take anyone's mother away from them. You don't have anything to be afraid of here."

He turned to Elice. "Izzy is yours?" he asked, the condemnation in his eyes.

And yours. "Yes," she said, knowing Micha was doing the mental math that would take him back to Izzy's conception. She would have to find a way to stop him.

"My daddy's a brave soldier," Izzy offered innocently, not understanding the dynamics going on between the two adults.

"And who is your daddy?" Micha asked.

"He's tall and he's brave and handsome too. Mama says so."

"I see," Micha said softly, brushing a lock of the little girl's hair from her eyes.

Then he stood and looked pointedly at Elice, who felt his gaze burn through all the defensive walls she'd surrounded herself with.

"Let's go into the parlor," Elice said softly, not wishing to explain but knowing she'd have to offer him something tangible to hang onto.

"Come on, Izzy," Elice placed the little girl's hand in her own and together they walked into the parlor. They walked together, just as they would weather this storm together.

The parlor had once been an elegant sitting room for the Weld family. Five years was not a long time and if everything had been normal, the room would look just as wonderful as it once had. But Yankee soldiers had been through this house more than once. The arm chair Micha sat in had graced the room for eight years, but now a bayonet had ripped through it. She and Bertha had mended it best they could. The knick knacks that had been set lovingly on the tables and counters had all been stolen or broken, and the paint on the wall was peeling now. She couldn't afford the luxury of paint or wallpaper even if the Union boats had let a ship through. All the ships that made it through the barricade carried weapons and food for the troops.

"Maybe I should take Izzy to the kitchen for a snack," Bertha said, having lost her usual cheery disposition.

"He's nice. Mama said so," Izzy added as Bertha took her hand and led her from the parlor.

Elice watched the muscle in Micha's neck tick and his hands clench. "What are you angry about?"

"Wouldn't you be mad?" he returned. "Under the same situation--how long did you wait?"

Her hands in front of her, she shook her head with disbelief. "It doesn't matter. A lot has happened. A person has to survive. I did what I had to do, and I have no regrets." If she had planned to tell him about Izzy, the thought vanished with his crude condemnation of her actions.

"Is Izzy your brave soldier's daughter?" he asked, pacing the room finally to stand in front of the window that looked out on small lake and a gazebo.

Elice remembered the long lazy summer days when the water had been cold and the air hot. It had been a place to dream and plan futures that would never come true.

"Izzy's father is none of your business," she said through clenched teeth, knowing she lied, but not willing to tell him what he wanted to know--at least not yet. She had demons to erase from her heart and her soul before she could explain what had been such a beautiful yet painful memory.

"You're wrong. Everything that goes on here is my business," he told her, his voice taking on an edge she'd never heard before.

She strode to him, her fury growing. "Is that a threat, sir?" she asked as he turned slowly toward her. "Don't threaten me, Michajah."

"It's a promise, Elice. I hold your very life and wellbeing in my hands. You should take great care here."

"You want to pry into my private life then," she said, squaring her shoulders and readying for a battle she was unwilling to fight yet seemed to loom on the horizon.

He inhaled deeply, shaking his head. "No, but I do need to know if a man is going to be coming home. I don't like surprises."

"And you think I do? Don't you know your showing up on my doorstep was not something I eagerly anticipated?"

"You didn't seem too disappointed," he said.

"Disappointed," she said her heart pounding and her stomach churning. She sat down, barely able to breathe. Her face felt clammy and she swallowed hard to keep from fainting.

He poured her a glass of water. "Drink this. It will make you feel better."

No, nothing would make her feel better. Even the truth now that she'd let this go so far would not make anyone feel better. She sipped the water, holding on to the glass while he continued to pace.

"Tell me," he paused mid-stride and turned toward her. "About Izzy's father."

"What do you want to know?"

"Everything. You say he's a soldier. Confederate, I presume."

"Yes, no," she corrected herself, unsure what she should or should not say.

"You're not going to make this easy, are you?" he asked, running his fingers through his hair, watching her, and waiting.

"I don't know what you mean," she said. She couldn't think. She didn't want to play mind games with him. She didn't want to hear the recriminations he would silently say when he knew she'd married so soon after confessing her undying love for him. But he'd left her. Gone off to war without a thought--no, he'd put more thought into what he did than most of the people in her life. *For Izzy's sake I had to find a way to survive. Just as I do now.*

"Could we start with a name?" he asked, his politeness setting her nerves on edge.

She didn't want to tell him she'd married one of his best friends. A man he'd been so close to he'd called him brother. A lone tear slipped down her cheek. She wiped it away with the back of her hand.

"You love him that much?"

She looked at the ceiling then out the window, unable to look at the man she did love.

"Come on, Elice, meet me half way here."

She looked at him, tears welling in the back of her throat. "Charlie."

The silence between them seemed to stretch on forever. She could have sworn the tension was so thick she could have sliced it with a knife.

"Tickner?" he queried softly, as if he tried to hide his anger. They had all been friends once a long time ago.

She had always been wary when his voice lowered to such a deadly softness. The anger had never been directed her way before. She nodded and wiped away another tear.

"I see," he said. For a moment he left the room. The silence rose up to surround her. She didn't dare move. If she ran, he'd find her. Even when Yankee soldiers had swept through here, she had not felt this debilitating fear. Minutes later he returned.

"You don't see anything," she told him, rising and walking to him. "You have no idea."

"I've only asked for the truth here. Was our bed even cold before you slept with my best friend?"

I never slept with Charles. She shook her head, denying his anger, denying her own bitterness. "You have no idea."

He laughed and the sound echoed in the parlor. Nothing would ever be the same. *Of course, you ninny, did you ever think we would go back to the good old days of care free parties and unrequited love?*

"So, Izzy is Charles' daughter." She turned away again. Unable to tell him Izzy was not Charles' daughter.

"The truth, Elice," he gritted out. "Just tell me and I'll try to understand. I'll take care of you if Charles doesn't come home."

"Charles is dead," she told him bluntly. "He died in the first battle of Bull Run. He wasn't a very good soldier. Not like you."

"What is that supposed to mean?"

"Nothing. Everything. He was always your sidekick. If you would have gone to war with him, he would have lived. You would have made sure nothing bad happened to him. He would have had someone to guard his back."

"For your sake? I doubt that."

"No, it wouldn't have mattered. He wasn't as strong as you were--are. He liked poetry and art. He loved the finer things. When you were out riding or fighting or even drinking, he was painting. He didn't stand a chance against bullets and bayonets."

"I didn't know you were in love with him. If you were, you had a strange way of showing it."

I wasn't. "Izzy never saw him." How on earth was she going to skirt the truth without lying to him? She wasn't a very good liar. Indeed, she was shocked he hadn't seen through this lie already.

"What are you leaving out?" he asked.

"How old is she?"

"Three," Elice said. "She is three years old."

She watched him looking as if she was counting backwards and knew what his next question would be. But he didn't ask.

Instead he turned and once again walked from the room. She rose too and following in his footsteps, left the room. She walked to the gazebo and sat down, watching the breeze make ripples in the water and wondering what would happen next.

~ * ~

He stood at the entrance to the gazebo, hat in hand. "I was going to pick you flowers but..." He held out one small purple crocus, wondering where he would start--how he would begin to court her while trying to put the past in the back of his mind.

"The last time we were here you brought me..."

23

"Daisies if I recall," he told her with a smile.

"The crocus is beautiful." He gave it to her and for a moment she held the delicate spring flower in the palm of her hand. He leaned in through one of the openings and she put the flower in his buttonhole.

"Your smile is just as beautiful as it was then. Just looking at you and seeing your happiness lights up my day." He walked around the gazebo to the front and up the steps with a slow measured pace, watching her.

"Yellow daisies," she murmured as he sat down beside her. She gazed at him the way she used to look at him, her eyes shimmering and her smile making her so beautiful his breath caught and he had trouble speaking.

Picking up her hand and placing it in his, he turned it over. "You have calluses." He traced each one with a fingertip.

She tried to pull away, her smile as well as the beauty of the sunny day vanishing. "I haven't had a life of leisure. If that offends you--"

"Don't be absurd. As you've told me, you've changed. I want to make changes in your life now. I need to right some of the wrongs the war has done to you and your child."

"What about your home? Your family. The war must have taken its toll on them. Micha, I don't need or want charity."

"They're fine. The home wasn't touched and my sister is an avenging angel of mercy." He rubbed tiny circles on the underside of her wrist and reveled in her response. The passion in her eyes was enough to set him on fire.

"We can't pick up where we left off. Too much has happened," she tried to pull her hand away but he placed it on his chest.

"Hear my heart? It beats for you. I know nothing will ever be the same, but let me help. See what we can achieve together."

She rose, walking to the side of the gazebo facing the pond. "Remember when we used to swim here? The rope is still there." She pointed to the tree where the rope swing still fluttered in the breeze. She knew changing the subject would not deter him for long, but for the moment, it gave her a small measure of security and perhaps even peace.

He walked up behind her and rested his hands on the railing. She stood between his arms. She let her head fall back on his chest, leaning into him, and for the moment, letting him shield her from the wrongs dealt her.

"I'm sorry," he told her. "I'm apologizing for all that happened to you."

She turned to face him, her fingertip tracing his jaw. "You can't apologize for something you're not sorry for. You believed in the preservation of the Union. You believed what you did was right. I'm never going to question your purpose. It is done and in the past."

"Still, I seek forgiveness. No one deserves to lose their husband in war. No one should have to bring up a child without a father." He paused, wondering if he dare tell her his plans. Yet she deserved to know. "I've sent some of my men for supplies."

She broke away from him, facing him with her arms crossed in front of her. "I don't want your charity. I've survived everything that has been thrown my way. I--"

"Hush now," he placed a finger on her lips. "Let me do this for you. It's not charity. I don't want you to lose everything you've worked so hard for. My men have already repaired one of the fences. We will do more."

He watched anger flush her cheeks. He knew she would react this way, but he hoped she would come around to seeing things his way. He loved her. And if not for the war, he was sure they would have wed. He hoped they would make a home for themselves here. He thought perhaps there had been a good reason when she turned to Charlie. He didn't think she'd loved him. If he lived here, the land would not be stolen from her from the surge of humanity who was sure to swoop to the southern states, looking for the next victim to their greed.

She turned away from him again. Her silence told him more than he wanted to know.

"This isn't going to be easy, is it? How can I convince you?"

"After Charles died, I prayed you would come back for me. I watched the sun set every evening and wished I could see you riding along the horizon, waving and yelling the war was over. I had grandiose ideas of life being just the same. Crazy, wasn't I? I thought the world hadn't changed."

"We can't pick up where we left off, but if you allow it, we can start over." He pulled the hair away from the back of her neck, lightly massaging her stiff, strained muscles.

"We can't pick up at all. You have to go." She sighed and leaned into him, seeming to revel in his ministrations.

"Of course we can."

"What about Izzy?"

"I'll adopt your daughter. And I'll love her as if she is my own." He turned her again, so very hesitant and for the first time in his life unsure of Elice and her feelings toward him. He wanted her to love him again. He needed her to be part of his life. He still loved her, had never stopped loving her.

"Can you really be happy knowing I married Charles?" she asked her hands on his chest as if she meant to push him away.

"If you're by my side, I can be happy."

"When we go to bed at night, the thought of him beside me won't bother you?"

"I won't lie. The thought will always make me angry. But our relationship is about us, no one else."

She shook her head then moistened her lips. Her face took on a far away expression as if she couldn't erase the other man from her mind or her bed.

"What about you?" she asked. "Did you ever sleep--fall in love?" Her eyes shimmered with moisture.

"No, I've never fallen in love." *Except with you.*

"Really," she said softly as if she remembered her times with Charles. He could no longer think of him as his best friend. "He married me to help," she told him.

"You can believe that if you want. I don't for a second. Why would he marry you unless he loved you and you loved him?"

She looked down for a moment, long sooty lashes lowering to shield her eyes. "He did."

"No," he said, and put a finger beneath her chin. He didn't want her looking down again. He needed her looking at him. He wanted her to look forward, not backward. He needed to see her indomitable courage.

Her hands rested on his shoulders and he brought his hands up to cradle her head. She was soft and so feminine. Her beauty went soul deep. She was kind and considerate. She had always taken a stand for creatures and people less fortunate than herself. He loved her. He had loved her from the moment he first set eyes on her. She was four years younger than he was, and so he'd had to wait for her to grow up. He had been eighteen and she was only fourteen. At the time, he hadn't known it was love. He'd thought her cute and vivacious. But there was always something about her that tugged on his heart strings. Then he waited until she was nineteen to court her. She had been twenty when they first made love in the moonlight.

His thumbs rested at the base of her neck. He felt her pulse quicken. He moistened his lips, watching her, waiting for her to say no or yes. He lowered his lips to hers with the gentlest care.

Her sweet scent, vanilla, filled him. Her softness was an aphrodisiac he could not deny. She didn't pull away and he thanked God for that. Slowly, he deepened the kiss, letting his tongue run along the seam of her lips, silently begging her to surrender to his gentle care. His own pulse thrummed with anticipation and his heart sped. He needed to stop this before he frightened her.

Yet he couldn't. He needed her too damn much. Her soft siren's sound sent another wave of heat pulsing through him. She opened for him. He explored her, tasted her, and he wanted her more than he'd ever wanted anything. But his feelings went beyond want. He needed her. He needed her to cleanse his soul, to erase the horrific images he'd seen--the ground covered in blood and bodies. Everything saturated--the drums, the bugles, the rifle shots and the screams of men and horses as they lay dying.

He closed his eyes and let his mind wander back to the beautiful woman he held in his arms. The sweetness he knew once again, a sweetness he'd dreamt of every night.

Her tongue touched his and he heard himself moan. Her fingers rose from his shoulders to run through his hair. He didn't want to let go of the moment. He traced her teeth, the inside of her mouth, touched every part of her and remembered a time when he'd been deep inside her warmth.

A shot rang out and then the repeating rifles of his men beat a rapid staccato. He pulled away from her, survival instincts taking hold of his body. He brought her down to the ground, shielding her with his body then easing his way to see what was going on.

"What the devil," he said. Then, "Stay put."

Chapter Four

The hell I will.

Elice watched Micha run low to the ground in the direction of the gun shots and yelling. She wanted to put her hands on her ears, needed to hear the peaceful silence of the winter day. Instead she followed, doing as he did, keeping low and trying to stay behind whatever cover she could find until she reached the house. Her heart beat a rapid staccato beneath her ribs. Sweat beaded on her forehead.

She had done this same thing more than once, and she never wanted to run and hide again. She never wanted to worry about her daughter living through the day again or having to hide in the cellar. Micha turned from the house and moved toward the shooting.

"Micha, what--where are you going--doing?"

"I told you to stay at the gazebo," he stopped behind a tree, his back against it as he held out his arms to her. She ran into them. He pulled her close, tucking her head beneath his chin. "You have to take care of yourself--for Izzy."

"I don't have to be reminded of my daughter," she felt guilty and chastised all at the same time.

"I didn't mean you did, but this could be dangerous."

"Go inside with me, please," she said. She didn't want to lose him again. She didn't want to lose anyone else she loved. "Don't go."

His laugh sounded small and bittersweet. "I'm a soldier. This is what I do." He ran his fingers through her hair, pulling her closer even while he was pushing her away.

Lord, but he smelled of the mint scented soap she'd given him to bathe with. She inhaled a long breath as if the needed oxygen would give her the courage she didn't possess. "What are you going to do?"

"I'm going to find out if my men are all right. There shouldn't be any troops around here, confederate or union. All our correspondence has signaled the legitimate troops are in other parts of the countryside. But there are always deserters to consider."

"And then?" she lifted her head to look into his eyes. He had the most beautiful eyes, deep, dark and so brown. She could drown in their secret depths. She had done that very thing once a long time ago, a lifetime ago.

"And then I'm going to find you and we're going to have a talk. We need to," he stopped. More gunshots broke out. She hadn't even realized it had been quiet for the last few minutes.

"Go," she told him. "Do what you have to do and then come back to me."

"Find Izzy and Bertha."

"They'll be fine. I'm sure they've gone to the cellar." She touched his cheek, felt the slight stubble there and she prayed he would stay safe.

"Where Izzy hid for a day and a half? You must have been so frightened of me. I thought you could trust me."

"Men change," she said. He kissed her quickly on the cheek and let her go. Life changes and it doesn't seem to get better. Although she admitted to herself that perhaps with his return, life would be easier. She didn't want to hope too much. She didn't want her heart to break again.

"Stay down," she heard him say and when she turned to wave at him, he was gone. Her heart skipped a beat, and she felt the quick and sudden rise of tears to the back of her throat. She swallowed down the fear and the terror. Gun shots erupted again. *Okay, I've been through worse. Get on my feet and do what I have to do.*

She ran then. She ran and stumbled her way to the house, staying low and trying to keep the fear from freezing her in her tracks.

"Izzy," she cried out. The back door slammed behind her as she ran through the house to the entrance to the cellar.

"Izzy," she called out again. Her little girl's name echoed in the tiny, dark space. "Izzy, Bertha, anyone here." She called their names even though she knew they wouldn't leave their hiding place.

The cellar smelled of damp earth. Elice stopped, curbing her blind panic to a calm she didn't comprehend. She rubbed her arms in an attempt to ward off the cold fear seeping into the marrow of her bones. "Izzy, it's me. Bertha, it's okay. You can come out."

Met with dead silence, Elice's heart beat wildly. Cold sweat ran between her breasts. "No," she whispered into the darkness.

"No." My God, had she lost her mind? "Duck pond," she whispered, feeling giddy at the remembered password. "Duck pond," she said a bit louder.

Before she could see anything in the blackness, she heard a giggle then a flicker of light from a lantern being lit.

"We didn't think you were ever going to say it," Izzy giggled again. "Did you forget, mama? You made me practice saying it so many times. I didn't think anyone would ever forget."

"I did forget," she closed Izzy in her arms. Elice gazed at Bertha who was shaking her head. "I was so afraid, I forgot." She pulled her tighter, closing her eyes and praying for Micha. "Where is Henry?"

"Henry stayed in the barn. Land sakes, child. I'm not surprised. With so much going on out there and half the rebel army swooping down on us--where's your Micha?"

"I don't know. You two scoot now and get back in there. I'm going to find out if it's safe to come out. I don't hear any shelling and I suspect Captain Brooks' troops got rid of the Confederates. He should be back shortly, and it will be like nothing ever happened."

"We shouldn't be wishing for the Confederates to lose," Elice said as she stood by the door to their hiding place.

"We're wishing the war to end, that's all. Don't you start feelin' guilty about anythin', child. This old war has gone on far too long, and it's time for people to stop shooting at each other."

"All right then, I'll be back as soon as I know it's safe." Elice shut the door behind her and the tiny flicker of light floating from beneath the door vanished when Bertha extinguished the flame.

Nerves stretched tight, heart beating hard, Elice made her way upstairs with cautious footsteps. Before she stepped into the hallway, she inhaled then held her breath. The door squeaked on its hinges as she pushed it open. Peeking out the small crack, she didn't see anything nor did she hear anyone. Cautiously, she stepped into the walkway. No one appeared. The silence greeting her sent a chill down her spine. She couldn't hear bullets or men.

"Mam."

"What! Oh my, God." her hand went to her throat, her hand trembled and she stumbled, throwing her hand against the wall to stop her downward fall.

"I'm sorry. I didn't mean to frighten you"

Elice swallowed hard and waved her hand in front of her face. *You didn't frighten me, you terrified me.* "Say no more. I'll recover. Private Thompson, is it?"

"Yes mam," he said. "The captain wanted me to tell you they were chasing the Johnnies and he'd get back to you later. He also said he had some things to do before he saw you again, but his troops were going to stay here and guard the house. Not to worry, everything will be fine."

She nodded. *Not to worry, if it were only that easy.* "Then it's okay to let my little girl and Bertha come upstairs?" she asked watching the boy in front of her, a boy who had turned into a man faster than he should have.

"How old are you?" she asked.

He blushed.

"Never mind. I guess I've forgotten my manners. Can you come have a cup of coffee? It's your company's coffee. Micha brought it."

"No mam, I've got to get back to the troops. I was just sent to relay the message."

"I understand." Elice said softly. She leaned against the wall and watched him before she ran down the steps. "Duck pond," she called out.

Izzy and Bertha tumbled from the room. "Can we have dinner now?" Izzy asked.

"Of course, child, I'll go see what the nice captain left for us. I haven't had so much food in the cupboard since before the war. We might even get a choice," Bertha said with a little cackle that might have passed for a laugh in a happier time.

"I'm going to watch the road for a little while," Elice told them. "I want to make sure what the private said is true. Trust is a new concept for these parts."

"Where's Captain Brooks?" Bertha asked.

"He's left." *Seems to be the story of my life. My men always show up, kiss me once then leave.*

~ * ~

"My God, it's Jedediah." Micha pinned the man dressed in butternut to the ground. When he rolled him over, he saw the man clearly. At one time they had been friends. They had grown up part of the privileged south. They had attended the Virginia Military Institute together.

"Micha?"

"Do I let you up and send you home, or do I put you in chains and send you to a prison camp?" Micha wondered, staring at a man he hadn't seen in five years.

"God, it was so long ago. We were wrestling on this very land, but it hadn't meant life or death then."

"No, it didn't. I can't seem to recall much from those years. You don't look so good. Why were you at the Weld place?" Micha asked, helping his friend up from the ground and dusting the dirt from his own pants and shirt.

"Why are you?" he countered. "She's married. You can't have her."

"Widowed," Micha said softly, the words echoing in his chest like a sorrow-filled song. He didn't want to think about her wedding another man. Didn't want to know she hadn't really loved him. Micha turned from his friend, looking in the direction of the Weld home.

"I didn't know," he said. "Still doesn't give you leave to go snoopin' around her. She's a fine lady and the way I see this situation, you too had your chance and you chose to leave her. You're just going to hurt her again."

Micha's fists tightened. He bent over to pick up his hat, giving himself a moment for the surging anger he felt to cool down. He inhaled and stared hard at Jed. "The way I see it, you don't have any rights to the lady either. And at the moment, being nice to me is going to determine just where you go when you leave here."

"I was heading home. The war won't last much longer so if you send me to a Yankee prison camp, I guess it doesn't matter. I'll be home before the year is out."

"You want to bet your life on that?" Micha asked.

"I'm not usually a gambling man but yes. The south can't hold out much longer," Jed said. "I served my time. I'm taking the uniform off and planting my spring crop if you give me a chance. If not," he shrugged, "at least I'll be alive."

"No more yelling about state's rights or--" Micha walked to the campfire his men had built in preparation for the night.

"No," was Jed's reply. "What are you going to do with my men?"

"Haven't decided," Micha said. He wanted to send them home too. But he wasn't sure how his commanders would look at the idea. If they promised not to pick up arms again, maybe he could justify sending them back to their families.

"Best you make up your mind pretty soon."

"Why?"

Jed shrugged. "Could be more of us coming, more who wouldn't take lightly to the imprisonment of some of their own--by their own."

Micha motioned for Jed to sit down. They watched the sparks from the campfire float lazily into the darkening sky. They listened to the night sounds both of them had heard so many times waiting for the battle of the next day. This time there wasn't going to be a battle. This time everyone was going home alive.

"If there are reinforcements, I hope they are in better condition than your men. Coffee?" he asked.

"Captain Brooks, the wagon's here," one of the pickets called out.

Micha rose and strode to the wagon which was piled high with all kinds of things, a feeling of guilt washing over him. He should have talked to her first, told her exactly what was in the wagon. The attack had given him good reason to ride out to meet the wagon load his sister had sent to Elice. He just didn't know how she was going to respond to the gifts. Hell, it wasn't charity. He meant to settle down--join her. When he'd sent the letter, he'd thought he would be living here. He'd thought he and Elice would start their relationship where they had left off five years ago. He wasn't sure when he'd become so stupid.

Jedediah stood beside him, "Good luck, pard. I wonder if she's going to think too highly on the charity here. She's a proud woman."

"You don't have to tell me about Elice. I'll figure out something," Micha said, closing his eyes and thinking about the last couple of days he'd spent with the woman he loved. His gut tightened when he thought about the hardships she'd been through, but the memory of her lips beneath his stole his breath. If he closed his eyes, he knew he could remember everything that had ever mattered to her. Knew he could remember how she felt in his arms and beneath him.

Jed cleared his throat and set a hand on his shoulder. Small comfort to a man who had left the woman he loved alone. But then most of the men he knew had left their women. Lord, but he remembered times when he wanted to write to her, but he was so exhausted he couldn't move even enough to write a damn letter.

Jedediah didn't alleviate his worries.

"You decided what you going to do about me and my men?" Jed asked as the darkness seemed to enclose them.

"I'm going to let you go home. But you all have to promise not to pick up arms against the union."

~ * ~

"I can't wait to get home to my wife," Charlie said.

"You think she's going to welcome you home with open arms? A coward? A man who faked his own death then ran tail between his legs to his grandparent's home in Boston?"

Charlie tossed a stick into the fire. "She's my wife," he said dryly. "She doesn't have a choice."

"You said you never slept with her. Hell, you told me you and your unit rode off right after you married her."

"I'm going to change that." he said, standing so quickly he dumped his plate onto the ground.

His friend shook his head. "You're a bigger fool than I ever thought possible, Charles Lee Tickner. But I told you I'd come down here with you, and I'm going to see this through. I'll help you rebuild if you have to. I'm sure you have enough money to pay any back taxes on the land and your home when the war ends."

"She'll need me," Charlie said.

"She'll want someone she can trust and can lean on in hard times. Someone who isn't a coward."

"Micha?"

"Someone who she loved," his friend reminded him.

"Whose side are you on?" Charlie whirled on his friend, his fists clenched at his side, his anger boiling inside. "I couldn't kill--people. I couldn't. And when I watched a man jump up and down in glee when he killed his first Yank, I lost my meal but when I watched him discover it was his brother--"

"I'm sorry, Charlie." David Goodloe put his hand on Charlie's shoulder. "I'm sorry for everything. I'm here for you. I just don't want you get your hopes up too much."

Chapter Five

Elice watched the men struggle with the wagon and the mud. She heard the counts and the grunts as they pushed to remove the wheel from the wet ooze. She smiled a small little smile and swept her hair from her eyes, wrapping the length into a knot to hang down her back.

"What are they doing, mama?"

"It seems they are trying to push a wagon from the mud." Rain dripped from the eaves and a chill wind whipped around the corner. What had appeared to be an early spring had turned into a wet, soggy day. She rubbed her arms in an effort to warm herself.

"What's in the wagon?" Izzy ran to the porch railing and peered over the edge.

"Army things," Elice said with a shrug. "Let's go inside before you get too wet. We'll fix them something to eat."

A loud shout and cheers rang out in the early afternoon downpour. "They got it out of the mud," Izzy said. "Look."

"My goodness, they did indeed," Elice said, watching as Micha strode away from the men and walked toward the house. He was covered in mud, and as he closed the distance a wicked grin crossed his handsome, devil-may-care features.

"Don't you even think to come in this house, Michajah Brooks!" She backed up, her hands held in front of her as if she could keep him at arms length.

"I wouldn't dream of it. I just wanted you to welcome me home." He spread his arms wide as if he meant to give her a hug.

"No, you don't," she shook her head, knowing if he wanted to, he would have her covered in mud within a second.

Izzy clapped her hands and squealed in delight. "He wants to kiss you, mama. You have to let him."

One dark eyebrow inched upward and his smile widened. "Listen to your daughter. She's very intelligent."

"If I kiss you, Micha, it won't be in front of your men and my daughter." She set her hands on her hips and tried for an indignant expression.

"Just a peck?" he asked. "A small kiss and then I'll get washed up."

"Promise?" she asked, wishing he wasn't quite so muddy. She didn't dare show her real feelings in front of Izzy.

"What, you don't trust me?" he asked her looking as if the thought hurt him.

"No, I don't," she said clasping her hands in front of her and pursing her lips in a spinster-like pout. "I can recall several times I came up the loser in this same type of encounter." She leaned forward and gave him a quick kiss on the cheek, then danced away from him just in time to keep from becoming a muddy mess.

He let out a roar of laughter. "You win." He leaned a bit closer and whispered, "We could have shared a bath." He straightened and winked.

Elice felt the rise of heat to her cheeks, looked at Izzy to see if she heard, then breathed a silent sigh of relief when it appeared Izzy hadn't heard a word of the exchange. "You're horrible," she whispered back.

"Am I?" he asked.

"What's in the wagon?" she asked, trying to change the subject to something a little less threatening. When he was so playful, she felt vulnerable.

"Things," he said with a shrug. "Guess I need to get back and help them unload."

"You're avoiding me now, Micha Brooks. I know you well enough. You don't want to tell me what you brought here because you know I'm not going to like it. Fess up, Micha." She stepped forward. He wiped mud from his face with an equally dirty sleeve.

"I am," he told her seriously. "Let me get cleaned up and then we'll talk about it."

"I'm not going to like it."

"Well--I'm hoping you're going to love it. But I'm not holding my breath. Quit scowling at me, Elice. I only have your best interest at heart."

"Michajah--"

He threw up his hands, looked at the wagon and then as if giving up, "The wagons are full of things you need."

"Like--"

He ran his hands through his hair, "Paint, nails, fabric--"

"I don't want your charity. I have money. I'll pay you," she told him, wiping her sweaty palms on her apron.

"With confederate script?" he asked. "That money is not worth anything--not even the paper it's printed on."

Tears welled in the back of her throat. She forced them away. "I will not be your charity case. I have money--Yankee dollars."

"You are not paying for anything. Think of it as a gift."

"I'm not your--"

"Good God, I never thought anything like that. Don't you even go there, Elice Weld. We slept together one time. We were kids."

She wiped away the tears, but she couldn't vanquish the anger or the humiliation this gesture had caused. The pain went straight to her heart. "Just go away." *Is that what he thought of my love? I was just a kid.*

She turned from him and walked through the house into the kitchen, trying to ignore the tears welling in the back of her throat. Mechanically, she brought out pots and pans; the food for dinner followed. She didn't have grounds to accuse him of such things but what could she think? She wouldn't be bought and paid for. She wasn't going to let him into her bed even though she loved him.

Elice sat at the table in the kitchen, waiting for Micha to return. The walls were cracked and the paint chipped. The fencing had long ago been torn apart and used for firewood. She had buried all their silver trays and candlesticks as well as a bag of gold coins. She had little use for money over the past years. Everything had been bartered for, nothing paid for. Stockpiling food or anything else had only resulted in the loss of the item. If the confederate armies didn't take it, the Yanks did.

"I'm sorry," Micha said. He stood in the doorway; his hair slicked back, his dark eyes shimmering with emotion.

"I am too," she told him. "Sit down, eat, and we can talk about this. Know from the start I'm not about to take anything without paying you."

"I don't want anything in return. My sister, Cara, sent the wagon load. You'll have to pay her." He shrugged as if the conversation were over.

"It isn't that I don't appreciate all you have done, and I can pay you. But I may need the money later. I wasn't planning on using it now."

"I don't want your money."

Her heart fluttered beneath her ribs. She was always so close to tears when she talked to him. She had loved him for all of her life. What was she supposed to do? If he wanted to sleep with her, how would she ever resist him? If he was even nice to her, she would give him her heart as well as her soul.

He reached across the table and held her hand, his thumb rubbing gentle circles on her wrist. She met his gaze, more determined than ever to stay strong. But while he looked at her, her heart melted. She wanted him to hold her, to comfort her, and to some how convince her everything would work out.

In the end, she knew nothing would work out. He would be called away. Many had said the war wouldn't last but a few months. How did he know it would be over soon? The South seemed to have the ability to keep on fighting despite the insurmountable odds.

~ * ~

He set his napkin on the table. "Walk with me."

She watched him, her brows furrowing in concentration. "All right." She rose and without saying a word walked through the door he held open.

"Thank you," he said, relieved he would have a chance to talk to her. Once she cooled down, she was usually reasonable.

"Don't placate me, soldier," she said. "Where are we going?"

He walked beside her and motioned for her to take his elbow. He whistled a tune, a pleased and happy man for the moment. "Let's go see what my sister sent. I only have a general idea."

"I don't--" she began.

"Hush, just wait until you see what is there. I'll draw up a contract and you can pay me back when you have the money. I'm not in a hurry." He stopped and turned to her, grinning. She touched his chin with a slender finger and the moisture in her eyes stopped him.

"I will pay you back," she told him. "I will."

He watched her clench her fists at her sides. She was furious with him for assuming too much, but he sensed the beginnings of forgiveness in her. "I wouldn't have it any other way."

She looked at him. She had to tilt her head back to see him. "I want you to know I do this under protest. Even if I accept what your sister sent, I can't possibly…"

"My men will help. They are all on leave. We've been discharged but asked to stay in the vicinity. They'd rather fix fences and paint than fight. We've seen enough..." *blood.*

For a few more minutes they walked toward the wagon. His heart beat hard against his chest and his palms felt sweaty. He couldn't ever remember being this nervous.

She leaned over the side and rummaged through the contents. She made little noises over different items as she searched through the wagon. When she pulled out a doll and turned toward him, her eyes filled with moisture.

"How did she know?"

Micha shrugged. "My sister has always made it her business to know what was happening to her friends. I think she always considered you a dear friend."

"The wagon really is from her and not you?" she asked.

Micha had the good sense not to tell her the truth, but he

supposed his expression told Elice what he didn't want her to know. "We both sent the wagon. I told her to get what she thought you would need."

"She did a very good job," Elice said, wiping a solitary tear from her face with the back of her hand.

The sun peaked from behind dark clouds, sending warming rays to the earth. She stood with the sun silhouetting her, and he couldn't help but think, *My God, she's so beautiful she steals the breath from my body.*

He held out his hand to her and she put hers in his. For a moment, he reveled in the feel of it enclosed in his own. He brought her close and wrapped his arms around her, holding her for a few seconds too long, but she didn't object and so he tucked her head beneath his chin, memorizing the moment.

Looking up, he said, "Unload the wagon. Put the fabric and dishes in the house and the rest of it can go in the barn. Best get busy before it starts to rain again."

"I can help," Henry emerged from behind the barn, his rifle in hand, a huge grin on his face. He walked with a slight limp, dragging his left foot. Micha remembered when Henry walked without a limp. He also remembered the day a slaver caught him down by the river and thought Henry was a runaway. He'd caught Henry's ankle in a trap.

"Thanks," Micha told him. Without saying anything else, Micha took Elice's hand in his and walked toward the pond and the gazebo. He liked the peace and the serenity surrounding the tiny structure. The lapping of the water on the shore always soothed his soul, and right now he wanted Elice to himself. He felt as if he'd reached a milestone where they were concerned--a healing. If nothing else, he felt as if they had a chance to pick up the pieces of their shattered lives.

Elice leaned into him. He heard the sound of the wind whispering in the trees and a chatter of a squirrel. A few ducks swam in the pond and dipped beneath to forage for fish. Near the center of the pond a fish jumped.

"Have you taught Izzy how to fish?"

Looking toward the pond then back to Micha, Elice shook her head. "It doesn't seem we've ever had the time, and I never wanted her away from the house. Henry has done the fishing."

Micha picked up a rock. He tossed it a couple of times and then he skipped it across the water, the ripples spreading out in concentric patterns across the pond.

"I remember when I saw the elephant," he paused and watched the water.

"Elephant? What?" she asked. "What is seeing the elephant?"

He shrugged again. "It's a euphemism for the first time a soldier sees battle, when he's in the line of fire."

"I can't imagine." She put her hand on his back.

The gesture warmed him to the core. He skipped another rock. "All the congressmen and their wives--all the socialites in Washington, everyone--they rode out in their carriages to watch the Union forces push back the Confederates."

"That's quite a tall tale," she said.

A smile formed on her so kissable lips. Micha shook his head. "It's no story. When the Confederates pushed back the Union army, all hell broke lose. The carriages turned tail and ran back to Washington. Not everyone made it though." He paused in thought, a lump forming in the pit of his stomach. "I saw things I never want to think of again, yet sometimes at night--"

"You don't have to think anymore, just feel," she said softly, running her hand up and then down his arm.

"I can't stop the dreams."

She put her head on his chest, and he ran his fingers through her hair, wishing he dared kiss her again, knowing he would anyway and damn the consequences. She could only deny him.

"About a year ago, it rained every day for a week and the mud was several feet deep. I think everyone felt just like me, waterlogged. I don't know how they did it but they stayed happy. They sang songs, some of them played cards, and some wrote letters."

She moved away from him, and he felt the chill settle in the depths of his soul. She strode closer to the pond.

"Did you write any letters?" she asked, turning to him, her expression dangerous and flushed.

"I did," he knew she was angry. "My God, Elice, you were a married woman." He ran his hands through his hair. "What did you want me to do?"

"You didn't know I was married," she told him. "Did you write any letters to me?"

"I have them in my haversack."

"Might I have your permission to read them?" she asked letting her chin raise a notch, even as the sun disappeared behind a cloud and the day grew stormy.

He nodded. "We should be getting back." He felt the first rain drop on the hand which he held out to her. But she didn't take his hand.

"Why didn't you send them?" Her chin tilted upward and she made a wad of her apron with her fingers.

"Ah, Elice, do we have to go into the reasons?"

Her stormy grey expression matched the changing afternoon. "I would like to know. I suppose you can tell me whatever you choose."

He shook his head, knowing he didn't like what he was about to tell her, knowing now he'd been wrong about her, but also knowing that maybe deep in his gut, he knew she had moved on. "The way we parted--"

God but he remembered that day. The hours played in his mind over and over and to save his very life he could not have done it any differently.

"You could have told me how you felt about me or did you have any feelings at all, Micha?"

"You were quick enough to marry my best friend. I suppose neither one of us really cared that much. I must have just been a stepping stone for you."

She gasped. Her hand flew to her throat. "You think so little of me. We--you--you--made love to me in that very gazebo." She turned and pointed at it. "How dare you imply--"

"That you didn't love me," he said slowly. "I thought you did. Until you yelled at me and told me you never wanted to see again and that you hoped I died in battle. I thought you loved me with your heart and soul."

Chapter Six

"I never wanted you to lose your life," she whispered.

She turned from him, afraid to confront him with the truth, yet knowing she would have to tell him about Izzy. For the moment, she couldn't keep from crying, wouldn't keep the tears from falling once more for the man she'd loved and for the man who had left her--the man she had lost.

He inhaled a swift, deep breath. His eyes shimmered with what she thought must be anger. "That isn't what you told me. I went to war believing you hated me for everything I stood for, for the man I was."

Elice drew herself up stiffly, trying to think of something to defend her actions but unable to justify anything. "I just wanted to convince you that you were wrong. I wanted to have everything my way."

He laughed softly and she turned back to him.

"You think this is funny?" He tried to take her hands in his, but she wouldn't allow it. She wasn't ready to give him an intimacy that would tell him everything she had ever felt about his leaving her was in the past.

"No, nothing that has happened in the last years has had even a hint of funny to it."

He shrugged his broad shoulders, and she wished she could read his mind.

"I don't know what you want now. I don't understand why you came back here, bearing gifts as if you were a king," Elice said, feeling angry, ashamed, guilty and so many other things. Now she couldn't stop shaking.

He smiled at her, looking at her sideways as if he were also searching for the right words. "You were always spoiled. You were a spoiled child and when you grew into a beautiful young woman, you were still spoiled. You thought you could snap your fingers and you would have the world at your doorstep. And I adored you. I adored everything about you."

"How could you adore a spoiled brat?" she asked in such a hushed tone she was sure he couldn't hear her.

"I knew you would change. Your parents, before they died, gave you everything you asked for. When a woman has children, well then, her life changes. She will be the parent and she will love and cherish and yes, spoil her little girl." He looked at the house as if he were thinking of Izzy.

"I haven't had a chance to spoil Izzy. And I would like to think I would be a better parent than that."

"Spoiled by love--" he mused, lifting a strand of hair from her face and gently placing it behind her head.

"I was spoiled both ways, my parents loved me unconditionally, and they also gave me everything I asked for. They shouldn't have done that."

"Probably not." He leaned over and kissed her forehead.

"You're laughing at me again," she whispered, but she didn't mean to move away from him. She needed him more than she'd ever thought she would need another human. Even though she needed her daughter, this was so very different.

"No, I'm just thinking about your little girl and all the hardships the two of you have had to endure. Tell me about her."

She placed his hand in hers and led him up the steps to the gazebo. "It's starting to rain," she said as if she thought to keep from talking about Izzy. But truth be told, Izzy was all she ever wanted to talk about. He would guess soon that Izzy was his daughter if he hadn't already. She looked like him a little. Oh, she had her eyes and her coloring, but Izzy had his dimples and his smile. She was easy going but when she decided on something, even a team of horses pulling with all their might against her couldn't change her mind, just like her daddy. She had to tell him before he confronted her.

They sat down. He still held her hand in his. "I don't know where to start."

"When was she born?" he asked, his thumb tracing gentle circles on the inside of her wrist.

She suddenly couldn't think. Heat rushed through her and what was once a normal beat of her heart escalated to a rapid staccato. She didn't know if the sensations she felt were because of his question or his ardent attentions to her wrist and now her arm.

She inhaled swiftly--for courage--she thought or *because he is flirting dangerously with me*. "She is a Valentine baby. February 14, 1862."

"She'll be three years old in a couple of days," he asked with a bit of awe in his tone.

Elice wiped another tear away. "I don't have anything for her," she whispered. He brought both her hands to his lips and kissed each knuckle.

"What would she like?" he asked. "Perhaps I can send for something. It might not be here in time, but--"

She shook her head and tried to draw her hand away from his, but he wouldn't allow her. "No, you've already done too much. I can't accept anything else."

"I haven't done nearly enough," he said, his voice a little husky and his fingers working a magic all their own.

"What is that supposed to mean?" She was drawn to him like a moth to a flame and nothing short of a disaster could break the spell he wove around her.

"Hush, it doesn't mean anything except I wish these last years had turned out differently." He ran a finger along her cheek, smoothing it lightly tracing her eyebrows and down her neck. He held a strand of her hair between his fingers. "So soft," he murmured.

"What did she say first?"

"Mama, I never taught her anything else. She called Henry, Hey, Hey."

Micha laughed. "When did she learn how to walk?"

"Almost a year after she was born. She pulled herself up on the old table that used to be in the parlor and toddled to me. I held my arms out for her, and she went right into them."

He sighed softly, looked to the pond and then back to her. "What aren't you telling me, Elice? I know there is something." He brought her close and kissed her softly on the lips--a soft kiss--a teasing butterfly kiss that meant nothing yet foretold everything they might share together.

She brought her hand up touching his cheek. The stubble of a day's growth was there. "I--" she looked down. How she wanted to tell him everything. "It's--" she choked up and the sobs wouldn't stop. He pulled her close, holding her, easing the pain he had caused and yet knew nothing about.

With a gentleness she'd known before, he touched her tears.

"Stop, please don't cry. I won't ask any more questions." He kissed her softly once more everywhere, on the tip of her nose, her closed eyelids, her eyebrows. He feathered soft kisses down the column of her neck. And he demanded nothing in return.

She ran her fingers through his hair and reveled in the softness of the dark black strands. He'd always had a bit of the pirate look to him. If she could only bring herself to force the words from her lips, she'd feel--

His lips settled on hers, working their magic. She ran her fingers up then down his back, pulling him closer, even while she heard soft sounds in the back of her throat. He ran his tongue across her lips, and she opened for him, rejoicing in the moment. Even if she knew the moment would come to an end all too soon.

His hands settle on her rib cage just below her breasts. She heard him groan roughly in the back of his throat. She heard the harsh beat of the rain drops on the top of the gazebo and the whistle of the wind whipping through the tiny structure. She shivered but leaned into him, seeking his warmth and comfort. She had been alone for so long.

He trailed kisses across her collarbone and lower, slowly opening the tiny white buttons of her blouse. His lips sent her pulse skyrocketing and her entire body softening to meet the hardness of his.

"Micha," she said softly. But she didn't know if she wanted to tell him to stop or to carry her up to her room.

"Elice," she heard back. "Is everything all right? Should I stop?"

It was just like him to ask. "Please," she whispered, returning his kisses with ones of her own. She kissed him on the neck then brought his head back up to meet her lips. She dipped her tongue into his mouth and explored, tasting, relearning everything about the man Michajah Brooks, once the love of her life. He was still the love of her life.

An inferno swept within, passion as well as a need to spend an eternity with him filled her. He wove a magical spell around her, urging her to return the passion completely. She felt his hard, muscled form pressed tightly to her. Wondered at his strength and courage of convictions. It was that same strength she'd fallen in love with so many years ago. Today, in the gazebo, during a February rainstorm, she would remember this moment forever, no matter what else occurred between them. She should tell him to stay, to give her everything that had once been assumed. But that was the past and this was the present. Micha gave her strength and confidence to meet whatever troubles would still come her way.

She wanted him desperately. She needed what she knew he alone could give her.

His hands swept higher. This time when he pressed his lips to hers, they were neither soft, nor gentle, nor persuasive. They were a brand demanding, hot and searing. He urged her to respond, an urging she didn't need yet reveled in. Her breath was ragged. Within the safety of his arms, she forgot all her fears and remembered only the evocative, mercuric heat that seemed to radiate from his very core.

She felt as if he'd drugged her soul, bewitched her. It was as if he filled her with liquid fire, and need, and with a slow beating tempo. He kissed her and kissed her. The tempo beat throughout her, and she could no longer resist the emotions and the conflicts surrounding their lives. The wildness entered her mind and her soul, kidnapping her heart. She felt his body through the layers of clothing between them. She felt the savage power that was Micha. She willed herself to turn him away, yet she could not deny herself this pleasure. His hands had undone the buttons of her bodice.

"Tell me to stop," he murmured softly, yet his words held no conviction. For a long moment he held himself back. "Hell," Micha said through clenched teeth. "I can't take you here in the gazebo with the rain pounding all around us.

"Why? You did once before." *Yes and I conceived a beautiful little girl on that very day.*

"Miss Weld, Miss Weld, a letter for you." Micha's adjutant shouted, running their way.

~ * ~

"Put the letter on my desk," Micha said, not wanting this time with Elice tainted with business and not understanding the letter was not for him.

"It is for Miss Weld," Micha's man said.

Elice flushed crimson, keeping her back to the man and quickly trying to refasten the buttons Micha's nimble fingers had undone. "That's okay, put it on his desk. I'll get it later," she mumbled.

"On my desk," Micha said again, watching his adjutant turn away. "He's gone," he said, touching a finger beneath her chin and lifting it to see into her eyes. "You're so beautiful," he said, softly kissing her once more.

"What will your men think?" she asked, sounding breathless and panic-struck all at the same time.

"That we are in love," he told her softly. "Don't' worry that he will say anything. I have trusted him with my life more than once. He will be the epitome of discretion."

She inhaled a ragged breath. "It's late," she said, "and do we dare make our way through the rain? We'll be drenched."

He laughed, "I will dry you off when we reach the house."

"Incorrigible man."

He saw a twinkle in her eyes he had missed when he first arrived. The sight gave him hope that between them all was not lost. "Come," he stood and held out a hand. "We should check on Izzy then

I'll make sure you don't catch a cold from the chill."

"I haven't agreed to anything."

"Haven't you?" One eyebrow rose thoughtfully. "But I think you have. You can deny me--us--tonight but what about tomorrow or the next night. It is inevitable. Do you love me?" he asked, hoping she would let down the barriers that guarded her heart.

She looked at him, a sadness simmered in the depth of her eyes when he asked, yet he still saw the shadows of the past years. They were shadows he hoped to vanquish. *I have never stopped loving you, Elice Weld.* But he had to stop himself. Her name was Tickner.

"You can say no anytime," he told her, watching her as she rose and came into his arms again. Yet she held herself away from him, still trying to dress herself. "If you fasten all those buttons, you're just going to make more work for me when we get to our room."

She flushed a beautiful shade but she smiled at him. "Let's go, Captain Brooks." With that said, they dashed from the gazebo and toward the house, laughing as if they were young lovers and there were no troubles in the world. The rain sluiced down and still they laughed and ran. Puddles were no obstacle. He stomped in them as if he were a little boy, flirting with his first girlfriend.

The kitchen door swung open. "My lands, children, you're soppin' wet," Bertha said.

"We'll dry off upstairs," Micha said, swinging Elice into his arms and taking the stairs two steps at a time.

"Don't get everything wet."

Elice buried her face in Micha's shoulder, laughing softly. "I don't think I've ever been so embarrassed in my entire life," she whispered.

"Let's check on Izzy." He set Elice down by the door to Izzy's room. Together they walked inside. She was curled up in a tight little ball, her doll cuddled next to her sound asleep.

"She's so precious," Elice whispered, pulling up the blankets and tucking them in around her little girl. She bent down and gave her a quick kiss on the cheek.

"May I," Micha asked.

Elice smiled at him. "Of course."

Overwhelmed with emotions he'd never felt for a child, Micha bent over and kissed Izzy's cheek. He suddenly felt as if the years had indeed been whisked away, and Izzy was his daughter. He wished it from the depth of his soul and his heart.

Backing out slowly, Micha closed the door behind them. Elice grabbed a couple of bath sheets from the closet and accepted his hand as they walked to the master bedroom, the room he'd so callously taken over when he arrived. He winced at the thought of his actions, yet he knew he wouldn't have done anything different. He'd calculated his return to the minute detail, all the while praying what he did here would work in his favor. Patience was not one of his best attributes, but he knew it would take every ounce of it to win Elice over to his side. He prayed tonight he would win her hand in marriage.

Shivering, she started to towel dry her hair. He started a fire in the fireplace. Flames licked upward, warming the room. "Come here," he said.

She walked slowly to him. He reached out to her, taking her in his arms, nibbling light kisses down the column of her neck and across her collarbone. She ran her hands up his chest, unfastening his shirt and slipping it off his shoulders so he could shrug out of it.

Holding her as he did now, he forgot all the obstacles in this path they were taking and remembered only his most evocative dreams. The wild, rugged tempest that raged inside her seemed to sweep inside him. He wanted her so, yet he knew she had been married to another man, a man he'd once called his friend. But that man was dead, had died an honorable death. By what he did here, did he make light of that death? He felt as if she filled him with liquid fire, and need, and with a slow beating tempo. He kissed her and kissed her.

He freed her from the restraints of her clothes, and his palm swept over her nipple while he curved his hand and cupped her breast. A sweep of fire shot through him when she touched his chest and ran her hands the length of his back. He was amazed by her fragility and the sweetness of her touch. His hand barely touched her breast. His lips barely fell against hers, and the tip of his tongue rimmed her mouth and her inner lip.

He lifted his head. Her lips were moist, and they parted for him almost as if she were as desperate as he was to breathe. Her hair cascaded down the length of her back in wild disarray, loosened from its ribbons by his exploring fingers. Her breasts were bare.

He pulled away, studying her, questioning, even challenging her. "Elice," he whispered her name. His hands bracketed her neck. His thumbs gently stoked her chin and the line of her lips. "You have the softest lips I have ever kissed."

"Micha..." She left off staring into his eyes as he gazed into hers, wondering what the future would bring them.

He laughed and kissed her once more. He noticed her hesitancy and prayed she would come to him, would lie with him with no regrets. "Say no if you wish, Elice. You can say no anytime." God, but he didn't want to hear those words.

"I want you, Michajah Brooks. I need you so much there are no words," she whispered.

"Would that I had never left you," he murmured softly, feathering butterfly kisses down her neck and across her collarbone."

Her fingers brushed across his nipples and he groaned. Good Lord but she could do things to him he'd never imagined.

He swept her into his arms and carried her to the bed, coming down beside her. Before she could say anything, his lips closed over a nipple, sucking, caressing. Heat spiraled, and her nails bit into his flesh. He had lost control of his heart, perhaps his very soul.

"You are so beautiful," he told her. At that moment, he believed he must have died and gone to heaven. He could have never imagined these feelings, so deep and raw they overpowered all that he was.

Her flesh was ivory, her breasts tipped with the softest rose. Scents of vanilla would linger in his memories forever.

"Elice, touch me," he whispered to her and it seemed she did.

She whimpered as he directed his attention back to her breasts then the delicate contour of her neck and her ears.

"Do you want me?" he asked.

"Oh, yes," she whispered.

He needed her to want him as much as he wanted her, and it seemed she did. He clenched his teeth in a valiant attempt to hold back, to make this night perfect for her. He wanted her to feel as much pleasure in their lovemaking as he would.

His fingers brushed the soft curls at the apex of her thighs. She was soft and moist. He stifled a groan. Gently, he eased himself between her legs, spreading them wider. He sank lower and lower against her, creating a havoc and a tempest within his blood. She had mesmerized him, enchanted him, bound him to her with some magical spell. He stroked her belly. The hot damp trail of his mouth followed. Ever lower he moved, caressing her, all of her, his fingers brushing the triangle that guarded her innocence, then exploring intimately, parting her, stroking her, bringing her to what he hoped was heaven to her.

Her fingers gripped his shoulders, her nails biting into his flesh. Within seconds he felt the sultry heat inside her. She was damp and hot and ready.

"Micha, please."

Chapter Seven

A moment later he was inside her. One move filled her then he held still, watching her as if she meant to say no. She would never tell this man she loved, no. Never.

"Are you all right?" he asked, his gaze one of concern and love.

"I want you," she whispered. Smiling, she lifted her head slightly and brushed a quick kiss on his lips.

"Are you sure?" he asked, rocking slowly. Her hips rose against his. She ran her hands down the length of his back, feeling his muscles bunch and dance beneath her fingertips.

"Please, Micha," she said. "Don't stop now." All she wanted was to feel loved again after so many years.

Her fingers entwined in his hair. God, the longing she had for him. She needed him with a fire and passion unlike any she had ever known before. Even the first sweet time he'd made love to her, she had not felt this way.

On his elbows, he rose above her. She opened her eyes. The strength she knew he possessed told her he would always care for her, protect her, and shield her from anything bad that could possibly come her way. Even if he never told her he loved her, she would want him for the rest of her life. She didn't need the words.

He locked his fingers with hers. Then he began to move, a slow stroke then another. She watched him, not wanting to miss a moment, but then the passion and the hunger swept through her. She closed her eyes, reveling in the fire he engulfed her in. She moved against him, responding stroke for stroke. He lowered his head, his lips touching hers, then lower, forming over one breast; gently, sweetly.

"Easy, Elice," he whispered.

He kissed her again and again and moved within in her with more force and passion. She felt the fire ripping and burning within her, she could take no more of the sweet, sweet pleasure. Her nails dug into his back, she buried her face against his sweat-sheened chest. Theirs was a primal dance, as old as time, and sweetly fierce.

A muffled cry suddenly tore from her. She rocked violently, her fingertips tearing into his shoulders. Then she lay shaking beneath him.

"Micha," she whispered, her voice trembling, her body weak with pleasure.

A thunder swept through his body, "Elice," he cried out. "God." His body filled hers even more completely. His very life flowed into her. After-tremors seized him, rushed through him again and again, until at last he groaned.

She clung to him, her fingers warm against his heated flesh. "Micha." While he watched, she moistened her lips and she let her eyes close for a brief second.

For that short moment, she thought he might tell her he loved her, but he stopped and pulled her close. They lay together, neither one feeling the need to talk, listening to the rain fall against the windowpane. Finally, he rose from the bed bent over and gave her a quick kiss on the cheek.

"Sleep," he told her. "I will check on the household then I have a few papers I have to go through. When I'm finished, I'll come back and join you."

She sat up, pulling the covers high in a moment of shyness, as if he hadn't seen and touched all of her. "Would you bring me the letter?" she asked, wondering who would be writing to her and suddenly becoming very interested.

"Yes, but wouldn't you rather rest?"

She shook her head, her hair spilling around her shoulders. "It might be important," she told him as she watched him pull his clothes on before blowing her a kiss and walking out the door.

"All right then, I'll bring the letter to you."

She plumped the pillow and stared out the window. She had never felt more alive and hopeful of the future that lay before her. She heard his footsteps as he walked down the steps. He was so strong and handsome. Izzy would know her father. Her daughter would have someone--a man--a father in her life. Memories of the times before the war swept through her. Memories of the first time Michajah had made love to her. She'd conceived Izzy that day.

The day had been warm and sunny, filled with happiness. Her parents had ridden in to Chancellorsville to go shopping. She and Micha had been left alone. He was going back to school the next day. She smiled remembering how he'd been so careful of her, knowing it was her first time. The sky had been so blue, and there had only been a couple of wispy clouds floating past the sun. After they had made love in the gazebo, they went swimming and he'd made love to her in the water. The feeling had been sinful, decadent, and filled with passion.

At that moment, the world had been perfect, her life perfect. And then Virginia seceded and Micha joined the union forces. They had fought. He hadn't even come home to say goodbye. He'd known she'd hated the idea of him becoming a Yank. She'd considered him a traitor. How far away those days seemed--and meaningless now that everyone had lost so much.

Many weeks later, she'd discovered she was pregnant. She hadn't known what to do. She refused to use her pregnancy as a weapon to bring him home, and so she had never told him he would become a father. Micha had refused to come home and join the confederacy. His beliefs had been more important to him than she was. But then she had been spoiled and pampered. She didn't think anyone had ever told her no.

She'd confided in Charles and he'd come to her rescue. He'd married her two weeks later and then he'd ridden to war too.

"Here it is," Micha strode to the bed then kissed Elice quickly before he turned around to leave.

"Thank you," she said.

When he'd left the room, she read the back of the envelope. Elice Tickner it said. Only a handful of people knew of her marriage to

Charlie. All but a couple had died. She ran her finger over the letters, her hands shaking. A strange fear spiraled up her spine. She closed her eyes for a moment, dreading the unveiling of the letter.

She listened to the sounds of the night. Somewhere below her, Micha moved through the house. The rain had stopped and outside a full moon poked its head out between clouds. A frog croaked. Nothing soothed her rattled nerves. She inhaled a rough, ragged breath before she slowly opened the letter. She felt a shadow pass over her and thought of the death of Charles.

The parchment was worn and the writing faded, but she recognized the bold scrawl. "Charles," she whispered into the night.

Dearest Elice,

Our commander says there will be a battle tomorrow. The men are cheering and saying we'll send the Yanks packing with their tails between their legs. They're ready to fight. It's strange but I don't feel any jubilation. I've been thinking about you and our hasty wedding. I love you, Elice. I know you don't return my sentiments, but I promise you when I return, I'll be the best most loving husband and father.

"The bugler is sounding taps. I have to turn the light out. My stomach is turning I'm so nervous about the fighting. The men who have fought out west tell me once you've seen the elephant, a soldier will be all right. I don't think that is going to be true for me. I wish Micha was here with me, I know he'd protect my back. Sometimes I think I'm a coward for feeling this way. The other men tell me it's just my nerves.

"Well, good night Elice. I hope this letter finds you well and happy. Take care of your precious baby. I will try to write again very soon.

Love,

Your adoring, Charles

Tears streamed down Elice's face. She couldn't stop crying. Rolling over, she buried her face in her pillow. Guilt and remorse swept through her. A life had been lost for no reason she could see or understand. No, thousands of lives had been lost. And with his death she was happy for the first time in years. She was happy at Charles' expense. He had died. And she had lived. Dear God that there had been some other way.

He was my husband and I never slept with him.

~ * ~

"Rise and shine, sleepy head," Micha said just as Izzy jumped and bounced on the bed where Elice was sleeping.

Micha opened the shade. Sunlight poured into the room. Elice pulled the covers over her head. "No," she said, weakly as if she knew her slumber had ended.

Izzy giggled. "Come on, mama, Micha made hotcakes for us. Bertha and Henry already ate. They'll get cold." Izzy dove beneath the covers with Elice and snuggled against her mother, something Micha would have liked to have done if Izzy hadn't been in the room with them. His intentions were far from innocent.

Micha fell on the bed beside the girls, tickling Izzy and Elice. Elice emerged from beneath the covers, pillow in hand. She clobbered Micha on the side of the head with her pillow. Giggling, Izzy did the same. They fell into a pile on the bed, the girls ganging up on Micha. He laughed, holding his arms in front of his head in defense.

"Enough," he cried. "Enough. You win."

And when they stopped, he laughed again. Izzy climbed on top of him, tickling him. Breathless, she finally quit. Elice watched them, a smile forming on her beautiful face. Micha prayed he could always make her happy--put a song in her heart for the rest of her life. He prayed too the war would come to a quick end, and he could convince Elice to become his wife.

"We have to let your mother get dressed," Micha said, pulling away and standing up beside the bed.

"Alright," Izzy said.

"Let's go set the table," he held his hand out to the little girl he wished with all his heart were his own. It didn't matter though. He would always treat her as if she were his very own child. He remembered a night four years ago. He'd seen a little blond girl with beautiful blue eyes running down the steps in this house. But that had been something he'd seen in a dream.

"Hurry," he turned to Elice. "We don't want to spend one minute longer than we have to without you."

Elice waved them away. Micha closed the door to the room and swept Izzy into his arms, carrying her piggy back style down the steps to the kitchen. Izzy giggled all the way.

When they reached the kitchen, he set her on the counter. "I'm not supposed to be here," she said seriously. "Mama won't like it."

"Oh." Chastised by a little girl with the prettiest blue eyes, eyes just like her mother's. "Well then, I'll just put you here," he swept her into his arms again and this time he set her on a chair.

"You don't want me to help?" she asked.

"Of course I do. I just don't know what big girls like you want to do. Why don't you tell me?"

"Mama taught me how to set the table," she said wiggling out of the chair.

He leaned against the counter, his arms crossed and watched her with the most giddy feeling he'd ever felt.

"It smells good." Elice slipped into the kitchen and Micha handed Elice two cups. She poured coffee, sipping it slowly before looking up from the cup to smile at him.

Micha set the flapjacks on the table. Elice dished up Izzy's food. They ate and chatted as if they were a family.

"I'll do the dishes," Micha said, standing up.

"No, you cooked. But you can keep me company. Izzy, go find Bertha. She will give you some chores and then you can play."

"I'll dry," Micha said, stepping close behind her. He put his arms on either side, kissing the long column of her neck. He felt her response, the tiny shiver of delight. She turned in his arms and kissed him softly. The kiss deepening with each moment, he explored and tasted and touched. Her soapy fingers wound into his hair.

"Micha," she said. "I have to show you the letter."

He pulled back, "Is everything all right?" He saw the moisture fill her eyes as well as the sadness. "I don't want to see you cry."

"I know. Give me some time," she told him softly, wiping the tears away.

The euphoric giddiness he'd felt for such a short time was replaced with weariness. He'd known from the first moment he saw her again she was hiding something.

"The letter was from Charles," she said as if that was enough information.

"I thought he was--"

"Dead?" she said. "He is. The letter was posted in July, 1861 before the first battle of Bull Run."

"It just got here now?" He felt as if a knife had been stabbed in his back. He didn't want her to be reminded of her first husband and of his death.

She nodded, tears welling in her eyes again. "You can read it if you want."

He shook his head. Hell, but he wanted to read it. He wanted to burn it too. "No, when you feel like it, you can tell me what it said. I'm going to go find Izzy."

He turned and walked out of the kitchen, wishing the letter had arrived when it should have arrived three and a half years ago.

"Izzy," he called out. "Izzy, where are you?"

"In here with Bertha, making Valentines."

"Valentines," he paused. *Was it almost Valentine's day?* "May I join you," he asked, settling on the floor where the two were cutting red hearts and pieces of lace before sticking them on paper.

Izzy nodded and Bertha grinned at him. "You fixin' on makin' one for Miss Elice?" she asked.

"I suppose I should, but I don't know how. Can you show me?" he asked Izzy. "I'll make one for you too."

"It's easy." she reached for different materials and showed him how to do everything. He worked and watched the little girl. She smiled at him and, in shock, he realized she had the exact same two dimples he had.

"I do think you make mine look silly," he said. "Yours are beautiful." He looked at Bertha and he knew his imagination played tricks on him. She nodded as if to confirm his suspicions. Izzy was his. How could he have been so stupid? They'd only been together one time before he left. *Fool. It only takes once.*

He rose. "Can you keep mine safe until Valentine's Day? I have to go talk with your mother."

Izzy nodded and kept cutting different shapes with Bertha. He strode from the room and into the kitchen.

"It's time for the truth, Elice."

~ * ~

"Jedediah, Jedediah Jackson," Charles Tickner called out. He dismounted and strode to his friend's home.

Jedediah opened the squeaky door and stood in the opening hands on his hips. "Charles?" he asked, his voice questioning.

"It's me."

"I thought you were--"

"Dead," he finished the sentence for Jedediah. "I'm very much alive and I'm home. That's what counts."

"Well, come in. I don't have much, but I can give you some of my famous hickory coffee. You been to see Elice?"

Charles ran his fingers through his hair. "That's just it. I haven't and I'm not sure I'm going to see her. We were married but the minister is dead and we--" he shook his head, unwilling to finish the sentence.

"Micha is back. He's living at the house."

"I know. I went by there before I came here--couldn't stay away. I--" he swallowed. "I'm a deserter. I turned tail and ran. No woman is going to want a man like me when she has Micha," he said, the bitterness overwhelming him.

"You are her husband," Jedediah reminded him.

"In name only," Charles said. "What can I give her?"

"Your love. Did you know you have a little girl?" Jedediah asked, sipping his coffee and staring at Charles as if he was taking his full measure.

Charles shook his head. "She's not mine. I don't know if I should be telling anyone this. But Elice was in trouble, pregnant, and I married her to give the little girl a name. Didn't want the child to be called a bastard."

"That was very noble of you. So the little girl has to be Micha's. Well, that does complicate things."

Charles felt the same fear that had given him nightmares for the last four years spiral down his spine. "She never loved me," he said bitterly.

"Where have you been?" Jedediah changed the subject. "Prison?"

Charles shook his head. "Worse."

"Nothing is worse than a Yankee prison camp."

"That's where you're wrong. I ran. I ran up north to my uncle's place. I lived and worked there. I kept track of Captain Micha Brooks. And when it appeared he'd be coming home, I decided to follow."

Suddenly he knew his intentions.

Chapter Eight

"How long have you known Izzy is my daughter?" Micha asked as he sipped his coffee while he sat across the kitchen table from Elice. He set the cup down, drumming his fingers on the old and well nicked wood. His dark eyes shimmered with anger and even frustration.

"What are you talking about?" Elice asked cautiously, not wanting to volunteer anything she didn't have to volunteer. She looked toward the parlor where she knew Izzy was playing then back to Micha.

"Come on, Elice, you know what I'm talking about. I shouldn't have to spell it out."

She stiffened, not liking the position he put her in even while she knew it was justified. "Maybe you should," she said softly, looking at the dark liquid in her cup.

"If Izzy is my daughter, I have a right to know the truth. Were you ever going to tell me? Or did you think I wouldn't care?"

She winced at the questions as well as the not-so-subtle accusations. The growing anger she saw in his dark brown eyes sent chills down her spine. "Yes, I wanted to tell you. I was waiting for the right time."

"How long have you known?" he repeated, his voice rough, his hands clenched.

Elice felt her nerves unravel and snap. *How long have I known?* Since forever, too long, not long enough. "That's not fair. You left me." She didn't want to remember the fear and the upheaval of those days. A few days after Micha had ridden off not even looking back or writing, her parents died in a carriage accident.

"I know, but it's got to be told now. Don't you think it's about time?" He rose and paced the room, running his long fingers through his hair, turning to face her and with infinite patience waiting for an answer.

All Elice heard was the roaring in her ears and the echo of her heartbeat beneath her ribs.

"I wanted you to know," she said, "You left. You didn't write to me. For all I knew you were dead. I wouldn't have heard. I'm sure I wasn't important enough to be notified. Why, we'd slept together but that was all. We'd made no promises for our future. I didn't want to think about you."

"My sister would have written you if anything happened to me. I was here after the battle of Chancellorsville. You could have told me then."

"I was too terrified you might take her away from me."

"I'm not a monster, Elice. I would never take a child from its mother," he roared.

"What makes you think Izzy is yours?" she asked, surprised by her words. "I don't want to bait you, but why do you think she is yours?" Elice sipped her coffee, wishing there was something stronger in the drink, knowing that idea wasn't wise. She couldn't keep her hands from shaking.

He sighed, "Why are you playing these games? Izzy has my dimples. She looks a lot like my sister."

"Other people have dimples."

"Charles doesn't. Are you saying you slept with more than the two of us?" he asked, his words ragged around the edges.

"What will you do if I confirm your suspicions?" Elice asked, once again moisture pooling in the back of her eyes. She forced the tears from her eyes and tried to keep her hands still. She could barely speak let alone think.

"Good, God, Elice, do you know me at all? I'm not going to hurt you or Izzy. Even if she isn't mine, I will help support her. And if she is mine, I'll--"

Elice's chin rose. "I told you before I don't want charity. If Izzy is yours, you'll--"

"If Izzy is mine--"

"Yes."

"Ah, hell." Micha strode from the room. She watched him walk outside and stand by the pond. He was so still, she was afraid. *I should be afraid. For four years I've wanted nothing more than to tell him and now that I have my chance, I freeze.*

She watched him from the kitchen window, her fingers gripping the countertop until her knuckles turned white with the pressure. *Tell him everything. Tell him you know she's yours because you've never made love with anyone but him. Tell him.*

Hours seemed to pass but it was only a few minutes before he turned and made his way back to the kitchen. His face was flushed and a small vein in his neck pulsed.

"You're angry," she said.

"You noticed?" he asked, his voice edged with sarcasm.

She inhaled a ragged breath, her hands folded in front of her. "Izzy is your daughter. I've known for a long time. I've always wanted to tell you, but you didn't ever seem to care enough about us to write. I'm sorry but I had to think of her first."

"It wasn't like you ever expected Charles to come home. And you couldn't have believed a child was better off without a father."

"No, but this way I wove a picture of her father, and she had someone she could believe in--someone she could hold close to her heart. I always prayed you would come here. I never expected you to-- not after the way you left me."

"If I'd known I'd had a child, I would have been here to help. To give you money."

"For the child," she murmured. "Money for the child. What about love?" Her anger escalated, her nerves unraveled, and she wanted nothing more than to throw her dishcloth at him and run from the house.

"You're damn right. I would have moved heaven and earth for Izzy," he said, his voice heavy with sincerity. "I would have loved her."

"But not for me. Micha, I don't know if I could have endured knowing you were here for your child but not for me too. I was selfish. I was never willing to let Izzy lose a father because of my insecurities."

"We have to tell Izzy," he said.

"Tell her what?" Elice asked. "That her father is the dark, handsome soldier that died in the war. Or should we tell her he's the man who abandoned her mother and never looked back."

"Ah, hell, I don't know. We can explain things to her," he said.

"And when will she understand? She's only three years old. She won't understand anything except you abandoned her and I've lied to her."

"What do you me want to do--to say? I won't let her go on believing her father is dead, or that I don't care about her."

"I don't want that either. Let me think about it. Let's get through her birthday then we'll decide."

"No, I want her to know today. Waiting will only make it harder. I don't see any reason why we should put this off any longer."

"You're positive you want to be her father," Elice whispered uneasily, wishing she could play the devil's advocate and make him think about this longer. She'd always dreaded this moment.

"If you're positive she's mine. I understand a few dimples doesn't make it so, wishing won't make it so either."

She turned away from him. "I'm sure," she said.

"Look at me. How are you sure?"

"Ours was a marriage of convenience. I never slept with Charles."

~ * ~

Micha inhaled, a breath that was long and slow, thinking about everything Elice told him about her short marriage to Charles Tickner. "That's incredible." It seemed one of his wishes had just come true.

She watched him, tears in her eyes and he couldn't help but wonder who the tears were for--a lost love--his or Charles.

"He married me to give Izzy a name. I knew I was pregnant, and he knew Izzy was yours. I don't think he loved me but he did want to help. He didn't want there to be any recriminations for your little girl. I think he married me more for you than for me."

"Don't have any delusions. All the young bucks were half in love with you, Elice. I was the lucky man who thought he had your love. And I threw it away," he said, his fist coming down hard on the old table top, rattling the dishes and sending one coffee cup to its side, a stream of dark liquid cascading to the floor.

Elice laughed, but the laughter was hollow to his ears and bittersweet. "We were married, he gave me a quick kiss on the cheek, then he, too, rode off to war, whooping and hollering about the Yanks they were going to kill. No one understood what would happen and that Yanks would just keep coming."

"A kiss," Micha mused thoughtfully. All these nights he'd wondered if Charles and Elice had slept in the same bed he and Elice had just made love in. He wondered about the gazebo and if they'd shared hopes and dreams while watching the water lap against the shore. He swore that no matter how many years it took, he would make everything up to Elice. He never wanted to see another tear

"That was all," she murmured, "a kiss on the cheek. He wrote me several times. The letter I received yesterday--" she broke off, brushing tears from her eyes. "It seems I have to mourn his loss all over. And yet his death has made this so much easier for us."

"You have no reason to feel guilt or betrayal. You did not kill him," he told her, wanting to reach out and pull her into his arms.

"They sent me the death certificate but never the body. I don't know where he is buried."

"Can I see the certificate?" Micha asked.

She nodded and walked to the parlor desk where she kept all the papers she'd ever received and brought it back to him.

"Do you have a wedding certificate?" he asked.

She shook her head. "There wasn't time. The minister said he would send one. But he rode off to war too, and I never got anything from him. I don't even remember signing anything."

"Then you're not really married," he said, his heart filled with a joy he didn't want to admit to and yet, and yet the relief escalated with each moment.

"I said my vows before a witness, the preacher, and God," she murmured softly. "I felt married, and I felt as if I had betrayed you. But I didn't think you cared."

"Look, Elice, I don't mean to be difficult when this so emotional for you. But it doesn't appear your wedding was legal," he paused. "Why didn't you give Izzy Charles' last name? Why didn't you take his name?"

The silence lasted forever before Elice finally answered. "Because Izzy is yours. No one else knew. And almost everyone who had any idea or who would ask questions--they're dead too. When he died…"

Micha sat down then stood up. He paced with restless anticipation--an eagerness to learn the truth swept inside. A million thoughts surged through his head. His wishes and his dreams were about to come true.

"Don't go anywhere, Elice."

"What," she asked, standing. "Where would I go?"

"I don't know," he told her. "Just don't go anywhere, I've got an idea."

"If whatever you're planning involves me, you'd best tell me. I've had enough scatterbrained ideas I don't want to be privy to any more."

"Stay," he held up his hands. "Just stay here. I'll be back in a second with something I hope will make you happy."

Micha ran from the room and raced upstairs to rummage through one small bag. He swore and cursed then pulled out a small box. He opened it and a ring with a solitary diamond sparkled in the sunlight. In another box, he found the matching wedding ring. His heart beat escalated and sweat beaded on his forehead. He was terrified and yet confident. Elice had to say yes. Some of the feelings they once shared existed, he was sure. She had made love with him, had slept in his bed. She hadn't said she loved him, but he didn't expect the words would come easily. She had been through so much and when he'd arrived here, she'd had few expectations. He closed the lids to the boxes and shoved them in his pocket.

Inhaling a deep breath, more for courage than anything else, he walked more sedately down the steps to the parlor. Before he entered the room, he straightened his clothes and paused for a moment.

"Elice," he called out. "Can you meet me in here for a moment?"

She walked from the kitchen. Sunlight rippled through her golden hair. She stopped when she saw him, cocking her head sideways a whimsical expression crossing her beautiful face. "What is it? You look like a school boy with some big secret."

He walked to her then bent down on one knee, keeping his gaze riveted on her. He saw her gasp of recognition then she caught her lower lip beneath her top teeth. He watched her swallow and breathe deeply.

"Elice," he paused, watching her face and praying what he read there was a good sign, "will you marry me?"

Anticipation swept through him. For a quick moment, he closed his eyes and waited, afraid she would say no then he looked at her with open eyes and high expectations.

"Yes," she whispered. "Yes, Michajah Brooks, I will marry you. When?" She held her hand to her mouth.

"Today," he said. "Today, if all goes well. Go upstairs and find your best dress. I've a dress in the trunk my sister sent that will fit Izzy. My girls will be so beautiful. Now you get ready and I'll go into town and fetch the minister."

Whistling, Micha strode from the house, his heart beating and his pulse racing with untold excitement.

"Private! Private Thompson," Micha called out, feeling as if a burden of gigantic proportions had been lifted from his chest.

"Captain?" Private Thompson fell in behind him and was trying to catch up to him. "Sir."

"Hitch up one of the wagons. We're going into Chancellorsville."

"Sir, yes, sir, I'll have it here in a minute."

The private raced to do the Captain's bidding. Micha went inside to make sure everything was as it should be, and he hadn't just imagined all this. "Bertha, there you are. Elice and I are getting married in a few hours. Put together whatever you can for a celebration meal. Help Elice and Izzy get ready and make sure old Henry is around. He always seems to be hiding out in the woods. My men will make sure there isn't any trouble."

"Land sakes," Bertha clasped her hands to her bosom. "She said yes?" Bertha danced a little jig. "I'll make this a day to remember."

"She did agree. And she made me the happiest man alive. Now go on and do whatever you can. Get food from my soldiers, I'll give them the orders that you can have whatever you want."

Bertha didn't waste anytime. She raced up the stairs to see to Elice as fast as her old legs could carry her.

"Wagon's ready," the private called out. "Am I going with you?"

"Get in." Micha picked up another man for a guard and the wagon rumbled off.

~ * ~

Charles and Jed sat inside the shabby and worn-down mansion that had been in Charles' family for generations, eating hardtack and drinking commissary. The day wore an unexpected brilliance. Sunlight filtered through the broken window panes.

"She's going to be mine, I tell you," Charles said after taking a long swig of the whiskey Jed had in his haversack. "I tell you, I'm going to ride over to the Weld's place and take back what's mine." He took a long pull then belched. "Excuse me," he said as if manners made a difference in this dreary world.

Charles stood and swayed. He felt as if the floor was about to rise up and meet his face.

"Easy, pard, I think you've had enough to drink," Jed told his friend. "Best you sleep this one off before you do something you might regret."

"Don't want to sleep without my wife." Charles stumbled out the door and toward the barn. "I'm going to saddle up my horse and ride over to the Weld plantation and claim my wife."

"You're in no condition to do anything like that. You need to be sober. You can't even think straight right now," Jed told his old friend. "I don't think she's going to let you in her bed, and it wouldn't surprise me if old Henry sent a round of buckshot through your fine tweed pants."

Jedediah followed Charles.

"Goin' over there. You comin' with me?" he asked, his words slurring into one huge mush. Charles stumbled again. His head clearer now than a few minutes earlier. He deserved his wife, by God. She shouldn't be sleeping with the enemy. Micha Brooks was a damn Yank. It didn't matter he'd been in the midst of Yanks hiding for all these years.

"You got your marriage certificate?" Jedediah asked Charles. "No use going over there if you don't have proof of the wedding."

"Never got the certificate," Charles mumbled and swayed against the barn door.

"Then Elice has it. If she doesn't want to produce it, it's yours and my word against theirs."

"Then I'm going to watch her lie if she says anything to the contrary. We're married." Lord but his head pounded. He grabbed the commissary and took another long pull. He needed the courage. For so long he wanted to die. He'd thought several times that putting a bullet through his head would end his misery. Now all he wanted was to kill Micha and his lying wife.

"Micha might kill you," Jedediah said, hoping to stop Charles from making a fool of him at least until the morning when he was thinking more clearly.

"Don't care. If I can't have Elice, I don't want to live. He'd be puttin' me out of my misery."

Charles stumbled into the barn, ignoring everything Jed had told him. After the third try, he was on his horse. When he looked to his side, Jedediah rode beside him.

"Couldn't let a friend ride to his humiliation alone."

Chapter Nine

"Are you ready?" Micha asked Izzy. Kneeling beside her, he looked into her smiling blue eyes. "Are you ready for me to be your father?"

Izzy watched him, her eyes shining. Elice's heart turned over with joy. Izzy nodded. "Yes."

The minister and his wife Linda stood in front of the fireplace in the parlor, holding his bible and appearing solemn for the occasion. Elice recognized the man. He'd lived in the Chancellorsville for as long as she could remember. She thought he might have even married her parents.

The father shifted slightly and cleared his throat, nodding for Micha to walk to him. Micha offered her his arm and she smiled at Izzy who stood beside the father as if she were a maid of honor. Bertha and Henry stood beside her, and one of Micha's men stood on the other side of the father.

They walked slowly even though she wanted to hurry. Some foreboding thought of doom swept through her, and she fought to put the shadow of fear outside. She wanted to remember the joy of this day. But a knot formed in the pit of her stomach. Happiness had eluded her for so long it was difficult for her to envision this day and very difficult to believe nothing would happen to change the joy to sorrow.

She had married another and she had never buried his body-- never would. She felt a betrayal of her first marriage, and yet she had not loved Charles. Linda nodded encouragement. Elice lifted her chin, moving forward toward the father, the husband, and forward to her future and a new life.

The papers for their marriage had already been filled out and signed. This was a formality of sorts, yet she wanted to say the words. She wanted the minister to pronounce them husband and wife. She needed to give her vows of loyalty and love to Michajah Brooks--the man she would love forever.

She found herself in front of the fireplace at Micha's side. The father bowed his head and spoke a few words of encouragement. He looked around the room at Micha's men. "Is everyone here?"

"Yes," Micha said while she nodded. Oh, yes, everyone who mattered to her, everyone she loved stood in this room.

Oh, Lord, but this was so real. Elice felt relief and joy, yet she also knew fear and it seemed as if the room closed in around her, as if she were caught in a magical dream. She had wished for this to happen most of her life. She didn't want to awaken from the dream.

It was happening, now, right now. Micha spoke his vows in a strong clear voice as if he had no doubts or fears that what they did here this day was right.

Elice barely managed to whisper her own. But she meant them just a strongly as Micha.

He held out a ring to her. "It was my mother's," he told her. He set it on her finger next to the engagement ring she'd only worn for a few short hours. It fit her perfectly and she was amazed he had carried this with him for so long. Then Micha was instructed to kiss the bride. His fingers were gentle as he slowly lifted her chin.

His lips molded over hers, imparting a molten fire that thrilled her and left her shaking and wanting more as Michajah's mouth lifted from her. He smiled at her, and touched her cheek with a calloused fingertip.

"I now pronounce you husband and wife," the father said.

She was married to Captain Michajah Brooks now. Izzy would know her real father. Sunlight filtered through the window on this wonderful February day.

"You're mine now," he said. "I will never let you go."

"Just as you are mine," she told him. "Just as Izzy is yours also."

Micha left her side and was giving all his attention to the father who handed him the signed marriage certificate.

Bertha and Henry were shaking hands with Micha's men and everyone was laughing and talking. Linda gave her a motherly hug of encouragement.

Micha strode over and wrapped his arm around her shoulder. "I'm going to be a very possessive husband. And Mrs. Brooks, I don't intend to let you out of our bed for a week. I can't wait until everyone leaves," he whispered, kissing her earlobe and sending little shivers of passion sweeping through her.

Izzy stood beside them and Micha swept her into his arms, tickling her and laughing with her, his daughter. "What would you like to eat," he asked giving her a quick kiss to the cheek.

"Everything," she said. "Are you really my daddy now?"

"I am. And I will never let anything bad happen to you." he set her down. "Now, go get Bertha to give you a plate of food. Don't eat too much. You don't want to get sick," he warned.

Elice laughed. "You're already acting like a proud papa."

"I hope so." He walked with her to the dining room. The table was laid out with an assortment of food, much of which came from his wagons. There was wine and cheese. Bertha had made bread and there was an assortment of coffee cakes.

"Glass of wine?" he asked as he poured a glass for both of them. When he finished, he handed Elice the crystal glass. He guessed Bertha had unburied these for this occasion, and he guessed when they were done, they would go back to their hiding place.

He held the glass aloft. "Here, here," he said. His men turned and lifted their glasses. "To Mrs. Michajah Brooks and Izzy," he said, grinning at them.

Elice could not stop smiling. Micha was so handsome in his dress uniform, and Izzy looked happy too. She had done the right thing. Everything had seemed so rushed but now it felt so good. Tomorrow was Valentine's Day and they would celebrate Izzy's birthday. She'd be three years old tomorrow. What a beautiful gift she was.

Micha's adjutant lifted his glass in a toast to them. "Here's to the newly married couple. May the future bring good luck, peace, and many children." he winked at her, a broad grin on his face.

Elice felt blood rush to her cheeks. Micha threw his head back and roared with laughter. One of his men began a ribald tune on his fiddle, and his other men clapped their hands in time to the music.

"Dance," they all cried out.

Michajah bowed low and swept her into his arms, dancing to the wild polka, spinning and lifting her to the music until she was winded. "Stop, please," she laughed. He set her down and kissed her. It was a day time kiss, but one that left his men laughing and calling out for more.

Three rapid fire shots rang out. Elice screamed. Micha pulled her down to the ground. Bertha fell atop Izzy.

"Michajah Brooks!"

"Stop," they heard the much lower voice from outside.

"Get out here you coward. Michajah Brooks."

Micha crawled to the window and peered out, careful not to bring more rifle fire into the room. His men had already spread out around the room. He motioned, giving hand signals to his men. They responded like a well-oiled machine.

A horse whinnied and pranced around the front porch. "Elice!"

"God, it can't be," Elice whispered.

"It's Charles," Micha said. "He's come back from the dead."

~ * ~

"Don't shoot, Charles. I'm coming out," Micha called, as he motioned for a couple of his sharp shooters to move upstairs. "Don't shoot anyone unless there is no other choice. Do you understand?" The men nodded, grabbing their rifles and heading up the steps.

"No."

Micha turned to Elice, holding on to her shoulders. "You know it's too dangerous for you outside. Let me try to talk some sense into him. Please, Elice," he begged, wondering if she would do his bidding.

"I have to talk with him. I need to know what happened, where he was all this time." Elice pushed past Micha and through the front door, the sound of it banging shut behind her, terrifying him.

"Elice!' Micha lunged to stop her but was too late. Micha flew past her and put Elice behind him. "Go in the house," he ordered. He felt as he did when he first saw the elephant, terrified, excited, confused, emotions ripping through him at a pace he'd never before felt.

"I can talk to him," she told him. "I can make him put away his gun."

"I'm not going to risk your life." Hell, he'd just begun what he thought would be the happiest day of his life, and now Charles was back from the dead. He looked like the living dead. Nothing about his demeanor led him to believe the son of a bitch would negotiate. He was crazy looking, wild-eyed, and out-of-control.

"You're a coward, Michajah Brooks. Go away and leave my wife alone." Charles slurred the words. His horse pawed the air. His face contorted but he clung to the horse as well as his gun while the horse bucked, whirled, and pawed the ground below.

"I know different, Charles. Where have you been and why did-- my wife now--believe you were dead?" Micha's nerves were strung taut. He'd been in tighter situations but never in one that put his wife and daughter in jeopardy. He'd seen men like this on the battlefield. The sight put terror in his heart. They were half mad, crazy with fear, and they didn't care if they lived or died.

Charles' face paled but he whirled on his horse and fired two rounds into the air. Warning shots from his men hit the dust around the horse's feet. The horse pawed the air again and whinnied in fright. Shadows danced in the yard and a soft breeze picked up, sending debris swirling in tiny cyclone-like figures.

"Let him answer," Micha called out to his men. "I want to know what his excuse is. Where have you been?" he asked again.

Elice moved to Micha's side, but he blocked her path with his arm. "I want to know too. Where were you? Why did I get a letter telling me you died? Why, Charles? All these years, why didn't you write me? You could have told me you were still alive. I would have understood."

"Would you? You would have wanted me to come home--or

maybe not." Charles shrugged. "I couldn't go into battle. I thought I'd die if I had to shoot at anyone one more time. My God, Elice, you don't know what I went through. I didn't want to come home a coward."

"But you did come home a coward--a deserter--a liar," Elice bit out.

Micha felt Elice's body shake next to him, as she clung to him. "Please, Elice, go inside. I don't want you to get hurt, and I'm sure Charles doesn't either. I need to reason with him."

"He's not going to reason with anyone," Jedediah said. "I already tried that. I tried to talk him into going back to his uncle's place in the north, but he wouldn't listen. He's crazy--mad at the world and himself."

"He's going to have to do just that. He can't ride into Elice's life and expect to pick up where he rode out." Hell, those words sounded just like what he'd expected to do. But their stories were different.

A shadow passed across the scene unfolding in the front yard. Clouds gathered above, threatening rain. "What makes you think she can make you happy, Yank?" Charles asked. "She's my wife."

Elice pushed forward, standing beside Micha for a second. "Would the two of you quit acting as if I'm not here?" He turned and holding onto her shoulders, he saw the tears in her eyes and knew this was hurting her more than anyone else. He needed to fix this, make her happy again. He'd thought he'd be able to put a song in her heart.

"Bertha," he called out. "Can you talk some sense into her?" He swept her into his arms and carried her inside. Hell, he felt as if he was the main attraction in a three ring circus.

"Won't do no good, but I'll try," Bertha said, but before he could close the door, Elice was back on the porch standing side by side with him.

"Michajah Brooks, this is just as much my problem as it is yours. Now let me stay. You know you can't keep me inside unless you hogtie me." She turned to Charles. "Do you have the marriage certificate, or was our wedding as much a sham as your death? Was the man who married us someone you picked up on the way to my home, or was he a real preacher?"

"Don't know. He said he was a preacher, a travelin' man. Said he was on his way out west to convert the Indians."

"You need to go inside where it's safe," Micha said.

"No," she whispered.

"It would be a whole lot easier for me to let you stay if there wasn't a possibility of shots being fired," he paused. "Charles, why don't you get off that horse of yours and come inside. We can talk there."

Charles whirled the horse in a tight pattern. "Don't want to talk. I want to take my wife and go home." He fired his gun one more time. "She's mine, Brooks, and I'll die before I let you have her."

Micha felt another spiral of fear snake up his spine. That was what he was afraid of. He was terrified Charles would kill every one of them then take his own life. War had changed him. He wasn't sane any longer.

Jedediah leaned forward on his horse. "Charles, give me the gun. Let's go in and talk. Besides my stomach is grumbling and I'm damn sure I smell some of Bertha's best cooking."

Two more warning shots flew down from the window, kicking up dust. It was a reminder to Charles. Micha wanted Charles to understand the Union soldiers would fire on Charles if he tried anything or even looked as if he would shoot the gun at the house. Charles was a dead man if he tried anything. Clouds gathered above them and a few drops fell, hitting the earth. The rain was about to start in earnest. Micha wanted to bring this under control without an incident and soon.

Charles rode closer to the porch. Micha stepped back to shield Elice. "Never had a marriage certificate, but you said the vows, didn't you Elice." He sneered at her, his voice rough with sarcasm. "You promised to love me but you never did, did you. You never loved me. You always loved Micha. I was the fool, wasn't I?"

She didn't answer. She backed up, shaking her head.

He felt her sorrow as much for Charles as for the empty promise she made that day so long ago. He knew Charles was right. Elice had never loved Charles.

"You knew what you were getting into when you agreed to marry her. She was honest from the start. You wouldn't want her if she didn't love you."

Shaking his head, "She's my wife, for better or worse."

"One couldn't find a worse situation than this."

"I'm taking her home."

"I am home," Elice said.

Micha didn't dare let down his guard. Charles was itching to shoot him, Elice or both of them. "Charles, if you get down off the horse and come inside, we can fix this. I know we can." But he knew nothing would fix this for Charles. He'd kill him before he'd give up his wife and child. No man should be able to fake a marriage and a death then end up on the shiny side of life.

"Did you even care when you got the letter?" Charles asked Elice. "Did you mourn for me?"

"Who sent the letter, Charles?" Her voice was stiff, her shoulders squared and even though there were tears in her eyes, Micha knew she fought for her identity, fought to understand her part in this.

Trouble was this was all Charles' making. There wasn't a damn thing she could have done to change the way this was turning out.

Charles sneered, "I did. I sent it." He laughed and it sounded demonic to Micha's ears. "When I got back that night, I volunteered to write to the loved ones of the men who did die. I wrote and wrote and pretty soon, I figured it would be easy to write to you. I knew you would recognize my handwriting so, I printed the letter."

"I can't believe you did this. It's so cold-blooded."

"I figured I could find my way up north. I even stole a uniform off a dead union soldier so I could blend in better."

"Charles, that's horrible," Elice said.

"At the time, I didn't think so. I watched someone stick the man who was fighting next to me. There was blood everywhere. My God, Elice you don't know. You can't understand."

"But I do," Micha said. "I know and I can't believe you could do such a horrible thing. You could have resigned your commission and come back here. You could have seen that Elice would not have suffered so terribly."

"I gave her my name. And look what she did. She married the first Yank who came her way. She's a whore."

Micha's fists clenched. "Be careful what you say and what you imply. You--a deserter--come in here shooting up the yard. I can have my men do anything I please."

"Micha, no," Elice said. "Let it be."

He guessed he couldn't, and he knew he wouldn't do anything to the man he once called his best friend. This had turned out to be a bittersweet day. "Charles, you have no marriage certificate. The minister who performed the ceremony died in the war. How do I even know if the marriage was legal? Go back up north. Start a new life and leave us alone."

The words were easier to say than he thought they would be. But Charles didn't move. He looked suddenly sadder then more wild-eyed than he'd been.

A single shot rang out. Charles fell from his horse. Blood stained the earth where he fell.

"No, Charles," Elice ran to him, stumbling on the steps. She cradled him in her arms and Micha felt sick to his stomach. "You couldn't do this to yourself. How could you shoot yourself?" she whispered and rocked.

Micha watched her rock with Charles' head in her lap, knew she whispered to him but he couldn't hear the words. She would never believe he didn't give the orders for his men to shoot.

"He killed himself?" Jedediah said softly. "I had no idea he was so distraught. I just thought he was drunk."

Elice looked up. "He shot himself," she said, brushing back the hair on his forehead, rocking and sobbing. "He didn't want to kill anyone else. He was always such a gentle soul."

Micha walked to Elice. "Come on. Let my men prepare him for burial. He would have wanted to lie in his family's plot.

Her face a mask of sorrow, Elice rose. Taking the hand Micha offered she walked with him to the parlor. He poured her a glass of brandy. She sipped but Micha didn't think she saw anything in the room, not the decorations Bertha had made for the wedding, not the food that still sat on the tables uneaten.

"Izzy, come here. Your mother needs you. Will you stay with her while I do some chores?"

Izzy nodded and climbed into her mother lap. "I love you, Izzy," he heard Elice whisper as he walked outside to see to Charles Tickner and his real burial.

"My God," he murmured shaking his head and looking at Charles for the last time. "He's dead."

Chapter Ten

"What's wrong, mama. Why are you crying? The funeral for Uncle Charles was today." Izzy sat on her mother's lap, playing with Elice's hair. "You shouldn't cry on my birthday."

Elice wiped away her tears and forced a smile, knowing her daughter was the most important person in the world. "I know. It's just so much has happened. I'm going to leave you here for a few hours. Bertha will take care of you then we'll celebrate your birthday. We'll have a real birthday party."

"With cake and everything?" Izzy asked.

"Yes," Elice smiled. "With cake and everything."

Everything--Elice thought. I should be happy. I have everything I could possibly want. Charles shouldn't have died the way he did. Jedediah found a note in his pocket. He'd meant to kill himself all along. He'd been so ashamed of himself, but he'd had to get drunk first. When he was drunk, he couldn't think straight. He hadn't meant to ride here to the farm and terrify everyone.

"Who is Charles?" Izzy asked, squirming a little on Elice's lap. But Elice didn't want to let her go so soon. She needed to hold her, to reassure herself Izzy was alive, and the aftermath of yesterday was only a nightmare. It was her birthday today. She was three years old. How time flew, and how slowly it had seemed to go at the time.

Elice hugged her little girl. "Charles was a dear friend. He did me a favor a long time ago, and I will always thank him for his sacrifice."

"What did he sac--"

"Sacrifice? He did a very noble thing and when you're older and you can understand, I'll tell you. For now all you need to know is he was a poet and an artist and the war hurt him in ways no one will ever understand. It changed him. He couldn't kill another human being, and he couldn't accept that part of himself. When everyone wanted the South to win the war, he couldn't be part of the war.

"Bertha and Henry will be here with you while I'm gone. I love you, Izzy. No matter what happens, I want you to always remember that." How easy it was to tell Izzy she loved her. How hard for her to say the same words to Micha even though it was true long before Izzy was born.

"Micha!" Izzy scooted off her lap and ran with arms wide open. Micha caught her up and twirled her around while she giggled. "Are you going with mama?"

"My dear, I believe you've grown since yesterday. You look a year older if I do say so myself."

"Do I?" Izzy giggled. "Twirl me again."

Micha did then set her gently on the floor, steadying her to make sure she wasn't too dizzy. "Yes, I'm going with your mother. Whenever you want, you may start calling me daddy. I want to be your daddy very much." He tapped her little button nose with the end of his finger.

"Daddy," she said to him, looked at the ceiling then back at him. "Daddy," she said again, an impish grin on her beautiful little features.

Micha picked her up and after sitting down, he set her on his lap. Elice sat next to them in another chair. She hoped and prayed Izzy would understand why Micha had not been around.

"Your daddy and I have some things to tell you." Elice breathed in deeply and placed Izzy's hand in her own. She looked at Micha who nodded for her to go on.

"What?"

"Well," Elice began, "Remember when I told you your father was tall, dark and handsome?" She watched the grin grow on Micha's face.

"You said that? Did you mean it?" he asked, cocking one eyebrow, his lips twitching as if he wanted to throw his head back and roar with laughter. "Tall, dark and handsome. I like that."

"Mama never lies," Izzy said. "My daddy is handsome just like you."

Elice loved the picture the two of them made. Their dimples were not the only likeness. "Izzy," Elice said. "Micha is your real daddy. He had to leave to fight in the war, and I never knew if he would come home to me."

Izzy stared at Micha with wide-eyed wonder then she looked back at her mother.

"Your mother's letters never reached me. The mail wasn't very reliable during the war. My cavalry unit was always on the move. I didn't know about you until a few days ago when she told me."

"Would you have come to see us if you had known?" she asked.

"Yes, and if I couldn't make it home, I would have sent you presents every year on your birthday," he told her, giving her a hug. "I love you, Izzy. And I'm never going to leave you and your mother alone again."

"Can I get down now?" she asked, giving him a quick hug before wiggling off his lap. "I love you too," she turned and ran outside, "Bertha! Bertha, I've got to tell you something."

Elice smiled at Micha. He placed her hand in his. "That went better than I thought," she said.

"She's still so young. She had no idea all we went through to get to this point. We can tell her more when she gets older. For now I think we've told her all she can understand." He rubbed little circles, tantalizing circles on the underside of her wrist, reminding her all they shared the night before, the tears and the love.

"Are you ready to go to the funeral?" Elice asked softly, a tear slipping from her eye. "Best we get started so we can get home to Izzy. I want to get this over with."

"You don't have anything to feel guilty about. The war changed us all. Charles seems to have seen the worst even though he escaped most of it. I hate to think war is natural to any man, but some men did fare better than others."

"I need to mourn him. He was sweet and kind and gentle. He

helped me when I needed him, and I think I took advantage of his generosity, only I didn't see it that way at the time." Elice leaned into Micha for emotional support. She'd never had anyone she could really talk to, anyone to confide her deepest troubles too.

"We will mourn his loss and we will go home to our child. We will make new memories." They walked hand in hand to the wagon bearing the body of Charles Tickner to his new home. They would meet the minister at Charles' home. He was the minister that wed them only yesterday. They would say goodbye to a friend for the last time.

Throughout the funeral the rain never stopped. Jedediah was there. Other than that, Charles was laid to rest with only his three friends present. The coffin was lowered into the ground and for the moment, it seemed to put the past to rest.

Micha turned to Elice, "It's time to move on. Let's go home and celebrate all we still have and the love we share."

~ * ~

"Surprise!" Izzy, Bertha, and Henry jumped out from behind their hiding places, laughing and shouting at Micha and Elice when they walked into the parlor.

Bertha stood with her hands in front of her, grinning and Henry yelled and danced a little jig despite a bum leg. Even though rain poured from the sky, Elice felt an all-consuming joy. Micha swept Izzy into his arms and danced around the room, joining Henry.

The table was filled with platters of Virginia ham and stuffed eggs. Bertha had made a plum pudding, pulling out some of the dried plums from the basement. And there was a cake, a carrot cake that was Bertha's specialty.

"This is so grand," Elice said stepping into the middle of the room and finally seeing the presents. There had to be at least ten wrapped boxes. She looked at them and lifted each one separately, finally looking over her shoulder at Micha. "You are going to spoil her."

"I intend to do just that. I'm going to make up for lost time."

Elice shook her head, "Today. And after today you've got to act like a father, not Santa Claus."

"I seem to remember a mother who received everything her heart desired." His happiness grew. The world was almost one he could live in and understand. The war would end soon and all could live in peace once more--one nation, united.

"And I was spoiled. I won't have my daughter--" He cut her off with a quick kiss then finished.

"Our daughter," he corrected her with a laugh, hugging her and holding her close to his heart.

"Our daughter spoiled."

He bracketed her face with his hands and looked into beautiful azure eyes that seemed to shimmer with pleasure. "I don't see that happening, Elice. I love her to death but hopefully and God willing, she will have brothers and sisters. I can be a doting father, but if I have to spread it around no one will be spoiled."

"Promise?" she asked, cocking her head sideways.

"Promise. I promise only to spoil her mother." He kissed her slowly, promising more to come when the sun set and their daughter was put to bed.

Izzy tugged on her mother's skirt. "Can I open my presents now?"

"This one is from your mother," Micha said, letting her go for the time being. Elice slanted him a wry look.

He grinned and nodded, telling her in the only way he knew that everything was alright. Izzy tore through her presents. They had all been meant to help Elice out. His sister had sent them in the wagon when he first arrived. A doll, a couple of dresses, charcoal for drawing and the list went on.

"Thank you," Izzy wrapped her arms around each of them. "Now we have the valentines."

"Valentines?" Elice asked, looking once more to Micha.

"We made them a couple of days ago." He handed Izzy, Bertha and Henry valentines made by the father-daughter duo.

"I don't have anything." Elice whispered. "I didn't even think--I forgot." Her forehead furrowed into little frown lines.

Micha winked. "I cheated there too," he whispered, close to her ear. "I made one for you to give Izzy." He watched the color rush to her cheeks, and her hands settle there to cool them from the heat.

"Thanks," she whispered back.

He watched the pulse thrum just below her ear, and his thoughts went to the wedding night. Parts had been bittersweet because of Charles' death, but he felt the renewal of life and knew the Charles he'd known growing up would have wanted it that way.

"Now, Izzy, Bertha will get you something to eat then why don't you go play? I want to share my valentine with your mother."

"Bertha will come too?" she asked.

"Of course, child," Bertha and Henry left with a wink to Micha.

"There has been so much haste and I wanted everything." He knelt beside her and held her hands in his own. He looked into her eyes again and inhaled a long breath. "Elice, I asked you to marry me, but I overlooked one small detail."

"What was that?" she asked, looking puzzled yet at the same time as if she knew the answer to her question.

"I have known you for a long time. We were children and I always thought you were spoiled and incorrigible but I was always intrigued. When we grew older, I found I couldn't keep my eyes from wandering your way no matter how hard I tried."

"Oh, really. You teased me so much. Sometimes I wanted to hit you."

"But you didn't. Why was that?"

"My mother taught me it wasn't right to hit other people. So I gritted my teeth and tried to ignore you."

"Which you couldn't," he said empathically. "I couldn't ignore you either. Elice, what I'm trying to say is that I love you. I have loved you forever."

She touched the side of his cheek, her expression softening. "I think I have always loved you too."

"My God, I thought I'd never hear those words. He swept her into his arms and whirled her around the room, her feet never touching the ground. "I love you, I love you, I love you," he said.

"I love you too, Captain Michajah Brooks.

He kissed her, not wanting to ever let her go. But when the kiss finally ended, he sobered and said. "You and my daughter are the greatest gifts a man could ever wish for. Thank you, Elice, for never giving up on me."

~The End~

ABOUT THE AUTHORS

C. L. Kraemer has been a gypsy all her life. From her military child beginnings to her might-not-get-this-chance-again attitude after she left home, she's seen most of the continental United States as well as Hawaii and Alaska. She hopes to travel the world but is content to stay close to her family in the great Northwest. Three novels written under the nom de plume Celia Cooper, *Old Enough to Know Better*, *Sun in Sagittarius/Moon in Mazatlan*, and *If Only* were gifts from the writing gods. A fourth novel, *Cats in the Cradle of Civilization*, written as C. L. Kraemer is her first venture to the mystery genre followed by *Healthy Homicide* written as C.L. Kraemer. The winds of writing have directed her to concentrate on the fantasy and sci-fi worlds in the near future.

~ * ~

For years Genene Valleau has been fascinated by the puzzle of why some people collapse under life's traumas and others emerge triumphantly stronger. Her dramatic action stories explore the lives of heroes and heroines who overcome those traumas, often using touches of humor. With *Chasing Rainbows,* one of the novellas in this anthology, Genene jumps funny bone first into romantic comedy. Writing this story was such fun that another humorous novella is in the works for 2011.

~ * ~

Born in Medford, Oregon, novelist Christine Young has lived in Oregon all of her life. After graduating from Oregon State University with a BS in science, she spent another year at Southern Oregon State University working on her teaching certificate, and a few years later received her Master's degree in secondary education and counseling. Now the long, hot days of summer provide the perfect setting for creating romance. She sold her first book, *Dakota's Bride*, the summer of 1998 and her second book, *My Angel* to Kensington. Each fall, Christine returns to the classroom-and the pool-as a math teacher and high school swimming coach. Her teaching and writing careers have intertwined with raising three children. Christine and her husband of 32 years live in Salem, Oregon.

www.ingramcontent.com/pod-product-compliance
Lightning Source LLC
Chambersburg PA
CBHW061937170626
46813CB00006B/2441